Enclave

David Roscoe

chipmunkapublishing
the mental health publisher

Published by
Chipmunkapublishing
PO Box 6872
Brentwood
Essex CM13 1ZT
United Kingdom

http://www.chipmunkapublishing.com

Chipmunkapublishing gratefully acknowledge the support of Arts Council England.

To Mum and Dad

Chapter 1: The Smallest Acorn

Timothy Bruce slowly, silently, turned the handle to his front door and gently pulled it open. He winced as the hinges squealed and then silently cursed himself as the bottom of the door hit his foot. Clumsy.

Just as he was about to leave the flat he heard one of his neighbours unlocking their own door, about to come into the passageway. Timothy quietly pushed his door shut and waited inside, listening. He could hear someone leaving their flat, slamming then noisily locking the door before heading off down the passageway.

He had no idea who it was, had no idea who any of his neighbours were. Despite living in the same building for almost five years, Timothy Bruce had barely exchanged a dozen words with his neighbours and little more with anyone else.

The corridor once again silent, Timothy emerged and set off to perform his task.

****

Several doors further down the corridor, inside another unknown flat, a man sat motionless in a chair. The two-room apartment was completely devoid of furniture except for the chair and dusty, never raised blinds on the windows.

As Timothy passed his door the man's eyes flicked open and looked to the wall behind which Timothy silently passed. The man, dressed in a dark green trench coat and heavy military-style boots, rose and moved to his own front door, his face set in a permanent scowl. He waited a few moments before exiting the flat and silently following Timothy down the corridor.

****

Moments later Timothy Bruce emerged onto the Bexhill-on-Sea High-Street. It was a dull autumn evening with a hint of drizzle in the air. Timothy always found himself at odds with this time of year. While he found the weather depressing, the streets did begin to quieten as winter set in.

It was no accident that almost all of the shops were closed and the streets were all but empty, for Timothy had chosen the time to leave his flat very carefully. It was too late for most shops to be open, and too early for the pubs and clubs to get into full swing. For the next hour or so the streets were his, with but a few people wandering home from work or getting their groceries.

Groceries.

That was what brought Timothy out on one of his rare trips into town. The need for food and other supplies.

Money was not really a problem. After his family's death in a car accident Timothy learned of a trust fund set up by his parents upon his birth. The fund had been linked to a joint insurance policy in his parent's names and ensured that, in the event of their deaths Timothy and his younger brother John would be able to support themselves.

As the only surviving member of his family Timothy inherited the family home which he lived in for a couple of years before everything started to go wrong. For the first year he was so depressed and shell-shocked about being left alone in the world that he left his job and lived on his inherited funds. Gradually the sadness lifted and for a short time he enjoyed his life, travelled around the world and did all the things people do when they suddenly find themselves wealthy.

Of course, such a lifestyle is unsustainable and before very long he came to realise his funds were quickly running out. First to go was the family home. The modest three-bedroom house was sold and he moved into his current two bedroom flat in the middle of town.

The second year after the family tragedy marked the beginning of a much harder phase in Timothy's life. First came the worries about money. He realised that, far from being wealthy, he was haemorrhaging his savings at an alarming rate. Soon he was down to the trust fund set up by his parents, its monthly amount equivalent to the minimum wage paid to someone on a twenty hour a week job. Even with the flat paid for, it was barely enough to get by and Timothy's lifestyle changed with it. He went out and socialised less and less and gradually started on the road to becoming a recluse.

So used to not having to work for a living, Timothy found it difficult to find a job and the longer he left it the harder it became. He eventually found work in a warehouse but by then his depression and increasing inability to interact with others made the job unbearable. He left and never worked again.

That was four years ago and since then Timothy Bruce has existed on his trust fund, paying bills and services and using whatever money was left to buy food.

Timothy pulled a small piece of paper from his pocket and examined it minutely. The scrap of paper had only a half dozen items on it and he knew the list by heart, but he still stared at it. He found that scrutinising the list took his attention away from what he was about to do: enter the shop.

He used four different stores in the town, alternating between them. He did this because he didn't want anyone to see him buying the same items each week for fear they would think him odd. He had no idea why that should bother him, but it did. Also, in the past when he'd gone to the same shop each week the staff there began to recognise him and so, quite naturally, enter into idle chatter: something else he desperately wanted to avoid.

He approached the store, took a deep breath and, forcing himself not to break his stride, entered. Once inside he looked at the list again. The words hadn't changed of course, though his unfocused eyes probably wouldn't have noticed if they had. The automatic action was simply a way to avoid making eye contact with anyone.

He approached the canned vegetable section and scanned it for special offers and out-of-date stock.

****

At the far side of the store a trio of teenagers argued with the cashier. The large woman was refusing to sell them alcohol unless they provided proof of I.D., and the youths, though clearly underage, were not about to give up.

"We jus' want some fuckin' beers, bitch!" the tallest of the kids was saying. Tall and gangly, with bony hands and sporting just a marijuana emblem t-shirt despite the cold weather, this was clearly the ringleader of the gang. His outburst elicited snorts of amusement from his two friends, further encouraging him.

"We buy here all the time!"

"Well not from me you don't," the woman snapped, not in the slightest intimidated. "And watch your language." It was clear this woman wasn't going to back down.

Taken aback by her response and enraged that she was making him look small in front of his friends, Marijuana Boy lashed out at the chocolate display beside the till, knocking sweets and chocolate across the floor.

"Fuck you bitch!" he shouted and, turning to his friends, added, "Lets go." He led them towards the exit, making a big show of stamping on the chocolate strewn across the floor. The other two obediently followed, jeering at the woman and stamping their feet. One of them sniggered as he drew a half-smoked joint from his pocket and lit it.

****

As far away as he was, the events at the checkout went unnoticed by Timothy Bruce, but not by the man wearing the long green coat and combat boots. It was no accident that he was standing where he was, allowing him an unrestricted line of sight to most of the store, including the tills and Timothy Bruce, currently looking for bargains on the 'reduced to clear' shelves.

The man in green was an expert at not being noticed, of blending in. But if anyone had happened to look at him now, they would have been surprised by his expression. As he gazed at Timothy Bruce his face was a mask of disgust and hatred.

Green Coat grunted to himself as he watched the youths leave. He spared a final glance at Timothy then, decision made, turned and followed the three youths from the store.

****

Timothy soon completed his shopping and headed for the checkout. Much to his horror a short queue had formed while the woman on the till finished picking up crushed chocolate and sweeping up the spill from split sweet packets.

Even this small event filled Timothy with anxiety. Should he stall for time, pretend to continue shopping until the queue had gone? Or could he…?

Suddenly gripped by uncharacteristic bravery, Timothy forced himself forward and joined the end of the queue. Normally such action would be out of the question, the idea of standing in a line with these four strangers filled him with dread, but today he forced himself. A step forward. A personal victory.

The queue moved quickly, despite the cashier sharing the saga of the foul-mouthed yobs with each customer in turn, elaborating it with each retelling. Soon it was Timothy's turn and he listened with polite interest. He paid for his items and accepted the receipt.

As he left the store, he realised that his 'Thank you' to the cashier was the first time he had spoken in five days.

He left the store feeling quite buoyant. His task was almost complete – all he had to do was get home. He had surprised himself by joining the queue and was glad that he'd done so. It had been a good day, but he just wanted to get home as quickly as possible, before something happened to spoil the good feeling.

But then, from somewhere behind him, a gruff voice called out.

"Oi, mate! Hold up a minute!"

He wasn't sure the voice was directed at him, but rather than find out he began to walk faster.

"Oi! Dick head!" the voice called again, louder this time, angry. "I'm talkin' to you!"

Certain now that the shout was meant for him, Timothy's brief feeling of success was replaced by an all-too-familiar pain in his stomach. He walked quickly until he rounded the corner and, once out of sight, broke into the fastest run he could manage.

****

Peter Mitchell, 'Mitch' to his friends, was incensed.

For several weeks he had been trying to get some credibility for his gang. There were only the three of them so far but he had big plans. His father had started from nothing and he was determined to do the same.

Mitch's father was Robert 'Bob the Breaker' Mitchell, a much feared and respected local villain. He had watched his father build his 'business', seen the way people feared and respected him and decided he wanted some of the same.

By the age of six Mitch was charged with assault for attacking his schoolteacher and expelled from school. His father had given him a severe beating for that. Not for the attack, but for getting caught. Several days later the teacher's house was burnt to the ground while Mitch and his father watched from a car. The bruises from his beating still raw, Mitch listened while his father lectured him on the finer points of intimidation.

"Never go off half-cocked," he had said. "Always plan ahead and always, always hit as hard as you can. When you make a move it's never aimed at just your enemy, it's a message for anyone else out there thinking about taking a swipe at you. Do what you have to, but do it cold. Think about the best way to hurt them with the least exposure to yourself. Do something different every time so they never know where you're striking from. Never underestimate anyone. Even the quietest, most timid person can surprise you. People are petty and hold grudges. When you hit them they need to know that you've hit them and they need to be too scared to even think about pissing you off again."

His father's words echoed through Mitch's head as he watched the quiet, wimpy looking man walk briskly away, ignoring him. He often thought about his father's many lectures, about little people being able to surprise you, but right now he just didn't care. He was far too angry. The fact that the man was clearly much older, in his mid thirties Mitch guessed, he was obviously a wimp and there were three of them.

All he'd wanted was for the guy to go into the shop and buy some beers for him and his gang. He wasn't even going to rough him up despite that fat bitch in the shop pissing him off so much. But now, in front of his friends, this little shit had just blanked him and scuttled away.

Well, fuck him. Now he was really pissed off and someone was going to pay. He could sense his friends, Tone and Hollow, losing respect for him. Soon they would be giggling in that annoying way they had, disrespecting his authority. How was he going to get a gang going if his first two recruits acted like this?

He had to do something to regain control of the situation. He had to stamp his authority and that little prick up ahead was going to be the one he did it to.

Mitch was just about to order his friends to follow him into a jog to catch up with their target when a calm voice spoke into his ear.

"Why don't you chavs just keep it down, eh?"

Mitch turned to find a man wearing a long, green coat standing just a couple of feet behind him.

The man in green spoke quietly, showing no concern at being outnumbered three-to-one. He was in his thirties, of average height, a little shorter than Mitch and about the same height as Tone and Hollow. His build was unimpressive, his features ordinary and not in the least bit intimidating.

Mitch suppressed a sigh as he noticed Hollow jump slightly. He would have to have a word with him about appearances.

He himself hadn't noticed the man approach, but he'd suppressed any surprise, and felt pleased with himself about that.

Timothy Bruce disappeared around the corner, completely forgotten, as Mitch stared at the man in green.

Here was someone he felt he could deal with even if his two friends weren't with him. This would be the perfect opportunity to gain some respect.

Mitch remembered something else his father had drummed into him.

"Never get your hands dirty when you have people to do it for you. No point having a dog and barking yourself."

So, with the confident smile of the teenage general he thought himself to be, Mitch took a step backwards, between Tone and Hollow, and said, "Shut this prick up."

Five seconds later Mitch's smile had gone and he was fighting for his life.

As Mitch would have put money on, Tone was the first to make his move on the man in green. He walked straight up to him and aimed his hardest punch at the man's face.

Tone felt confident in his attack because he'd spent a lot of time practicing on his punch-bag and anyway, the guy wasn't even looking at him. He knew he had a good, hard punch. This should be over in a second.

Green Coat grabbed Tone's fist in his right hand. He didn't deflect it or dodge it, but caught it. The fist stopped dead.

Before Tone could even register surprise at what had happened, Green Coat was moving, moving faster than Tone would have thought possible. With his right hand still holding Tone's fist, Green Coat used it to deliver a terrific blow to the left side of Tone's nose, smashing the cartilage from his face. Before Tone's head even began to jerk sideways, Green Coat's fist continued in an arc, bringing his elbow across Tone's jaw and shattering it.

Mercifully unconscious, Tone dropped to the floor and only now did the man in green release his victim's fist.

Hollow didn't even have time to react. As he stared down at Tone's face, at the gory hole where his nose had been and the horribly twisted, broken jaw, he caught a glimpse of movement from their victim-turned-attacker. The man dropped to the ground with what seemed to be faster-than-gravity speed and lashed out with both feet. One hooked behind Hollow's ankle while the other smashed heel-first into his kneecap. Hollow gasped, too shocked even to cry out as he looked down at his leg, bent to at least forty-five degrees against the normal direction of the joint.

The force of the blow made Hollow's body lurch forwards, but before he came anywhere near hitting the ground the same foot that had shattered his kneecap came up and dealt him a terrific blow to the chin. His forward motion was immediately reversed and the last thing he felt was the back of his head hitting the concrete before he, too, lost consciousness.

Mitch looked down at his fallen friends, at Tone's mutilated face and Hollow's horribly twisted leg and blood-spattered mouth. The sight before him was ghastly, but not as ghastly as the look on Green Coat's face.

The man, standing again, was smiling at him.

With no time to think, Mitch lashed out with a desperate swing to the jaw. The man didn't even flinch and Mitch watched helplessly as he lazily swatted his fist away and stepped in. Almost nose-to-nose now, Mitch braced himself, trying not to imagine the terrible things this man could do to him from this range.

The man burped in his face, chuckled, then put his hand over Mitch's face and pushed him backwards.

Mitch landed on his backside with a spine-shaking jolt. For the briefest of moments he sat there, stunned, before he noticed the man in green was laughing.

"My god! You kids are pathetic!" he said, pointing at Mitch's fallen friends then waving his hands around mockingly, "Playing 'gangsta' on da' streets. Geez."

He then stopped and looked suddenly sad and his voice softened. He squatted down and stared at Mitch sitting on the pavement before him and spoke quietly, as though thinking aloud.

"He was right, this *is* getting boring." But then, just as suddenly, the moment of introspection ended and he stood, his voice raising to its previous level. "I don't suppose you have a knife on you, do you? You might be able to take me down before I..." he looked Mitch up and down as if making a decision, "... oh, I don't know... break both of your legs?"

Mitch felt helpless. He had no doubt this man could do exactly what he'd threatened. He looked around desperately, hoping to spot someone, anyone, to beg for help. But the drizzle-soaked streets were empty and he already knew from his own personal surveys that there were no CCTV cameras in the area. It was one of the places he'd designated safe should he ever want to rob anyone.

Knife.

Mitch thought about another of his father's lectures.

Once, when he was eleven years old and just starting out at secondary school, a bully a few years his senior had started to make his life difficult. Coming from the oldest class at his previous school, Mitch had got used to being at the top of the food chain and it was some time since he had been on the receiving end of bullying.

A failed attempt at standing up for himself had ended in a couple of serious and humiliating beatings, one at the hands of the bully and a further one when he got home. Weakness, even at the hands of someone several years older, would not be tolerated by his father

So Mitch took a kitchen knife to school, hoping to scare the bully into line and regain his father's respect. But he was caught with the knife long before he could face the bully and, once again, the police became involved.

After his father succeeded in talking the police out of bringing charges he took Mitch home and gave him another severe beating. Between stinging blows across his back with his leather belt, Mitch's father lectured him about carrying weapons.

"Never," he was shouting, punctuating each word with a blow with the belt, "Never carry a weapon unless you plan to use it. Don't use a knife to cut someone; they will just come back for revenge. A knife is for killing. Were you going to kill another child for bullying you?"

By now Mitch had managed to crawl into a corner where he was cowering and sobbing uncontrollably. His father took a step back, panting heavily from the exertion of the beating. He wiped sweat from his brow and stretched to get the kinks from his back. Suddenly calm, he continued the lecture in a more neutral tone as he returned the belt to his trousers.

"Do you ever listen to anything I tell you?" he'd asked, but never waited for an answer. It wouldn't be intelligible anyway, the way his son was snivelling. "You need to think things through. This isn't a movie. You can't just threaten someone and expect them to run away, never to be seen again. They're much more likely to come back with friends. Or the police."

Robert 'Bob The Breaker' Mitchell sighed and began pacing the room, sparing occasional disgusted glances at his son cowering in the corner. Mitch always hated this. Even though the beating had ended, he knew his father was now warming up to one of his famous, unending lectures. He sometimes wondered if this was why his father had got the nickname 'breaker', talking people to death rather than the generally accepted theory that he liked to break legs.

But once he had returned the belt to his trousers, Bob stood over his son and stared at him until Mitch finally met his gaze.

"Never," he said in an oddly level voice, "never let me catch you with a knife again." And with that he straightened up and, after holding Mitch's gaze for a few moments longer, turned and left the room.

Mitch had stayed where he was for a long time, waiting for the pain of the beating to subside before finally standing. No matter how much Mitch respected and feared his father, he hated him as well. What he wanted more than anything was to get out from under his shadow and become his own man.

And here he was now, several years later and into his mid teens, just starting to get his first gang together. Once again he was in pain, sitting on the ground and looking up at the man who had knocked him down.

But this wasn't his father, this was some stranger mocking him, asking him if he was carrying a knife. Suddenly, all of the pent up hatred he felt for his father came bubbling to the surface. All those years ago his father had told him he didn't want to catch Mitch carrying a knife ever again. Well he hadn't caught him, even though Mitch had carried one every day since that beating as a secret act of defiance.

Anger welled up inside Mitch. Anger at his father. Anger at this man in the green coat. Anger at the stupid bitch in the shop. He grunted as he slowly tipped forward onto his hands and knees, making a big show of how much the fall onto his backside had hurt. The man in green didn't move, even though the top of Mitch's head was almost touching his knees at this point. His face hidden, Mitch smiled to himself as he surreptitiously put his hand in his jacket pocket and wrapped his fingers around the torpedo knife he always kept there.

In one sudden movement he drew the knife, depressing the switch on the handle as he swung it to plunge hilt-deep into the side of Greencoat's calf.

At least it would have gone into the man's calf had he not launched into one of his impossibly quick blurs of motion.

The left leg rose several inches from the ground and almost instantly came back down, smashing Mitch's knife hand against the pavement. Greencoat ground it under his heel, crushing Mitch's fist.

Stepping back, the man in green looked down at Mitch with a disappointed expression on his face.

"Try again." He said with a deep sigh.

Mitch looked down at his hand. It was shaking uncontrollably as the knife fell to the pavement, dribbles of blood falling from between exposed bones.

Desperate now, he did his best to ignore the pain as he grabbed at the weapon with his left hand. Not allowing himself time to think, Mitch lunged forward, putting all of his weight behind a desperate thrust towards his opponent's stomach.

Again, Greencoat didn't bother to move out of the way. Instead he caught Mitch's knife hand in his left and held it in place, the point of the knife centimetres from his stomach. Mitch couldn't understand how his lunge had been stopped so completely and suddenly.

They locked eyes, Greencoat's level and cool, Mitch's wide and disbelieving. This appeared to amuse Greencoat, who smiled.

"Game over," he whispered.

Mitch watched helplessly as Greencoat took a step forward and, without releasing Mitch's left hand from his own, struck at the inside of Mitch's left elbow with a chop from his right hand. At the same time he pushed up with the left. The result was a sweeping of Mitch's knife hand up and round into an arc, the end of which saw the knife plunging through Mitch's right cheek, skewering his tongue and exiting through his left cheek.

Only now did Green Coat release Mitch's hand and take a step back to survey his handywork.

It didn't seem possible, but Mitch's eyes were now even wider. He looked down as he tried to comprehend what had just happened. Then he let out a quiet whimper, along with little spurts of blood and shards of broken teeth, before his eyes rolled up into his head and he passed out.

The man in green looked down at the three bodies lying around him. He glanced at his first two attackers and grunted before turning his attention to Mitch, still holding onto the knife sticking through his face. A smile played across his face.

"Well, Sol," he muttered to himself, "You can't begrudge me this one." And with that he stepped forward and brought his booted heel down onto the teen's chest, driving shattered ribs into his heart and killing him instantly.

With one final look up and down the street to ensure no-one had witnessed anything, he reached for his wristwatch. Still glancing around the street, he held all three of its side buttons down before pressing it's toughened glass face. The glass depressed slightly and, with the low pop of air rushing into a vacuum, the man in green disappeared.

****

Timothy Bruce closed his front door behind him and leant against it, gasping for breath. He let the bag of groceries slip from his trembling hand as he tried to force his breathing to slow. He wasn't shaking from exertion so much as fear. He triple-locked the door and wedged a chair against it for good measure before allowing himself to slip to the floor where he hugged his knees and strained to listen for any sounds in the corridor outside.

When no sounds came he stood on shaky legs and walked through to the bedroom where he stripped down to his T-shirt and pants and climbed into bed. He curled into a tight foetal position and lay there trying desperately not to sob, afraid to make any noise. It was always cold in his flat but he soon warmed, the sweat from his body making the duvet feel clammy against his skin.

There was no chance he would sleep this early in the evening, but at this time of year he often spent much of his time curled up in bed to keep warm, reading library books and wishing forward the end of another day. He knew the next day would always be the same pattern of boredom and routine, but it was somehow comforting to see the days pass, hoping that one day something would happen to change his life, to make it more bearable.

After a few minutes he remembered the bag of groceries he'd left by the front door. It took several minutes for him to will himself back out of the bed to recover them, walking slowly through the cold and gloomy flat, avoiding the floorboards he knew would creak. He collected the bag and took it through to the small galley kitchen and opened the fridge door. He'd once heard that empty space in a fridge cost more money to run so he'd filled two of the three shelves with balled-up bubble wrap, leaving the third shelf empty for food. He filled the near-empty space with his groceries, including the fruit and vegetables, and closed the door.

As he turned to return to the bedroom he spotted something on the table that brought a smile to his face. A small torch sat there, next to a packet of budget-priced batteries. The torch, which he used to read under his bed covers at night, had the night before run out of power. For days he'd been struggling to read under the feeble glow of its power-starved bulb, but last night it had finally stopped working.

Timothy forgot how cold and depressed he was and rushed to change the torch batteries. Once done, he looked into the end of the torch and switched it on, smiling to himself as he blinked away the spots before his eyes. Tonight he would be able to read under proper lighting.

He hurried to the bedroom and climbed into bed, savouring the warm space he'd left there minutes before. For a while he just lay there, his every muscle and joint straining to contain the sudden happiness he felt. Forgotten for this brief moment were his fears and anxieties. He was safe and alone, the rest of the world held at bay behind his bed covers. For the moment at least, Timothy Bruce's entire world consisted of nothing more than himself, his torch and the library book. He reached for the book, feeling the cold air prickle his arm before he drew it back into the cosy security of his bed.

Timothy pulled the duvet over his head, carefully ensuring there were no gaps for the torchlight to leak through, then switched the torch on and began to read.

Soon he was safely lost in the book, the world outside no longer existing.

Chapter 2 – All in a Day's Work

A phone was ringing.

Ted Kane sat up in bed and rubbed his eyes. His mind was instantly awake and alert but his eyes needed that little extra help in the mornings. Especially after the amount of scotch he'd gotten through the night before.

Before he swung his legs over the edge of the bed and reached for the phone, his mind automatically ran through its standard checklist:

Was he in any immediate danger?

Should he be reaching for a weapon?

Where was he?

The answer to the first two questions being 'no', he gave the third some thought and was mildly surprised to find himself in the familiar surroundings of his Cambridge apartment.

A gentle groan came from the other side of the bed and he remembered why he was there. The girl lying beside him was called Clare and he'd picked her up at the Club the night before. He didn't usually bring girls back to his own apartment in case they became clingy and got ideas about them becoming a couple. That would be inconvenient in his line of work.

But he didn't need to worry about the girls he met at the Tuesday Club. Anyone who could get in knew the score.

Entry was only granted to retired soldiers and partners or, more specifically, retired SAS and their partners. Kane had long since left the Regiment for MI6, and frequented the Clubs to keep in touch with old comrades. Any single women there were usually the widows of Regiment officers who had died on a job. They were the only civilians allowed in.

The Tuesday Club wasn't open to, and barely even known of, by the general public. Run by Former SAS themselves, the Clubs were a safe haven for members to share war stories without the worry of giving away official secrets.

The Tuesday Club was one of seven such clubs dotted around the United Kingdom, each named after a day of the week. It was a rite of passage for members to 'Do the Week': visiting each Club on the day that bore its name within a single week. But even getting to and finding each secret Club was a challenge in itself as each corresponding one was located hundreds of miles from the last. And god help you if anyone discovered you were trying to 'Do the

Week' because turning down or failing to finish a drink resulted in failure and instant expulsion from that particular Club, making any future attempts impossible. Also, the custodian of each Club spoke frequently with the other six and together they conspired to stop anyone completing the challenge. Many members were forced to drink themselves unconscious on the first day while making the attempt. But those who were successful became senior members and received a set of seven specially engraved pewter tankards, one kept behind the bar of each Club. Anyone seen drinking from one of these exclusive vessels was accorded the suitable level of respect and was never asked to pay for a drink again.

It was over the rim of such a tankard that Ted Kane had spotted Clare. He'd seen her a few times before at the Tuesday Club and tried to recall who she'd been there with. Drawing a blank, he simply asked her. Her late husband was a Scottish officer, imaginatively nick-named 'Jock', who Ted had met in Belize. He couldn't remember much about the man but managed to piece together enough half-memories to maintain a level of small talk.

Jock had recently been killed on a job in Africa and, as was often the case when a member of the Regiment died on a mission, Clare wasn't able to find out any details about his death. Ted was impressed with how she was coping and could understand what Jock had seen in her. Because of the life they led, it was always hard to find a woman to settle down with. Clare was clearly a strong woman who understood the consequences of marrying into Jock's dangerous and secretive life.

A few drinks later they were heading back to Ted's apartment. He didn't feel guilty about sleeping with the woman. She knew her own mind and it had probably done her good being able to talk freely to someone who knew what she was going through. And looking at her now, lying naked on his bed, he didn't regret a thing.

Reluctantly, Ted picked up the phone, glancing at the clock as he did so. It was just after five in the morning.

This had better be damned important.

He held the phone away from his mouth while he noisily cleared his throat and winced at the resultant stab of pain to his temples.

"Kane," he croaked.

"Sounding good Teddy Boy!" a cheerful voice boomed back, making him wince and hold the phone a little further away from his ear.

"Morrison. Morning wanker," said Kane with a grin.

"Aren't we all mate?" the voice replied with a theatrical sigh.

"Not today I'm not…" Kane muttered proudly as he spared a quick glance at Clare, still asleep next to him. "And if this isn't important I'm getting back to it. That should give you a couple of hours to get out of the country before I get hold of you…"

"I keep telling you Teddy, I don't bend that way," the voice chuckled then instantly became serious. "Besides, I think you'll want to hear this."

All trace of levity gone, Kane sat a little straighter, his headache forgotten.

"You've found him?"

"Get your knickers on mate. I think I have."

****

At about the same time Ted Kane was being rudely awoken in Cambridge, Robert 'Bob the Breaker' Mitchell was beginning his day in Bexhill, on the south coast directly south of London. After his usual five hours of sleep he'd called for his driver before going downstairs to the restaurant on the ground floor of his apartment block. He owned the entire building, including the restaurant beneath, having consolidated his entire fortune into the development years earlier.

Rather than take the lift from his seventh floor penthouse, he walked his usual route of taking the stairs on the west end of the building and along the corridor to the east stairwell where he went down to the next floor. He continued the process until he finally reached the ground floor where he entered the restaurant through the kitchens. Robert Mitchell used his morning walk, taking in every hallway in the building, to both meditate on his plans for the day and ensure the building was in good order. He paid a lot of money to keep the hallways immaculate, with fresh flowers on every floor and every chrome light switch and lift button polished to a mirror finish. He liked to keep an eye on every aspect of his businesses.

His tenants were all retired pillars of the community, former local politicians, council officials and other professionals who could both afford his luxury prices and bring a little prestige to the building. Besides, it didn't hurt to keep a few experts in various fields close at hand. No empty apartments were ever advertised, no agent's signs were erected. The only way to get into the exclusive complex was by word of mouth and an interview with Robert Mitchell himself.

De La Warr Towers was a separate community in the heart of the small seaside town, populated by the elite of the county. It was the realisation of Robert Mitchell's every ambition, from his own twelve-room suite on the top floor right down through the twenty other smaller, though no less impressive, suites, to the restaurant and down into the private basement garage where every resident's car was cleaned and polished each evening.

But now he'd reached the position he'd fought so long and so hard for, Mitchell felt a strange feeling of emptiness. It was the fight he enjoyed, not the victory. He needed a new goal, a new campaign.

He walked through the kitchens, where everything was spotless and tidy, and into the restaurant where he nodded at the day manager before sitting at a window table. Within moments a mochachino and a couple of warm croissants appeared in front of him. The day manager, Bradley was his name, wasn't being rude by not speaking to his employer. He'd worked for Mitchell long enough to know he appreciated silence at this time of the day. It was enough that he had the coffee machine and croissants warmed and ready for his arrival.

Mitchell tore off a piece of croissant and popped it into his mouth as he gazed out of the window. His blacked out Cadillac Escalade was already outside with his driver dutifully standing by the rear door, his hands clasped before him. Mitchell felt a small pang of guilt as he looked at the man standing in the drizzle, but not enough that he would rush his breakfast. He worked hard to hide any such emotion, anything that might make him look weak. He was fortunate to be a big man with broad shoulders and an intimidating scowl to call upon when needed. He had learnt from an early age that he could easily intimidate people with a few words and a scowl and it was second nature to him now. He didn't particularly enjoy intimidating people, it just got quicker results.

Parked behind the car was a flatbed lorry carrying three large bottle-recycling containers. They were the circular type, with several rubber-shielded holes for bottles on the top surface. He smiled grimly to himself as he thought of the day's first piece of business.

His gaze drifted past the lorry towards the seafront. Across the road stood the De La Warr Pavilion, a 1930's master class in white Nuevo architecture. On the side of the famous theatre and gallery was a neon sign baring the legend 'We Must Cultivate Our Garden'. It was a reference to supporting local artistic talent but Robert Mitchell had adopted it as his credo, thinking more about empire building than art.

It was low tide and through the drizzle he could just make out a lone figure digging for lugworms on the waterline. Mitchell idly wondered if the man on the beach was happy. He couldn't imagine how dull someone's life would have to be to look forward to digging up worms and then fishing with them from a cold grey beach.

But at least the fisherman had a hobby.

All he had were his various businesses and the daily routine of checking up on his managers, ensuring nobody was cheating him. And the greater the wealth he acquired, the greater his paranoia grew.

Not for the first time Robert Mitchell wondered why he couldn't be happy. He'd accomplished everything he'd ever set out to do. He had money and properties and the respect of those around him, but still he couldn't really define what it was his life was missing. His then wife, Gloria, had explained that maybe he needed to have children and so, after years of cajoling and nagging from her, Peter was born.

He wondered where his son was now. Most likely smoking cannabis at one of his waster friend's houses or passed out in a gutter somewhere.

Robert loved his son very much, but at the same time he found raising the child to be the most frustrating thing he had ever undertaken. Businesses could be shaped and moulded, employees bullied and flattered into what you wanted them to be, but Peter refused to cooperate at anything. And the older he got the harder he became to control.

Gloria had disapproved of his treatment of the child. So much so that when Peter was three she filed for divorce. Mitchell's team of solicitors tied her in knots and managed to make her look like a negligent parent and he not only won the custody case but also succeeded in gaining a restraining order against her. He hadn't really wanted custody at the time, but it simply wasn't in his nature to be beaten at anything. He had shown some kindness though, and provided Gloria with enough money to live a comfortable life in Canada.

Lately his son had been spending a lot of time with a couple of boys called Tone and Hollow. Nicknames, obviously, but

Mitchell couldn't care less what their real names were because he didn't like them. They were sheep, with no apparent wills of their own, and followed Peter around. Real brown-noses and no use to anyone.

It was time to find Peter a position in one of his businesses. He was sixteen now and hadn't done a minute's work in his life. He made a mental note to talk to him later.

Robert Mitchell finished his breakfast and took out one of his cigars. As he snipped the tip off with his cigar cutter Bradley silently moved over and placed a leather-bound document wallet on the table. He then removed the empty cup and plate, leaving the saucer for Mitchell to use as an ashtray.

Mitchell lit the cigar, took a long, luxurious pull on the expensive Havana and blew a thick cloud of blue/grey smoke across the restaurant. Another daily ritual, this was Mitchell's way of sticking his middle finger up to the government. He had smoked a cigar in his restaurant every day since the smoking ban had come into effect. He'd be damned if some do-gooder hippies were going to tell him he couldn't smoke in his own place.

The cigar also served another purpose. While he smoked he would enjoy watching Bradley stand uncomfortably off to the side, waiting for him to open the folder containing the restaurant's figures from the previous day. Mitchell's mood would depend upon those figures and, as always, he enjoyed trying to divine whether they were good or bad by watching Bradley's body language. He slowly finished the cigar and stubbed it out on the saucer. He then opened the file and glanced through the figures.

They were good, very good.

"Excellent Bradley," he said in a flat tone, carefully devoid of emotion. "You must have been busy last night."

"Very, sir." The manager replied in the same flat manner. He must have been relieved but he wasn't showing it. "We had another party in from one of the office leaflet drops. And we managed to fit everyone in without turning away any regulars."

"Very good." And without another word he closed the file and stood to leave. Bradley was a very good manager and as long as there were no problems Mitchell was happy to let him get on with it. He found that keeping staff at arms length and feeling a little uncomfortable produced the best results.

Maybe that was where he'd gone wrong with his son. Perhaps he'd let Peter get too comfortable. He would definitely have to talk to him later.

Robert Mitchell left the restaurant and walked to the car. His driver, Ralph, waited until the last moment before opening the rear door. The drizzle had turned to rain and he'd already been lectured about letting the interior of the car get wet. Mitchell nodded to the three men sitting in the cab of the lorry as he climbed into the car.

The car pulled away from the curb, closely followed by the lorry, and set off through the town. Mitchell chose one of the newspapers from the seat beside him and glanced at the headlines.

It was because he was reading the newspaper that he was completely unaware of events unfolding on one of the streets they'd just passed. Police cars, moving without the need for 'blues and twos' at that early hour, had sealed off a section of road. Other officers had begun to erect a large white tent on the pavement.

A few minutes later the car arrived at its destination. Galley Hill marked the end of Bexhill's seafront road at the eastern edge of the town. The car pulled into the car park while the lorry turned onto the public green area at the top of the hill. Deciding that he had wasted enough time keeping people waiting for one day, Mitchell exited his car as soon as the driver opened the door for him. An umbrella appeared over his head and he surprised the driver by taking a hold of it himself and heading off towards the parked lorry.

"Bring our guest," he commanded over his shoulder.

By the time he reached the lorry his men had already attached the on-board crane to the first recycling bin. The crane was activated and the container slowly rose a couple of feet from the flatbed at an awkward angle and swung there, the glass inside crashing and grinding together.

The driver arrived at Mitchell's shoulder with his 'guest' being led none too gently by the arm.

And what a comical sight the guest was.

The crane operator sniggered into his hand and immediately glanced at Mitchell, expecting some form of rebuke at his lack of professionalism. But to his relief his boss was also grinning widely. A look of realisation crossed the crane operator's face, followed by more, slightly forced, chuckling. Clearly the object of this exercise was humiliation. Soon Mitchell and his four men were all laughing at the top of their lungs.

Recently released from the spacious trunk of the Escalade, one of the largest production cars on the market, was the shivering form of Jerome Kline. The thin, middle-aged businessman, usually smartly dressed and perfectly groomed, was standing before them completely naked. His hands were cuffed behind his back and a bright red ball-gag was securely strapped around his head. His face was a riot of colour, with bright blue eye shadow, oversized fake eyelashes and bright red cheeks crudely painted over a basecoat of thick white face-paint. Someone had even added a large black beauty spot to one of his cheeks.

Kline was raging with anger, trying his best to scream at his captors through the ball-gag. Spittle and drool dribbled down his chin as he ranted, held firmly in place by Mitchell's driver.

After a few minutes Mitchell stopped laughing and stepped up to the man. The driver held both of Kline's skinny shoulders in an iron grip and struggled to keep the raging man still.

"Well," said Mitchell, looking Kline up and down, "aren't you a picture?"

He turned and nodded to the man working the crane arm. Under that man's deft control the crane lifted the swinging bottle bank away from the lorry. It rocked gently until it reached the ground where its rocking movement was abruptly halted as one edge of its base dug into the ground. The crane operator let the container come to rest on its curved side while the other two men rushed forward to jam wedges under its leading edge. The lifting chains were unhitched and the second bottle bank was prepared for lifting.

All the time this was going on, Jerome Kline was forced to watch, incensed. Mitchell alternated his attention between his men working and Kline's feeble attempts to escape the grip of the driver.

Both sights pleased him.

Kline was furious and helpless. The ball gag was an inspired decision, both adding to his humiliation and keeping him from talking. Mitchell preferred not to be interrupted at the best of times but it was especially important now. The last thing he wanted was Kline displaying any bravado or defiance. He wanted him as helpless as possible.

He was also pleased with the smoothness of the operation. He had called the four men together the night before and explained what he wanted done and told them to work the details out among themselves. They had done so and the operation was proceeding with a smooth efficiency.

Soon two of the three bottle banks were resting on their sides along the top of the steep hill, both held in place by wooden wedges with ropes attached. The third stood on its base off to one side. At a simple nod from their boss, two of the men grabbed the ropes and yanked the first two wedges clear.

The bottle bank began its roll down the hill, slowly gathering speed. The noise was deafening as the broken glass inside crashed and ground together. Everyone winced at the noise at first, taken by surprise at the sheer volume. But soon the men were whooping as the bank disappeared down the hill. It's abrupt stop when it reached the wall of an abandoned warehouse was met with a further cheer before all eyes turned to Mitchell for his permission to set the next one free. Mitchell spared a glance at Kline to ensure he was paying attention and then nodded at his men. The second bank was released and set off down the hill on a similar course until it hit a mound of earth and veered off. It rolled towards the warehouse's empty car park where it struck a concrete bollard, tearing it from the ground before coming to rest in a pile of abandoned pallets. The impact didn't make as much noise as the first bank and this was greeted with groans of disappointment from the men.

Mitchell turned and nodded at his driver who shoved the still raging Kline toward the third bottle bank. Kline was still trying to put up a fight, but there was little he could do with his hands cuffed behind him. Close to the bank he was stopped and held in place once more. Mitchell moved to stand before him and looked him right in the eye. He waited patiently until Kline's attention was assured before speaking.

"A few days ago," Mitchell began, his voice gentle as though beginning a bedtime story, "I came to you with a very kind offer to buy your recycling business. You were very rude to me." He waited a few beats, a look of disappointment on his face as a fresh wave of muffled curses erupted from behind the slobber-covered ball-gag in Kline's mouth. Mitchell sighed and shook his head slowly as he turned and nodded to his three men, now standing menacingly around their victim. Without the need for further instruction, one of them went to the lorry while the other two busied themselves with opening the top hatch of the remaining bottle bank. The first man returned with a stepladder and set it up next to the open hatch.

Realisation fell across Kline's face and his eyes widened in terror as he launched into a fresh bout of desperate thrashing in a vain attempt to escape. His aggressive rantings quickly turned into muffled pleas for mercy. Mitchell stood aside as the driver, now needing the help of the other three men, manhandled Kline toward the stepladder.

Kline, now being carried clear of the ground by the four men, each with an iron grip on their assigned limb, reached the bottom of the ladder. He was roughly dropped onto the ground where his captors stared down at him. He waited for the inevitable, utterly defeated

The four men laughed and walked away.

Kline lay there for a moment, unable to move. Finally he summoned the courage to turn his head to see where everyone had gone. The three men from the lorry had climbed into the cab where they were laughing amongst themselves. The one sitting by the nearest window blew Kline a kiss. The driver was walking back towards Mitchell's car. But still standing a few feet from Kline's prone body stood Mitchell himself. He lit a fat cigar and drew on it heavily before turning it in his hand and staring at the glowing end with satisfaction.

Kline remained quiet, all of his fight gone and feeling suddenly exhausted.

"My next offer for your business," Mitchell said mildly, "will not be as generous."

Kline lay shivering as he watched Mitchell walk away, seething with anger and cursing him with every breath.

But just before he climbed into his car, Mitchell's phone rang. He answered it and spoke for a few seconds before exploding with rage.

"What!" he bellowed, making his driver jump. "I don't give a shit about his fucking friends…! Where the fuck are they now…? Right!"

Kline watched as Mitchell threw his phone into the car and snapped something to his driver as he climbed in. The driver looked shaken as he closed the door and rushed round to the driver's door. The vehicle roared away, closely followed by the flatbed.

Kline grinned to himself as he watched them speed away. He didn't know what had enraged Mitchell so much, but whatever it was he hoped it was serous.

****

Three hours later Ted Kane was in Bexhill-on-Sea, walking towards the police incident zone. He had already made his apologies to an understanding Clare and driven her home before embarking on the one hundred and thirty mile drive to Sussex.

The street was taped off and several police and unmarked forensics vans flanked the site. Even at this early hour uniformed officers were on the scene, holding back onlookers and reporters as Kane approached and began to gently force his way through the small crowd. When he finally reached the tape a young constable raised his hand to his chest, stopping him from coming any closer.

"I'm sorry sir," the officer said politely, "but as you can see, this is a restricted area."

Kane was just reaching for his MI6 I.D. when Morrison's cheery voice called out from further down the street.

"It's all right Phil, he's with me."

The officer swallowed visibly and looked up at Kane with what looked like a mixture of fear and respect and instantly pulled the tape upwards to let him through.

"I'm sorry sir, I didn't realise." He stammered as he stepped aside. By now Morrison had arrived and placed a hand on the young officer's shoulder.

"No need to apologise Phil," he said to the young man, "You're doing a good job here. I'll be sure to tell your sergeant."

The constable looked as though he'd just won the lottery.

"Thank you Agent Morrison!" he said.

"Please," Morrison said with a warm smile, "It's just 'Al'. Now, back to work!"

"Yes sir!" And with that the young police officer returned to his position, his chest swelling with pride.

Kane smiled and shook his head.

It was typical of Alfred Morrison to be on first name terms with everyone within hours of arriving. He wasn't the most intimidating man to come from the British army. Standing at little over five feet tall he looked more like a train-spotter than a former member of the world's toughest elite fighting force. But that had made him the perfect choice on undercover operations in Northern Ireland and elsewhere. Morrison's pre-military life of petty crime had given him unique skills and whichever unit he was with never went without the latest kit. What he couldn't get through sweet-talk he simply went back and stole. The British army was known in the world's military community for never having enough kit, so Morrison was a godsend. During their last tour in the Gulf together, he'd explained to Kane that he especially enjoyed 'borrowing' from the Americans because 'they have all the best toys and so many of them that the odd one or two going missing don't even register.'

On one job together, their four-man SAS patrol were on one of their famous 'Scud-busting' missions in Iraq. They'd successfully located and destroyed their targets and were making a fighting retreat to their pickup point when they found themselves in danger of being surrounded. It was then that they discovered their British-issue satellite phones didn't work. Morrison took out an American version he'd 'borrowed' and proceeded to use secret U.S. I.D codes to first call in an air strike onto their pursuers and then arrange for a pick-up by the U.S. Air Force. No-one ever found out where the kit and codes came from and no-one ever asked. Such is the way of the SAS and such was the way of Alfred Morrison: never taking anything for granted and always making an escape plan or two of his own.

Kane looked at his friend as they walked towards the white forensics tent at the centre of all the fuss.

"So," he said, "what's with all the arse-licking and 'agent' crap from the bobby?"

"Oh, that?" Morrison said with a look of exaggerated innocence, "Phil's a good kid but a bit by-the-book. I just gave him a flash of the MI6 card and spun a bit of the old James Bond secret agent crap. He lapped it up."

Kane grinned. When he'd been approached to join MI6 upon leaving the Regiment he'd been under no illusion that the life of a secret agent had nothing to do with vodka martinis and bikini girls. Mostly it was routine surveillance stints and long hours of paperwork. So far Kane had found very little of interest in the job.

But occasionally there were cases like this one.

As they reached the tent, he turned to Morrison.

"So, what do we have here, Al?"

Morrison didn't say anything, he just held the tent flap open for Kane to enter. Stopping just inside the entrance, Kane quickly began scanning the area with a well-practised eye. Morrison took up a position behind his friend, remaining silent until Kane had surveyed the area.

The tent was quite small by forensics standards, covering about twenty-five square metres, and there wasn't much to be seen within. Portable lighting shone upon two white-clad and masked forensics officers who were quietly returning various tools to their boxes and preparing to leave the area, their jobs done. Kane glanced at two chalk outlines on the pavement surrounded by various blood stains, each with a small numbered marker next to it. Only when the forensics officers rose to leave did Kane move over to examine the single body in the tent. He crouched over the corpse for a closer look while Morrison allowed the two men to leave before closing the flap behind them. He waited in silence, allowing his partner uninterrupted time to examine the area for himself.

Kane guessed the victim's age to be in the mid teens and he was in a terrible state. His chest was caved in and blood covered his t-shirt and the ground immediately around him. His right hand, lying out beside him, was mangled, with several of the fingers broken. But by far the grizzliest injury was to the boy's face. The left hand was still holding the knife that had been thrust into his right cheek, through his mouth and out the other side. The victim's eyes were open but had rolled upwards so far that Kane couldn't make out what colour they were.

Kane turned to Morrison and pointed at the two chalk outlines. "I take it these two survived" he said, a statement rather than a question. There was no other reason to remove two bodies and any survivors would have been examined and removed for medical attention. Not all chalk outlines meant fatalities.

"Barely," Morrison replied, "They've been taken to the Conquest A&E in Hastings. One should pull through alright, but the other one…well, it doesn't look good."

"Hmm. And were their injuries just as… flamboyant?"

"By degrees, yes. Looks like our man warmed up on those two before really having some fun with matey here. Oh, one other thing," Morrison added as though it was just an afterthought. "While the two survivors were being attended to, one of them mumbled something about a man in a green coat." Kane straightened up, his examination apparently over for now. A tight grin played across his face as he glanced round the tent once more.

"Well?" Morrison asked after a few moments, "Do you think it's our man?"

"Yes, I think it is. Looks like his trail just warmed up again. Good work Al."

Alfred Morrison grinned as he pulled the tent flap open with a theatrical flourish. "Only type I do matey."

Once outside the tent Kane lit a cigarette and passed it to Morrison before lighting one for himself. Morrison took his without a word and the two men stood, smoking in silence for several minutes and looking up and down the street. The rain had started to fall more heavily now but neither man seemed to notice.

"Have you noticed," said Kane without looking at his friend, "there are no CCTV cameras on this street?"

"I have, yes."

"So, either our man is very lucky or pretty well organised. Possibly a local boy. Either that or he's had time to stake the street out. He couldn't have checked the whole street for cameras from a single static position before the attack."

"My thoughts exactly," replied Morrison, and the two men fell silent again as they finished their cigarettes.

"Well," said Morrison, dropping his cigarette butt and grinding it under his heel, "we'll have to go in my car. I'm not sure your piece of crap will get us all the way to Hastings."

Chapter 3: Perks of the Job

The Grand Canyon was a truly wonderful sight.

No matter how many times he laid his eyes upon it, Deblanc always felt as though he was seeing it for the first time. He had explored much of the world and so far this was his favourite place. Not only was the Grand Canyon National Park arguably the most beautiful place on earth, but at over fifteen million acres it was also a very easy place to find solitude.

Deblanc sat in a cave high up on the canyon's northern rim, watching the Colorado River, thousands of feet below, continuing to eat into rock three billion years older than that of the cave in which he now sat.

A squirrel scurried into the cave entrance, where it stopped and stared at him. Deblanc remained motionless and stared back at the timid creature. Nobody ever came to this part of the Canyon and it was probable that he was the first human being the squirrel had ever seen. The thought made him happy. It was likely that no human had ventured into this cave for hundreds of thousands of years. It was his now.

He often came here to quiet his mind after violent events such as those four hours ago in Bexhill. He had no fear of the worlds' various authorities, he knew he could deal with any situation this world could throw at him. But it was always easier and far less complicated to take his leave and visit one of his many hideouts.

He had already been to one of the apartments he kept in nearby Las Vegas to change his clothes before spending a pleasant hour or so touring his favourite casinos and bars. Over a hundred Las Vegas surveillance cameras had recorded him in the first two hours after the Bexhill incident. The perfect alibi should he need it.

And all he had to do now was enjoy a moment of quiet introspection before…

"Deblanc." His name was uttered by a quiet, ancient voice.

The squirrel didn't hear the voice of course, projected as it was into a microscopic receiver implanted in the tympanic membrane of his left ear. It was a good system with just one flaw. While the incoming signal was completely silent to any other person or known listening device, the system's microscopic sending component, located in the cartilage of his larynx, could only be activated by physical vocalisation. With practice the user could lower the volume of his voice to near inaudible levels, but it was almost impossible to send without making some sound.

Deblanc sighed, his moment of solitude gone. It didn't matter how long he had to himself, any interruption was always greeted with the same stomach-twisting sensation of disappointment and anger.

He was instantly irritated. Irritated with the caller, irritated with the world and irritated with the squirrel.

"What do you want, Sol?" he said loudly and watched the squirrel scurry away, a metaphor for his disappearing calm. Of course, it wouldn't of mattered if he'd shouted at the top of his lungs, there was no one nearby to hear him and the caller himself would be receiving through a comm system identical to his. The system was self regulating, adjusting its volume thousands of times a second to ensure a comfortable level no matter how loud or quiet the sender's voice and whatever the level of environmental noise at either end of the transmission. But what it *could* convey was the tone of the sender's voice and Deblanc's irritation was obvious.

"Once again," the emotionless male voice droned, "you have failed to report before the designated deadline."

"I've been busy."

There was a slight pause before the voice continued.

"I am aware of the events in Bexhill, Deblanc, just as you are aware that any such activity must be reported immediately. I am also aware that you are currently sitting in a cave in Arizona and have been doing so for one hour and seventeen minutes. You have not been busy."

Deblanc didn't know what annoyed him more; the invasion of his privacy, Sol's eternally emotionless voice or being treated like a child.

"You will come to the Keep immediately," the voice said "and wait for me there." And with that, the connection was cut.

Sol's other annoying habit was his ability to surprise.

Deblanc hadn't been invited back into the Keep, Sol's base of operations, since he'd first been recruited several years previously. And he wouldn't be ordered back unless for a very important reason, something more important than another lecture about his methods.

He had a very bad feeling about this.

****

Alfred Morrison guided his silver Audi estate into the staff car park of Hastings' Conquest Hospital. He found a space and reversed into it. Nobody with his experience of covert operations would ever drive forwards into a parking space; you never knew when a quick getaway might be needed.

He reached over and selected a 'visiting doctor' security pass from the glove compartment and placed it in the window. This drew a wry look from Ted Kane.

"What?" Morrison demanded with exaggerated innocence. "I'm a trained medic aren't I? Patched you up enough times."

"No argument there," Kane replied as he took out his cigarettes. "I was just wondering if there's a situation you *haven't* got a fake ID for?"

Morrison nodded towards the cigarettes. "Not in the car mate," he said as he reached back to retrieve a laptop from the rear seat. "Look, if you came into the office every now and then you'd be able to get your hands on all sorts of cool stuff too."

Kane grunted and climbed out of the car. He lit a cigarette, passed it over the car roof to Morrison and then lit one for himself. As he did so he glanced at the child's booster seat in the back of his friend's car. He often wondered how Morrison managed to maintain a normal family life while doing a job like this. He tried to remember the name of the child but couldn't.

"How's the kid doing?" he asked as they walked towards the hospital entrance. "She'll be walking soon won't she?"

"Sky's just turned three, of course she's bloody walking. Talking too." Morrison turned to look at his friend. "Small talk and children. Not two of your greatest strengths Ted."

Kane grunted and the pair walked and smoked in silence.

Usually, Morrison would aim to turn such introspective moments around with a change of subject or quip of some kind, but he knew what his friend was probably thinking about and chose to allow him the quiet moment.

Morrison and Kane would usually take every opportunity to take cheap shots and digs at each other, such was the nature of their professional partnership, but that had changed after an unguarded moment from Kane a while back.

Morrison didn't know much about his friend's love life and really wasn't interested. He didn't understand how anyone could reach their early forties without making a commitment to one relationship or other. He and his wife had been married for eight years and he'd never been happier. He simply couldn't imagine life without his wife and little girl to go home to. What would be the point of such a fruitless life?

One evening, while he and Kane had been on a stakeout together, huddled in a freezing hire car outside some five star hotel in Oslo, Morrison had brought the conversation round to married life once again. He did most of the talking as usual, and eventually his monologue ended on the question of whether Kane ever saw himself settling down or not? Kane had been in a more sombre mood than usual, sitting in that freezing car for so long couldn't have helped, and said something so out of character that Morrison actually looked at his friend to make sure it was Kane sitting next to him and not some impostor.

Staring dully out of his side window and with his voice barely audible, Kane had muttered "I've already found and lost one soul mate, it would be greedy to assume there was another one out there somewhere."

The conversation was killed stone dead of course, but the words were out. Kane was obviously embarrassed by the uncharacteristic dropping of his guard and Morrison decided to pass on the opportunity to rag him about it. Gathering information was his specialty and he was very good at it, but Morrison doubted very much that he would ever get anything further on the subject from Kane.

By the time they reached the hospital door both men had returned their thoughts to the case at hand.

Their quarry, known only by the name Deblanc, had remained beyond their reach for several years. He had first crossed Kane and Morrison's path during an investigation into an explosion in London's Docklands. An apparently deserted warehouse had exploded for no apparent reason during a property developer's survey. The investigation later showed that the surveyor was there without the permission of the owners, owners that were never traced. The unfortunate man was there at the request of an over-confident property developer, too eager to cash in on the early-millennium property boom to wait for permission.

But the reason MI6 became involved was the nature of the explosion. The building was completely vaporised, every brick reduced to dust, every girder melted to slag. It was as if an atomic bomb had been detonated within London's city limits.

But not a single person reported hearing a sound and no damage was reported to any property, vehicle or even shrub outside the immediate blast zone. One minute there was an empty warehouse, the next there wasn't. There wasn't even the faintest trace of radioactive residue and the only reason a time could be put to the explosion was that the surveyor was talking to his office on his mobile phone at the time.

The mystery of the warehouse remained just that, a mystery with no clues until Morrison caught a lucky break. Among the hundreds of hours of CCTV footage taken from the roads surrounding the warehouse he spotted a solitary figure wearing a dark trench coat. He didn't think anything of it until he noticed the man stop a few hundred yards from the warehouse. He appeared to stare at something off camera for a couple of heartbeats before turning back the way he'd come. And all this happened seconds before the warehouse was vaporised. The man in the trench coat had clearly seen something.

Morrison brought the footage to Kane's attention to see if his friend could get anything else from it. And of course he did. By comparing the time on the CCTV footage Kane noticed that the man in the trench coat, once walking away from the warehouse, put his hand in his coat pocket at exactly the same moment as the surveyor's mobile phone went dead; the assumed time of the explosion. But with no evidence of foreign involvement in the warehouse events, the case was passed from MI6 to MI5, Britain's homeland security division.

Several months later the case was returned to MI6 when someone matching the man's vague description appeared on a CCTV camera in the small Spanish seaside town of Platja D'Oro. Morrison and Kane were reassigned to the case and immediately set off for Barcelona. It was while they were transferring from the airport to Platja D'Oro that their mysterious quarry struck again, striking at the Interpol field office dealing with the case. Every piece of information regarding the case was destroyed, but far more disturbing was the fate of the Spanish officers stationed there. Every member of that six-man team had been killed in a variety of grotesque and flamboyant ways.

With no surviving witnesses the case had gone cold again.

But then another lucky break: The day before Kane and Morrison set off for Spain one of the Interpol officers had had his laptop stolen from his car. He hadn't informed his office and the matter wouldn't have come to light had Kane not found a ransom note from the thief in the agent's apartment. Assuming that a leak within Spain's intelligence services had led their quarry to the field office in the first place, Kane and Morrison set about retrieving the laptop themselves. Which they did without too much trouble. It had been stolen by a local opportunist who had tried to sell it on to the newspapers.

The laptop contained little new information, but the Spanish agent's investigations had managed to provide a name: Deblanc.

The two agents cleared their desks and from that moment on concentrated fully on finding Deblanc.

One thing was clear. Deblanc was a very careful man. Whenever a lead presented itself it quickly went cold and they were yet to get a decent picture of the man's face. Only the bizarre circumstances in which he was brought to the various authorities' attention and the grizzly trail of death he left behind linked each occurrence. There seemed to be no pattern or reason to his actions.

Unfortunately, leads were so few and far between that it wasn't long before Kane and Morrison were forced to take other cases and over the years Deblanc slowly slid down MI6's priority listings.

But Deblanc was never far from the minds of Ted Kane and Alfred Morrison.

The two agents entered the hospital and set about locating the two survivors. Without a word Morrison headed for the information desk while Kane headed for the nearest 'You Are Here' poster to familiarise himself with the hospital's floor plan. In their years of working together the two men had leant to play to their individual strengths; Kane's almost perfect memory and tactical prowess the perfect compliment to Morrison's ability to gather information and deal with people on a personal level. By the time Morrison approached Kane he had pretty much memorised the hospital layout.

"They're both on Norman ward," Morrison said, "off the A&E department. One critical and one talking." He held up his laptop, "With any luck we should be able to get a photo-fit pieced together."

"Yeah," Kane grunted as he led the way. "Be nice to finally see what the bastard looks like."

Kane's pace quickened as he felt the thrill of the hunt coursing through him, raising his pulse rate. They had spent so long chasing Deblanc, seen so many of the man's atrocities, that the hunt had become deeply personal. So many times they thought they'd got a line on him only to have their hopes dashed and their quarry disappear yet again. But today they were one step closer to their prey. Today, after years of fruitless chasing, they might actually get to see the face of their tormentor.

As they approached the ward however, it quickly became clear that something was wrong.

The first clue as they passed through the ward door, was the unmanned nurses' station. At this time of the day it should have been bustling with staff preparing to give patients their morning tests and readying them for breakfast. But all was silent. Kane and Morrison looked at each other with concern before splitting up to check the ward. Morrison stepped behind the nurse's station and instantly called Kane over.

"What do you make of this?" he asked as his colleague approached. Kane followed his nod down onto the desk where he saw a pile of mobile phones and walkie-talkies.

Both men reached beneath their jackets and drew their sidearms. Something was definitely amiss.

Each man taking one side of the short corridor leading to the main ward, they walked slowly, their weapons held in front of them, arms rigid and always pointing in the direction of their intense gazes. The whole ward was eerily silent save for the occasional bleep from various machines.

Kane motioned up ahead where he'd spotted a private side room with its door wedged closed, a broom jammed through the handle. Morrison nodded his acknowledgement and the two men silently continued along the corridor, checking rooms as they went, with Kane keeping a wary eye ahead and Morrison one behind.

Soon they reached the wedged door and stopped. The side room had a small window in the door but it had been covered with a 'Have you cleaned your hands?' poster on the outside. The rough angle of the poster and the thick gaffer tape used to hold it there was all wrong.

Kane nodded first to Morrison and then the door while he held up his left hand, flat, with its palm down. He then jerked his thumb at his own chest, pointed two fingers at his eyes then aimed his flat palm, side-on this time, further down the ward. Morrison nodded. He would wait there to cover the door and ward entrance while Kane would secure the rest of the ward before they investigated the sealed room.

Kane returned less than a minute later and with no more than a thumbs-up with regards the ward. He pointed his gun at the poster on the door and nodded to his colleague. Morrison pointed his own weapon in a similar direction and leaned forward to grab the corner of the poster. At a further nod from Kane he ripped the poster free with one swift action and let it fall to the floor. There was a female scream from inside.

Kane peered down the length of his gun through the small window for less than a second before lowering it and pulling the broom free.

"Stand back!" he shouted as he kicked the door open. This resulted in further screaming, this time from several different voices. Kane entered the room, his weapon in the ready position, while Morrison turned to cover the entrance of the ward. A second later Kane's voice sounded again.

"Clear!"

Morrison allowed himself to relax slightly. He lowered his gun and followed Kane into the room. Within were a dozen hospital staff, several patients and an elderly woman sitting up in the room's single bed. Everyone but the old woman looked a mixture of terrified and relieved, while the woman herself appeared to be having a much happier time.

"Well," she beamed, completely unaware of the tense situation playing out around her, "I've never had so many visitors!"

****

Just over twenty minutes later local police officers were on the scene and the debriefings were underway. Kane had made himself scarce, taking the time to step outside for a cigarette. He didn't need to be there for the debrief: people were Morrison's field. He took the time to pace and concentrate on lowering his pulse rate. He was feeling pretty angry and knew from past experience not to get involved with debriefing civilians. Morrison's investigations went a lot quicker without him hovering like a dark cloud waiting to spit thunder.

After several minutes, and two more cigarettes, Morrison returned, his laptop tucked under his arm. Kane lit another cigarette and handed it to his friend.

"Ta," he said as he took it. "Well, it's pretty much as we assumed. Either someone else has an interest in our man Deblanc or that was the biggest damn coincidence I've ever seen." Morrison nodded towards a picnic table and opened the laptop as the two men moved towards it.

"This is what we have," he began as they sat down at the same side of the table. "Three men entered the ward and claimed to be related to one of Deblanc's victims. They were allowed into the patient's room where they demanded he be released into their care. The nurse told them it was impossible because of the patient's condition, he paused as he drew on his cigarette.

"And?" Kane prompted.

"And that's when they went loud. They rounded up the staff and walking patients, took their phones and walkies and locked them up with that thoroughly pleasant Mrs. Wilkinson."

"I know all that," Kane sighed, beginning to sound weary, "Do we have any leads on the bastards?"

Morrison smiled, keeping Kane in agony a moment longer.

"Yes we do. Piecing together details from several of the witnesses I've managed to get a positive ID on one of the snatch team. I assumed advanced military training and began my search through the Sandhurst database. And here he is."

Morrison pressed a few keys on the laptop and turned it to face Kane. The screen showed the military record of one Gregory Lindros, a soldier wearing an officer's uniform of the Royal Logistical Corps. Beside the photo the man's military history detailed his chequered career right up to his dishonourable discharge for 'misuse of military hardware'.

"That was quick work, Al." Kane said as he scanned the screen.

"Oh, you know," his friend replied, his face a study in exaggerated modesty, "You just need to ask the right questions. And it helped not having your ugly mug unsettling the poor bastards. They've been through enough. Plus," he added, pointing to the screen, "he is quite a memorable-looking chap isn't he?"

That was an understatement. Rather than looking like an officer, the man on the screen was the caricature of a thug. Atop an impossibly broad neck sat his shaved head with its thick brow and dark scowl. His nose had clearly been broken at least once and his left eyebrow was almost gone, replaced by a tight network of pale blue scars that continued down onto his cheek. It was a face you were unlikely to forget.

"So," asked Kane when he'd read all he wanted to, "How do we get a hold of this charmer?"

"Ah, well, that's the problem. Since he was thrown out of the Army he fell off the radar. No criminal record, no National Insurance or P.A.Y.E. activity, no driving licence, no passport, no nothing. He obviously isn't dead, so best guess is he's connected to organised crime, most likely an enforcer."

Kane pushed the laptop away in disgust, his anger returning.

"Great. Another dead end." He reached for yet another cigarette and, finding only one left in the packet, looked up at Morrison. His friend grinned and held out his hand.

"Oh, come on!" Kane pleaded. But Morrison's grin only widened as his hand reached out further. Kane sighed, lit the remaining cigarette and passed it to his friend. "You're killing me." He muttered as he screwed up the empty pack and threw it on the ground.

"Deal's a deal." Morrison replied as he drew deeply on the cigarette, blowing smoke rings into the air. "Ah," he purred in mock ecstasy, "This is a particularly good one."

Kane grunted loudly and glared at his friend. "So, where next?" he demanded, all business again. "Back to square one?"

"Not entirely," Morrison replied. "We still have the other survivor, the one still critical." He nodded back toward the building. "I've posted a couple of uniforms in there with him. Babysitting duty. When, or if, he comes to, he may be able to give us a description of Deblanc. Though to be honest, the chances of him being able to talk in the near future are pretty close to zero. Or," he added as though an afterthought, "we could just go get this Gregory Lindros chap…"

"The other dead end," Kane grunted.

Morrison grinned as he turned the laptop back towards himself. While finishing his cigarette he tapped away at the keyboard for a couple of minutes.

"One day," he began as he stubbed the cigarette out on the picnic table, "you will learn to truly appreciate what a genius I am."

He turned the laptop back to face Kane.

Kane looked at the screen, now showing an Ordinance Survey-scale map. In the centre of the map a red dot was flashing.

"What's this?" Kane demanded as he stared at the screen.

"That," Morrison replied triumphantly, "is our new best friend, Mr Gregory Lindros, just arriving at Sainsburys in Eastbourne. Looks like he's doing his shopping."

Kane stared at his friend as if he'd just turned water into wine.

"Tell you what," Morrison continued as he closed the laptop and stood, "Why don't we go and say hello?"

"But…?"

"And while we're there, you can get some more fags."

"How…?"

But Morrison was already heading for his car. Kane followed in his friend's wake, shaking his head and grinning.

Chapter 4 – Hereford Cocktail

Deblanc opened his eyes and winced at the bright light surrounding him, not shining down upon him, but physically surrounding him. There was no indication of where the light came from; it was simply there, illuminating every nook and cranny of the room.

The reception room itself looked no different from the last time he had visited Sol's Keep. Measuring about a hundred metres on each side, the arrivals chamber was a featureless white cube containing a huge variety of chairs, couches and beds spread evenly throughout the space and along three of the blank walls. The furniture was made from a shiny white plastic, the chairs and couches fitted with overstuffed, plain white material. The fourth wall was an immaculate, seamless expanse of white, completely devoid of feature or interest. But it was towards this wall that Deblanc glared, arms folded across his chest, his back rigid.

"Come on, come on," he demanded at the wall.

After a few moments a pale blue, glowing spot appeared halfway along the wall, about a metre from the floor. The spot remained steady for a few seconds before swiftly expanding into a glowing oval, two metres high and one wide. Through this shimmering portal stepped the slight figure of an elderly man clad in a pale grey, collarless suit. Despite appearing to be of pensionable age, the man was clearly both fit and healthy, his bald head free of wrinkles and with piercing blue eyes as sharp as any Deblanc had ever seen. The Portal disappeared, the white wall showing no sign that it had ever been there.

The man stood, matching stares with Deblanc, his neutral expression facing Deblanc's angry glare. As ever, it was Deblanc who blinked first, further angering himself.

"Well?" he finally demanded of the older man, "What's so important?"

The man remained silent.

"If this is about Bexhill, I had to do something before those yobs caught up with your precious little pet!"

Still the man remained silent, calmly regarding Deblanc and ignoring his anger. Deblanc glared back a moment longer, his anger peaking. The man watched silently as Deblanc snorted loudly and began pacing, clenching and unclenching his fists.

"All right!" Deblanc snapped, "Perhaps I was a little…vigorous with them. But you can't tell me the world wouldn't be a slightly better place without those parasites prowling the streets."

The man remained silent until Deblanc stopped his pacing and his attention returned. The two men stared at each other a moment longer before Deblanc's shoulders sagged and he sighed loudly.

"Alright," he sighed in a quieter tone, "you're right. I went too far and endangered my mission. Happy now?" Still, the man remained silent. Deblanc tried again. "You know as well as I do that after a fright like that, Timothy Bruce will be hiding under his bed for days. He's secure. No problem."

Silence filled the room and the two men regarded each other a few moments longer. This time Deblanc blinked much sooner and stared at the floor, deflated.

"The well-being of this planet's society is not your primary concern, Deblanc," the man finally spoke, his voice calm and level though not lecturing. "You are well aware of this, just as you are aware of the importance of Timothy Bruce."

"I know that, Sol." Deblanc sighed.

"And you know the time restrictions we are working under."

"Yes."

"Actually," Sol began as he moved to one of the chairs and sat down, suddenly sounding old and tired, "that is why I ordered you to the Keep." He motioned to another chair and waited while Deblanc sat to face him.

"I have just heard from one of our automated stations in sector six. The Brachyurans are closer than we thought." He looked Deblanc straight in the eye. Was that fear Deblanc could see in the old man's face? "Much closer."

That was a surprise, and not a pleasant one. Deblanc had no idea what to say or do, not even what to think. He was shocked to his core.

The two men sat in silence. This changed everything.

Deblanc had hated his mission, the endless and tedious task of watching over the pathetic Timothy Bruce. He knew how important it was and how much faith it showed on Sol's part to trust him with it, especially in the face of his own frustrated insubordination.

But no matter how much he hated his mission, Deblanc knew it to be a relatively safe one. He knew it was little more than a period of waiting for the mission proper to begin. His frustration and anger was in part due to his helplessness in the greater scheme of things. He felt suddenly impotent, like a school bully facing the move from primary to secondary school where he would become a small fish in a much bigger pond.

"So what's the plan?" he said in a quiet, almost pleading voice, suddenly aware of how insignificant he was and how much he relied on Sol's guidance. "Do you want me to bring Timothy Bruce in?"

Sol stood, the action filling Deblanc with a small feeling of hope. Sol would know what to do, he always did.

"Not yet." Sol's voice was as calm and even as ever, "There is something I require you to do first. A task that you may feel more suited to your talents."

Deblanc felt a small thrill of excitement, pleased to be free of his Timothy Bruce duties. Finally, something to break the monotony of the past few years. He looked past Sol toward the wall through which his master had recently emerged. Sol followed his gaze and smiled.

"No, Deblanc," he answered the unasked question, "It is not yet time for you to return to the Keep proper. Your mission will be taking you back to the surface."

Deblanc stood, the scowl returning to his face. Sol smiled and stepped forward to place his hand on Deblanc's shoulder.

"Do not worry, Deblanc," he said, "I think this particular task will be much more to your liking."

****

Ted Kane sat quietly as Alfred Morrison drove them towards Eastbourne, an unopened carton of cigarettes lying across his lap. Morrison had agreed to stop for 'essential supplies', but not to wait for his friend to open them before getting back in the car. Morrison smiled as he glanced down at Kane's finger tapping the carton. It had been almost an hour since the man's last cigarette but that wasn't the only reason for Kane's agitation.

"Alright, alright," Kane finally burst out, "I give in! How the hell did you know where Lindros was?"

"Ah," Morrison replied, impossibly smug, "you wouldn't ask a magician how his tricks were performed, would you?"

Kane glared back. “Yes, I would.”

Morrison regarded him briefly. “Probably at gunpoint,” he muttered. Kane’s glare increased in intensity. “Alright then,” he continued. “It was very simple actually. I figured they would have left in something of a hurry and most likely with a wheelchair for their passenger. So I checked the car park CCTV and spotted three men loading a patient into a Landrover Discovery. I got lucky and captured the number plate.” He turned to face his friend. “With me so far?” he asked in his most patronising tone.

“OK,” Kane sighed, “that’s pretty straightforward. But how the hell did you track him to Sainsburys? I don’t see any use in the number plate of a car that unlikely to be registered to our invisible man.”

“Now *that’s* the clever part. I could see it was a top of the range model so I ran the plate through the vehicle database and guess what?”

“Go on…”

“It has satellite navigation.” Morrison announced in triumph.

“Ah,” Kane breathed, realisation dawning.

“Yep.” Morrison tapped the similar unit on the dashboard. “Got the vehicle’s return signal codes and routed them through to here.”

Kane craned his neck to look at the small screen. It showed a flashing red dot, similar to the one he’d seen on Morrison’s laptop.

“You see,” said Morrison, “not so impressive when the magician explains, is it?”

“Still, not something I’d have thought of.”

“Nope,” Morrison agreed as he tapped the screen again. “But we’re coming up on the target, so it’s over to you. What’s the plan?”

Kane thought for a moment. “Neutralise his two friends and take Mr Lindros away for a quiet chat, see what he knows about Deblanc. And I suppose we’d better take the kid back to the hospital after we’ve debriefed him.”

“Assuming his condition hasn’t deteriorated under their tender care. He was pretty badly banged up before they moved him.” Morrison reached over to the SatNav and increased the screen scale. “We’re less than a mile from Eastbourne hospital, we’d better drop him off there. Phone ahead and order up some uniforms to meet us there.”

Kane pulled out his mobile phone and did so. When the call was over Morrison announced that they were a couple of streets from their destination.

"How do you want to play this?" he asked.

"Find a spot where we can see their car and park up." Kane replied as he checked the load of his sidearm. "We'll see how it looks and take it from there."

Morrison suddenly yanked the car over to the side of the road and stopped. Before Kane could put words to the question his raised eyebrows were already asking, Morrison tapped the SatNav screen.

"They're on the move," he said.

Morrison re-holstered his weapon and pointed forward.

"Let's go."

Morrison waited a few moments before moving off.

Tailing another car was a delicate and skilful job for which he was well trained. Unlike in the movies it's not a simple case of driving behind the target and hoping they don't notice you. Special care was needed, especially when the target had military training. Instead, with the advantage of their satellite navigation tracking, they could follow some distance behind, out of sight, using the screen as a guide. The only problem came when the target arrived at their destination and switched the car engine off, ending the SatNav feed. Kane would be keeping a constant eye on the screen, giving Morrison directions and be ready to memorise the spot when the red dot disappeared.

While both men watched that dot, Kane opened his carton of cigarettes and removed two packs. He reached down to put the rest of the carton under his seat. He chuckled as he examined one of the packets then held it up for Morrison to see.

"Have you see this?" he asked.

Morrison glanced at the packet and saw that the usual black and white, printed government health warning had been replaced with a photograph of a dead body along with the text 'Smokers die younger'.

"Yeah," he replied, "They started putting those on a while back, trying to scare people out of their dirty little habits."

"Well," said Kane as he showed his friend the other packet, "they've failed with me on this one."

The second packet showed a different picture, this one a microscopic view of some sperm with the text 'Smoking damages sperm and lowers fertility.'

"Now, that," Kane said with a grin, "sounds like a damn good reason to keep smoking. If you ask me, the government should keep quiet about that one. Sounds like a double assault on teenage pregnancies."

Morrison let the comment pass. He was used to Kane's blunt opinions. The man never had an overabundance of tact.

"You know it's already backfiring?" Morrison said. "The photo warnings are only just starting to filter through and already there are websites for people collecting the packs, like when they used to make cigarette cards. Probably buying more fags than ever."

Kane harrumphed as he looked at the dead body picture again.

"Think I'll stick to duty frees."

Some minutes later the red dot disappeared, its last location blinking on an industrial estate just outside Eastbourne. Morrison guided the car in that direction while both men compared their own vehicle's location icon to the spot the red dot was last seen. As they passed the spot, a nondescript wholesale warehouse catering to the drink's trade, both men were careful not to look directly at the building while Morrison maintained the steady speed of a car just passing through.

Morrison parked the car several warehouses away and both men exited the vehicle. As soon as his feet touched the ground Kane opened a packed of cigarettes, lit one and passed it to Morrison. He then lit one for himself while his friend busied himself with unlocking the rear hatch of the estate car.

"So," said Morrison as he wrestled with the boot's deadlocks, "What's the plan?"

"Recon first, then take it from there. We need to get the hostage out alive and bag Lindros for debriefing. We'll see how many X-rays he has with him and what sort of threat they present." He drew on his cigarette as he watched Morrison open the boot and pull aside the carpeting to reveal the spare tyre compartment beneath. Instead of a tyre however, the compartment held a large holdall. "We know we have at least one target with military training, Lindros, and probably the other two members of his snatch team. We don't know how many more people are in the warehouse, what their experience is and whether we can expect more to arrive. But we don't have time to wait for reinforcements, so it's down to us."

None of these details were news to Morrison of course, but Kane detailed them anyway and Morrison didn't feel in the slightest bit patronised. It was in their training to vocalise every aspect of an operation before going in. Both men had to be on exactly the same page and if there was the slightest chance that one of them had missed some piece of information, no matter how small, things could very quickly turn sour.

"Splendid," Morrison muttered around the cigarette. He hefted the holdall out of the tyre compartment, pushed the carpet back in place and placed the bag on the flat surface. "Might I suggest we invite them out for cocktails?"

Kane grinned expectantly as he looked down at the holdall.

"Toys?" he asked.

"All manner of shiny new toys," Morrison grinned, then turned serious again. "We're agreed we have to go in *now*?" he asked.

"I think so, yes." Kane regarded his friend for a moment. "We both have a veto of course, so I guess it's up to you."

The usual procedure would have been to put in a call for backup before entering such a potentially dangerous situation, but both men were acutely aware of the limited time they had. The captured hospital patient was by far their best lead to Deblanc and Lindros' involvement warranted further investigation. The chance to secure both sources of Intel with such a strong element of surprise on their side was too good an opportunity to pass up. Both men knew from their long and varied experiences that chances sometimes had to be taken to secure their goals. And chances to secure a line on Deblanc were so rare.

"Alright," said Morrison, his mind made up. "Let's go to work." Both men cast their eyes about the area to make sure they would be undisturbed as Morrison opened the bag and drew out a submachine gun. "For sir," he announced as he handed the weapon to Kane. "A factory fresh FN P90 USG with improved optical package. I was saving it for your birthday, but what the hell…"

Kane turned the compact weapon over in his hands, a smile creeping across his face.

"USG?" he breathed, "American spec. How the hell did you get hold of this?"

"Well," Morrison replied with exaggerated modesty, "West Midland Police are trialing the standard model at Birmingham Airport and I know the guy who puts in the orders from Belgium. I convinced him this would be a better choice."

"And he just took your word for it?"

"I saw how much you liked them when we were training SWAT in Washington last year, and you're such a difficult person to buy for..."

"You could have wrapped it, wanker." Kane grinned as he checked the weapon's action and reached into the bag for a couple of extra 50-round magazines.

"Your gratitude is most touching," Morrison sighed as he passed Kane a webbing harness for the weapon. "I'm filling up."

Kane removed his jacket and shoulder holster and dropped them into the back of the car. He then put the webbing on over his shirt. Resembling the skeleton of a vest, the webbing allowed the wearer to secure the butt of the compact weapon to a point just below his right shoulder with a short length of strapping. This allowed the wearer to let the weapon hang down the side of his chest, easily concealing it beneath a jacket while at the same time making it easy to bring the butt up to the shoulder for firing. He then slotted his sidearm into the webbing's built-in underarm holster as he watched Morrison draw a 9mm MP5K machine pistol from the bag.

"You still have an eye for the classics I see."

"Stick with what you know, mate," Morrison replied as he removed his own jacket and secured his weapon to webbing similar to Kane's. "These little babies have served us well over the years."

Kane couldn't argue with that. Morrison's gun was the compact version of the Heckler and Koch weapon made famous by the SAS in the Iranian Embassy siege of 1980.

"And for our friends inside," Morrison announced with a flourish, "one Hereford Cocktail."

Kane grinned widely as he looked at the two items held out before him.

"Nice. Let's give the place a quick once-over."

****

The warehouse was little more than a storage and distribution depot for wine and beer, with a main area for storage and a smaller room at the front of the building being used as an office. The main storage area was huge, its maze of racking as high as a three-story building. Half a dozen articulated lorries were parked inside, with several forklift trucks dotted around the loading area.

Outside, Morrison's car had been moved as close to the building as they'd dared, the rear hatch open and ready to receive their targets.

Kane and Morrison gained access by picking the lock on one of the fire exits at the rear of the building and then split up to approach the office from opposite sides, Kane along the left wall and Morrison the right. Their intention was to incapacitate anyone they found in the main warehouse on the way but so far they had not seen anyone.

Kane moved slowly between the racking, weapon raised to his shoulder, his every sense alert. Across the warehouse he caught occasional glimpses of Morrison as he paralleled his route. Ahead he could hear low voices coming from the direction of the office and a look towards Morrison confirmed that he, too, had heard them. Both men dropped into a crouch and strained to hear the voices, but they were too muffled to pick out individual words. Morrison pointed to his ear and shook his head. Kane nodded and signalled forward, his mind running through scenarios and drills, preparing himself for whatever they found ahead.

Kane found his path blocked by an untidy pile of empty pallets and rather than risk making noise by climbing over them, decided to bypass them by ducking beneath some empty shelving to the right. When he'd completed the manoeuvre he looked across to Morrison to make sure he was still parallel to his partner and not falling behind. But Morrison was nowhere to be seen. Kane cast his gaze about, looking for either Morrison, or… there. Someone was approaching Morrison's last-seen position, from up ahead. Morrison must have seen him and taken cover.

From his position of concealment Kane watched the man approach the spot where he'd last seen his friend... and pass it. Kane frowned and was just starting to wonder what Morrison was playing at when the warehouse worker suddenly dropped out of sight with a low grunt. Silence followed and Kane smiled to himself. He shouldn't have doubted his friend. All those years in and out of the office clearly hadn't dulled his reflexes.

Kane waited a few moments, scanning the area ahead while he allowed Morrison time to conceal the unconscious worker. The warehouse remained silent, no cries of alarm were issued, no sounds of running feet or weapons being cocked. Everything appeared fine until something caught Kane's eye. A booted foot was sticking out from behind a shelving unit a dozen or so metres ahead of Morrison's position. There was no way he could have incapacitated someone that far ahead and returned in such a short amount of time. Something was wrong.

Kane desperately looked over to where Morrison was, hoping to warn his colleague, but he was still nowhere to be seen. That was worrying too. He should have secured the man by now and re-established visual contact with Kane.

Something was definitely wrong. Kane decided to make his way across the warehouse and investigate. But as he moved forward, using the layout of the staggered shelving as cover from the office end of the warehouse, his path took him closer to the booted foot he'd seen a moment before. Now, closer to the boot, he noticed something else about it.

It belonged to Morrison.

Kane's blood ran cold as he fought down the urge to rush forward to check on his friend. The situation had changed drastically. He was facing a person or persons unknown, clearly with military training, in unfamiliar surroundings. The standard military procedure would be to make a strategic withdrawal and reassess the situation.

But Kane wasn't standard military. Kane was former SAS.

He silently set off towards the office, straight toward the enemy. His every instinct screamed at him to run to his friend's side, but that was the most likely reason he'd been left out in the open. He would deal with any hostiles then check on Morrison's condition once the area was secure. Rushing to Morrison's aid now wouldn't help either of them.

Knowing that at least one assailant was present at Morrison's side of the warehouse, Kane kept to the left and made his cautious way forward.

Soon he was near the front of the building and close to the office. He hadn't heard any voices since Morrison went down, but decided to check the office area anyway. His intention was to secure the area before working his way back once he knew his rear was safe.

But as he rounded the last corner his weapon was suddenly snatched from his hands. The unseen assailant grabbed his wrist and wrenched him forward. As he fell past the assailant he felt a hand shoving his shoulder, propelling him across the concrete. Kane tipped himself forward and allowed his momentum to throw him into a roll. He came up into a crouch and reached beneath his arm for his sidearm. But it wasn't there.

"Looking for this?" a calm voice asked.

Before Kane stood a man of average build, holding up the weapon in question and giving it a mocking shake. In his other hand was the P90, held by its barrel by the side of his body, butt downwards. Kane strained to see who it was but the man's face was hidden by shadows. Whether by luck or design he stood beneath some recently broken lights: glass littered the ground.

Kane stood slowly, his hands raised slightly. As he rose he glanced around, taking in his surroundings. In the office he recognised the scar-faced Lindros and his two colleagues sprawled out on the floor. The open concrete area he now found himself in led off in several directions into the warehouse's maze of shelving. But none of those exits were anywhere near enough for him to have any chance of escaping. He placed his hands behind his neck.

"That was a pretty neat trick," he said. "Learn that at Ninja school, did you?"

"Oh, no, no," the man replied calmly, not in the least bit arrogant. "Just a little something I came up with just then. *You're* the one with all the training," he continued, his manner almost reverent. "I was watching you and your friend work. I must say, I was very impressed with your technique."

"Well, I'm not quite done impressing you yet…"

As he spoke, Kane reached down below his neck and grasped at the two objects secured to the webbing there. The two ingredients of a Hereford Cocktail.

Stun Grenades, or 'Flashbangs', have long been an important part of the SAS armoury. Invented by the Regiment themselves in the 1960s, the devices have become a staple of military forces the world over. While not a grenade in the true sense of the word, the device's detonation results in a blinding flash of light equivalent to seven million candles coupled with a deafening bang measuring up to one hundred and eighty decibels. This double assault on the target's senses results in temporary blindness, deafness and severe disorientation: ideal for subduing targets in an enclosed space.

Another such non-lethal weapon is the Sting Grenade. Not as widely used as the Stun Grenade, this weapon follows the standard design of a fragmentation grenade. But instead of steel shrapnel the Sting erupts into a shower of hard rubber balls, incapacitating nearby targets.

Members of the SAS unofficially referred to the simultaneous use of the two devices as the 'Hereford Cocktail' in honour of the Regiment's home.

And it was one of these ‘cocktails’ that Kane now held behind his neck. He pulled the pins from both grenades with his thumbs and waited as long as he dared before tossing them straight at the man’s chest and throwing himself down, putting his back between himself and the twin detonations. Kane clamped his eyes shut and jammed fingers into his ears, bracing himself for the pain he knew the rubber shot would soon bring to his shirted back.

He wasn’t disappointed. The double blast came almost instantly, assaulting his ears and making his back and legs feel like he’d been attacked with a giant meat tenderiser. The double boom echoed through the warehouse before being replaced by a fierce buzzing in his ears. He allowed himself a couple of seconds to shake off the worst of the cocktail’s effects before slowly turning over to see how the other man had fared. As bad as Kane was feeling, back tenderised and ears buzzing, it brought a smile to his face to think about what state…

The man was still standing there, in exactly the same spot, Kane’s confiscated weapons still held carelessly by his sides. But now a look of amusement was playing across his face.

Kane groaned and slumped onto his back. He immediately regretted it and winced as the fresh welts met the concrete.

“Oh crap,” Kane muttered aloud, finding himself out of ideas. He suddenly felt very old and tired. “So, what happens now?” he asked.

“Well, how about you take your shoes off for me?” was the man’s surprising reply. “And when you’ve done that, we can get on with the introductions.”

Kane scowled at the man, but with no better ideas coming to mind he sat up and began unlacing his boots, slowly, playing for time and hoping something would come to him. Sitting on the cold concrete, aching all over, unarmed and with his assailant holding both his weapons and standing well out of reach, it wasn’t an ideal situation to be finding himself in.

No plan of action came to mind and soon Kane was sitting in his socks, the boots sitting neatly by his side. The whole situation was becoming more surreal by the minute.

“I don’t suppose you’ll let me check on my colleague?” he asked hopefully, nodding his head in that direction. He was genuinely concerned for Morrison and the chance to get up and stretch out his muscles could only be a good thing. But he was to be disappointed.

"There won't be any need for that," came the man's maddeningly calm answer. He then stepped out of the shadows and squatted down to look Kane in the eye.

"My name in Deblanc," he said as he pocketed Kane's sidearm and extended his hand for Kane to shake, "I believe you've been looking for me?"

Before Kane could process this surprising piece of information, Deblanc's hand rolled into a fist and struck him a terrific blow across the jaw.

Kane was unconscious before he hit the ground.

Chapter 5 – Rude Awakenings

Gregory Lindros awoke to the annoying sensation of someone kicking his thigh. Usually he would wake quickly, instantly alert, no matter what the situation. But on this occasion he was somehow aware but not yet awake, his thoughts came to him slowly: the mental equivalent to wading through mud.

The blows against his thigh increased in intensity until they were all he could focus on, a bright spot in the darkness. The brightness grew with each blow until it filled his awareness, shaking his world. Suddenly he was awake.

"All right, all right…" he groaned, his voice slurred. Wincing against the light assaulting his eyes he attempted to raise himself onto his elbows. He made it half way before slipping back down, the back of his head impacting the concrete.

"Fuck…" he muttered, the word too weakly spoken to carry any anger. He lay still a few moments longer, his eyes clamped shut, before the kicking resumed, harder this time.

"Get up Lindros!" a voice boomed, sending daggers of pain through his head. Lindros forced his eyes open.

Standing over him was the impressive bulk of Robert Mitchell, looking all the bigger to Lindros from his vantage point on the ground. Mitchell looked furious, a truly frightening sight, but Lindros would never let himself cower before anyone. Fighting through the pain in his head, the numbness he felt throughout his body, Lindros rose and finally stood, face to face with Mitchell.

Mitchell silently glared at Lindros, ensuring his full attention before speaking again.

"What the hell happened here?" he demanded, louder than Lindros felt necessary.

Lindros looked around the room, the… warehouse? Yes. He'd brought the kid, Hollow they called him, from the hospital for questioning. He remembered it had all gone according to plan and he and his two men were waiting in the office for Mitchell to arrive… and then…ah.

"There was someone else here," he began. "He… came out of nowhere." He looked around, finally coming to full awareness, "He took down Griffith and Higgins… and me."

"Yes he did." Mitchell said, straining to keep his voice level, "He took you all down."

Lindros remained silent, desperately trying to piece together recent events. Gradually his confusion turned to embarrassment and finally anger, not helped by his throbbing headache.

"Clearly you didn't tell me everything about this op," he said, matching glares with Mitchell, though feeling suddenly aware of the man's 'staff' standing at his shoulders. But no matter, they were just a couple of thugs, low-grade muscle. He was in no doubt that he could take them out if required. Mitchell could play the 'I'm in charge' glare game for as long as he liked, it wouldn't work on him. From the corner of his eye he saw Griffith and Higgins slowly coming to. Good, that evened the numbers up.

Mitchell had also noticed Griffith and Higgins returning to their feet, but didn't show any concern. Lindros had to hand it to him; he was a cool one. But this macho silence wasn't getting them anywhere, so when Mitchell didn't respond to his accusation, Lindros pressed on.

"Why don't you just tell me what the hell is going on?"

"My son was murdered," said Mitchell through clenched teeth, slowly and over-emphasising every word. "The boy I ordered you to retrieve from the hospital was one of two witnesses. He was going to tell me who did it, but you let him get away."

Lindros turned to look around the office, searching for conformation. The wheelchair was still sitting in the corner where they'd left it, empty of course. He didn't chide himself for not noticing it before; his priorities were to himself and his men.

But the facts changed their employer/employee dynamic. He knew Mitchell was a levelheaded man, but adding family into the equation made him and his temper very dangerous. He would have to tread a little more carefully.

"I'm sorry to hear that," he replied in a softer tone, "but that doesn't explain the guy in the green coat showing up and…"

"What?" Mitchell cut him off. "Say that again."

Lindros reviewed his previous sentence. There was only one pertinent fact.

"The assailant was wearing a dark green trench coat."

Lindros watched as Mitchell began pacing the room, fists balled, a fresh fury gripping him.

"What did he look like?" he demanded, visibly shaking with anger. "Would you recognise him again?"

"No." Lindros replied bluntly. He knew his answer would anger Mitchell further, but lying would be pointless. He felt his body tensing, sensed the need to defend himself. Mitchell was quickly losing control of his temper and Lindros had dealt with too many of his type to catch himself unprepared when they finally snapped. Fortunately, Mitchell retained enough of his senses to remain goal-focused.

"New job," Mitchell said suddenly. "Find this man in the green coat and bring him to me. *Don't* kill him. He's not getting off that easily."

Mitchell locked eyes with Lindros a few heartbeats longer, then turned and stormed out of the office.

There was no question of the job being an offer: it was an order. But that was fine by Lindros. He'd let Mitchell's contempt slide this time. He also had a score to settle with Mr Green Coat. But he needed more information.

"Who is he?" he called after Mitchell's retreating back. Mitchell turned and glared back.

"The man who murdered my son," he spat out.

"How do we know that?"

Mitchell stormed back across the room to stand in front of him again, even closer this time and obviously struggling to control his anger.

"You know because I said so!" he raged, sending spittle across Lindros's face. "Now do it!"

Lindros held his silence as he watched Mitchell leave room once more, this time turning over a desk and sending it's computer crashing to the floor.

"Someone clean this place up!" he shouted as he slammed the door. His two bodyguards looked at each other before one of them claimed the job with a nod. The other hurried after his employer, looking more than a little worried.

Lindros stared at the remaining bodyguard while his own two men stepped forward to take up positions behind his shoulders.

"Well?" he asked Mitchell's man, "what's the deal with the green coat?"

"On the way here," the man started, visibly relieved that his boss had gone, "we heard from our man stationed at the hospital. The other witness regained consciousness for a short time and was questioned by plainclothes cops. All they could get from him before he blacked out again was that the attacker was wearing a long, green coat."

****

Ted Kane opened his eyes and instantly regretted it. His jaw ached, his head ached and his eyes felt like they were on fire. His first thought was he was suffering from a particularly bad hangover but he dismissed the notion when he didn't feel the usual nausea.

He forced his eyes shut, fighting back the bright light. His forearm rose to cover his face as he forced himself into a sitting position, swinging his feet round and onto the floor. It was as they touched the ground that he realised his boots were missing, not an unexpected discovery considering that he was in bed, but one that sparked a memory.

Deblanc had asked him to take his boots off.

Recent events at the warehouse came flooding back to him, a tidal wave of memories crashing against his mind and shocking his body to full alertness. As he forced his stinging eyes open, wincing but still pushing, the first things he noticed were his boots sitting neatly on the ground in front of him. Beside them, to his relief and surprise in equal measures, were his weapons. The machine gun and sidearm, along with the combat webbing containing spare magazines for both weapons, lay neatly on the ground as if arranged for a publicity photograph.

The room was huge and, for the most part, featureless. Everything was a glaring, spotless white that interfered with his depth perception and made it difficult to estimate the room's size. It seemed to be a cube in shape, with a neat arrangement of chairs, couches and beds, like the one he'd found himself on, draped with clean white materials. The room didn't have any doors or windows: at least none that he could see. Nothing so much as a crack or seam could be seen on any of the walls or flooring. And where two such surfaces met they curved onto each other so there were no sharp corners, making the room look like a giant plastic sandwich box.

Kane rose and put on the webbing before checking each weapon carefully. Suddenly wary of some kind of trick he double-checked their mechanisms and firing pins to ensure they were ready for use. Satisfied, though with rising confusion, he secured the pistol in its holster while he looked around at his surroundings, trying to work out where he was. He kept the P90 in his hand, its familiar weight making him feel slightly more confident.

Kane took out his mobile phone and, unsurprisingly, it showed that no signal was available. He put it away and began a more detailed search of the room. He'd got in there somehow, so there had to be a way out.

As he turned around, scanning the blank walls once again, something caught his attention. The one wall clear of furniture had a pale blue spot of light glowing on it. It sat there for a moment before expanding into an oval. Kane instinctively took refuge behind a couch and brought the P90 to his shoulder, covering the direction of the glowing wall while all the time glancing about the room, wary of the light being some kind of diversion.

An elderly man stepped through the glowing oval. It winked out behind him, leaving him standing before the blank wall, coolly observing Kane and the weapon aimed at him. The two men silently stared at each other until Kane rose and slowly moved towards the older man, the weapon remaining at his shoulder. At less than two meters from the man, Kane halted and slowly lowered his gun. They stared at each other, neither wanting to be the first to speak. After a full three minutes the old man smiled and nodded to himself. Was that a subtle sign of approval?

"Thank you for not shooting me," he said in a crisp, well-spoken voice.

"Did you save me from Deblanc?" Kane asked, his tone gruff, ignoring the comment. He knew he'd already be dead if the man meant him any harm and he certainly wouldn't have let him keep his weapons.

Just as the man was about to reply, Kane turned and loosed half a dozen rounds into one of the over-stuffed chairs. The shots hit the chair in a satisfyingly tight cluster, the sound echoing throughout the huge room. To his credit, the man didn't flinch or jump for cover; his only reaction was the slightest raising of one eyebrow.

"Sorry," said Kane, not sounding the least bit apologetic. "Just checking."

"Can I take it that you are satisfied?" the man replied, his smile gone.

Again, Kane ignored his words. "I asked you a question," he said flatly as he took out a cigarette and lit it, not bothering to ask if the man minded.

Ignoring the cigarette, the man motioned towards a couple of chairs with a sweep of his arm. "Shall we sit?" he said, again refusing to answer Kane's question. "We have a lot to get through and my time is limited."

Kane grunted and sat down. Clearly there was a battle of wills underway and one of the best ways to bring a close to such time wasting nonsense was to deny the contest itself. Kane was an impatient man at the best of times and today wasn't turning out to be the best of times. He crossed his legs and carefully propped the P90 against his thigh in such a way that it pointed at the empty chair opposite. He flicked ash onto the spotless white floor as the man took the seat, apparently choosing to ignore both the weapon and the ash.

"My name is Sol," the man began, looking Kane in the eye. "And it was Deblanc that brought you here. At my request." If he was expecting a reaction from Kane, he was going to be disappointed.

"Where is Morrison?" Kane asked flatly, keeping the direction of the conversation in his favour. Sol wasn't taken aback by Kane's interrogational tone. If anything, it appeared to amuse him.

"Your friend is both safe and well," Sol replied. "Any time now he will awake in his car, several miles from the warehouse. In his hand he will find a note in your handwriting asking him to return home and wait there until he hears from you again."

"And when is that likely to be?" Kane asked, a threatening tone to creep into his voice. He rested his hand on the P90, subtly reminding Sol of its presence.

"That is entirely up to you of course," Sol replied, as though stating the most obvious of facts. "You may leave this very minute if you so wish, though I would request a few minutes of your time first. I'm sure you have many questions."

"And why should I believe anything you say?" Kane demanded.

Sol smiled again, a genuine, warm smile.

"You are a highly trained soldier. I am an old man." He leaned forward and gently tapped the barrel of the P90, still pointed at his chest. "And you are armed," he nodded at the chair Kane had shot at minutes earlier, "with a working weapon no less."

"And you," Kane replied with forced politeness, "are the only one who knows the way out of this room."

"Ah," said Sol with genuine embarrassment, "good point." He sat back in his chair and gave an exaggerated shrug. "So, where does that leave us?" he asked, amusement creeping into his voice. "An act of faith perhaps?"

Kane sighed and moved the P90 to the ground, carefully ensuring it pointed away from Sol.

Sol smiled and held his arms wide. "Ask your questions," he said.

Kane stared blankly. Where to begin?

He decided to move away from the subject of Deblanc for the time being. As desperate as he was to track the man down he could feel that line of questioning leading down a cul-de-sac. Sol was clearly working with Deblanc and pushing the matter of their relationship might cause the old man to turn defensive, ending the conversation and cutting Kane off from his only source of information. He decided to learn as much about this place as he could before steering the conversation back to what he was really after.

"How about you tell me where we are and what this place is?"

"The room we are now in," Sol began, "is the reception chamber of a much larger network of rooms that form the Keep, my base of operations. We are approximately three thousand kilometres beneath the surface." He motioned towards the room's walls. "Beyond these walls is a molten sea of iron and nickel, in the range of around five thousand degrees Celsius. The outer core of the planet is liquid, with a complex system of eddies and currents that make the answer to your question of 'where' we are a difficult one to answer. To be honest Mr Kane, I really have no idea where this chamber is at the moment."

Kane stared at Sol in silence for a moment, trying to decide whether the old man was crazy or the entire situation was an elaborate practical joke. The former seemed the most likely, though that didn't explain how he'd come to be there. But something else struck him as odd.

"How do you know my name?" he asked.

"Your interest in Deblanc brought you to my attention," Sol replied simply. "Your ability to track him was very impressive."

"Okay," Kane said at last, "let me get this straight. This secret underground base of yours is floating around somewhere in the Earth's mantle…"

"*Under* the mantle," Sol stressed, wagging his finger at Kane and taking on a lecturing tone. "We are in the outer core. The mantle is the solid layer *above* the outer core…"

"Alright," Kane cut Sol off, "outer core then. So, if this base floats about in this five thousand degree sea of liquid metal, thousands of miles below ground… just how the hell did I get down here?"

Sol regarded Kane for a moment, as though deciding just how much information to give him. Then, decision made, he continued, speaking slowly to emphasise the importance of what he was saying. "I have Portal technology that allows me to move from room to room and from the Keep to the surface."

Kane held his arms up and threw his head back, a coarse eruption of fake laughter escaping from his lips. "Of course!" he burst out, "Portals! So obvious when you think about it! Why would anyone make something as simple as a door when you can have magic Portals instead?"

Sol frowned back at him. "Your sarcasm is unnecessary," he said. "The hundreds of rooms that make up the Keep are not physically connected. They each float freely about the outer core, remotely connected by Portal generators."

"Right…right," Kane replied, trying hard to sound serious. "I can see why doors would be a problem."

Sol continued, ignoring Kane's sarcasm. "Chambers such as the one we now occupy are grown within the molten sea of the outer core and allowed to move about freely. They are little more than flat-sided bubbles. Even if physically joining them were possible, it would severely reduce their structural integrity: the tidal forces at work here are really rather impressive."

Kane still couldn't bring himself to believe him, it all sounded like the ravings of a madman. Yet Sol appeared both calm and rational.

"All right then," he began, deciding to let Sol's explanation stand for the time being. "How do these Portal things work?"

Sol thought for a moment before answering. "Please," he said in an apologetic tone, "don't be insulted when I tell you that my explaining the theory behind Portal technology to you would be akin to you travelling back in time and trying to explain the inner workings of your mobile phone to a Neanderthal."

Kane was taken aback for a moment, but found it difficult to feel insulted. Despite his gut feelings he found himself warming to Sol.

"But I can certainly tell you *what* they do," Sol said with a smile.

"Well," Kane replied with false timidity, "if you think my feeble little brain can cope with it…"

Sol chuckled. "I'm sure it can, Mr Kane.

"Simply put, a Portal device transforms the target into an energy signal. It then transmits this signal to its partner device. A Portal can only send the target to its matched pair, though they can be joined together into multiple units to form a Portal hub, such as the ones used to travel between these chambers. With me so far?"

Kane stared back for a moment, deciding whether he could believe, let alone understand, what Sol was saying. He decided there was no harm in humouring the old man and hearing him out. Besides, he had just seen Sol materialise in a seamless room with no doors or windows.

"I think so, yes," Kane replied. "But I don't suppose you'd be willing to prove it to me? You know, just to be sure my Neanderthal brain has got a grasp of it."

"Of course," Sol replied. "You will be leaving this room by the same means by which you arrived." But Sol looked embarrassed as he continued. "Unfortunately," he began, "there are a couple of… limitations with Portal technology that have yet to be addressed."

Oh great, thought Kane, *here we go. This is where he says I have to* believe *in the 'Spirits of the Portal'.*

"Firstly," Sol continued, ignoring Kane's sudden look of concern, "the Portal process transfers the subject's body and anything it is in direct contact with into energy. But if the subject is in contact with an object over a certain mass, the system ignores that object and leaves it where it is."

"Fair enough," said Kane, looking about the chamber, "you wouldn't want to teleport a super tanker into one of these rooms I suppose."

Sol smiled proudly. "The Keep has many rooms more than capable of holding such a vessel," he said. "However, I'm talking about larger objects such as, say, the bedrock of the planet."

"Ah, yes, I see how that would be a problem."

"Indeed. But the system is also restrictive in much smaller ways. Shoes, for example, when worn with socks of sufficient length and so not in contact the wearer's skin…"

"...which is why Deblanc made me take my boots off. And why my webbing and weapons were removed…"

"Just so, though we can make clothing and equipment ourselves from materials that can pass through without physical contact with the subject. They also have other useful applications, but they're not important here."

"Why don't you tell me them anyway?" Kane said, his voice a little peevish.

Sol looked a little taken aback, but nodded and continued.

“”The opening of a Portal can be quite attention-grabbing,” he said, “especially in areas of poor lighting. Our work here often requires us to go unnoticed and the sudden flash of blue light caused by an opening Portal can easily give us away. The materials we construct for our clothing allows us to contain a Portal, to literally open it *within* the subject’s clothing, transporting the subject along with anything, or anyone, in contact with the subject’s skin. This does come with certain limitations unfortunately. Portals can be opened within the Keep by merely *thinking* the correct commands: devices built into the Keep’s walls measure thought-waves in the same way that your television receivers decipher digital information. All that is required to control Portals within the Keep is a simple and painless brain implant and some basic training on its use.

“However,” he continued, “*outside* the keep extra apparatus is required. A small control circuit must be carried, in contact with the skin. But this can easily be built into a watch or bracelet.”

Kane remained silent as Sol spoke. Despite his reluctance to believe what he was hearing, the soldier in him couldn’t help but imagine the tactical advantages such a device would bring.

“Also,” Sol continued, “outside the Keep you can only exit a Portal at a previously prepared site.”

“‘Prepared’?” Kane prompted.

“Seeded with a field of a particular radiation, a radiation that is very hard to detect unless you know exactly what you are looking for.”

“Radiation?” Kane muttered, sounding worried.

“Harmless radiation,” Sol assured him. “It can be delivered simply but degrades over the course of a few years.”

“You said there are two problems…” Kane pressed.

“Yes,” Sol paused, marshalling his words. “The other limitation is… mental in nature.”

“Oh great,” Kane sighed loudly. “Are you going to tell me it only works if I *truly believe*…?” But much to his relief, Sol chuckled lightly and waved the comment away.

“Oh, no, no, nothing like that. I can assure you the technology is based on pure science, not witchcraft and magic. However, the process of disbodyment does present certain… psychological challenges.” Sol let the comment hang in the air for a moment. Kane remained silent, a neutral expression on his face as he waited for Sol to continue.

"The experience of Portal travel effects different people in different ways. There doesn't seem to be any pattern to this, though certain meditative techniques have had a limited success in overcoming them."

"Effects?" Kane asked quietly, a feeling of concern growing in his gut. "Would you care to elaborate?"

"Tell me, Mr Kane," Sol said, sitting back and steepling his fingers, "have you ever spent any time in an Isolation Tank?"

"No." Kane's answer came without hesitation. He'd always found the trendy desire to lay in a soundproof, lightproof, saltwater-filled box an odd one. During the escape and evasion phase of his SAS training he'd experienced limited sensory deprivation first hand and it wasn't pleasant. Why would anyone pay to undergo it?

"Well," Sol continued, "used correctly, the benefits of such sessions in combating physical and emotional ailments can be quite extraordinary. For short periods of time the patient's brainwaves move into the Theta range, more commonly experienced in the moments before sleep. The Theta range of brainwave activity is where the brain is at it's most creative. I use the Portal experience myself for meditative sessions.

"However," he continued, his voice suddenly becoming grave, "so total is the sensation of disbodyment during Portal travel, that the conscious mind can lose all sense of time. Simply put, for some people the passage through a Portal, while lasting a little under one second in real time, can literally feel like an eternity, an eternity devoid of sensation of any kind."

Sol stopped talking and watched Kane as the concept sank in. Kane considered what Sol had told him, though still not entirely sure whether anything the man had said was true or just the ravings of a madman. A madman with a wonderful imagination, but a madman none the less.

Kane's feeling of unease increased as thoughts of unending sensory deprivation crept into his mind. He'd seen colleagues crack under a few hours of such treatment, their personalities never quite the same again.

But that was assuming all of this was true. It sounded too farfetched to believe. Yet he had seen Sol walk through an apparently solid wall…

"And that, I'm afraid," Sol continued, his voice filled with apology, "is why Deblanc was forced to render you unconscious before your transit to the Keep."

Kane was reminded of his aching jaw and felt a sudden surge of anger. He remembered the hunt for Deblanc and his determination to catch the man, a callous murderer with no regard for human life. And now he appeared to be part of something much bigger, something that Kane was having trouble believing, let alone understand. But before he could question Sol further the man held up his hand for quiet, a look of concentration on his face. He cocked his head to the side as though listening to a distant voice that Kane couldn't hear.

"I'm afraid our meeting will have to be cut short," Sol said, rising to leave. "But I promise you, I will be in touch soon." He turned to walk towards the wall through which he had arrived.

Kane rose and followed him, retrieving the P90 on the way. "That's great," he said, fighting back his frustration at Sol's dismissal. "What am I supposed to do?"

"Once I leave this chamber a harmless anesthesic vapour will be released, rendering you unconscious. You will awake in your home, feeling rested and unharmed."

He looked at Kane with a genuinely apologetic expression. A pale blue point of light appeared on the wall behind him and blossomed into the glowing Portal through which he had originally appeared. "I am truly sorry to have to leave so suddenly, Mr Kane. You must have many questions. I can promise you that I will answer them all when time permits and if you can accept your new reality, I would like to offer you a position here." Without waiting for a response he turned toward the portal.

"Sol, wait," Kane said, holding out his hand. "It was nice to meet you." Sol turned to take the hand and shook it, smiling warmly.

"Mind if I bum a lift?" Kane asked suddenly.

Before Sol could respond, Kane shoulder-charged him into the glowing Portal.

Chapter 6 – Recruitment Drive

Deblanc passed through the front entrance of the apartment block and began climbing the stairs. Normally he'd curse at the sight of the faded 'Out of Order' sign that adorned the single lift door, but today the five-story climb allowed him a little extra time to gather his thoughts.

Sol was right, his side mission to recruit Kane had been a welcome diversion. He'd even had the chance to vent some of his persistent frustration by removing some 'live obstructions' at the warehouse. Usually Sol would lecture him about excessive force and the need to remain covert in all his dealings, but time was quickly becoming more and more limited and, while that was certainly a terrifying prospect, it did allow him a lot more freedom to get jobs done his way.

And it had been nice to see professionals at work. The two men he'd been sent after, Kane and Morrison, were clearly highly experienced and extremely brave. They'd entered the warehouse without knowing what they faced and with next to no planning time. He wondered if he would have had the courage to do so if he didn't enjoy his own, unique abilities. Probably not, though that was a fact he would file away deeply in his mind where not even he could find it again.

But the day's amusement was now at an end. Now he had to perform a task that he had dreaded for some time: the recruitment of Timothy Bruce.

For months he'd been tasked with watching over the pathetic specimen and ensuring his safety. It was a tedious and thankless task, far beneath what he felt to be worthy of his skills and abilities. The recent incident with the three youths from the supermarket had been the first time he'd been able to break the pattern of frustration in a long time. Maybe that was why Sol had cut him some slack. Deblanc had braced himself for a lecture over the incident at the very least, but Sol's revelation about the Brachyurans would also explain that away. That was a real slap in the face, making Deblanc feel like a petulant child, more concerned with his own comforts while a devastating war raged outside the door.

But on the plus side, bringing Timothy Bruce in would end his babysitting duties and he could look forward to more interesting commissions.

Deblanc arrived at Timothy Bruce's front door and stopped. He stood there for a while, listening for signs of life from within. Finally, he heard the almost silent sound of pages turning and then the gentle creaking of bedsprings.

Good. He was in. Not that Deblanc expected anything different. He raised his hand and knocked on the door, loudly, three times. He waited several seconds, listening intently. No more sounds came from behind the door so he knocked again, harder this time. Still no response.

Deblanc took a step back and kicked the door open with one savage kick. The door flew open with enough force to swing it through a full one hundred and eighty degrees and onto the inner wall of the flat, breaking it away from its hinges. Splinters of wood rained down onto the carpet before the door itself slowly fell forward and onto the ground. A broken chair bounced off the opposite wall; apparently it had been wedged behind the door. Deblanc waited a second, enjoying the carnage before entering.

"Timothy Bruce!" he boomed, a cruel grin on his face, "I have come for you!" He walked slowly towards what he knew to be the bedroom, his every step an echoing stamp on the ground. When he reached the bedroom door he stood there, silhouetted in the doorway and staring at Timothy cowering in his bed.

A library book clutched to his chest, Timothy sat there trembling, his eyes impossibly wide. He watched, paralysed with fear, as Deblanc held out his hands in the style of Frankenstein's monster and slowly shambled towards him.

That was when Timothy passed out.

Deblanc grinned as he stepped up to the bed. Well, at least that saved preparing him for Portal travel.

****

At the same time Deblanc was introducing himself to Timothy Bruce, Alfred Morrison was waking up. He found himself in the front passenger seat of his own car, parked at the entrance to a field overlooking the South Downs. He had no idea how he'd got there and why his head hurt so much, so he sat for several minutes gathering his thoughts and looking out across the fields and the English Channel beyond. It was only then that he noticed the note in his hand.

Written in Kane's spidery scrawl, the note told him, in no uncertain terms, to go back home and wait there for further instructions. But while the note appeared to be written in Kane's hand and the bluntness was certainly in character with the man, something about the note was niggling at Morrison.

Over their many years working together the two men had slipped into a countless number of habits and eccentricities. Like a married couple they enjoyed a variety of secret in-jokes and routines known only to them.

Like the cigarette thing.

During much of their time in the SAS Morrison had been the unit's sniper and Kane his spotter, giving wind and distance readings when needed. Often, a sniper would be on station for several hours, even days, before the shot could be taken and during that time the weapon operator would need to remain vigilant. It was during such times that Kane would light a cigarette for Morrison and pass it to him under his camouflage scrim. It was completely against standing orders to smoke in the field but the SAS hadn't become feared the world over by following the rules. Though they obviously drew the line at smoking at night.

It was on one such mission in Iraq that Morrison claimed he could score all three required kills with a single shot. He'd won a similar bet earlier in the tour when he'd managed to get a single shot through two targets at once. Kane told him three was impossible because, even if he did get a clear shot with all three targets lined up correctly, the bullet would be too slowed and deformed after passing through the first two targets to guarantee the third kill.

Kane raised his powerful monocular to his eye and surveyed the target area again. They were in the middle of the desert, holed up at the base of one of the rocky outcroppings that punctuated the gravel plains in the north of the country. A little under one and a half kilometres across the sun baked land before them he could see the small 3-man anti-aircraft battery, the image shimmering in the mid-day heat haze. No way could Morrison make such a difficult shot under those conditions. The artillery piece was partially covered with camouflaged netting, hiding it from casual observation while the three-man crew milled around, tidying supplies and cleaning weapons. They were pretty well spaced out.

"I tell you I can do it mate," Morrison had insisted, his eye staring unblinking through his rifle sight.

"Bollocks," said Kane as he placed a lit cigarette between his colleague's lips. "Look, if you do, you'll never have to buy another fag as long as we both live. And I'll even light each and every one for you, you cocky wanker."

Morrison grinned and gently squeezed the trigger of his Tac-50, sending the 50. calibre bullet on its journey across the dessert. Kane watched through the monocular and waited for the bullet to reach its target, wherever that may be. He cursed himself for not establishing with Morrison what *he* would win when his friend didn't make the shot.

He needn't have worried.

Moments after leaving the rifle, the bullet hit its intended target; the chest of one of the three Iraqi soldiers. But rather than instantly falling down, the soldier's chest erupted into a ball of blinding white light. Within seconds the man was dead, his torso a blaze of flame and smoke. His two colleagues rushed over to help him, desperately beating at the flames with shirts and blankets, anything that came to hand. As Kane watched, the man on fire suddenly exploded, instantly killing the other two.

"Silly sod had a phosphorus grenade next to a frag on his webbing," Morrison muttered around the cigarette. "Probably didn't even know the difference. Bloody kids."

Kane was just about to comment when the anti-aircraft post exploded, sending a huge black mushroom of smoke billowing into the windless blue sky.

"And there go the secondries," Morrison grinned. "We'd better make ourselves scarce." Without another word both men belly-crawled backwards until they were safely behind a ridge of rock where they rose to their feet and jogged away from the scene, chuckling.

The shot was Morrison's personal best, but Kane took a great deal of pleasure in later pointing out that it was a full kilometre short of the confirmed military record, held by some Canadian called Furlong in Afghanistan.

But Morrison had won his bet and from that day forward Kane was as good as his word, always lighting him a cigarette without any fuss, even if it was his last one.

Morrison's attention returned to Kane's note and focused on the reason why it felt wrong. Another little quirk of their relationship was the constant trading of insults. Even a short, terse note like this would have contained some dig or gibe. At the very least he would have addressed it to 'wanker' or 'tosser', not 'Morrison'.

Either Kane was under duress when he wrote it, or someone had forged it. He had no idea what either notion meant and why he had been delivered from the warehouse unharmed. He considered whether his instruction to return home was a trap, but dismissed it quickly; if whoever had orchestrated the note wanted him dead or captured he would be already. Maybe they wanted him to lead them to his house so they could threaten his family? Possibly. Perhaps they wanted him away from Sussex? His home in Cambridgeshire was over a hundred and twenty miles away. Well, either idea wasn't an option. If Kane genuinely wanted to get a hold of him he would use his mobile number and Morrison wasn't about to abandon his friend to whatever trouble he'd got himself into. And even if their phones weren't secure, he and Kane had certain code phrases to let the other know.

He would return to the warehouse and investigate the scene, looking for clues to Kane's fate.

His mind made up, Morrison screwed the note up and threw onto the floor as he climbed over to the driver's seat. Relieved to find the keys in the ignition he started the engine and turned round in the seat, ready to reverse the car out of the field entrance.

And that was when he noticed the body on the back seat.

****

Twenty minutes later Morrison screeched his car to a stop outside the A&E entrance of Eastbourne General Hospital. The two plain-clothes police officers he'd phoned ahead for were already at the door, waiting for him with a couple of paramedics. As soon as the car stopped the two medics rushed forward and opened the back door of the car to begin their assessment of the patient.

"You two!" he shouted at the police officers as he climbed from the car. "This boy does not leave your sight. He's a witness to a murder and the subject of an MI6 investigation into possible terrorism." He wasn't of course, but it was amazing how the mere mention of terrorism galvanized people these days. And the simple use of the word 'possible' freed Morrison from any chance of litigation later.

He had been surprised to find the boy in the back of his car and had to assume Kane put him there. No other possible explanation came to mind. The boy was unconscious but seemed to be stable despite being moved about so much. He remained Morrison and Kane's only lead to Deblanc. All Morrison could do now was stay next to the kid and wait to hear from Kane.

The drive to the hospital had given him time to think about Kane's note and what secret meanings it might hold and what to do about it. Little came to mind; it was a most frustrating development. But there was one other thing he could try. He took out his mobile phone and sent a message to Kane. A single full stop. It was a signal they'd often used to inform the other that they were safe without risking the attention a ringing phone could bring: Both of their phones being set to vibrate only for text messaging. The correct responses would be for Kane to send a single comma if he agreed they should avoid contact or a hash if he was in danger and needed help. If everything was fine he would simply phone back. Of course, if no response came he would be back to square one.

Morrison returned the phone to his pocket and followed the medics and police officers into the hospital. With any luck he could still get some information from the boy.

****

Alfred Morrison was so deep in thought as he entered the hospital that he failed to notice the figure watching him from just twenty feet away. If Morrison had noticed the figure he would have instantly recognised him as Gregory Lindros, the man Robert Mitchell had recruited to kidnap the very boy he was now escorting into the hospital.

Lindros didn't recognise Morrison, the only other time they had been this close together was as two unconscious forms left in Deblanc's wake at the warehouse. It wasn't Morrison that Lindros was there for, but the boy being carried into the hospital. But that didn't mean he wasn't interested in him now. He'd come straight to the hospital after his dressing down by Mitchell in the hope that someone had taken the injured kid there. He'd sent his two men to other hospitals in the area. It was a forlorn hope but all he had to go on.

The only description he had of Deblanc was that he was wearing a green coat. The man he now watched didn't, but he was clearly mixed up in this business and had official standing with the authorities. If he wasn't Deblanc he might be able to lead him to him.

Lindros phoned his men with instructions to meet him there, then followed Morrison into the hospital. As he walked he pressed the inside of his bicep against the comforting bulge of his sidearm, sitting in his shoulder holster. One way or another he wouldn't be leaving the hospital until he had the information he wanted.

****

As has already been described, while Portal travel lasts for less than a second in real time, the effects on the individual are not so easy to quantify. For the average, unprepared mind, entry into a Portal can mark the beginning of an eternity of torment: endless floating in a soundless, sightless limbo.

But Deblanc's mind was far from unprepared and could never be described as average. In fact, his time in Portal transit was more precious to him than anything else he could think of: time within his own mind, free of the irritating rabble that inhabited the world.

Within the safe environment of the Portal, Deblanc was literally the master of time. If he so wished he could keep his mind in this place for anything up to a mental eternity, or emerge right that very 'second'. Either choice would return him to the real world, and his destination, within a real-time second of entering the Portal. But no matter how long Deblanc decided to spend in transit, emergence was always met with the same feelings of deflation and disappointment, the real world crashing in on his perfectly ordered mental landscape.

The more time Deblanc spent in Portals, the harder the return to the real world became. Sol had warned him of this when he'd trained him. He'd explained how Deblanc's mental profile would allow him greater control over the perception of time within the Portal and how, during that time, he would experience a greater level of mental clarity, free as he was from all physical distractions. Deblanc used the time to plan and scheme. He prided himself on always being supremely prepared for whatever the next stage of his mission might be, whatever awaited him at the other end of the Portal.

But today was destined to be different.

As he materialised in the reception chamber of Sol's Keep, the unconscious form of Timothy Bruce slumped against him, Deblanc had just enough time to see Ted Kane shoulder-charge Sol through the exit Portal. He released his grip on Timothy's hand and charged across the room. Timothy's body slumped to the ground, momentarily forgotten as Deblanc leapt through the air, desperately diving for the rapidly closing Portal. But as quick as his actions were, he couldn't outrun the speed of a closing Portal and in that instant his life became a fraction of a second away from ending.

He realised with horror that if he continued on his headlong trajectory towards the Portal it would certainly close before his body had fully passed through. The portal would close, taking his top half with it.

Fortunately for him, Deblanc's reactions were so fast that he literally didn't have time to dwell on that eventuality. Instead, he dispassionately analysed his situation and acted upon it. Gone was the hope of chasing Sol and Kane through the Portal. All he had to worry about now was survival.

Deblanc thrust his left arm out, aiming the flat of his hand at the edge of the closing blue glow before him. It struck near the edge of the Portal and he tried to use the impact to bounce himself clear. He succeeded, but not without twisting his wrist awkwardly against the wall. He was vaguely aware of a wrenching tear to his wrist before his face impacted with the wall, mercifully above the closing Portal.

It was fortunate for Deblanc that he lost consciousness then. Had he not, he would have seen his right arm pass through the ever-shrinking blue glow. He would have been forced to watch the Portal snap shut, taking his arm, to a point above his elbow, away and to the other end.

The Portal completed its closing cycle and Deblanc's unconscious, armless body fell to the ground.

Chapter 7 – Into the Portal

If there was one thing Ted Kane didn't like, it was having his destiny put in someone else's hands. That was why, when Sol was spinning him his 'Magic Portal' story, he'd decided to take matters into his own hands. He couldn't bring himself to believe the story, though he had to admit Sol's walking through an apparently solid wall was a good trick. But he remembered Morrison's comment about apparent magic always being revealed as simple tricks when the secret was explained. *Probably some sort of trap door and light show,* he thought to himself.

And when Sol announced he was going to leave and that Kane would be 'rendered unconscious', well, that was just too much to take. So he'd grabbed Sol's hand (better safe than sorry) and shoved him through his 'Portal' thing.

And now he was beginning to regret it.

Really regret it.

As soon as he entered the Portal, Kane was plunged into the most perfect darkness he had ever experienced. His first reaction was to try to open his eyes but they didn't respond. He tried to raise his hands to his face but he couldn't feel them. But more than that, he realised he wasn't even *aware* of them. He tried to look down at his body, but he had no control over his neck. He had no control over any part of his body.

Then there was the total and utter lack of sound. Kane couldn't even hear his own heartbeat and when he realised he couldn't *feel* it either, or feel the action of his lungs, panic threatened to overtake him.

Despite his years of military training, or perhaps because of it, Kane was no stranger to panic. The man who didn't feel some level of fear throughout his military career wasn't mentally fit to wear the uniform. The secret was to hide it and nurture it, to seize the adrenaline it produced and turn it against whatever was causing it. Unfortunately, in that featureless limbo there was nothing to turn it on.

Kane was put in mind of his HALO training. High Altitude Low Opening parachute jumps were a staple tactic of Special Forces the world over. Exiting aircraft at heights of up to forty-five thousand feet and waiting until the last possible moment to open the parachute was a good way to insert troops into hostile territory without bringing the aircraft within range of anti-aircraft fire. It was during the long free-fall, when the jumper reached terminal velocity, that panic presented its greatest risk. There were no second chances at timing the opening of the parachute and no time to open a reserve, had there been one, if the main chute failed. Waiting for that small window of opportunity was, for Kane, the most stressful time he could remember.

Portal travel felt exactly the same, except that the falling and waiting could continue forever if what Sol told him was true. Yes, it certainly felt like the old man could have been telling the truth after all. But where did that leave Kane now?

He tried counting seconds in his head to see if he *could* gain some sense of time. But it seemed that Sol was telling the truth about that aspect of Portal travel as well. There was simply no way to guess how much time had passed.

Time *appeared* to pass and gradually Kane began to accept his situation. All traces of his earlier panic had gone and he began to amuse himself by going through training scenarios in his mind, thinking again about HALO jumping. How long ago was that now? Years? Decades?

With nothing better to do, he imagined himself falling towards the ground, waiting to open the 'chute at the last possible moment. He imagined looking at the ground rising up beneath him, the air buffeting his body as he fell. He imagined the sensation of falling, of feeling the front of his webbing pressing into his chest and stomach. And, some unfathomable period of time later, he realised that he could actually *feel* those things. Furthermore, without him noticing, the darkness about him had receded and he was suddenly aware of his surroundings. He actually *was* falling towards the ground! He could see green fields beneath him. Huge fields of maize like the ones he'd seen when HALO training in Kansas years before.

But rather than being seized with a fresh terror at his predicament, he felt joy. This was something he *had* been trained for.

Ted Kane let out a loud, uncharacteristic whoop of joy and tucked himself into a forward roll as he fell through the air towards the cornfields of Kansas. He plummeted towards the ground, yelling and whooping at the sudden exhilaration coursing through his body. Yes, he realised with a mental grin, he had his voice back, was fully aware of his own body again. How long had he been imprisoned in that sightless, soundless nothingness? Weeks? Months? Years?

There was no way to tell but focusing on his training appeared to have been a breakthrough.

But of more immediate concern, or rather, interest, was his continued freefall. It seemed to Kane that he had been falling for an inordinate amount of time. He'd covered a lot of subjects in his mind, had thought about many things in great detail. Surely he could use that as a base level for estimating the passage of time?

He considered the matter for a while, during which time his mind wandered off subject innumerable times. He imagined counting the seconds to detonation on a hand grenade fuse, something he'd done a thousand times. But that didn't seem to work. Next, he looked down at his watch and tried counting off the seconds on the sweep hand. But, before his very eyes, the passage of that flawlessly accurate mechanism was fluctuating wildly.

As he watched the sweep hand begin to speed up once more, he glanced over the top of his wrist and became suddenly aware of the ground rushing up to meet him. He focused on the watch again and the second hand began to slow, and with it his apparent airspeed. He practiced concentrating on the watch face, trying to control the advance of the sweep hand. Gradually he found the mental discipline to control its speed.

But he was still falling towards the ground.

Feeling strangely disconnected from is surroundings, somewhat bored by his predicament, he focused on the ground and willed himself to travel faster, willing the moment of 'chute deployment forward. The moment finally came and he pulled the ripcord, opening the 'chute and slowing his descent with a violent lurch. A normal HALO jump's open-'chute time could be measured in a handful of seconds, but he appeared to hang there for an age. Frustrated, he tried focusing on the crop fields below and mentally increasing his speed.

But he over-did it and began to fall much faster and almost instantly hit the ground with a sickening impact, breaking both of his ankles and dislocating both his hips. He could feel the sticky warmth of his blood soaking through his trousers and imagined it pooling in the dirt around him. He dared not look and laid there in helpless agony, unable to move.

That went well.

The crop field he'd landed in was tens of thousands of acres in size; so vast he'd not been able to see the edges during his free-fall. Any chance of finding help would require him to crawl for miles through the young, foot-high maize crop. And it hadn't occurred to him before, but he'd apparently been HALO jumping on his own. There was no sign of any other jumpers, no one to report him missing. And there was no chance of spotting the plane he'd jumped from, even if there had been one.

Kane lay back and closed his eyes, thinking how nice it would be to return to that dark, silent limbo again. He'd felt nothing back then, and while it had been terrifying at the time it was a lot better than the unbearable pain he now felt. He'd suffered broken limbs before, but this was something else. Normally the pain didn't present itself fully until some time after the event, temporarily held at bay by adrenaline. It was as if his body was refusing to release the chemical into his system. The heightened sense of falling he'd experienced earlier had now been replaced by an equally intense awareness of his body, of the pain his injuries were producing.

Kane looked down at his legs, twisted and misshapen by his hard landing. He slowly raised himself up onto his elbows and tried to drag himself backwards and instantly regretted it. He couldn't move his legs, his hips were dislocated and useless. Where the hell was his adrenaline? And why hadn't he passed out?

And that gave him cause to think. How long had he been in this Portal now? He would guess weeks or months. He hadn't slept or eaten, yet was neither tired nor hungry. Not even thirsty. And the sun hadn't gone down once.

But, right now, that was the least of his worries. A quick check of his webbing produced a basic first-aid kit but no morphine syringes and nowhere near enough bandage to sufficiently wrap both ankles. The lack of morphine was an unwelcome surprise. To his knowledge, all military medical packs carried the pain-killing drug. Strange.

Drawing his combat knife, Kane reached back and drew in his parachute. After cutting it into strips he reached down to remove his boots and socks before slowly beginning to wrap his ankles with the reinforced silk. He couldn't help grinning to himself as he worked. When he'd reached down to collect his P90, just before launching himself at Sol and into the Portal, he had slipped his hand down the inside of his boots, pushing the top of each sock down so that his leg was in physical contact with the leather of his boots. He'd felt silly doing it at the time, but decided it couldn't hurt. If Sol's stories *were* true he didn't want to find himself without boots.

It was just as he began work on his second ankle that he realised he shouldn't be able to do this. And it should be hurting a lot more. A hell of a lot more. It was highly unlikely that he would be able to reach his ankles with two dislocated hips. Without him realising, the pain throughout his body had receded. In fact, he was feeling pretty good.

Taking advantage of the reprieve he reached forward and drove his knife through his trousers next to his right ankle and into the hard ground beneath. Easing himself up onto his elbows again he took a deep breath and jerked his body back along the ground. After a few such attempts he felt his right hip pop back into place. Suddenly exhausted, Kane fell back onto the ground and lay there sweating. After a few attempts to raise his leg he was rewarded by the sight of his foot slowly and shakily appearing beyond his chest.

His feeling of well being increased to one of almost euphoria and re-socketing his other hip was much easier. Once done, he lay back and laughed loudly. He really felt great.

While he'd been attending to his second hip Kane had been giving a lot of thought to his experiences within the Portal. It appeared he had a greater deal of control over his surroundings than should be possible. It could just be his heightened feeling of well being, but he felt like he could do anything.

Reaching forward once again, Kane unwrapped the makeshift bandages from his ankles and stared at them. Both were a swollen mass of purple/green bruises, yet he still felt light-headed and pain-free. He continued to stare at his ankles and thought back to his earlier freefall experience, back to when he'd been able to control the flow of time. As he stared he felt a tingle in his ankles. In his peripheral vision he became aware of the maize swaying in the breeze. As he concentrated on his feet the maize began to sway faster and faster until its green tips became nothing more than a blur of motion. The tingling in his ankles increased and before his eyes the swelling began to reduce. Faster and faster he increased the passage of time until his ankles looked to be the right size again and finally, the bruising reduced and disappeared.

Satisfied with their size and colour, Kane slowly rose to his feet and tested each ankle by putting more weight on each one in turn. Apart from a slight numbness, most probably due to a lack of use, his ankles felt as good as new. His hips felt fine too. He quickly put his socks and boots back on.

Kane stood there, staring out across the field, wondering what to do next. He couldn't think of a time when he'd felt this good, so filled with energy and childlike excitement. He chose a direction at random, the field looked the same in every direction anyway, and set off at a flat-out run. The ground beneath him became a blur as he crashed through the maize and leapt over dips in the ground. He continued on his ballistic course until something tugged at his awareness.

Kane didn't know how, but he was suddenly aware of a *something* off to the side. He couldn't see, hear or even smell anything out of the ordinary, yet there it was, silently calling to him. He altered his course and headed towards it.

Soon (or was it a long time later? He still couldn't estimate time) he came upon an open area of ground, free of crops. Instead, a glowing blue oval about one metre wide and two metres high hovered just above the ground. He stopped and stared at the thing, instantly recognising it as a Portal, or more accurately, the original Portal through which he had passed to get here. He knew for a fact that it was the same one because there, frozen at the point of entry, were the static figures of Sol and himself.

Kane stood and stared at the image of himself, suspended in mid shoulder-charge, frozen at his point of impact with Sol. He grinned, remembering the moment he'd decided to test Sol's wild claims, and was pleased to see the look of surprise frozen onto the old man's face. He also noticed that the image of himself was still holding onto the P90 and wearing the same jeans and jacket, not the HALO pressure suit he currently wore.

Kane positioned himself behind the figures and peered through the Portal.

On the other side of the blue oval was a different room, similar in shape and colour to the one he and Sol had spoken in, though markedly different in size and content. This new room was huge, bigger than any aircraft hanger Kane had ever seen, so massive that he couldn't make out the far side or ceiling. Its walls and floor were as spotlessly white as those in Sol's reception room and this chamber was apparently also perfectly cuboid in shape. He could see banks of what looked like computer consoles with oversized screens suspended above their keyboards, the design of which Kane had never seen before.

Spread all about the room were huge machines, the function of which Kane couldn't even guess at. Some were as big as a garden shed while others appeared to be the size of several-story buildings. All were cube or cuboid in shape and a uniform dark grey in colour. Their sides were mostly flat and smooth, though many of them had open panels revealing inner workings that Kane couldn't quite make out from his vantage point.

Dotted about the room and suspended in mid air were several objects looking something like elongated motorcycle helmets. Protruding from various points on the device's bodies were a variety of arms and manipulators. Clamps, grabbers and probes of various shapes and sizes sat among what Kane could only describe as metal tentacles. They all sat, floating perfectly still in the air, as if frozen in time. And then Kane spotted something that made him realise that, from his point of view within the Portal, this new room actually *was* frozen in time.

About thirty metres across the chamber, and standing perfectly still before one of the strange computer terminals, stood a woman. Tall and with a muscular frame, Kane estimated the woman to be in her late thirties. Even frozen as still as she was, the expression on her face and the way she stood before the console, gazing into one of the strange monitors with her hand poised over the keyboard, belayed to Kane a sense of supreme confidence. This was a woman in authority, maybe even over Sol. While Sol had come across as a genial old gentleman, polite and patient, this woman certainly had a military bearing. Her dark hair was cut short enough to sit clear of the high collared, pale grey jumpsuit she wore. Her clothing was spotless, right down to the flat-soled boots it was neatly tucked into. The various flat pockets adorning the outfit did nothing to disguise her trim Amazonian figure. Kane had to shake his head to stop himself from staring at the woman.

Moving to the other side of the Portal, Kane peered through and saw what he'd expected to see: Sol's reception room, looking exactly the same as it had when he'd leapt at Sol and carried them both through. On this side of the Portal there was no evidence of the figures of Sol and himself, he could see the reception room perfectly clearly, without the obstruction the bodies presented when he peered through the other side at the new room.

One thing that did catch his attention was a tiny, pale blue glow floating about a metre from the ground behind the spot where he and Sol would have been when they'd entered the Portal. It was the same colour as the Portal itself, but tiny in size. Kane didn't remember noticing the spot when he'd spoken with Sol and decided it looked like a second Portal opening.

It occurred to Kane, though he had no evidence to confirm his theory, that if he pushed these static forms of Sol and himself through the Portal then he would complete his journey and emerge in the new room. It felt right somehow, like it was an obvious fact.

The longer Kane spent in this weird place, the more he was ready to accept the bizarre at face value.

He gave the figure of himself a gentle, experimental shove and was rewarded by its slow, steady movement towards the Portal. Moving perfectly parallel with the ground, the image of himself and Sol moved smoothly as though on a conveyor belt. He kept a hold on the figures and drew them back to their original position where they stopped as though reaching an invisible buffer.

Satisfied that his theory was worth a try, Kane prepared to push the figures completely through, bracing himself for whatever effect the move had on him personally.

But then he stopped and let go.

If Sol was right about the passage of time within the Portal, then Kane could spend as long as he wanted here, doing whatever he wanted. He decided to spend some more time practicing with his newfound abilities and exploring this strange place.

Gathering intel: Morrison would be proud.

Kane stared out across the fields, wondering where to start. He had all the time in the world but not one clue with what to do with it. Once again, a military-based idea was the first to present itself.

He considered the tactical advantages of Portal travel. Obviously, the ability to travel from point to point in an instant would be a priceless asset for any military organisation. Add to that the endless planning time the traveller had once inside the Portal and the ability to gaze through the opening to gather reconnaissance on the exit area. It all added up to a very useful tool.

Kane turned and took another look through the glowing oval, at the new room and woman within. There was something about her that made his attention wander, made him want to complete his journey and meet her.

Dragging himself away from the view, Kane took the P90 and its spare ammunition clips from the image of himself and turned his back on the Portal. He needed something to do. Flipping the weapon selector switch to single shot, he reached down and selected a clump of hard soil from the ground with his left hand. He then shouldered the weapon in a one-handed grip and tossed the clump of soil high into the air. He hit it with his second shot. That was pretty good, but he'd thought of a way to improve his technique.

Throwing a second clump, he concentrated on slowing time as he had earlier. The clump slowed in the air as it continued on its trajectory. This time, when Kane brought the weapon up to the firing position his movements were slow, though very smooth. His body was slowed down in time just as the environment was. But his mind was still working at what he perceived as its normal rate. Even though his body was slow to do his bidding, when it did move, it did so with faultless precision.

His first shot cut the clump of soil cleanly in two, the next two shots cut those two halves in two and his final four shots shattered the remaining pieces, reducing them to a shower of dust. Kane was under no delusions that this technique would be useless to him back in the real world, but it couldn't hurt to practice his aiming. Besides, it was fun.

Next, he switched the weapon's selector to fully automatic. In this mode the gun would deliver fifteen bullets every second. Selecting a particularly leafy clutch of the maize crop, Kane once again concentrated on slowing his perception of time, then took aim and squeezed the trigger. Rather than the usual hammering buzz the weapon made in this mode, Kane heard the stream of bullets leaving the barrel as a series of separate bangs, each making its own echo as it passed through the sound barrier. At the end of their twenty-metre journey each round struck a different leaf on the chosen shrub, a leaf he'd mentally designated.

With a huge grin making his face ache, Kane selected another shrub and repeated the procedure, this time not stopping until the shrub was little more than a ragged twig standing over a pile of leaf fragments. Kane removed the weapon's magazine to check the number of rounds and grunted with surprise to find it still contained its full complement of fifty.

Returning the magazine to the weapon he pointed it towards the ground he pulled the trigger. The bullets poured from the weapon and began to drill a small hole into the soil. Kane maintained pressure on the trigger and slowly began moving the weapon in a spiral pattern, moving out from the centre of the hole. When the hole was about the size of a bucket Kane released the trigger and again removed the magazine. It was still full.

He grunted again. While he was still having fun, the inexhaustible supply of bullets in the P90 served as a stark reminder that none of this was real. He was still within the Portal, trapped in a timeless world of his own imagining.

He already had a theory on how to get back to the real world, into the new room with Sol, but instead of testing the theory he'd stayed and played with his gun. Why had he done that?

If Sol was to be believed, and it was certainly beginning to look like the old man was telling the truth, time spent in the Portal didn't count in the real world. Kane could stay in the Portal for as long as he wanted, without growing older in the real world. While that was a type of immortality and sounded like a dream come true, being trapped here alone in an unending field of maize didn't sound like a fair trade. A man like Kane needed a purpose. He felt like he'd learnt a lot since entering the Portal, this was a wildly different place from the sightless, soundless limbo he'd originally endured. Who was to say what he could conjure up with more experimentation?

But Kane was never a patient man. He needed more information and Sol was the only person to get it from. Or possibly the woman…

Returning to the Portal and the image of himself and Sol, he held his breath and gently pushed them through.

Chapter 8: If a Job's Worth Doing

Robert 'Bob the Breaker' Mitchell stepped from his car and instantly felt dirty. The Wentworth Council Estate stretched out before him, looking dull and tired in the day's dreary light. He'd grown up on the very same estate and as a child had sworn to get out as soon as he possibly could. But rather than filling him with a sense of achievement, reminding how far he'd come, his visit made him feel angry. Anger at being reminded of his roots, at having to breathe the same air as these people again.

How could anyone live like this?

During his father's generation many people lost their homes to German bombing in the war. Social housing reached its peak in the post-war years and those presented with such a home were, for the most part, grateful. They looked after their property, tended the gardens.

But now?

Mitchell looked up and down the street, shaking his head. Every lawn in front of every identical pebble-dashed monstrosity was an ankle deep mess of weeds and litter. The only differences were in the type of rubbish: a burned sofa here, a car up on bricks there. It was just the sort of place that hooded figures would congregate on street corners, glaring at passers-by. But none were on duty today, just a few children playing with a grimy dog. The hoodies were probably sleeping off the previous night's alcopops.

Even in the fifty-odd years of his lifetime Mitchell had seen the damage a succession of governments eager to win votes by being perceived as the most caring, most generous had wrought on his country. Teenagers having babies, thinking it would get them a free house and free money for the rest of their lives, destroying any incentive to work. A couple of generations down the line and that belief was so firmly ingrained that the current generation of pregnant teenagers saw it as their god-given right to live on handouts.

But instead of gratitude for the country's hardworking taxpayers, there was instead a siege mentality, a resentment and hatred of anyone who made the effort to improve their lives, to better themselves through hard work. Rather than a sense of pride and any attempts at self-improvement, vandalism and perpetual aggression had become the tools of choice in an attempt to bring everyone else down to their level.

As social experiments went, Mitchell felt that one lesson should have been learnt years ago: don't indulge parasites.

It made him feel sick to be there, but he had grown tired of waiting to hear from Lindros and decided to take matters into his own hands. Truth be told, he was starting to lose faith in the man.

Mitchell was not in the best of moods.

He turned to his driver, still holding the car door open.

"Stay with the car," he ordered, eyeing the children with the dog suspiciously. His Escalade was probably worth more money than these people saw in ten years. "This won't take long."

Without waiting for a reply Mitchell turned and walked briskly towards house number seventy-three, eager to get this piece of business finished as quickly as possible.

His march was halted by a loud buzzing sound coming from around the corner. Two mopeds came into view, each carrying a pair of hooded youths. As soon as they saw the Escalade the lead bike changed course and headed straight for it, obediently followed by the other. Mitchell watched as his driver moved to the rear of the vehicle and positioned himself between it and approaching mopeds. He stood there, arms folded, glaring at the approaching youths. As they neared the vehicle and slowed down, Mitchell's driver simply stared at the lead youth and slowly shook his head. Without stopping, both bikes performed a neat u-turn and headed off in the opposite direction.

Well, thought Mitchell, *at least somebody still knows their place*. But as soon as the mopeds were about thirty metres away they all started waving middle fingers at the driver and shouting obscenities. *Hmm. Perhaps not.*

Mitchell walked to the front door of number seventy-three and knocked heavily. It was a solid, weatherworn door, the type without any panel detail and likely chosen for strength rather than aesthetics. Instantly, a dog began barking and a thumping sound came from the other side of the door. Obviously the dog was eager to meet him even if the occupant wasn't. Mitchell waited a handful of seconds after the dog finally stopped barking before knocking again, louder this time. Again the dog flew into a frenzy but still no-one answered. His anger rising, Mitchell hammered on the door, not stopping until he heard human signs of life from within.

"Who is it?" a gruff voice demanded.

"Open the door," Mitchell shouted back, "or I'll kick it in."

"Who is it?" repeated the gruff voice, much louder to be heard over the increasingly frenzied dog. In response Mitchell took a step back and kicked at the door. If it were possible, the dog began to sound even more ferocious. After several such blows the voice within relented.

"Alright, alright. Fuckin' hell." There was the sound of fumbling with several types of locks and slide bolts before the door finally opened. A small, wiry man was within, holding onto the studded collar of the dog, struggling to hold it back. As Mitchell had suspected, it was the obligatory Staffordshire bull terrier, looking something like a beige shark's mouth with a bandy leg at each corner. The creature was fighting to free itself, desperate to tear into whoever had dared disturb it.

Mitchell eyed it coolly before slowly turning his attention to the gaunt, unshaven figure holding it back. The scrawny, tattooed man looked almost as aggressive as his dog but Mitchell saw in his eyes that the bravado and posturing was hiding a deeper layer of cowardice.

"If that dog so much as breathes on me," Mitchell said, his tone level and threatening as he looked the man in the eye, "I will thumb both of its eyes out and then shoot you in both knees."

The man looked taken aback, confused even.

"You... you're not the Bailiffs then?" he stammered. Mitchell just glared. The man looked up at him, trying but failing to maintain an air of indignant authority in his own home.

Well, the Council's home, Mitchell thought to himself.

"I'll just put Bogey in the back then," the man said, pulling the frenzied creature towards the kitchen. Without responding, or waiting to be invited, Mitchell entered the house, closing the door behind him, and walked through to the sitting room.

It was just as he'd imagined. A huge, flat panel TV sat in the corner of the small room, surrounded by some of the cheapest, shabbiest looking furniture Mitchell had ever seen. And there, cliché of clichés, in an ashtray sitting on the arm of the centre armchair was a still-burning joint.

Mitchell was staring at the joint as the man entered the room. He sheepishly rushed forward to stub it out and hide the ashtray behind a picture frame, ignoring the irony of the large bong sitting not two feet further along the shelf. The dog continued to bark in the kitchen.

"So," the man began, trying to regain a sense of authority, "if you're not the bailiffs, then…"

"Shut up!" Mitchell cut him off. "Your name is Anthony Holloway." It was a statement, not a question, yet the man felt compelled to answer.

"Yes I am, but…"

"I said shut up."

That was more than Anthony Holloway was willing to take. Although much smaller than Mitchell he stepped up to him and puffed up his feeble chest in an effort to appear more intimidating.

"Who the fuck do you…!"

It didn't work. Mitchell pushed Holloway onto the armchair and leaned forward, grabbing the man's throat in an iron grip. He held him in place, staring into his widening eyes for a few moments, ensuring he had his undivided attention before speaking again. Holloway's bony hands clawed at Mitchell's in a feeble attempt to free himself.

"Your name is Anthony Holloway," Mitchell repeated, "and your son is Jamie Holloway, also know as 'Hollow'. Correct?"

The man, finding himself unable to speak, struggled to nod his head, his eyes betraying the fear of what this man was going to do to him.

Mitchell released his grip and stepped back while Holloway watched in helpless terror as he reached inside his coat. Holloway tried to push himself further back in his armchair, shaking with fear. He had no idea who this man was or what he'd done to upset him, but he knew for sure that this was the end. He tried to summon enough backbone to fight his corner, but his legs refused to function. Instead, his bowels voided themselves.

But instead of the expected gun, Mitchell pulled out a tight roll of twenty-pound notes. He waved them under Holloway's nose for a moment, savouring the greed on the little man's face.

"There is something you're going to do for me, Holloway."

****

Alfred Morrison groaned as the pound coin once again dropped into the coin-return tray at the bottom of the coffee machine. He swore under his breath as he retrieved it and turned his back on the machine before his desire to kick it became too strong. He looked up in mid swear and locked eyes with a nun carrying a charity collection tin.

"Excuse me Sister," he said sheepishly as he dropped the coin into her tin. "Too much caffeine." The nun tutted and continued on her way.

Morrison looked to the ceiling and let out a long sigh. He'd only been at the hospital for a couple of hours but it was already getting to him. The boy, since identified as Jamie Holloway, 'Hollow' to his friends, had yet to wake up. And despite leaving the hospital building several times to switch on his mobile phone to call his wife and check for messages, Morrison had yet to hear from Kane. It was very frustrating and, while he handled frustration better than Kane ever would, it was really starting to get to him.

The two plain-clothes officers were still stationed in the Holloway boy's room with strict orders to contact Morrison the second he awoke. There really wasn't anything else he could do there.

Decision made, Morrison checked in with the officers one last time then headed for his car. Once inside, he opened his laptop and began researching a theory he'd been working on while pacing the hospital corridors.

Even assuming the kidnapping of the Holloway boy had something to do with him being witness to the Bexhill murder, it was unlikely that Deblanc had organised the kidnapping for two reasons. One: Deblanc had always worked on his own in the past, and two: Deblanc never failed.

So the question was: Who had organised the grab? Who would benefit from it?

Fingers flying across the laptop keyboard, Morrison keyed up database after database, cross-referencing profiles and police records. Soon, the name of Deblanc's victim appeared on the screen: Peter Mitchell.

Morrison had already viewed the files but read through them again anyway, checking for anything he might have missed. He then brought up Gregory Lindros's file again, checking for any links between the two files. Instantly a name flashed up: Robert Mitchell.

He'd come across the name a couple of times already, but this link to Lindros, as a suspected employer, was far too much of a coincidence. Obviously Mitchell had employed Lindros to grab Holloway, most likely to interrogate him with a view to going after Deblanc himself.

Closing the laptop and replacing it in the secret holder beneath his seat, Morrison switched on the engine and set off for

Mitchell's last known address. It was a long shot, but if Mitchell didn't have any new information to share, at least he could warn him about Deblanc.

Glad to be doing something other than pace hospital corridors, Morrison hit the road without looking back.

If he had looked behind when he drove along the exit road he could have saved himself a journey. Gregory Lindros was two cars back, following.

And he'd brought friends.

****

Lindros was really beginning to clutch at straws.

He and his two men had scouted the hospital, had checked out the room in which Holloway was located and decided another kidnapping wasn't worth the risk. Security had been put in place to prevent another such attempt. Hospital porters milled about the area as well as the two plain-clothes officers. Lindros also noted that the room in which the boy was placed had been carefully chosen. If they did manage to grab him, they still had to transport him through a warren of corridors to get back to the car park.

So Lindros looked for another source of information and decided that the man who appeared to be in charge of the boy's security must know something of value. Why else would an apparently high-ranking operative be taking such an interest in the case?

His moment came when the man in question finally left the hospital on his own. So he rounded up his two men, Griffith and Hawkins, and here he was now, following the target and waiting for the best time to make his move.

Lindros had done a few jobs for Robert Mitchell since he was drummed out of the Army and they'd always paid well. Usually his tasks were restricted to gathering information on his business rivals and using old army contacts to secure weaponry for Mitchell's bodyguards. But sometimes he was required to get his hands dirty, as with the recent hospital abduction.

In the army, Lindros had carefully tailored his career to avoid placing himself in any dangerous situations while taking every opportunity he could to make extra money on the side. He'd done quite well, making black market deals and pilfering from supply stores wherever he could to build up a nest egg with which he planned to retire in his early thirties. Unfortunately, it all came tumbling down when he got too greedy and fell foul of an internal investigation. His assets were seized, he was thrown out of the army and spent just over two years in prison.

Naturally for someone of his kind, the whole sorry story filled him with anger rather than remorse. It was everybody else's fault. His time inside wasn't wasted and by the time he was released he'd set up a network of suppliers and clients and networked among the various strata of criminals. In fact, he was working for Robert 'Bob the Breaker' Mitchell several months before his release.

Mitchell paid well, very well, and Lindros had begun to rebuild his nest egg. He only needed a few more steady months of work before he could call it a day and retire to somewhere with a bit more sun. It was only because he was so close to his goal that he had quietly taken Mitchell's recent dressing down and continued to work for the pompous man. The simple fact was he needed Mitchell's patronage for the time being and for as long as that remained the case he would continue to bite his tongue.

But when the day came that Mitchell was no longer a part of his plans, well, he would see a very different side to Lindros.

Bringing his mind back to the matter in hand, Lindros watched the silver Audi estate of his target continue towards its destination, wherever that might be. He stared at the car in silence as it approached the town of Pevensy, past the very stretch of beach upon which William the Conqueror had arrived in 1066, on his way to the Battle of Hastings and the history books.

Griffith and Hawkins remained silent in the back of the car, their eyes darting about suspiciously, eternal vigilance being the cost of their profession. They were good men, quick to follow orders and tough fighters. They also looked the part, their appearance often being enough to intimidate away the need for physical action.

Decision made, Lindros reached over to the glove compartment and drew out a flat, blue light unit and positioned it on top of the dashboard. He addressed the two men over his shoulder as he speeded the car up slightly, gaining on Morrison's vehicle.

"Okay," he said, "here's how this is going down..."

****

Alfred Morrison's attention was caught by a flashing blue light in his rear view mirror. The driver of the car behind was also flashing his headlights and waving at him through the windscreen, gesturing for him to pull over. The flashing blue strip on the dashboard identified him as a police officer.

Morrison turned off the road and pulled into a pub car park, wondering what the flap was about. His first thought was some kind of breakthrough in the Deblanc case, but surely he'd have been contacted via mobile phone if that were the case? He lowered the driver's side window and waited.

The other vehicle pulled in and parked several metres behind Morrison's car. Morrison watched in his rear view mirror as three men exited the vehicle, two from the rear and one from the driver's side, and approached his car. The driver confidently strode forward but the other two looked anxious and shifty as they approached in a wider arc, one on each side. Morrison's danger sense prickled and his eyes narrowed as he stared at the approaching driver in the mirror. He looked familiar.

It was Gregory Lindros, the man he and Kane had attempted to chase down at the warehouse.

Morrison's whole body tensed, his every muscle becoming taught and ready for action as adrenaline flooded his system. His mind was already running through scenarios, weighing his options and assessing his resources. He had his 9mm handgun secured in the glove compartment, but everything else he had was locked in the boot of the car. He was glad he'd taken a moment to check on them while he was stuck at the hospital waiting for the Holloway boy to wake up.

Any thought of the men's approach being friendly in nature disappeared as he watched one of the approaching men reach under his coat to remove a semi-automatic pistol.

Morrison had kept his engine running, standard procedure when entering unknown situations in a vehicle, leaving him more options if the situation turned nasty. His easiest option would be to duck down, gun the engine and make a break for it. But that wouldn't gain him anything other than escape. And he knew could do better than that.

Keeping one eye on the two men approaching from the rear, Morrison waited for Lindros to come level with his window. Lindros apparently didn't know that Morrison would be able to both recognise him and know his role in recent events or he would certainly of drawn his weapon before getting this close. And that gave Morrison the upper hand.

Lindros walked up to the window and casually leant on the sill. Morrison was intrigued to know what Lindros was going to say, how he'd play this out, but he wasn't going to get the chance.

Waiting for the moment when Lindros opened his mouth to speak, when his attention was fully focused on distracting Morrison as his two men got into position, Morrison grabbed his forearm with both hands and dragged his torso into the car. At the same time he floored the accelerator, sending the car lurching forward, driving blind with Lindros furiously struggling across his lap. Instantly, bullets began pouring into the car, shattering the rear then the front windscreen.

Morrison freed his left arm and brought his elbow down several times onto the back of Lindros's neck, stunning him long enough to make a grab for the steering wheel and put the car into a sudden right turn, bringing Lindros between himself and the approaching gunmen. The shooting stopped, but he would only have a few seconds before they got close enough to take a clear shot. He could see them running at full tilt towards his car.

Elbowing Lindros on the back of the neck several more times to keep him quiet for a few more precious seconds, Morrison wrenched at the wheel and stamped on the accelerator. Gravel sprayed from the rear wheels as he aimed the car straight at the gunmen. He grabbed at the glove compartment and drew his sidearm from its hiding place. Lindros managed to get his head up just as Morrison brought the gun around and fired a few blind left-handed shots through the windscreen. His wild shooting did nothing other than make the two men dive for cover but actual the firing of the gun, right next to Lindros's ear, draw a satisfying scream from the former soldier. Morrison's own ears were ringing but he'd had the advantage of knowing when the shots were coming. He grinned to think of the earache Lindros was now suffering.

For the next few moments he could focus his attention on the two gunmen. The fact that they'd opened fire first made the task easier as he was now officially acting in self-defence.

Morrison brought the butt of his weapon onto the back of the man's head before dropping it onto the passenger seat, freeing his hand to grab the handbrake. Grateful that his car was an automatic, Morrison gunned the engine briefly before yanking on the handbrake and wrenching at the steering wheel, swinging the tail of the vehicle round and into one of the gunmen. The man made a satisfying scream as he was knocked down, which rose in pitch as the rear wheel went over his legs.

One down.

But as he began looking around for the second gunman, Morrison became aware of a sudden and intense pain in his lap. He was so shocked by the sudden agony that it took him a moment to realise what was happening. His eyes widened and began watering as he realised Lindros was sinking his teeth into his crotch!

"Dirty bastard!" he screamed as, more by reaction than any planning on his part, Morrison slammed the breaks on, sending Lindros's head crashing into the steering wheel before his body fell backwards and out of the car. Morrison slouched forward and, fighting back the urge to vomit, just had enough time to grab his manhood with both hands before he felt a pistol barrel being pressed against his temple.

"Not one fucking move," the second gunman sneered.

****

Naturally, a crowd had cautiously gathered once the gunfire had come to an end. The entire shootout had been watched by people inside the public house and others in nearby shops and on the street, but that didn't worry Lindros. Griffith had already gagged and cuffed Morrison and checked him for weapons.

Once his head stopped spinning and he'd recovered his senses, Lindros took control of the situation, acting with all the authority his former military position had once given him. He helped the limping Higgins into the back of Morrison's vehicle with the willing help of two men from the gathering crowd. Higgins had a badly broken leg, but was lucky it hadn't been both.

Glancing over to ensure the fake police light was still flashing in the windscreen of his own car, he thanked the men and asked them to remain at the scene until his backup arrived to begin debriefing the witnesses. But right now, he explained, he had to get his injured man to the hospital and secure the dangerous criminal, meaning Morrison.

These two pub-goers, chests puffed up with pride at their perceived positions of authority, dutifully began bossing people around, leaving Lindros and his men free to deal with Morrison and make their escape.

Securing Morrison in the boot of his vehicle, Lindros drove away from the scene while Griffith drove Morrison's Audi, with Higgins stretched out in the back, along behind.

As he drove along, heading for the Eastbourne warehouse once more, Lindros's mobile phone rang. It was Griffith in the car behind.

"What?" he snapped.

"Higgins' leg is in a bad way," Griffith replied, "I should take him to a hospital for treatment, say he was in a traffic accident or something."

"Oh, brilliant," Lindros snapped. "How long do you think it'll take them to link him to that fracas in Pevensy? We take him to the warehouse and set the bone there. We have morphine and medical supplies there." And with that, he snapped the phone shut.

Griffith was a good man and he had a point. The car had gone over Higgins' ankle and made a pretty mess of it. He would be lucky if he ever recovered full use of it. But that wasn't the reason behind Lindros's anger. He'd been caught out by Morrison in what should have been a simple hold up. They'd outnumbered him three to one, yet he appeared to be ready for them. And Lindros had only managed to get away with it by resorting to a pretty desperate act, which he didn't want to think about.

He wondered if anything would ever taste the same again.

Lindros continued to drive, his dark mood increasing. He wondered if he was getting sloppy or if he'd just been having a run of bad luck. The recent events at the warehouse, when some unseen foe had sucker-punched him and his men, still stung. Perhaps it was closer to his time to get out than he'd realised. Yes, maybe this should be his last job for Mitchell.

His phone rang again. It was Griffith.

"Look," he shouted into the mouthpiece, "I fucking told you. We go to the warehouse…"

"I know that boss," Griffith replied calmly, ignoring Lindros's tone, even sounding slightly amused. "Me and Higgins were just wondering how you managed to get free of that bloke's car…?"

"Fucking warehouse! Now!" Lindros snapped the phone shut again, but not quickly enough to avoid hearing Griffith and Higgins roaring with laughter at the other end.

Chapter 9: The Keep

Ted Kane and Sol burst, there was really no other word for it, through the Portal and into the new chamber Kane had witnessed from the other side. When he'd dived at Sol and carried them both through, he'd done so with more vigour than was necessary because of the need to catch him unawares. Now, the pair entered the chamber and landed hard in an undignified heap on the gleaming white floor. Sol let out a surprised grunt as he hit the ground, though it could have been the end of his original cry of surprise when Kane had leapt at him.

Kane was stunned by the suddenness with which the Portal journey had been completed once he'd pushed the images of Sol and himself through. He sat on the ground, stunned as if someone had just shone a spotlight in his face in a dark room. He'd felt disorientation before, but this was something else.

But along with the disorientation was another, equally powerful feeling, coursing its way through his system.

He felt great. Really, really energised, almost high with a sense of well-being. But unfortunately, the feeling didn't last for very long.

A feral scream filled the air and something hard crashed into him, sending him flying into something else solid. Before he could regain his senses his wrist was grabbed and he was hauled sideways into yet another hard surface. Objects fell onto him, one catching him on the side of the head as he tried to understand what was happening. The world had gone crazy and the assaults on his body continued. He could offer no defence. Spots danced before his eyes as he forced them to focus, just in time to see a figure lunging at him. Another scream filled the air and he watched helplessly as the figure grabbed him by the throat and hauled his aching, stinging body onto his feet.

He found himself staring into the face of the woman he'd seen through the Portal. But any trace of femininity was gone, replaced by a mask of pure, bloodthirsty hatred. She held him up against one of the grey constructions, his feet clear of the ground, in a one-handed grip. Kane struggled to free himself, clawing at her hand with both of his, but to no avail. She was enormously powerful. He watched helplessly as she drew her other hand back and rolled it into a fist…

"Hold!" called out Sol, just now coming to his feet. "It's alright 23, let him go."

Kane watched helplessly as the woman, without once taking her hate-filled eyes from his, slowly lowered him enough for his feet to touch the ground. But she didn't release his throat or lessen the pressure of her grip.

"Who is he?" she demanded. "What's he doing here?" Her voice was surprisingly deep and angry.

Kane forced himself to take his eyes away from the woman's and peered over her shoulder. Behind her, Sol was indignantly smoothing his pale grey suit with the flats of his hands. He sighed as he looked at the damage the recent incident had wrought on this otherwise spotless chamber. Kane followed his gaze and glanced at the unidentifiable units and pieces of equipment strewn about their feet, his field of vision greatly reduced by the woman's grip holding his neck immovable.

"I didn't intend to bring him here just yet," Sol explained with another sigh, suddenly sounding very old. "I'd just made initial contact. But it would appear that Mr Kane here prefers to set his own timetable."

"Are you alright, Sol?" the woman asked over her shoulder. Her tone was lighter, sounding slightly relieved, but not the grip on Kane's throat.

"I'm fine my dear, but please, let our guest go. I don't know what he must think of us."

The woman narrowed her eyes further as she leaned in close enough to Kane for him to feel her breath on his ear.

"If you so much as touch Sol again," she whispered so only he could hear, "I will pound on you until not one part of your anatomy can be identified." With that, she released her grip and stepped back. Kane's legs buckled beneath him and he fell to the ground, both hands clutched to his throat, trying to massage some feeling back into it.

He watched in surprise as the woman shot him one final glare before turning around and rushing up to Sol. She changed before his bemused eyes from ferocious Amazonian to a giggling girl as quickly as though someone had flicked a switch. He shakily rose to his feet, still rubbing at his throat and coughing gently as he watched her lift Sol from the ground in a tight embrace, swinging the older man around as though he were an oversized teddy bear.

"Take it easy 23!" Sol laughed as he struggled to free himself. "I'm not as young as you anymore!"

"Silly!" she giggled, "You're younger than I am, remember!"

Presumably this was some kind of in-joke that Kane wasn't privy to. The woman was obviously in her thirties, about half Sol's age.

"How long have you been up?" Sol was asking the woman, holding her at arms length and smiling widely.

"Just a couple of hours," she replied. "I called you as soon as I'd made myself look presentable…" a look of sadness crossed her face as she looked him over. "But Sol," she said, "You've aged so. You've been doing everything by yourself again haven't you?"

Sol laughed away the comment. "Well, I have to make sure everything's moving along with the timetable don't I?"

"The timetable you made, or one Brakus replaced it with?" she asked with mock severity, wagging her finger at him as though scolding a small child.

"Don't worry about him," Sol assured her. "We've come to an… understanding. You really should spend a little more time with him, he's a remarkable individual."

The woman shuddered and cringed at the same time, turning her nose up at the very notion of whatever it was they were talking about. "Yuck!" she said, "he still gives me the creeps after all this time…"

Kane stood there uncomfortably, waiting for their bizarre greetings to end. He glanced about the chamber and realised that his peep through the Portal hadn't prepared him for it's sheer size. He couldn't see how such a huge space could possibly maintain it's integrity, so high was the ceiling without any visible means of support apart from the walls, so far away in the distance in all four directions.

Dotted about the chamber, floating freely throughout the space, were the objects that had reminded him of elongated motorcycle helmets covered in mechanical arms. He could now see that they were some kind of robotic drones, flying about the place and performing various tasks of construction both on and in the grey units. These grey constructions were dotted about the chamber, in all manner of shapes and sizes including the large one the woman had thrown him into. But to his surprise, the side into which he'd been thrown was split wide open and its innards had spilled out onto the ground. It was the only untidy thing in the entire, spotless room.

"Yes, they are surprisingly fragile, aren't they?" said Sol, drawing Kane's attention back to the people in the room. The woman was standing next to Sol, holding onto his hand like a little girl. *A very scary little girl*, Kane thought to himself. Now that he had someone to compare her height to, he could see that she was very tall and incredibly well built. Muscular, but still feminine.

"I might be surprised if I knew what they were," Kane replied as he stepped up to the damaged unit and poked at it with a fingertip. "Or even what it is they're made of."

"That would take a bit of explaining…" began Sol.

"I know, I know," Kane interrupted, "cavemen and MP3 players…"

Sol smiled. "Well, yes," he replied, "but can we now agree that everything I've told you has been true?"

"I think so, yes," Kane replied as he continued to glance around the huge chamber. "But the question remains, what am I doing here?"

The response to his question didn't come from Sol.

"That's a good question," the woman muttered, looking him up and down with a most unimpressed expression on her face. "What *is* he doing here?"

"Agent 23," said Sol as he freed his hand from hers and put it on her shoulder. "This is Mr Ted Kane. I was considering him for a place on our staff…"

The woman snorted and Kane found himself strangely disturbed by her derision.

"But," Sol continued, a smile creeping across his face, "what if I were to tell you that this man has just arrived here by Portal without any mental preparation whatsoever…?"

Kane didn't really understand the significance of Sol's statement, but it obviously meant a great deal to the woman because her whole attitude changed before his eyes. Her face softened and her every muscle seemed to loosen. Her proud, almost arrogant pose melted away.

But best of all, Kane watched as her expression changed to one of… well, almost respect. And Sol looked almost as proud of Kane as he was beginning to feel about himself, though he still wasn't really sure why. Sol had started to explain the workings and dangers of Portal travel, but had been cut off in mid explanation by his mystery caller. Kane remembered Sol's earlier warnings about being trapped in a timeless limbo, but he found his experience a lot simpler to deal with than Sol had implied.

Kane did feel a little proud of himself for negotiating the Portal so easily and was very happy to see a hint of the same in the woman's face. But he still had the uncomfortable feeling of being the only uninvited guest at a party.

"So…" he began, not really knowing how his sentence was going to finish. "Er... Miss 23 is it…?"

The woman chuckled, enjoying his discomfort, though this was the first time she'd addressed him with anything less than resentment.

"Just 23," she smiled. "Though if you want to address me by my full title, it's Agent 23." She and Sol exchanged half smiles and Kane again felt left out of some private joke. Not knowing how to respond, Kane was relieved when Sol spoke again.

"On the subject of introductions," he said before raising his voice and addressing the room as a whole: "Aren't you going to greet our guest, Brakus?"

Kane followed Sol's gaze, looking up into the massive space of the room. The ceiling was so high it felt like he was standing outside.

"I am very busy," a raspy voice announced, apparently from thin air. The voice sounded irritated and almost snooty, drawing a grin from Sol. Agent 23 though, cringed visibly.

"Gives me the creeps," she muttered to no one in particular, "that thing watching us all the time."

Kane strained to spot where the new voice had come from. There was no clue to its direction; it appeared to come from everywhere at once. He could see no evidence of speakers anywhere on the distant, plain white walls. The floor, too, was featureless as far as he could see. His attention shifted to the multiple-armed devices floating about the chamber, busying themselves with various tasks. Like worker ants they followed each other around the huge space, at various levels in straight lines. And the more he watched them the more order he saw in their actions. Most of them were busying themselves with the flat-sided grey constructions.

"No," said Sol, following Kane's gaze across the chamber. "The drones are simple construction devices. They merely do what they are instructed to do. Brakus is in a different chamber from this workshop.

"Brakus' voice is being beamed from his chamber into this one, where it is resonated through the chamber's surfaces themselves; the floor, the walls and the ceiling. The sound goes through an intelligent modulation process that varies the volume throughout the chamber based on where the recipients are, producing equal and comfortable audio levels throughout the chamber."

"I expect Brakus is in his control suite," Agent 23 added to a bemused Kane. "He usually is."

"Yes I am." The voice rumbled. "And currently attempting to carry out the work of several beings of even my intellect." Agent 23 rolled her eyes.

"He's a bit crabby isn't he?" asked Kane, surprised at how much he found himself wanting this woman to accept him as part of the team.

To both his surprise and concern, his comment made Sol and Agent 23 roar with laughter, leaving him feeling more of an outsider than before. But then, to his equally great relief, Agent 23 stepped forward to placed an arm around his waist and gently guided him across the chamber.

"You don't know how right you are," she said as she led him through the maze of grey units to a previously hidden seating area where tables had been prepared with various foods and drinks. "I'd only expected Sol to be joining me for refreshments, but there should be plenty for three of us." She looked at him with an amused smile. "I know how hungry *I* feel after Portal travel." She looked back over her shoulder, where Sol was quietly standing where they'd left him. "We'll let Sol deal with Brakus. I do believe he actually *likes* the guy."

Kane looked back at Sol just as the man addressed the mysterious voice again.

"I'll check in for a status check later Brakus," he was saying. "I need to bring 23 up to date and acclimatise our guest."

"I take it he will be joining your little *crusade* then?" the voice replied, sounding inconvenienced by the idea. The use of the word 'your' was not missed by Kane. *Who's side is this Brakus character on?* he wondered.

"Yes he will," Sol stated flatly, apparently choosing to ignore the sarcasm in Brakus' tone. "Prepare a standard equipment package for him."

"If I must," the voice snapped back, peevishly. "Is there anything else you would like me to do, should I manage to find a free second or two among my other duties?"

Sol grinned and motioned towards the grey unit into which Agent 23 had thrown Kane. "Yes," he said. "Divert a couple of drones to clear this mess up will you? It looks untidy."

There was no further comment from Brakus and Sol joined Kane and Agent 23 in the dining area.

Had Sol taken a moment to inspect the damage to the grey unit himself, had he looked through the debris the split unit had deposited onto the ground, he would have found something that didn't belong there.

The Portal had deposited Sol and Kane just in front of the unit and so fast was Agent 23's reaction to the perceived attack on her colleague by the stranger Kane, that no-one had had time to notice the other object that had come through the Portal with them. The impact of Kane into the unit had resulted in the object becoming buried by debris, debris that was now being collected and taken away by the drones.

A man's right forearm and hand, wrapped in the sleeve from a dark green coat, was being taken away and recycled with the rest of the flotsam.

****

Timothy Bruce awoke from his nightmare in a state of utter confusion and abject terror. He was used to waking up to a feeling of dread, he did so most days, but this time it was far more pronounced. He'd been dreaming about a stranger hounding his every move. No matter how fast Timothy ran in his dream the man would appear from around the next corner, a look of evil intent on his face.

A bright light burned his eyes, taking his mind off the tightness he felt in his chest, forcing him to squeeze them closed and hide them behind his hands. He could feel tears rolling down his cheeks, though he didn't know if they were a reaction to the light or whether he'd been crying. He'd been so miserable for so long that he reflexively wiped his face free of moisture every time he woke up.

The unusual brightness of wherever he was filled him with panic. Timothy Bruce was not someone who adapted to change very easily.

He moved from the foetal position he'd awoken in, the position he *always* awoke in, and slowly eased himself into a sitting position. It was a brave move on his part, exposing himself to whatever danger it was he was trying to remember, but he was too scared for rational thought. Slowly and gradually opening his eyes, he blinked away the last of the dancing spots to finally take a look at his surroundings.

The room was large and white and filled with various pieces of white furniture. He had no idea where he was and how he'd got there. He was sitting on the floor despite the selection of couches and beds in the room and was surprised to notice that, hard and shiny as it was, the floor wasn't cold to the touch.

Timothy rose and moved towards one of the white couches, his every move stiff and clumsy as the tension in his muscles fought to deny his actions. As he sat on the couch and looked around a sound caught his attention from across the room.

It sounded like a groan coming from behind of one of the couches.

He stood and raised himself up on tiptoe, summoning the courage to peer over the couch, but not quite enough to cross the room to take a closer look. There was a man lying on the ground, with his back to him. He could see that the man was in a similar foetal position to the one he himself had found himself in, but there was something wrong with the pose. Rather than being curled up as a source of comfort, the man appeared to be shaking gently, possibly crying.

Feeling a sudden kinship with the stranger, Timothy walked over to him and crouched to put a hand on the trembling shoulder.

"Are you alright?" he asked quietly, gently pulling at the shoulder to bring the stranger's face into view. But as soon as he saw it he let go and fell onto his backside in horror.

It was the man from his nightmare.

But rather than the ghastly expression from his dream, the man's face was pale and waxy with beads of sweat standing out on his forehead. The expression of pain on the face made him appear even more frightening somehow. His right arm was hidden under his left armpit, and Timothy could see that his left wrist was twisted at an unnatural angle and covered in bruises, apparently broken or at least badly twisted.

"H…hello Timothy," the man greeted him with a clenched grin. "How's…your day…going?"

Whether he was more taken aback by the man's attempt at humour or that he knew his name, Timothy wasn't sure. But he now recalled where he'd seen this man before. It was him that had broken into his flat, had invaded the only place in the world that he'd felt safe. Timothy sat there, wide-eyed and not knowing what to say. One minute he was safely tucked up in bed reading, and the next… It was all too much to take in.

"Look…" the man said with some difficulty, "I'm sorry that I…I gave you such a… fright earlier. But, believe…believe it or…not…" Here he stopped talking as the pain became too great for him to talk through. He took a few breaths before continuing. "Believe it or…not, I came…with news… good news that will…change your life forever."

The man slumped back with the exertion of speaking for so long, making Timothy wonder how badly the wrist was broken. Surely he was in a lot more pain than a broken wrist would cause?

As if hearing Timothy's thoughts, the man spoke again.

"I'm…going to need your…help to get us out of here, Timothy," he said as he raised himself into a sitting position and extend his right arm to examine the extent of his injuries.

Timothy found himself forcing back bile at the sight that met his eyes. As the man held out his arm, it took Timothy a few full seconds to realise what he was seeing. The arm was gone from bellow the elbow. *Completely* gone. Timothy was staring at the stump of an arm, looking something like the cross-section of a tree trunk. There was no blood that he could see, just a perfectly smooth surface showing the twin bones of the forearm in the middle, surrounded by layers of muscle and flesh, in turn surrounded by the thin, pale outer layer of skin.

"Yeah, it…really does hurt as much as…as you'd imagine," the man said with a forced smile, tucking the stump under his armpit as though embarrassed by it. "And the…punch-line is that this one," he said, holding up his one remaining hand, "is *really*…badly broken."

But Deblanc didn't stop there.

"Oh," he added, as though as an afterthought, "and the…control device I carry to get in and out of this…chamber was built into my watch…which I tend to wear on my right hand… Without it, there's no way out of this room."

Timothy had no idea what the man was talking about, didn't know what to say, so he remained silent. Everything had been so weird lately that he just accepted what the man said, no matter how farfetched and ridiculous it sounded. The man slowly moved himself back against a couch, the effort bringing more sweat to his face, and they both sat in silence for a few minutes before the man finally broke the silence.

"My name is…Deblanc, by the way."

"Hello, Mr Deblanc," Timothy said with some effort, his voice breaking half way through the greeting. This brought a grin from Deblanc.

"Just…Deblanc," he said. When silence once again filled the room, Deblanc made another attempt at getting Timothy talking. He needed him to feel comfortable and safe, to open up if they were ever going to get out of there. He was no use to Deblanc if he just clammed up and sat in a corner. "If you could…have any one thing in this world," he asked, "anything at all…what would it be?"

The question took Timothy aback. He'd become so used to having no control over his life that he'd long since given up on dreams and aspirations. So he considered the question for a little while before answering.

"A friend," he said at last, his voice small and feeble.

Perfect, thought Deblanc, *I couldn't have hoped for a better answer*. It was the most pathetic thing he had ever heard and did nothing to lessen the disgust he felt for Timothy Bruce. For months he'd been ordered to watch over the pathetic wretch, made to act as his secret guardian. But now, fate had turned the tables and it was he who needed Timothy's help.

He would have to endure the pretence of tolerating Timothy Bruce for the time being. At least until he no longer needed him.

Taking a deep breath, Deblanc spoke again.

"Well…that's the very least we… we can offer you, Timothy," he said, trying to sound earnest. "I came to your…flat with an offer…to join our organisation… I apologise for the misjudged…joke on my part, I didn't mean to scare you." He paused, waiting for Timothy to make eye contact with him before continuing. It was quite a long wait. "I…can promise you this…Timothy, your…life will improve in ways in which you can't…can't yet imagine." He forced a smile, trying to lighten the mood. "I'd offer you my hand in…friendship," he said, shakily raising his broken one, "but even my…good one's not up to the task at the moment…" Worried that he might have sounded bitter, speaking through teeth gritted against the pain as he was, Deblanc forced a small chuckle and smiled at Timothy. And to his relief, Timothy smiled back.

"Pleased to…meet you, Timothy." He said.

"I'm pleased to meet you too, Deblanc," Timothy replied with the first smile Deblanc had ever seen on the pathetic wretch.

“Well,” said Deblanc, “I suppose…I’d better explain where we are and how…we’re going to get out of here…”

Chapter 10: Coming to Terms

Robert 'Bob the Breaker' Mitchell knew he should be feeling at least a trace of self-satisfaction, the warm glow of a job well done. He had done, after giving the matter a few minutes of his attention, what Gregory Lindros with all his military training and intelligence gathering experience, apparently couldn't do. But all he felt, if anything at all, was the dull throb of anger making the veins in his temples pulse.

He now sat, unusually, in the front passenger seat of his car as the driver guided the large, blacked-out vehicle away from Eastbourne hospital. In the back seat sat Adam Holloway and his injured son Anthony, also known as 'Hollow', former friend of Mitchell's dead son Peter.

It hadn't taken Robert Mitchell long to convince Holloway to travel with him to the hospital and demand they discharge his son. Mitchell could have threatened the man into doing his bidding, but he really couldn't be bothered. Instead he'd waved a roll of banknotes under his nose and told him what he'd have to do to receive it. Mitchell didn't know how much money was in the roll and Holloway didn't even ask. When his eyes had widened at the sight of the money, Mitchell knew he had him.

They'd travelled to the hospital with Mitchell in his usual rear seat, next to a visibly excited Holloway. The man's original fear of Mitchell had evaporated the second he'd laid eyes on the cash, his sullen attitude replaced with a much more buoyant one: An attitude Mitchell found even more irritating. Holloway spent much the journey asking Mitchell how much the car was worth, how much the insurance was, his every question relating to money in some way or other. The very sight of the roll of cash had transformed the man's attitude, filling him with childlike excitement.

Unfortunately this new attitude came with increased confidence and ambition. As was so often the case when Mitchell recruited people like Holloway to do little jobs for him, the man saw it as the beginning of a lucrative new career. But Holloway had gone one step further and appeared to think he and Mitchell were now the best of friends. He'd even gone so far as to try giving him advice about the best places to invest his money. Mitchell had done his best to ignore Holloway, to hold his temper until the job was done and he could cut him loose.

And then there was the smell.

Simply put, Anthony Holloway stank. Mitchell had originally assumed the smell to be coming from the man's filthy house. The wiry little man smelled like he'd been wearing the same clothes for weeks. His thin, lank hair sat flat on his head with little dots of white among the greasy strands. An image of Golem from the Lord of the Rings movies crept into Mitchell's head as he tried to distance himself, leaning as far away from Holloway as he could. He wondered if the evening's valeting would rid the car of the smell and made a mental note to tip the valet boy well if it did.

Finally, the journey ended and Holloway got out of the car. Mitchell watched as he swaggered into the hospital with all the square-shouldered arrogance of a man who knew his rights. Mitchell got out of the vehicle and climbed into the front passenger seat so quickly that the driver didn't have time to get out and open the door for him. This seemed to worry the driver, who sat in awkward silence until Mitchell addressed him.

"What a revolting little man," his boss growled as he lit a cigar in an attempt to cover the smell left by Holloway.

All of Robert Mitchell's employees had been walking on eggshells since the death of his son, waiting for the big man's temper to finally break. Despite the occasional outburst they were still waiting for the inevitable rage to fully breach the surface. But so far Mitchell's temper had remained a brooding, sleeping monster, waiting for someone to press the wrong button.

While he waited for Holloway to return, Mitchell phoned Lindros, tired of waiting and looking forward to shaming him with news of his own success. Lindros answered the phone in a foul mood, apparently expecting a call from someone else.

"I said fucking drop it!" he'd bellowed before Mitchell had a chance to announce himself. Lindros was apparently driving when he'd answered the phone and something had clearly annoyed him. So much so that he was surprisingly rude to Mitchell, displaying a boldness never before seen in the man. The driver winced when he heard Lindros's tone but Mitchell appeared to find the exchange amusing.

Lindros had captured someone connected to the case and was transporting him to the warehouse for questioning, hoping to discover the identity of Peter Mitchell's killer. When he was informed that the Holloway boy was as good as secured, Lindros began ranting about how much effort the capture of his own prisoner had taken. He hadn't gone into details, Mitchell wouldn't have been interested in them anyway, but was vehemently loath to dump his prisoner, determined to gain some information from him. It was much more likely his determination was just to cover the embarrassment of being beaten to the punch. Not to mention he was likely hoping to secure a financial bonus for any information his prisoner could provide.

Mitchell gave the matter a few seconds of thought before deciding to meet with Lindros at the warehouse where they could question both of their 'guests'. He told Lindros to blindfold his prisoner and hung up. Half an hour later Holloway approached the car with his son in a wheelchair.

Holloway stopped the wheelchair by the vehicle's rear door and waited, stooping slightly to stare through at Mitchell's driver. The driver looked across at Mitchell for conformation that he should get out and help, but Mitchell just shook his head and lowered his window.

"Get in," he snapped.

The driver was relieved. He'd not wanted to help Holloway, not even wanted to go near to him. The man's attitude was turning towards arrogance and the driver could see it wouldn't be long before Holloway assumed he could order him around. He appreciated Mitchell making the man struggle with getting his son into the car, a reminder of who was working for whom.

Holloway eventually got the boy into the vehicle and discarded the wheelchair, pushing it blindly across the tarmac and into another parked car. The boy was in a poor condition, almost asleep with the pain killing drugs the hospital had been giving him. His head lolled about before finally coming to rest on his chest. Holloway senior had shown his son little care when getting him into the car, a task that had obviously annoyed him. He'd shoved and pulled at his son as if he was forcing a duvet into an under-bed drawer.

The task done, Holloway rushed around the back of the vehicle and climbed in the other side. The driver looked to Mitchell for permission to drive away, his left hand resting on the gear stick. But instead, Mitchell lowered the sun visor so he could regard Holloway in the vanity mirror.

"Aren't you going to put your son's seatbelt on, Mr Holloway?" he asked mildly. "He's worth quite a lot of money to you, you know."

Missing the sarcasm in Mitchell's voice, Holloway struggled with the seatbelt until he'd finally secured it in place. He looked up at Mitchell's reflection in the mirror. The two men's eyes met briefly before Mitchell raised his eyebrows. At his unspoken command Holloway sighed and fastened his own seatbelt. Mitchell nodded to his driver and pointed ahead.

"To the warehouse please," he said.

After several minutes of blessed silence, Holloway senior returned to his talkative ways and proceeded to go into great detail about how he'd gone about the task of collecting his son.

"Yeah," he said, "they tried to stop me taking my boy out, but I know my rights." On and on he went, wilfully ignoring the fact that no one was listening.

To the driver's surprise and relief Mitchell was sitting quietly, ignoring Holloway and staring with unfocused eyes through the front windscreen. The driver drove quickly, willing the journey to be over as quickly as possible. Was Holloway mad? Did he not have any concept of who Mitchell was, of what he was capable of when angered? He'd just lost his only son for god's sake.

Finally, Mitchell had had enough, but it wasn't the reaction the driver was expecting.

"Change of plan," Mitchell announced quietly. "Drop me off at the restaurant, then take the Holloway's to the warehouse. Leave them with Lindros and come back to pick me up." Though his words were calm and level they left no room for questions. This was what was going to happen. He turned to face Holloway senior, addressing him directly for the first time since leaving the hospital.

"My man Lindros will meet you at your destination and debrief your son," he said flatly. "You will stay with him until I get there, at which point you will be paid and then returned to your home."

"Are you sure you don't want me to come with you?" the man asked, his voice filled with disappointment. "I've got some ideas I want to talk…"

"That won't be necessary," Mitchell cut him off. "I'm sure you're concerned about your son and would rather be taking care of him." It was a statement rather than a question. Holloway looked crest-fallen.

"What about me?" he said, ignoring the comment about his son and beginning to sound whiney. "If I came to work with you…"

Mitchell's driver looked across at his boss and the two men exchanged knowing glances. They both knew that wasn't going to happen.

****

Ted Kane sat back in the deep couch and listened to Sol and Agent 23 talking together. He couldn't understand a lot of what they were saying, the technical details were all going straight over his head, but he did pick up on a few facts.

They kept referring to Brakus and Deblanc and another man called Kendrick, but nobody else. Were these the only people in their organisation? The name 'Agent 23' implied there should be at least another twenty-two agents somewhere about the place but they didn't refer to anyone else.

He also discovered that the various, and apparently fragile, grey constructions filling the room didn't appear to have a name as such, but were instead referred to by number. The one he had been thrown into and subsequently broken was referred to as number 45372, meaning there were an awful lot of them: Tens of thousands. He still had absolutely no idea what they were and why so many were being built. But whatever they were, they were obviously very important and at the centre of whatever this organisation was up to.

On that subject, Kane had very little information. Agent 23 and Sol weren't being at all secretive about what they were doing, something Kane found unusual and more than a little unsettling. The circles he usually moved in were obsessed with secrecy and 'need to know' levels of security. But here they spoke openly and freely, Sol apparently eager to share his secrets with him. Though, Kane reflected, if Sol's claims about them being so far beneath the surface were true it wouldn't matter if anyone found out about them. No one would be able to get this far down to investigate anyway.

He decided to let them continue talking rather than jump in with the hundreds of questions he needed answering. It seemed that Sol and Agent 23 hadn't seen each other for some time and had some catching up to do.

Kane looked across at his combat webbing and weapons resting on another chair, exactly where he'd placed them shortly after entering the refreshment area. Nobody had attempted to take them from him and neither of his new friends appeared to be armed. In fact, he reflected, Sol had shown him nothing but respect since they'd met and even Agent 23 appeared to have warmed to him since Sol's revelation about him passing through the Portal unharmed.

The food Agent 23 had organized had been a wide mixture of fresh fruit and vegetable dishes and baked items still warm from wherever she had prepared them. Kane had eaten several cake-like morsels before realising there were no meat-based products on offer.

Great, he thought, *vegetarians*. But the food was good and he ate well while Sol and Agent 23 nibbled between talking, for the most part ignoring him.

Kane sipped at a cup of fresh coffee, enjoying its warmth in his throat. It reminded him of something.

"Hey," he said suddenly and to no one in particular, "I haven't smoked in ages!"

Sol and Agent 23 stopped talking and both turned to look at him.

"Smoked?" said 23, as though she'd never heard of such a thing. Sol smiled at her before addressing Kane.

"I wondered how long it would be before you realised," he said, enjoying Kane's surprise and confusion. "Tell me, how long do you estimate you spent in the Portal?"

Kane thought about it for a few seconds, his brow lightly furrowed. "I don't know," he said slowly. "A few days at least. Weeks maybe…"

"Less than a second in real time." Sol reminded him. "But as I've already explained, the perceived passage of time varies with the individual."

"Weeks?" muttered Agent 23 as she regarded Kane with respect, "that's pretty impressive."

"Indeed," replied Sol before returning his attention to Kane. "And in those perceived weeks," he asked, "the thought of smoking never entered your head?"

"Actually, no." Kane replied.

"Well, even though your physical body spent only a second in the Portal, your mind experienced a much longer period of time, long enough to rid you of the mental element of your addiction." He paused and watched Kane take the information in, waiting for the question he knew would come.

"Mental aspect…" Kane muttered. "How about the physical addiction of my…smoking?"

"Another aspect of Portal travel is the health screening you undergo each and every time you pass through. The system scans your body down to the molecular level before converting you into an energy stream. When you are…ah… recompiled the system omits any abnormalities, anything that shouldn't be there." He looked Kane straight in the eye before continuing. "And that includes, Mr Kane, the tar you'd allowed to build up in your lungs. That's why you no longer have a physical craving for cigarettes."

Kane thought back to the feeling of well being he'd experienced after emerging from the Portal. Was that really what it felt like to be a non-smoker? How he'd be feeling each day if he hadn't taken it up in his youth? Of course, had he never smoked he wouldn't of known the difference anyway, but still…

Sol picked up a datapad from a nearby table and punched in a series of commands before addressing Kane again.

"Quite a lot of tar," he said with raised eyebrows, "and a small cancerous tumour from your left lung." He passed the pad to Kane who looked at the diagram of a pair of lungs on the screen. A blinking icon indicated a small dark area to the left of the left lung. Kane stared at the diagram for a moment, his eyes scanning the strange script dotted about the screen.

"What are these markings?" he asked, handing the pad back to Sol, "That's not a language I've ever seen."

"Ah," said Sol as he and Agent 23 exchanged embarrassed glances, "That's something I will have to come back to later I'm afraid." An uncomfortable silence followed, finally broken by Agent 23.

"Well," she said to Kane, "looks like you've kicked your little habit then…" As soon as she'd said the words she realised they sounded patronising. She winced as she watched Kane sit straighter in his seat, obviously annoyed by her comment.

"Yep," he said, "looks like I can start all over again."

Sol and Agent 23 quietly watched as he took out a cigarette and lit it. He drew in a long blast and instantly began coughing.

"Shit," he said as he stared at the cigarette, "looks like I really *am* starting all over again…" As one, Sol and Agent 23 stared first at him then the cigarette in his hand. Agent 23 wrinkled her nose as the pale cloud of smoke reached her.

"Perhaps you're right," said Kane, dropping the offending item into the dregs of his coffee. He then pulled out the packet and stared at it for a second as though saying goodbye to an old friend before crushing it and throwing it onto an empty plate on the food table.

"Anyway," he said, changing the subject, "I think it's about time you two told me just what it is you're up to down here and how I fit in…"

Sol and Agent 23 relaxed visibly. Glad the awkward moment had passed.

"I think that's a reasonable request, Mr Kane..." Sol began, only to be interrupted by the level, brusque voice of Brakus once again addressing them from thin air.

"Sol," the voice announced. "You need to get up here. We have an anomaly on the system."

Kane threw his hands up in exasperation. "Oh for fu..."

"Can't *you* deal with it?" Agent 23 snapped, cutting Kane off in mid swear.

"I will not waste my precious time with your trivialities," the voice replied tartly, effectively ending the exchange.

"I swear," Agent 23 muttered to Sol, "If he wasn't so useful I'd tear his ..."

"Now, now," Sol said calmly, patting her on the knee. To Kane's surprise she didn't appear annoyed or patronised by the action. "Let's take this as an opportunity to introduce Mr Kane to friend Brakus. Besides," he continued to Kane with a friendly smile, "I think the experience will help you to better accept the things we have to say."

Sol stood, followed by Agent 23. The pair stared expectantly at Kane, still sitting in his seat with a sour look on his face. Agent 23 stepped forward an offered him her hand.

"Come along Mr Kane," she said with a smile. "Have we got things to show you...!"

Kane smiled despite himself. This woman, who had so recently beaten him down without so much as breaking a sweat, was really starting to grow on him.

"Call me Ted," he said as he rose from the couch.

"Okay then, Ted," she replied as she led him after Sol, still holding onto his hand, "and you may call me 23."

Yes, she was certainly growing on him, but not so much that he forgot to pick up his webbing and weapons as they passed.

****

Robert Mitchell slammed the car door and turned away from the vehicle before Holloway had a chance to bother him again. The car sped away and Mitchell felt a spark of gratitude for the driver, freeing him from further contact with the foul little man. He'd had more than enough of the little wretch. He had other things on his mind.

He passed through his restaurant without so much as a nod towards the manager, strode through the kitchens and continued straight up the stairs, all the way to his penthouse. He closed the door behind him and leant his back against it. Sweat began rolling down his forehead. He held up his hand and looked at it intently. It was shaking, but not from the exertion of climbing so many stairs so quickly.

His son was dead.

Anger and the momentum of his search for the killer had sustained him up until now, but the day had worn on and the time spent in the car with Holloway jabbering away had proved almost too much. He slid down the door and by the time he came to rest on the thick carpet, tears were freely streaming from his eyes. He made choking sounds as he attempted to hold back sobs of anguish. He failed. His arms fell out to his sides as he lay there, legs straight out in front of him, and let out a howl of uncontrolled anguish. He lay there, letting his grief take full control until several minutes later he had nothing left. He stayed on the floor a while longer, feeling helpless, exposed and exhausted.

When he finally rose on shaky legs he went through to his bathroom where he removed his coat and jacket and splashed cold water onto his face. It felt good and went some way to replacing the energy he'd expended moments ago. He stood, shoulders hunched, staring into the sink. He was putting off looking into the mirror, afraid of what he would see. Finally he lifted his head to meet his own reflection.

He stared into his own eyes, his son's eyes, and a lump instantly formed in his throat as the grief threatened to overwhelm him once more. But he forced the feeling back, using it to replenish his anger. His face twisted into a snarl as his hand shot out, unguided, to send aftershaves and other bathroom paraphernalia flying.

His son was dead.

Gone.

And no matter how hard he tried to forget, he would be reminded each and every time he looked in the mirror. Someone was going to pay dearly for this. Dearly.

Robert Mitchell forced himself to stare at his reflection, into his son's eyes, forcing away the physical pain it caused. He stared, willing the pain to peak, daring it to make him break down again. But it couldn't. It was spent. For the time being he had beaten it.

His face set in an expression of grim determination, Mitchell turned away from the mirror. He showered and put on a fresh set of clothes before heading back down to the restaurant. He would wait for the car to return and then head over to the warehouse to see what Lindros had managed to learn from their guests.

No doubt the news of his son's death would have filtered through to his staff and business contacts by now and anyone who'd had dealings with him would know better than to cross his path for the foreseeable future. That suited him just fine. He had only one task before him now, to uncover the details of his son's death and deal with all those involved. Every other aspect of his life would be put on hold. Nothing else mattered.

And when Robert Mitchell put his mind to something he always got it done.

Chapter 11: Meeting Brakus

Ted Kane stepped out of the Portal with a lot more dignity than on his previous attempt. This time Sol had mysteriously created a Portal in the air near to the dining area and led the way through. Kane made a mental note to ask Sol how they were controlled and whether he could do it himself. It would be an invaluable tool back in the world.

As Kane entered the Portal he found himself once again in the Kansas cornfields. But this time he didn't want to hang around. He was getting fed up with all the delays every time Sol was about to explain what the hell was going on. In fact, he thought sourly, it was all starting to feel a little too convenient. Kane was a suspicious man by nature and Sol was just a little too good to be true. Always smiling and answering Kane's questions, most of the time anyway, apparently happy to divulge all his secrets without asking for anything in return.

As soon as Kane entered his cornfield he looked about for the exit Portal. Again, he didn't spot it so much as *feel* it some distance away and over a hill to his left. He broke into a flat run and shot across the field to the exit. It glowed before him with an image of himself frozen at the moment of walking through.

Kane stepped up to the image of himself and peered through to see where he was going to emerge. Sol was already through of course, and peering round the older man's back Kane saw another white room, again perfectly cuboid and again immaculate. But this time the size of the room was much more modest, perhaps fifty metres square. The room's space was broken up by a huge number of consoles similar to those in the construction chamber. They were everywhere, creating a maze of passageways between the control boards and hanging monitors. There were so many of these units that Kane found his view of the room greatly restricted and he could only judge its size by looking up to the high ceiling.

With nothing more to gain from peering through the Portal, Kane gently pushed the image of himself through… and instantly found himself stepping into the room. He moved to the side just as 23 emerged and sidled up to her.

"Just a couple of minutes this time," he said with some pride. She'd been impressed that he'd only spent days or weeks inside the Portal the last time, so he expected, and hoped, to impress her again. But he was going to be disappointed.

"Oh," she said quietly, placing a hand on his shoulder. "Well, never mind…" and then she was gone, wandering off into the maze of consoles.

Kane stood there, confused and horribly deflated. Sol watched the exchange quietly then walked up to Kane.

"The first trip through a Portal is a difficult and dangerous one," he explained. "The danger is that, should someone not have sufficient mental agility to navigate the Portal, he can stay trapped in the dark, silent limbo for a perceived eternity. Such a person would emerge with his psyche utterly destroyed: a vegetable." Sol let his words sink in before continuing. "23 was impressed the first time you passed through so quickly, but as time is irrelevant within the Portal… well, short trips are seen as a wasted opportunity."

Kane scowled at this, feeling like a child needing to have something explained to him over and over again. Sol had already explained as much.

"You will find that, with the proper training," Sol continued, "your time spent within the Portal will naturally increase. It will become something to look forward to." He smiled as he added, "There really is no limit to what you can do there."

But Kane was too embarrassed and angry with himself to pay attention.

"You said we were going to meet this Brakus character," he said flatly.

Sol seemed to recognise his annoyance.

"Of course," he said. "But before you meet him I think I had better first explain…" But before Sol could complete his warning, Kane stepped past him, his eyes wide and his mouth open in amazement. He had already spotted Brakus.

"Ah," said Sol.

Kane had stepped forward just far enough to see round the first bank of terminals and there, with his…*its* back towards him was what he had to assume was Brakus.

Kane had been around the world more times than he cared to guess, had witnessed things he would have thought impossible had he not seen them with his own eyes. But this? This was something new.

Kane's trained eye scanned the creature before him, taking mental notes and trying to make sense of what he saw. Brakus was, clichés not withstanding, a monster straight from a nightmare. He was little over three feet in height, or length depending on how you looked at him. It was difficult to decide because Brakus was floating a full two feet above the ground. His skin, or flesh, was a pale cream in colour with a slimy sheen to it. Tentacles hung down from its stubby body, with longer, thicker ones at the centre radiating out to slimmer, shorter ones along the leading edges. There was little shape to the body as such, just a formless lump supporting the mass of gently writhing tentacles. The head itself looked like a crab's carapace, armoured and dull brown in colour. A Mohawk of spikes crested the dome while further spines lined the edges. The dome's surface was covered in knobbles and short spikes except for an area on one side which appeared to have been ground flat in order to accommodate what looked like a tattoo of symbols similar to those Kane had seen on Sol's datapad.

Kane couldn't see the creature's face and, judging by the rest of him, he wasn't sure he really wanted to.

Apparently oblivious to the fact he was being watched, Brakus was busying himself with the terminal in front of him, several of the terminals in fact. As Kane watched, Brakus reached out with a selection of tentacles and manipulated several controls at once. On one of the screens Kane saw a view of the construction room in which the grey constructions were being prepared. As he watched, a Portal opened while several of the drones converged on one of the units. Thin beams of light lanced out from the drones and touched the unit, gently lifting it from the ground and moving it towards the Portal. Once the unit was through, the beams winked off and the Portal disappeared. The drones turned as one and retreated out of range of the camera.

The task done, Brakus withdrew all but one of his tentacles, using the remaining one to manipulate a final control and cutting the video feed to the construction room. Finally, that tentacle also returned to join the others, hanging and twitching gently beneath the creature's carapace head.

He turned then and Kane prepared himself to come face to face with Brakus.

But Brakus didn't have a face. The front of his head looked exactly the same as the back. And the sides come to that, with no evidence of eyes or ears or anything resembling facial features at all. Kane stared, desperately trying to think of something to say, but his mouth was dry and his mind was a blank. Brakus floated there, silently observing him.

"Aren't you going to say hello?" asked Sol from somewhere behind Kane. Kane had forgotten Sol was there and didn't know who he was addressing: him or Brakus. Fortunately, Brakus took the initiative.

"If I must," the creature snapped, the voice radiating from the creature from some hidden source. "Though my limited time can be much better spent on other duties." But he moved forward and extended one of his larger tentacles in the manner of offering a hand to shake. "Nonetheless," he said, "greetings, Mr Kane."

Kane slowly raised his own hand and made as to step forward and take the tentacle. It looked slimy and he suppressed a cringe as it approached his hand.

"No!" shouted Sol as he rushed forward to drag Kane away from the offered limb. Kane withdrew his hand and backed away from the tentacle, bumping into the advancing Sol and sending them both tumbling to the ground in a tangle of limbs. A strange noise erupted from Brakus. *Is that laughter?* thought Kane.

"Not very funny, Brakus," muttered Sol and he and Kane got back to their feet. But Brakus continued to make his strange version of laughter, his whole body quivering and his tentacles twitching beneath him.

23 came running back from wherever she had disappeared to and glared at Brakus.

"That wasn't very nice!" she snapped as she dashed towards Brakus. Kane noticed she was now wearing some kind of black apron made from what looked like woven plastic with elbow-length gauntlets to match. She grabbed at the creature, gathering all of its tentacles in her arms. Brakus struggled greatly but she soon had him pinned firmly to her chest and unable to move, his head wedged beneath her chin. Kane watched as she freed one of her arms and wrapped on its head with the free fist. "Not! Very! Nice!" she shouted, punctuating each word with a heavy crack to his shell.

Brakus made a series of strange, high-pitched noises that Kane took to be cries of pain. He turned to Sol with a questioning look on his face, unable to form a sentence sufficient to express all the questions he wanted answered. For once, Sol wasn't smiling.

"I'm sorry about that, Mr Kane," he began, staring at Brakus with a mixture of anger and disappointment. "Brakus is an enormously intelligent individual but he does sometimes forget his manners."

He stepped up to Brakus, now hanging motionless in 23's grip. He nodded to her and after a moment of indecision she slowly released her grip before stepping back, her glare still focused on the creature.

"Play nice, or else," she muttered as she stabbed a gauntleted finger at the creature.

Brakus floated in the air once more and his tentacles twitched one by one as though he was testing them for mobility.

"Say hello to our guest," Sol ordered the creature.

"Hello Mr Kane," the creature snapped, suddenly sounding like a sulky teenager.

"Uh, hello Mr. Brakus," Kane answered with a quick glance at Sol. "I guess I shouldn't shake your…ah…tentacle then?"

It was Sol who answered him.

"It wouldn't be advisable Mr Kane…"

"Please, it's Ted," he interrupted.

"Ted, then. Brakus here is a member of a race known as the Brachyurans," he said as he glanced over at 23, who was still glaring at Brakus. "Though some of us have a different name for them…"

"Crab heads," said 23, spitting out the words and glaring at Brakus.

"Yes, well," continued Sol. "As you may have already guessed, his race originated in a different galaxy from this one…"

"A vastly superior one," Brakus interrupted. "And it's not *Mr*. Brakus, it's just Brakus." He added snippily, aparently addressing Kane, though it was impossible to tell which direction his eyeless head was facing. "And *that's* just a name created by you humans," Brakus continued, snippily. "*Your* rediculous vocal arrangement is incapable of pronouncing my true name."

"Oh, I think I could probably have a go," said Kane, tiring of the creature's attitude. "What *is* your 'true name' then?"

His challenge was quickly met by a full three seconds of indecipherable noise erupting from Brakus, a series of oscillating tones rising and falling in pitch, wildly changing and appearing to come from several sources at once from beneath the creature's shell. The higher notes made Kane's ears ring.

"Brakus has five mouths," explained 23, her gauntleted hands over her ears. "And he likes to show off."

"Modesty would be dishonesty," muttered Brakus, his tone sulky. Kane had no idea what to say, the whole situation had become too surreal, but Sol came to his rescue.

"I had probably better explain," he said, "that the Brachyurans are a very intelligent and long-living race and, while

Brakus is over two hundred of your years of age, he is actually little more than a teenager by Brachyuran standards."

Kane winced at the thought of a human teenager with the knowledge of a two hundred year old. If human teenagers seemed unbareable when they thought they knew everything, what chance did Brakus have?

"Another thing you should know about Brachyurans, Ted, is that they don't have the same…moral boundries as you or I." Sol pointed at the tentacles hanging below Brakus's head shell. "Just like your Earthly jellyfish, they are equiped with a very powerful sting." Kane strained to stare at the tentacles and noticed they were covered in small, fine hairs. "Even so much as a brush against one of those apendiges will result in an extremely painful sting, possibly even temporary paralasis." Kane glanced at the protective apron and gauntlets worn by Agent 23, then glared at Brakus.

"Nice," he growled, but to his horror the comment was met by further peels of alien laughter.

"Brachyurans, not to put too fine a point on it," Sol continued, raising his voice to be heard over Brakus's alien chuckling, "enjoy seeing other beings in pain."

"Yes," 23 muttered to Brakus, "but you don't like it much yourselves, do you?"

"But," Sol said loudly before she could say anything more, "he does work very hard for us, doesn't he?" His last comment was directed at 23, but she either didn't hear it or pretended not to.

"If all of these unnecessary pleasantries are finally completed," Brakus announced, now sounding more petulant than authoritative to Kane's ears, "I *did* order your presence here for a reason." He drifted past 23 and back to one of his consoles where he extended several tentacles and began manipulating various controls.

Kane watched with interest, noticing for the first time how much the tentacles varied in size and thickness. A few of them were broad and looked solid and strong while others looked little more than thin wisps of hair. But, whatever their individual size, they all appeared to be incredibly dextrous and as Kane watched, Brakus sent them flying across dozens of controls at once.

One of the screens suddenly came to life, showing a cross-section of what Kane guessed to be one of the cube chambers. The usual unreadable language, which he now had to assume to be alien in origin, was present, dotted about the screen.

"One of the chambers is reading a point-zero-zero-three degree axial variance," Brakus stated flatly as though the fact held no interest to him whatsoever.

"That shouldn't be possible," said Sol.

"Nonetheless, it is." Brakus stated bluntly.

"Which chamber?" Sol snapped as he stepped up to the screen to take a closer look, his voice beginning to sound worried. It was the first time Kane had heard that in the old man's voice.

"Chamber Three-Delta-Kappa," Brakus droned, completely disinterested. As Sol approached the screen Brakus flicked a few more switches then moved to a separate console where he busied himself with repeating the procedure Kane had witnessed earlier. Another screen came to life, again showing a view of the construction room, drones busying themselves around the grey units.

Soon Sol was at work at the first console with 23 and Kane watching over his shoulders. More alien script appeared at various points on the screen.

"That's the reception chamber isn't it?" asked 23.

"Yes it is," Sol replied, his words coming slowly and uncertainly as he continued to study the readouts. "But I don't know why it should be listing...ah...here we are..." His voice trailed off as he continued to scan the screens. Kane looked over to 23 to see if she might be more forthcoming with what was going on.

"Someone's in there," she said, sounding surprised.

"It has to be Deblanc," muttered Sol, echoing her confused tone, "but that doesn't make...Ah," he said again after further button tapping. When he didn't say anything else, Kane and 23 glanced at each other, eyebrows raised.

"Well?" they both said in unison.

"Hmm? Oh, it looks like Deblanc entered the chamber at the exact same moment Mr. Kane, sorry, Ted, and I left. That's why I wasn't aware of him arriving. The alert tone would have sounded while I was within the Portal... And I *was* somewhat distracted at the time..." he added with a wry look at Kane.

"So he's been in there a good couple of hours then?" muttered 23 as she motioned over to Brakus with a jab of her thumb. "Would have been nice if Crabby had let us know."

Sol continued to examine the screen, ignoring her final comment. Finally he pointed to a series of symbols and turned to 23.

"It looks like he's grown tired of waiting for the next automated check of the chamber," he said. "That's not like him.

There must be something wrong." He turned his full attention to the woman before continuing. "Would you mind going in and seeing what's up?" he asked. "It's about time you met Mr. Deblanc and I really must spend some time with Ted here, bringing him up to date."

23 glanced at Kane then back to Sol. "Okay," she said, "but from what Brakus told me about Deblanc, I'm not sure we'll get along very well…"

"Since when did you ever agree with Brakus about anything?" Sol grinned. "Besides," he continued before she could reply, "I've asked Deblanc to bring Timothy Bruce in. Perhaps he's with him now."

This seemed to please 23, whose attitude changed instantly. "Oh, do you think so?" she asked, visibly excited.

"Well, I can think of one way to find out…" Sol replied with a grin. Without another word 23 turned and dashed across the room.

"Don't forget," Sol called after her, "Deblanc can't join us yet. And you know why…"

With one final glance at Brakus, still busying himself with his mysterious duties, Sol turned to Kane.

"I think," he said, "that you've waited quite long enough. If you'd care to join me in my private suite I would be more than happy to explain to you who we are and what it is we're doing here…"

****

Agent 23 dashed across Brakus's control room, leaving Sol and Kane to their little chat, though she would liked to have been present when the situation was explained to Kane. She felt slightly embarrassed by her initial contact with Kane, but not guilty. She'd seen an unidentified man attacking Sol and that simply would not stand. But Kane appeared to have taken it quite well, all things considered. He'd impressed her and that was a rare thing indeed.

She trusted Sol implicitly and would happily give her life to save his. She and Kendrick owed him their lives a dozen times over and she had no doubt that before their mission was over, Sol would have the chance to collect on that debt.

Moving over to one of the room's consoles she input a series of commands then stood for several seconds checking the display. Happy that the system had completed her orders fully, she activated a further control and turned to see a Portal opening behind her. She stepped through the Portal and it closed behind her.

A second later she exited the Portal and stepped into the reception chamber. She'd seen the state of the room before emerging from the Portal of course, but not the reasons behind it.

What she found were the unconscious forms of Timothy Bruce and Deblanc. That was expected: she'd released an anaesthetising agent into the room before summoning the Portal. But she could also now see the reason for the chamber showing up on Brakus's system. Every stick of furniture in the huge chamber had been moved to one of the walls and stacked against it. The extra weight at one end of the room was just enough to cause the point zero-zero-three degree axial variance noticed by Brakus. She had to hand it to Deblanc, it was a very clever way to catch their attention, though very labour intensive and too much hard work for a simple case of impatience.

She took a few steps forward and saw the reason for the urgency. One of the figures, she had to assume it was Deblanc from Sol's description, had one of his forearms missing. She examined the wound with a trained eye. It was an impossibly clean and straight cut to have been caused by anything other than a collapsing Portal. He was lucky. While the injury would certainly hurt like hell, the action of the collapsing Portal would have cauterised the wound, removing the danger of blood loss. Agent 23 put a couple of fingertips to Deblanc's neck to check his pulse. It was strong and regular; he was going to be all right.

She glanced briefly at Deblanc's remaining wrist, twisted and bruised badly, but dismissed the injury as inconsequential. His next trip through a Portal would set any broken bones and repair the damaged tissue, making the limb as good as new.

Her checking of Deblanc's condition complete, Agent 23 turned to look at the slumbering form of Timothy Bruce. It had been many, many years since she'd last seen him and it made her heart break to think about how much he'd suffered in that time.

"Don't worry kid," she said quietly as she brushed a lock of hair from his forehead, "life will be a lot better for you now."

Chapter 12: Once upon a Time

Kane sat down on yet another comfortable couch in yet another pristine, cube-shaped room and once again waited for Sol to tell his story.

The chamber was tiny in comparison to the others he'd already seen, just a dozen metres square. A large bed sat in the centre of the room, which Kane thought to be an unusual position for it but everything else, from the consoles and couches to the shower cubicle and wash stand, lined the walls evenly, giving the space a tidy, symmetrical look. Once again, everything was a pristine white.

Kane had already politely refused an offer of refreshments and waited for Sol to sit down. No more distractions: the time had finally come.

Kane's trip through the Portal to Sol's private chamber had been another quick one. He knew time had no meaning in there, but he was so fed up with waiting for Sol's explanation that he simply didn't want to delay it any further. Besides, what he did with his Portal time was up to him and nobody else's business.

Finally, Sol sat down facing Kane, marshalling his thoughts before he began to speak.

"This is not the first time I've told this story," he began, "I've told it many times before but it doesn't get any easier. I have found though, that the best way to proceed is to just jump straight in and get on with it…"

Finally, thought Kane.

"You do have one advantage, however," Sol continued, "in that you've already seen and experienced many things that will help you accept what I have to tell you." Sol smiled a private, bitter smile to himself. "Perhaps that's where I've gone wrong in the past," he muttered. The comment intrigued Kane, but he chose not to comment, deciding to let Sol continue uninterrupted.

"As you are probably now aware, none of the people in the Keep originated on Earth," Sol began. "Apart from you of course," he added, needlessly. Kane just nodded silently, letting him continue.

"We all, including Brakus, come from a galaxy that Earth astronomers have yet to chart, from a society that was old and space-faring long before your planet had cooled enough to bear life..."

"Okay, it's old, I get it," Kane interrupted. "Can we just get to the details please?"

Sol looked taken aback but Kane was used to life in the military where flowery language had no place in the briefing room. And his patience was running very thin.

"Well," said Sol, "on to the details then." He fell silent for a moment, gathering his thoughts anew. *Probably picking out the relevant bits*, thought Kane. "I appreciate your candour Mr. Kane," said Sol. Kane noticed that he'd reverted to the more formal tone he'd used earlier, but again he chose not to mention it in case it was a deliberate delaying tactic. The niggling voice in the back of Kane's head still refused to let him fully trust this man.

"I was once a military man like yourself," Sol began again. "I won't bore you with the details, except for my final mission which is where our story begins. We knew it was a suicide mission from the start, but it was what we'd been trained for and there was a great deal at stake." He paused, reliving the events in his head. An earnest sadness had come over him, but still Kane remained silent. "My world was under threat from Brakus's race, the Brachyurans, who wanted nothing short of our complete extinction.

"As I've previously explained, the Brachyurans enjoy watching other beings suffering physical pain. It's almost like a sexual thrill for them, though as a genderless race that isn't really an accurate analogy, though it does suffice. They are also, as you might have gathered from your meeting with Brakus, a very arrogant race. If they want something, they take it. If a being inconveniences them, they kill it. If they perceive another race as a possible threat, they destroy it. I think you get the idea?"

"Yeah," muttered Kane. "Big, bad space fascists."

"Accurate enough," Sol conceded. "Myself and my companions, Agent 23 and Kendrick, don't all come from the same planet, though our respective planets can be found within the same solar system: Rigel."

"Part of the Orion constellation," Kane cut in, happy to show off the knowledge he'd retained from a 'navigation by the stars' course he'd once attended. "His left foot, I believe?"

"Quite right," Sol replied, though not with the impressed tone Kane was hoping for. It was likely considered the most basic of general knowledge to a space-faring race of the sort Sol obviously came from. "The Rigel system has two life-supporting planets. I come from Rigel 3 while Agent 23 and Kendrick originated on Rigel 4.

"To cut a long story short," Sol continued, "the Brachyurans arrived in our system and began strip-mining Rigel 4 for resources. At the time, Rigels' 3 and 4 were at war and my government saw no reason to intervene. The Brachyurans were doing a very good job of decimating our enemy and we were happy to let them continue. But soon our leadership wondered what would happen when the Brachyurans finished with Rigel 4? Would they turn their weapons on us in the same way? So a peace envoy was despatched to Rigel 4 to make contact with the invading forces. As soon as the vessel neared the planet the Brachyurans destroyed it without warning. Obviously this concerned our leadership."

"Yeah," Kane muttered, "I bet it did."

"A second envoy was sent," Sol continued, ignoring the comment, "this time accompanied by a fleet of our finest warships. Our only warships actually," he added, his voice losing a little of its volume. "We'd seen the firepower and technology the Brachyurans possessed and knew our only chance was to attempt a bluff."

"I'm guessing it didn't work," Kane said quietly, sensing the older man was reliving a terrible memory.

"It did actually," came Sol's surprisingly cheerful reply. "It was a glorious sight, Ted. Thousands of cruisers, support vessels, troop ships. We even filled in some of the gaps with hastily painted pleasure yachts and cargo ships."

"You said 'we'," Kane pointed out. "Were you part of the command staff?" To his surprise, Sol laughed.

"Oh, no, no," he said, "I was a grunt, a new boy in the military, barely twenty years old at the time."

"So," Kane prompted, "they fell for your bluff…"

"…And a delegation set down on Rigel 4 to speak with their leaders. I was present as part of the honour guard." Sol stopped here and leant forward to put his elbows on his knees, his head hanging as he recalled the events. After a few silent moments, Sol raised his head again and Kane noticed his eyes were red.

"I tried to warn you about Brakus before you met him earlier," he said, "and I'm sorry that you went into that meeting cold. But believe me when I tell you, meeting a juvenile like Brakus can in no way prepare you for coming face to face with a fully grown Brachyuran. Brakus is approximately one quarter of the size he will reach. I warned you about his sting, but as painful as it most certainly is, it is nothing compared to that of a Brachyuran warrior. The slightest brush from one of their appendages means certain death. It is a quick death though. No venom or poison enters the victim's blood stream; he just dies from the sheer pain of it. The heart and brain simply can't process such agony.

"You saw how quickly Agent 23 subdued Brakus?" he asked. Kane nodded, silently, allowing Sol to continue uninterrupted. "That was only possible because of the brand you might have noticed on his cranial ridge?" Kane nodded and Sol continued. "A Brachyuran warrior's shell is almost impenetrable. None of our weapons had the least effect on the shell itself, not so much as a scratch."

"How about the rest of the body?" asked Kane. "The tentacles?"

"They *are* much more susceptible to attack, but the warrior caste employ an energy shield to protect everything below shell level."

"Energy shields…?" Kane began, but Sol held up his hand before he could complete his question.

"I know what you're thinking," he said, "but the shields in question stop *everything*: Light, heat, sound, oxygen: everything. So no, you can't have one. It really wouldn't do you much good. But back to the story…"

"Before you carry on," Kane said, holding his hand up. "What's the deal with these Brachyurans *floating* about the place? How can they do that?"

"As far as we can tell, they have the ability to alter their body's density, allowing them to adjust their weight. They float for locomotion, as you've seen, and can make themselves super dense. I've seen Brachyuran warriors drop themselves onto vessels and buildings, crushing smaller ones or falling through larger ones. They're very adaptable."

"'As far as we can tell'?" echoed Kane. "You haven't questioned or examined Brakus?"

"Brakus refuses to be examined," Sol replied. "He won't allow what he calls 'lesser species' to touch him. And he can no more explain how the process works than you or I could explain how we discriminate flavours or scents.

"But anyway, there we were, meeting the Brachyuran delegates on the homeworld of our mortal enemies.

"The negotiations appeared to pass smoothly and we had an agreement that no Brachyuran would ever set foot on Rigel 3 as long as we made no offensive moves towards the Brachyurans themselves. So we left Rigel 4 and returned home, our world safe and our enemies vanquished.

"Of course, it didn't turn out to be that simple. Time passed and gradually the fleet broke up to return to their usual stations. Months later, I was serving on a diplomatic vessel which had been invited to meet with the Brachyuran High Council. It was a strange meeting. It was very short and very little was said. We couldn't understand why we'd been invited but our leaders were just happy that we were keeping up a dialogue with the invaders.

"On the way back to Rigel 3 we ran into a Brachyuran picket vessel and they attacked us without warning." Sol paused, a faraway look on his face as he recalled the events. Kane kept a respectful silence for his fellow soldier. He knew how talking about combat effected a man. "Their first salvo destroyed our engines and communications array. Our gunners hesitated to return fire, not sure whether they'd be responsible for starting a shooting war with the Brachyurans and unable to contact anyone with enough authority to give them permission.

"We were boarded," he continued, his voice growing quiet again. "The officials on board ordered us not to resist, desperately hoping to find a diplomatic solution. The Brachyurans flooded through the ship, carelessly brushing against elite commandos and support crew alike…" He paused again, the pain of the memories clear on his face. "I'll never forget the death screams of our men, echoing throughout the ship.

"They passed straight through the ship and into the cargo hold where they found half a dozen prisoners from Rigel 4. We had no idea they were there, had no reason to have *put* them there. But there they were, and according to the Brachyuran captain, clear evidence of our betrayal. All deals were off. We were at war with the Brachyurans.

"The prisoners were in a terrible condition. Obviously they'd been in captivity for some time and suffering from malnutrition. They were gibbering wrecks and we couldn't get anything out of them. It was impossible that they'd crept aboard the ship by themselves."

Sol stopped and looked at Kane with interest, almost daring him to solve the puzzle of the prisoners.

"The Brachyurans sent them there through a Portal," he reasoned after a few second's thought.

"Exactly," Sol replied. "Though we weren't aware of Portals at the time. They are Brachyuran technology and they hadn't needed to use them during their invasion of our system. Sheer weight of numbers and superior weaponry had been more than adequate for the task.

"Fortunately, being a diplomatic vessel, our ship had more than enough escape pods for the surviving crew. They were launched as quickly as we could get into them, while the remaining commandos attempted to hold the Brachyurans at bay. I found myself bundled into a pod with a couple of my colleagues and launched on a random trajectory.

"We had no illusions. Our chances of survival were minute. Most of the escape pods were being launched empty to distract the Brachyurans from those containing our dignitaries and crew. But my pod survived and we managed to make it back to our planet several weeks later."

Kane remained quiet, wondering when the story would get around to why Sol and his friends were on Earth. He had a bad feeling about what those reasons might be and didn't want to think about Brachyurans arriving on *his* world.

Sol looked at Kane intensely, as though attempting to read his mind. He sat up straighter on his chair and squared his shoulders. Kane felt a twinge of embarrassment. Had he looked bored or impatient?

"Anyway," Sol continued, all business again. "We got back to our world and found it changed from the one we'd left mere weeks before. The Brachyurans had indeed arrived, but not as an invasion force. They instead used the diplomatic embarrassment of the discovered prisoners as leverage to demand resources and supplies from Rigel 3. After the original diplomatic mission to Rigel 4 they'd waited for us to disband the fleet and now they made it clear that any attempt to put it back together would result in serious consequences. Our leaders capitulated, fearing the same treatment that Rigel 4 had received. Simply put, they were stripping our planet of resources without so much as lifting a finger, or tentacle, of their own. We were doing all the work and delivering the materials to them on Rigel 4. Meanwhile, their forces were being used on Rigel 4 to exterminate the remaining resistance there." He sighed and rubbed at his eyes before continuing. Kane listened quietly, his unease steadily increasing.

"A group of us formed a resistance cell on Rigel 3 and began gathering intelligence on our new foe. We could see what was happening, where the situation was heading. The Brachyurans were making more and more demands on our world's resources while gradually pulling their forces away from Rigel 4 as that planet slowly died, reinforcing their military presence on our world. But our leadership still refused to see it. They were far too busy appeasing the invaders. We began smuggling refugees from Rigel 4 to boost the resistance's numbers, our differences forgotten by that time.

"Soon, we were ready to make our first strike against the Brachyurans. We'd wanted to start off small by quietly raiding supply depots to gather equipment and weapons, but an opportunity arose that we couldn't pass up." Sol rubbed his eyes again before continuing.

"There was something else we'd learned about the Brachyurans, something we hoped to use to exploit as a tactical advantage. As I've already said, they are a very arrogant race and they saw us as little more than cattle without the technology or intelligence to pose any significant threat. We hoped to show them the error of their ways." Kane grinned at Sol's final comment, but the grin was short lived. He appreciated Sol's bravado but knew full well his tale wasn't going to end well.

"We'd heard of a presentation ceremony being held on one of our island bases in our East Sea," Sol continued, shaking his head at the memory as though still unable to believe it had actually happened. "Our glorious leaders had arranged the ceremony to thank the Brachyurans for vanquishing our age-old enemies from Rigel 4." He shook his head again, a humourless, bitter grin on his face. "Even though we were obviously going to be next. Anyway, we'd learned something useful from our new comrades from Rigel 4. Because of their arrogance, Brachyuran warriors are rendered temporarily…well, dumfounded with indecision when they witness their leaders falling in battle. The chain of command is so central to their society and following orders without question is so ingrained in their military, that giving an order to a superior, even by mistake, is punished by death. When a leader falls, it can take a few moments for the next in line of command to be recognised and put in charge, leaving the warriors dumfounded. The effect doesn't last long, but it *can* open a small window of opportunity. The resistance on Rigel 4 had used it to some limited advantage on their planet.

"We discovered that the presentation ceremony was going to be attended by several of the highest-ranking Brachyurans, no doubt a propaganda move designed to further cement their illusion of benevolence. We hoped that killing at least some of their hierarchy might act as a rallying call to the people of our world and the fight-back could begin."

Kane sucked in a sharp breath. It sounded like a pointless and desperate move, ill conceived and suicidal. Again, Sol appeared to be reading his thoughts.

"I know, I know, it sounds ridiculous in hindsight. But you have to understand what we were going through at the time. If your world was threatened with destruction, would you, as a soldier, volunteer for a mission that could possibly save it, even if you knew it would likely end in your death?" Kane thought about it for a few seconds and realised he'd gone on dangerous missions for a lot less; sometimes just to save a politician from some embarrassment or other. The truth was, soldiers were all too often thought of as resources to be used, rather than human beings with families waiting at home. At least Sol and his colleagues were fighting for something they believed in and it was their own, informed choice.

"I suppose so," he said. "And *you* obviously survived…"

"I did," said Sol, though the fact seemed to sadden him. "I was one of only three survivors from a strike team of forty." Again, silence descended on the room. Kane had experienced so-called 'survivor's guilt' several times himself, but his personal experiences had been of losing one or two team mates, not thirty-seven. He could think of nothing to say.

"The mission failed of course," Sol continued. "In fact, it was such a failure that, mid-mission, we were forced to assassinate our own leaders instead."

That shocked Kane to the core. You don't just switch mission parameters halfway through, especially with a team of forty to keep up to date. He looked at Sol, confusion and disapproval written all over his face.

"There were reasons," Sol announced indignantly. "One of our team got close enough to the targets to use snooping gear and overhear an exchange between their leaders and ours. The Brachyurans knew we were coming and were all equipped with personal energy shields. It was a trap. There was no way our weapons would harm them and even worse, our man learned that our own leaders had orchestrated the entire mission, even the forming of our resistance group. Probably a misguided attempt to ingratiate themselves with their new masters." Sol paused, letting the revelation sink in. Kane was shocked and tried to imagine how he would react to such news. Suddenly the change in the mission's objectives didn't sound so unreasonable.

"We were compromised," Sol continued, his voice bitter. "It was just a question of how long we had before being overrun by

Brachyuran warriors and wiped out… or worse. But," he added, his voice filling with pride, "we weren't about to go down without a fight.

"Our man with the snooping gear took the initiative. He told us he was going to take out our dignitaries as a diversion, giving us a chance to escape. Even though he only came about half way up in the mission's hierarchy it was a statement rather than a suggestion. But under the circumstances, I don't think he was worried about facing a court marshal later. He gave us a couple of minutes to prepare before he ran into the room, shooting at anything without a defence shield."

Kane appreciated the tactic. Backed into a corner, there was only one thing to do: attack with aggression. The effect on an overconfident enemy, who thought they'd already won, could be devastating. But this was suicide, plain and simple.

"Myself and four others fought our way to a hanger where we hoped to secure a vessel for our escape. But we found more than we bargained for.

"Purely by chance we'd arrived at the very deck on which the Brachyurans had arrived for the ceremony. Security was tight but the Brachyuran's only sent Rigellian security forces against us and we managed to hold the ground until more of our forces could arrive. With their help we secured the deck then set about sabotaging every vessel but one in which to make our escape. There was also the Brachyuran dignitary's vessel in there, but we couldn't gain access to it, it was too securely sealed. While we were preparing for our departure the Brachyuran vessel opened from the inside. We braced ourselves for what we truly expected to be an impossible fight. If just one of their warriors emerged from the vessel equipped with one of their impenetrable defence shields, we would have been wiped out to a man."

Sol paused again and Kane waited patiently. This was obviously a pivotal moment in Sol's story. While Sol himself had survived, Kane read a sorrow in the man's face that told him whatever had happened next was something terrible, something Sol was loathe to re-live.

"It was an unarmed Brachyuran infant," said Sol, his voice conveying the surprise and relief he'd obviously felt at the time.

"Brakus," muttered Kane.

"Indeed."

"So you kidnapped him."

"Yes," Sol replied, his voice sounded strangely apologetic, which surprised Kane. He would have done the same thing himself: it was tactically expedient. Not only did they gain a valuable source of intel in Brakus, but also a hostage. It certainly wouldn't of hurt their chances.

"There wasn't much time for discussion," Sol continued. "My group was tasked with taking the prisoner away in the captured vessel while the other team covered our escape and destroyed the launchbay doors once we were away. Brakus was very young at that time and it wasn't too much trouble to secure him in a food crate and stow him aboard the ship. We knew we were leaving our colleagues to their doom, but their sacrifice wasn't in vain. We made good our escape.

"There's something else you need to know about the resistance group," he added. Kane thought he could detect guilt in Sol's voice, even fear, as if what he was going to say would shock or offend him somehow. Still, Kane remained silent, allowing Sol to continue at his own pace.

"The Brachyurans don't use torture to question their prisoners. They don't need to. They have devices that burrow into the brain and tear the memories for your head. There is no defence against it, no way to resist. And once they have everything they need they begin the physical torture, purely for their own enjoyment.

"Because of the infallibility of their techniques it was imperative that none of our people fell into Brachyuran hands. But as you will no doubt know, it's a forlorn and unrealistic hope. Things go wrong and people get captured. So we needed a way to protect ourselves."

Here it comes, thought Kane.

"We'd considered various versions of suicide pills, microscopic explosives planted in the brainstem, but none of them were infallible. An incapacitated soldier can't take a pill and the Brachyurans might have been able to detect and deactivate brain bombs. No, we needed to think laterally. Eventually our science division came up with the answer." Sol said as he stared at Kane, unflinching in his resolve to finish his story no matter how much it obviously hurt him to recall the events. "All of our operatives underwent a memory wipe before the mission."

Kane tried to let that sink in, tried to imagine how he'd feel about having his own memory wiped. He had to hand it to Sol and his colleagues; they were certainly dedicated. But the more he thought about it the more something didn't sit right with Sol's story. The confusion must have shown on his face because Sol raised his eyebrows in a way that suggested he was waiting for Kane to ask a question.

"If your memory was wiped," Kane said slowly, "how could you know about the events leading up to the Brachyurans declaring war on your planet?"

"Ah, yes," said Sol, "well, first of all, the procedure doesn't erase all memory. That wouldn't make for very good operatives would it? No, we'd managed to quite successfully map the brain and were by then able to target specific memory centres. Military training, general knowledge and anything else relevant to the mission were left alone. But a majority of memories, including all irrelevant personal ones and the wider reasons behind the mission, were targeted and erased." He looked at Kane with his eyebrows raised. "For example, I have no idea what my real name is. Before you ask," he said waving a finger at Kane, "'Sol' is a name that Kendrick chose for me. And I'd rather not talk about it if you don't mind."

Kane snapped his mouth shut. He would ask 23 later; see if she would tell him.

"But to answer your question…" Sol continued. "During our escape from the base we… well, we had a bit of a fight to get away and during that battle Kendrick received a blow to the head. It was a one in a million fluke but, for reasons we never really understood, it undid a lot of his memory wipe. He remains the only one of us with any memory of events prior to our final mission on Rigel 3. It was he who described what happened to me during the diplomatic mission to Rigel 4. I have no memory of those events."

Kane found himself feeling uncomfortable at the revelation, as though Sol, someone who he really didn't know at all, had told him a great personal secret. But Sol didn't seem fazed at all and Kane found himself respecting the man's candour all the more. Sol was either a completely honest and open man, with an almost childlike sincerity, or a master manipulator.

But something else was worrying Kane. He was marshalling his thoughts, deciding the best way to broach the subject when Sol read something in his face.

"Something else bothers you?" he asked mildly.

"Ah, yeah," Kane muttered. "Brakus…"

Sol waited patiently for Kane to ask his question. Finally, the soldier spoke.

"Look..." he began slowly, before shaking his head and jumping straight in. "How the hell can we trust Brakus?" he blurted. Sol's look of amusement made Kane feel suddenly angry. So he continued, not caring how rude he might sound. "He's one of these vicious aliens! The ones that wipe out civilisations because they might just become a threat some time down the line! Who's to say he won't take over *this* world? Lord knows he has the technology..."

Much to Kane's disgust, Sol's infuriating smile widened until the older man began to chuckle.

"I don't think it's very fucking funny!" Kane snapped.

"I'm not laughing at you, Mr Kane," Sol said. "It's just that I've had this exact same conversation with both Agent 23 and Kendrick. You military types are all the same!" But then his expression turned serious and he turned to face Kane. "Don't you worry about Brakus turning against us," he said. "Over the last few centuries of working together, we've come to an understanding..." Sol's voice trailed off as he saw Kane's shoulders slump ever so slightly. He saw a pang of disappointment in the younger man's face and felt one of his own at Kane's apparent lack of faith. But he forced a short laugh as he slapped Kane's shoulder.

"I'm not a stupid man, Mr Kane," he said suddenly. "I also have various other... uh, means by which to ensure his loyalty." Kane's head snapped round, his eyes narrowing with interest.

"Ways that are far more effective than donning plastic gauntlets and wrapping him on the head..." he added with a mischievous grin.

"Such as...?" Kane prompted.

"Let's just say it's in his best interests not to cross me..." came his cryptic reply. Sol's suddenly grim expression effectively ended that particular conversation. *For now, at least*, Kane thought to himself, determined to get the information sooner rather than later.

Sol was about to continue with his story when he straightened slightly in his seat. His head tilted to one side as though he was listening to a far away sound. He looked concerned.

"Okay," he said aloud as he rose from his seat, "we're on our way." He turned to Kane. "Agent 23 has returned with Deblanc and Timothy Bruce."

"Something's wrong," said Kane. It wasn't a question.

"Possibly," the old man replied, his attitude brightening slightly. "But I think it's alright. Besides," he added, with the familiar smile returning to his lips, "I think we've reached the best point in my little story for you to meet the final member of our merry little band."

Chapter 13: Hosts, Good and Bad

Alfred Morrison grunted as another fist flew into his stomach. He doubled over despite his best efforts and was once again rewarded by the loss of a fistful of hair to the second man, standing behind him. This process had been going on for some time now, one man punching him in the stomach while the other grabbed a handful of hair.

"That was a good one!" the man behind him shouted with a laugh. Morrison had to agree. He'd heard and felt the hair tearing from his scalp and could now feel a cool trickle of blood snaking its way down his forehead.

Morrison was blindfolded and securely tied to a chair, his ankles strapped to the chair's legs. All of his clothes had been removed, a standard interrogation technique designed to build on the prisoner's humiliation.

He could tell from the echo of the men's voices that they were in a large, mostly empty room. When they'd dragged him in he'd been aware of the third man, the one whose leg had been run over by his car, being taken into separate room. They'd secured him to the chair and left him alone while they attended to their colleague. Screams of pain had issued from the other room as they set the man's leg, making Morrison grin to himself. The screaming had slowly reduced until it finally stopped, but it was several minutes more before the men returned to begin work on him. Morrison paid close attention to everything he could hear and decided that the third man must have been sedated so his leg could be worked on.

One down, Morrison thought grimly.

He knew one of the men was Gregory Lindros, formerly of the British Army Intelligence Corps and wanted by himself and Kane for the original kidnapping of the Holloway boy.

Morrison was just beginning to lose the feeling in his stomach and scalp, a welcome numbness replacing the pain. It told him that these men weren't experienced in interrogation techniques, didn't understand the need to move around the body to inflict the maximum amount of discomfort. He was focusing on that thought, using it as a distraction, when somebody stamped their heel onto his unprotected toes. He screamed as he felt his toenails splitting and grinding into the bones beneath. He tried to curl them up, reduce the target size, but realised his mistake too late. The boot came down again, this time onto his curled toes, breaking several of them with one crushing impact. This time, his screams were almost drowned out by the laughter of Lindros and his minion.

Yeah, laugh it up you wankers, he thought to himself. *Just you wait until the tables are turned.*

It was a forlorn hope, he knew, but turning fear into anger was all he had to concentrate on. The questioning hadn't yet begun, but it was only a matter of time. He had to keep his wits about him until… what? He had no idea where Kane was and he couldn't rely on anyone else knowing he was in trouble. He'd have to get out of this one by himself.

The softening up period came to an end, shortly after his toes had been broken, when a car arrived. His tormenters left him alone and walked off in the direction of the car. Soon he heard voices, but they were too far away to make out individual words. Morrison managed to pick out two new voices in the mumbled conversation, bringing the total up to at least four and one possibly sedated. One voice sounded whiny and argumentative, obviously someone who didn't want to be there. *Possibly another prisoner* he thought to himself, though the tone of the voice didn't make him sound like a worthwhile ally.

When the voices disappeared with the sound of a closing door, Morrison found himself alone to contemplate his injuries.

Injuries so far, he corrected himself.

The toes on his left foot were severely fucked up. They were sticky with blood and he couldn't move them, but at least they still hurt like hell, so he knew they were still there and the nerve endings still functioned. The pain in his groin from Lindros biting him had now reduced to a constant, dull throb. He hoped *that* still worked too. He wasn't aware of any blood in his lap and chose to take that as a good sign. Other aches and pains covered his body: his torn scalp and bruised stomach and finally, the broad cable ties securing his hands had cut into his wrists and ankles quite badly.

He'd been constantly testing his restraints and found them to be very secure, though their sharp edges told him they were industrial cable ties rather than the stronger Plasticuffs used by the military and police forces. Fortunately, Morrison had been alert enough to flex his muscles as much as possible while the ties were being secured; ensuring they weren't too tight when he'd relaxed again. There was a story going around the Regiment when he was in the SAS, about a soldier who'd had the ties applied to his wrists too tightly during an interrogation exercise. They'd been so tight that he'd permanently lost the use of one of his hands. As with most things, there was a right way and a wrong way to apply the ties and Morrison wasn't about to rely on his captors' abilities.

Injury inventory completed, Morrison turned his attention to the situation in hand, weighing up his options.

It didn't take long.

He wasn't even sure why they'd gone to so much trouble to capture him. He knew Lindros had military training, but how he'd got hold of current military-issue weaponry for himself and his cronies he had no idea. He had to assume it wasn't coincidence that he and Kane had crossed paths with Lindros during their hunt for Deblanc: the man wanted for the murder of Holloway's friend. Perhaps Lindros was working for Deblanc? But if so, why grab Holloway? If they'd wanted to sever any connections to Deblanc's work they would simply kill him.

So they were most probably looking for Deblanc themselves. It wasn't much to go on, but Morrison might be able to use it when the interrogation finally began.

A door opened and the muffled voices returned briefly before Morrison heard the car door open and close and the vehicle moving away. *At least one less to worry about*, he thought to himself. But that tiny speck of hope evaporated when the next sound he heard was two sets of footsteps heading in his direction. He braced himself for a long day, a single thought running through his head…

Where the hell are you, Kane?

****

A little over half an hour later, a more focused Robert Mitchell stepped from his restaurant and into the waiting Escalade. His driver closed the door behind him and quickly walked round the vehicle to get into the driver's seat. Neither man spoke.

The vehicle moved away from the curb and headed towards the warehouse where, at that very moment, Lindros would be beginning to soften up his mysterious captive before the questioning could begin. Mitchell sat in silence with a scowl firmly fixed to his face, staring out of the blacked-out window.

The lingering smell of Holloway had gone, replaced by an artificial and equally powerful one of air fresheners. Mitchell appreciated the driver making the effort, but his mood was too dark for him to show any sign of gratitude.

The manager at the restaurant had told him the police had been there, asking for him. It was an expected visit but he was in no mood to waste his time with them just yet. He knew he couldn't put them off for long, but for the time being at least they would allow him time to grieve over the death of his son. Mitchell didn't have much trouble with the police, he was always careful about that. He never did anything himself that one of his minions could do in his place.

People like Lindros.

A grim smile worked its way onto Mitchell's face. Lindros had been a lucky find. One of his people had met him in prison soon after his expulsion from the army, bitter and shouting his mouth off about how unfair it all was. It didn't take long to secure his employment and it quickly became obvious there was nothing he wouldn't do if the price was right. As a result, Mitchell had been able to use him as a shield between himself and the police. It was one thing Robert Mitchell didn't mind spending money on.

Today was going to be a test of his and Lindros's working relationship. He didn't know who the mystery captive was or if he had any information about the murder of his son, but Lindros obviously thought there was a connection.

It was going to take a prestigious act of will for Mitchell not to get involved in the interrogation. Usually he would watch Lindros go to work on the blindfolded subject through the office window, distancing himself from the process. But today he wasn't sure he'd manage such detachment. Somebody knew who murdered his son and he wouldn't let anyone they questioned go until he was one hundred percent convinced they'd extracted every morsel of information.

If they let him go at all.

****

Timothy Bruce awoke with a start, instantly awake and fighting back a crushing wave of anxiety. He slipped into a deep-breathing exercise that would have impressed the most experienced of meditative therapists. Such people would be all the more impressed when they discovered it was a self-taught technique and he'd never visited a therapist in his life. It was survival, pure and simple.

The last few days had delivered upon Timothy levels of stress that even the most confident and able person would have trouble dealing with. But Timothy would be the first to admit that he wasn't normal, that his life wasn't normal.

He'd awoken to find himself lying on his back on a soft bed, staring up at a perfectly white ceiling dozens of metres overhead. He didn't dare move, terrified of what new horror his stinging eyes would fall upon. He heard a distant voice and quickly clamped his eyes shut, forcing a tear from between his eyelashes and sending it rolling down the side of his face. It tickled, but more worrying to Timothy was the irrational fear that the rolling tear would draw the attention of whoever it was he could hear in the room. He forced his breathing to become ever more shallow, willing himself to shrink, to drop from anyone's notice. All he wanted was to be left alone.

The voice spoke again. It was quite far off and he couldn't work out what was being said but he realised something else in that moment. The speaker would be talking to somebody else, so there had to be at least two people in the room. It was an obvious and simple fact but it terrified him. The first voice was female and soon she was answered to by a man's voice.

They were getting closer.

"I can't understand it," the woman was saying, "he doesn't appear to be injured but I can't get any response from him."

"Hmm," replied the man. He sounded older than the woman and more kindly somehow. But still Timothy remained still. They were standing next to the bed now and he could imagine their eyes staring at him.

"Timothy?" the man spoke gently into his ear. Timothy flinched, surprised by the sudden closeness of the man's voice.

"Ah," the man said, the voice moving further away as he straightened up again. "I think he's just coming out of it." Something in the man's voice calmed Timothy, making him feel *slightly* less terrified. It was as if the man knew he was pretending to be asleep and understood his fear.

"I think we'll let the poor lad have a little more time to himself, to wake up properly," the male voice continued. "Don't forget we've got an awful lot of things to go through with him." There was a pause and Timothy felt sure the old man was staring at him. "You know what?" he said to his colleague as they walked away, "I think he'll look back on this day and remember how much it changed his life, how much better things had become…" the voice faded away, leaving Timothy alone on the bed.

He lay there for several minutes longer, his eyes firmly closed. There was something in the old man's voice, perhaps the subtly raised volume, which made him think the final words had been said for his benefit. It felt slightly patronising, but that was better than frightening.

He lay there silently, listening for any other sounds. He could still hear voices in the distance and as he strained to make out the words he detected a third voice. It was another man. A chill went down his spine as he thought about Deblanc, the man who'd broken into his flat and later somehow lost an arm. Despite Deblanc making an effort to befriend him, he still didn't like him. He was far too confident. Timothy hoped the entire experience had been a dream, it felt too surreal to be otherwise but the details were too fresh in his mind. The new voice was slightly deeper than Deblanc's and its tone sounded authoritative yet confused. It sounded like the older man was in charge and the other man was trying to get answers from him. He didn't hear the woman's voice any more.

Slowly, carefully, he opened his eyes and stared at the ceiling.

Everything was white. He wondered if he was dead and this was heaven, or somewhere else… But he knew he'd lived a blameless life. Surely he wouldn't be sent *there*?

Timothy slowly turned his head to look at the rest of the room and instantly found himself locking eyes with a woman. He froze, wondering for a split second whether he should close them again or flee. But the woman had a kind face and was smiling at him.

"Hello Timothy," she said, her tone conversational and kindly. "You've had quite a day haven't you?"

He couldn't speak and just lay there, staring. She was sitting on a chair, white of course, leaning forward with her elbows on her knees, her face only a few feet away from his. She had a strange expression and her eyes darted around his face as if examining him. It made him feel uncomfortable but still he didn't say anything.

"Would you like anything to eat or drink?" she asked. Timothy nodded slowly. His mouth was very dry and he didn't want to talk in case his voice broke. The woman got up and moved over to a side table on which sat the remains of a variety of foods and drinks. She poured a glass of what looked like orange juice, only paler and returned to his bedside.

He sat upright to accept the offered glass and sipped at it. It wasn't orange juice, wasn't anything he'd ever tasted before, but it was cold and sweet and he liked it. The woman had returned to her chair and sat quietly, watching him. Her attention made him feel uncomfortable. He'd spent so many years trying to go unnoticed that he didn't know how to react.

She suddenly glanced to one side and held up a hand. Tim followed her gaze and caught a glimpse of two men, one old and wearing a similar grey outfit to the woman and one wearing more regular clothing. The two men moved out of his line of sight and were gone. But even when they'd disappeared Timothy felt exposed, like he was in danger and had to hide.

"I'll introduce you to them later, Timothy," she said. "I think you'll like them." When he didn't respond she leant forward and laid a hand on his knee. "I just want you to know," she said, looking at him with a warm expression of concern, "that you are safe here. In fact, I'd say that this is the safest place on the entire planet!" Her voice rose and a smile crept onto her face as she finished and Timothy grinned despite himself. "That's better," she said, "I knew you'd have a nice smile."

****

Sol led Kane into the construction area, away from Agent 23 and the man on the bed. As they rounded a bank of consoles and disappeared from sight, Sol noticed Kane craning his neck to have one last look at the couple they'd left behind. At first, Sol didn't know who Kane was looking at, 23 or Timothy Bruce, but then the disappointed expression on the man's face gave him away.

"No," said Sol, "that wasn't Kendrick. That was Timothy Bruce, another element of our mission here that I will tell you all about." He glanced at Kane again and was surprised that his expression hadn't changed. Kane was still looking over at 23 and Timothy, his brow furrowing slightly.

Sol shook his head and grinned to himself. Kane was looking at Agent 23, not Timothy Bruce. He hadn't foreseen *that* coming. Never mind, Kane would learn quickly enough.

"I'm about to introduce you to Kendrick," Sol continued, "and when I do, I'll be able to bring you both fully up to date."

Kane grunted. His mood had definitely darkened. "And then what?" he asked, sullenly.

"That's entirely up to you, Mr Kane," Sol replied, pretending he hadn't noticed the change in mood. "When you've heard everything we have to say, I hope you'll agree to join us."

"And if I don't?" Kane replied, his voice devoid of emotion.

Sol blinked, apparently taken aback by Kane's reply.

"Well, we'll send you back to wherever you'd like to go of course," he replied.

"Of course," Kane murmured. His tone was even but Sol noticed him unconsciously shifting the weight of his P90, still strapped to his chest.

They rounded a further bank of consoles and found themselves back to where they'd originally entered the chamber. On another bed lay the still form of Deblanc, exactly where 23 had left him. Sol had explained that she'd left him there for Brakus to attend to while she carried Timothy Bruce further into the chamber where he could be more gently eased into his new reality. Kane knew next to nothing about this latest arrival and from what he *had* learned, he didn't think he wanted to. Timothy Bruce sounded like a neurotic mess.

A Portal popped open in front of them and Brakus emerged and gently floated towards Sol. Kane caught a brief glimpse through the Portal and saw the creature's control room within. Brakus was carrying a small datapad in one of his tentacles.

"What is so important this time?" demanded Brakus, clearly still in a bad mood, though Kane was starting to think it was the creature's natural state.

"Deblanc has been injured," said Sol, indicating the figure stretched out on the bed beside him. "He's lost an arm and I need you to fix him up with a prosthetic."

Brakus let out a raspy sigh, or an equivalent thereof, and floated towards Deblanc's bed.

"Upgrades?" he snapped. Sol thought for a few seconds before answering.

"No," he said, "just a standard arm I think."

"You still don't trust him," Brakus stated as he hovered over to Deblanc's unconscious form and manipulated controls on his datapad. Sol ignored the comment and turned to address Kane.

"Time to introduce you to Kendrick," he said. Kane noticed that, although he was facing him, his eyes were looking over in Brakus's direction. The reason soon became clear when Kane noticed Brakus stiffen, all of his tentacles straightening briefly before he began furiously entering commands into the datapad with renewed vigour. As Kane watched, a couple of the drones moved down from the ceiling and lifted Deblanc's bed aloft on a pair of pencil-thin beams of light. A Portal instantly sprung to life and the bed floated smoothly through.

"I am extremely busy," Brakus snapped as he moved towards the Portal, "and there is no need for me to endure further *reunions*." He spoke the last word with obvious distain, as though the very idea annoyed him. Without another word he darted into the Portal and was gone.

As soon as the Portal disappeared Sol began laughing and turned to Kane.

"Though he would never admit to it," he said, "Brakus is scared to death of Kendrick." Kane just nodded his understanding, unsure why Sol should find it so amusing. He hadn't heard much about the mysterious Kendrick apart from him being the third surviving member of Sol's doomed mission and somehow having his memory wipe reversed.

"You said Kendrick was the final member of your group," Kane began, "I notice you didn't include Deblanc or this Timothy Bruce in that. How do they fit into your plans? And me, come to that?"

Sol thought about the question while he retrieved a datapad, similar to the one Brakus had been carrying, from one of the consoles.

"If you don't mind, Ted," he said as he busied himself with the datapad, "I'll just retrieve Kendrick…"

"Retrieve…?" Kane interrupted.

Sol stopped inputting data and one of his fingers hovered over a key, suggesting to Kane that just one more press was needed to finish whatever he was doing.

"The time distorting effect of Portal travel has many useful applications," he explained. "While Portal travel usually lasts a mere second or two in real time, they can also be programmed to reopen after a set time delay." Sol touched the final control and a new Portal opened in front of them. "Or when commanded to do so," he finished as a figure stepped from the Portal and into the room.

Kane stared at Kendrick, or rather, *up* at Kendrick. He was a huge man, easily seven feet tall, with impressively broad shoulders and arms thicker than most men's legs. His skin was darker than that of Sol or 23 and instead of their collarless grey uniforms he wore a simple, loose outfit in black. It's cut suggested a military design, though it wasn't close to anything Kane had ever seen before. His face was strong and broad with a solid jaw: the face of a soldier. He stepped from the Portal and Kane watched with interest as Kendrick cast a practiced eye about the room, taking in details with his darting eyes. He glanced at Kane, then at his gun before taking in the rest of the room, likely dismissing the weapon as being slung and not an immediate danger.

Within a handful of seconds Kendrick appeared to have familiarised himself with his surroundings and walked up to Sol without breaking his stride.

"Sol," he said, his voice deep and authoritative as he reached his colleague, examining his face as he spoke. Kendrick's expression suddenly darkened with a look of disproval.

"How long did you leave me inside?" he demanded, sounding angry and making Kane feel intimidated despite being armed.

"A little longer than you requested I'm afraid," Sol replied sheepishly. "But there really wasn't much for you to do, my friend. Brakus and I tended to the everyday running of things."

The big man stared at Sol for a few seconds, his expression murderous. As Kane watched, ignored by both men, Kendrick suddenly lunged at Sol with his arms outstretched, his hands curled into craws. Sol didn't react as the giant flew at him and Kane rushed to bring his P90 up and into a firing position, already thinking about the best angle to shoot at Kendrick without harming Sol.

He needn't have worried.

At the last moment, Kendrick's arms spread wide and he scooped Sol up in a bear hug, lifting the man clear from the ground and swinging him round. Kendrick's laughter boomed through the chamber, his voice deeper than any Kane had heard before. Kane lowered his weapon but kept his hand on the grip.

"You're an old man!" Kendrick was shouting, making Sol cringe at the sheer volume of his voice. Finally he set Sol down and stared at him with a serious look on his face. "How long have you spent outside the Portal?" he asked.

"Oh, just a few decades," came the older man's reply as Kendrick continued to stare at him, not saying a word. "Okay, three or four decades," Sol admitted. Kendrick continued to stare, though his expression had softened.

"How long do we have until the Brachyurans get here?" the big man asked, instantly serious.

"What was that?" Kane demanded before Sol could answer. "Those monsters are coming to Earth?" He glared at Sol. "And just when were you going to tell *me* this?" Sol opened his mouth to answer but it was Kendrick's turn to butt in.

"Who the hell's this?" he bellowed over his shoulder as he stepped towards Kane. Kane brought his gun back up as he stepped back from the advancing giant, years of training and experience taking control. But before his brain could make the decision to fire or not, a huge hand lashed out and wrenched the P90 from his grip, tearing the straps from his combat webbing. Kane stared at the weapon, looking small and ridiculous in Kendrick's huge paw, before he smoothly took a step backwards and drew his sidearm. It was clear of the holster and pointed at Kendrick's massive head before a piece of the webbing, torn away with the giant's grab at the P90, silently hit the ground between the two soldiers.

But the big man's charge had stopped as quickly as it had begun and he stood quietly, looming a few feet in front of Kane, staring at the machine gun, turning it over in his hands and examining it with a practiced eye. He glanced at Kane briefly, the slightest flicker of his eyes taking in the readied pistol, before he turned back to Sol, apparently dismissing Kane as any kind of threat. He held the P90 out for Sol to see.

"Is this current Earth tech?" he asked.

Sol nodded sheepishly.

"And how long do we have before the Crabheads get here?"

"We thought we had a little under twenty years," Sol replied quietly, looking at both men in turn. "But we've picked up a scout vessel just today. It's a lot closer..." Kendrick raised an eyebrow and Sol continued in a dull monotone. "Days, possibly hours," he said.

Kendrick scowled and turned back to Kane.

"I think," he said, "that your world is in a lot of trouble."

Chapter 14: Kendrick

Ted Kane stared at the back of Kendrick's head, his anger steadily rising. The giant man had just stated, in a matter-of-fact way, that the world was going to be overrun by technologically advanced, free-floating crab-headed jellyfish with a fetish for torture. And it didn't appear to bother him in the slightest.

And worse, seconds after breaking the news to Kane, Kendrick had spun on his heel as Agent 23 entered the area, shouting her giggly welcomes at the big man. Kane was then forced to endure a further sickening display of reunion while he stood to the side, apparently forgotten and ignored. Sol watched the pair with his infuriating smile as Kendrick scooped 23 up in his arms and spun her around in exactly the same way she had done to Sol.

Kendrick still had hold of the P90 and Kane found himself feeling naked without it, silently watching as the trio exchanged unintelligible techno babble.

Finally, he'd had enough.

"Hey!" he bellowed in his best parade ground tone. He waited until he had six eyes staring at him before continuing. "I know I'm the new guy here," he said, spitting out each word and leaving no doubt as to his mood, "but did I just hear correctly that those crab bastards are coming *here*?"

The three exchanged glances before Kendrick stepped forward to look down at Kane. He spoke over his shoulder to Sol.

"Who *is* this guy?" he asked.

Sol stepped up and gestured at Kane.

"This," he began, "is Mr. Ted Kane. Former Royal Marine, former Sergeant in the Special Air Service and currently an Intelligence Officer with MI6." He then turned to Kane and gestured at Kendrick. "And this," he said, "is Kendrick, formerly Agent 34. Kendrick is also the man in charge of operations here in the Keep."

Kane noticed Kendrick raise an eyebrow at the final comment, but didn't comment. It surprised Kane to hear Kendrick was the man in charge, but he supposed it made sense if he was the only one with his full memories intact.

"Say hello and play nice, boys," said Agent 23. But both men remained silent, neither wanting to be the first to greet the other. After a few seconds of silence Kane turned to Sol.

"Again," he said slowly, visibly fighting to contain his anger, "did I hear right that those crab-headed bastards are coming *here*?"

"That's right," said Kendrick before Sol could answer. "They're coming here. So how do you feel about you and me having a drink and trading some war stories?" He handed the P90 back to a stunned Kane. "And then," he continued, "I'll tell you how we're going to send the bastards back to where they came from."

"As easy as that?"

"Ah…well, maybe not *quite* that easily," Kendrick admitted as he glanced back at Sol and Agent 23, "but we've had quite a long time to prepare…" He suddenly stopped talking and stared at Sol. "We have *been* preparing?" he demanded of the old man. Sol looked at Agent 23 as though for support.

"Don't look at me!" she said, showing him her palms. "I've only been out a few hours myself…"

An uncomfortable silence descended upon the room, leaving Kane feeling like he'd been punched in the stomach. For all their advanced technology and astounding abilities these people were behaving like a bunch of teenagers in a clubhouse. It was more than he could take.

"What the fuck is going on here!" Kane demanded, stepping forward and glaring at each person in turn. In an instant he'd changed from a star struck and mostly ignored outsider and into the experienced military man he truly was. He marched around the trio, spitting out his words in short, sharp bursts.

"You people have come to my planet," he snapped, "most likely leading an advanced and vicious alien race in your wake. You send people on murder missions all around the world." This comment resulted in Kendrick and Agent 23 each raising an eyebrow and staring in Sol's direction. Kane noticed this, but didn't comment on it. "I've been kidnapped by your tame assassin," he continued, "and brought here. Then you tell me my world is in danger from said vicious alien race. And now," he shouted, his voice raising to its limit, "the three of you squabble like fucking school children!"

Sol, Kendrick and Agent 23 stared at Kane in silence. He glared back, his pacing finished and his anger beginning to subside. It was an awkward moment. No longer riding his anger he felt suddenly tired and conspicuous under three sets of narrowed eyes. He had to keep his momentum up.

"Just who the hell *is* in charge here?" he snapped, his voice slightly lower but losing none of its authority. He stared each person in the eye, one at a time, demanding a response. "Well?" he snapped when nobody answered.

Kendrick turned to Sol and Agent 23 with a big grin on his face and pointed at Kane. "I think I like this guy," he said, ignoring any of Kane's questions. Agent 23 sighed and rolled her eyes.

Until a moment ago Kane was seriously concerned that the big man might pick him up by the throat and throw him across the room. But his relief at Kendrick's attitude change was at odds with his disgust at the trio's lack of concern regarding the danger they'd put his world in.

"I think," said Sol, his voice infuriatingly calm, "we should all sit down, introduce ourselves properly and bring the whole group up to date." This last comment was directed at Kendrick. "Some of us have been inside for a long time and we have some new faces to introduce." He turned to Agent 23. "How is Timothy doing?" he asked.

"How do you think?" she replied, her voice slightly bitter. "He's a nervous wreck. I think we went a bit too far with him."

Sol nodded his understanding. "He will be fine," he said. "Brakus!" he called into the air. A moment passed before the alien's reedy voice replied, ever grouchy.

"What is it now?" the Brachyuran demanded.

"How long before Deblanc is up and about?" the old man asked, ignoring the creature's tone.

"Walking or fighting?" the voice snapped.

"Walking."

"Within the hour," the voice finished. Sol didn't bother replying. He knew Brakus would have already cut the connection.

"Deblanc? Timothy?" Kendrick muttered to nobody in particular, though he did glance at Kane.

"One hour then," 23 said as she turned and walked away from the group. "I'll get Timothy ready." She disappeared behind the bank of consoles heading towards Timothy's bed.

"Timothy?" Kendrick asked again, looking at Kane. Kane just shrugged and both men looked at Sol.

Sol held up his hands and dipped his head slightly. "I think it best if I explain everything at once when everyone is gathered together," he said. "Then we can raise all the questions we want."

Kendrick's shoulders sagged slightly. "I really want to shoot something," he muttered. Kane grinned.

"Well," he said as he passed his P90 back to the big man, "If you don't mind playing with a caveman's toy, you're welcome to have a go with this..."

Kendrick accepted the weapon and examined it again.

"You don't understand," he said as he removed the magazine and peered into the weapon's innards, "I meant that this thing was way more advanced than I was expecting... *Too* advanced if anything." He glared at Sol, but the old man had wandered away and was busying himself with one of the room's consoles.

"Then you're right, I don't understand..." Kane began. But he wasn't going to get an answer yet. Kendrick snapped the magazine back in place and lifted the weapon up to peer through its sights.

"You and me both," was the giant's infuriating reply. "Best wait until we're all filled in on the details."

Kendrick pointed the weapon out across the chamber and loosed a three-round burst. All three bullets struck a hapless drone, tearing open its side and sending it into a smoking, spiral decent. He lowered the weapon and nodded his approval.

"Sidearm?" he asked. Kane nodded and handed over his pistol. A Walther P99QA, the newest version of the weapon currently being carried in the movies by James Bond. This version had a larger, .40 calibre load and a 'Quick Action' feature, shortening the slide's blowback length to increase the weapon's rate of fire and accuracy.

After giving the pistol a quick once-over Kendrick transferred the P90 to his other hand and fired the pistol one-handed across the chamber. Again, three shots rang out and three shots hit their target. Another drone fell from the air and crashed down somewhere out of sight.

Without a word Kendrick stepped away from Kane and up to one of the nearby consoles. He removed the magazine from the P90 before placing the weapon onto the console's flat surface. As Kane watched, he removed a single bullet from the magazine and placed both the magazine and the bullet on the console next to the P90. He repeated the process with the pistol and then moved over to a control board. Kane stepped forward to see what Kendrick was doing with his weapons, feeling suddenly possessive of his property.

The big man entered a series of commands and a row of boxes appeared on the large screen hanging in front of the two men. Kendrick continued to enter commands while Kane watched the strange alien script appear at various places across the screen.

Kendrick grinned as he hit a final pad and an intricate grid of green lights began playing across the weapons in an intricate lattice pattern.

After a few seconds the lights winked out. Kendrick quickly reloaded the weapons before handing both back to Kane.

"I scanned their patterns into a construction program," he explained. "Drones are putting a few units of each together for us. Should be ready by the time the meeting's over." He pointed at the weapons in Kane's hands. "And I've made a couple of modifications to the design for the new ones," he added with a grin.

"Such as?"

"Nothing major. You'll see."

Kane held up the P90 and looked at it intensely, trying to imagine how the weapon could possibly be improved in such a short amount of time. He just grunted, not bothering to press the matter.

"About the meeting," he said as he returned the pistol to its webbing holster, "there's a favour I'd like to ask you…"

****

Alfred Morrison clenched his mouth shut and braced himself. The blindfold had risen up slightly on his face and he was now able to peek beneath it and see his legs. He felt strangely disappointed by what he saw. His thighs sported a random criss-cross of pink and red stripes, not unlike that of a miss-coloured tiger. There was some bruising beginning to appear between the stripes, but not nearly enough to warrant the amount of pain he was in. He felt sure they'd look much worse. He had to admit his tormentors had begun to show a little imagination in the last hour or so and this latest thing was a new one on him.

The dull rumble of a compressor was once again overshadowed by the whoosh of the power sprayer, the type used to clean cars, and he felt a light mist of cold water settling across his shivering body once again. It felt quite pleasant, truth be told, as it numbed his many aches and pains. He knew it was going to be a short-lived respite and he was right. Seconds later, what felt like a blowtorch crossed his back in a curving line. It was amazing how much pain a simple jet of water could produce.

For the last hour or so Lindros and his man had been taking turns tormenting Morrison with the car washing equipment and anything else they could find lying about the warehouse. From what he'd seen on his legs he could imagine how he must look. His entire body below the neckline had been attacked by the water jet and, to put it mildly, it hurt like hell. He'd long since stopped the macho routine of remaining silent; it just made them try harder. Now his screams were coming freely whenever the water jet crossed his shivering body.

And still they hadn't asked him any questions.

Lindros's colleague had made a passing comment earlier about 'when the boss gets here,' so Morrison had to assume the tormenting would continue at least until then. He didn't want to think about what would follow the mysterious boss's arrival.

Eventually, and thankfully, the sound of a car arriving marked the end of the softening-up process and Morrison was once again left alone on his chair, shivering violently. They hadn't noticed the slipped blindfold and he found that by tipping his head back as far as he could, a natural enough pose for someone who'd been through what he had, he could peek beneath it and get a glimpse of his surroundings.

It was the warehouse that he and Kane had targeted earlier that very day, so at least he knew the layout. The voices he'd heard earlier would have become muffled when they'd gone into the office. He was now in the open area in front of the office where those within were most probably watching him through the window, so now wasn't the time to make any sort of move, even if he could.

He continued to test the strength of the cable ties binding his wrists. They weren't showing any sign of weakening and his struggling was only making them cut into the flesh. But he knew the discomfort to his wrists was nothing compared to what would be coming once the interrogation proper began. The working over they'd given him with the power washer had sapped a lot of his energy and he found himself having to dig deep to continue his struggle with the cable ties.

As he worked on the ties he listened, looking for any clues as to what was going on. He heard a car door open and close and distant voices in conversation. He strained to hear details but the only name he heard was the one he already knew: Lindros. The voices ceased with the closing of the office door and Morrison sat there, silently waiting, his mind racing. He didn't have long to come up with a plan.

****

Robert Mitchell stepped into the warehouse office and stared at each of the people in the room in turn. No one said a word, his expression made sure of that.

Lindros met his eye coolly, the most self-assured person in the room. His man, Griffith, stood to one side and only looked up briefly to nod acknowledgement of Mitchell's arrival before looking out of the office window once more. Mitchell followed his gaze and saw the mystery guest, tied to a chair in the warehouse. Griffith wasn't taking his eyes off him any longer than he had to. *Good,* thought Mitchell, *at least someone was on the ball.*

Lindros's other man, Hawkins, was stretched out on the office's only couch, his leg bandaged. He looked to be dozing, probably dosed up on morphine.

Because Hawkins was on the couch, Jamie Holloway, fresh from his hospital bed, was sitting on an office chair in the corner of the room. He was awake but slumped forward in the seat, obviously still in pain. His father stood next to him, but wasn't paying the boy any attention. He was looking out of the window at the prisoner when Mitchell entered the room, but as soon as he saw him, his bored expression changed to one of excitement.

The creepy little man walked over to Mitchell with his arms out, as though intending to give the big man a hug. Mitchell didn't move. He didn't have to. Lindros stepped forward and punched Holloway in the stomach, bending the man in half with a surprised grunt of escaping breath. Without breaking his stride, Lindros lifted the man back upright by the armpit and none to gently deposited him into an empty chair.

Mitchell glared down at Holloway, daring the man to look up and test his mood. But the little man was far too busy trying to regain control of his breathing.

Mitchell turned and met eyes with his driver, standing in the office entrance, and nodded once. The driver performed a quick about-face and returned to the car where he took up position next to the driver's side door. He folded his arms across his chest and looked out across the industrial estate, keeping lookout.

Mitchell returned his attention to the people in the room.

"This is what's going to happen," he said, his tone leaving no room for argument. "Nobody is going to leave this warehouse until I am satisfied I've learned as much as I can about the murder of my son from Jamie here," he pointed at the boy, still slumped in his chair, "and our mystery guest out there," he jabbed his thumb in the direction of Morrison in the warehouse. "Mr Lindros will begin the… interview with our guest, while I talk to Jamie."

At the mention of his son's name, Holloway looked up at Mitchell with an expectant smile on his face. But the smile quickly disappeared when he saw Mitchell was looking at his son and not him. He glanced that way himself, his face a mask of annoyance. His expression wasn't missed by Mitchell, who found a new level of loathing for the wretched little man.

Mitchell turned back to the teenager.

"Jamie," he said, his voice suddenly softer. The boy looked up, fear on his face. "Are you feeling up to a little walk?"

The boy nodded feebly and slowly rose from his chair. Seeing an opening, a chance to get some time with Mitchell, Holloway also got up from his chair and went as if to help his son. But it was too little, too late.

"Not you," Mitchell snapped without even bothering to look at the boy's father. "You wait here." Holloway hesitated for a few seconds, desperately thinking of something to say to ingratiate himself with Mitchell.

"Sit!" Mitchell snapped.

He sat.

Mitchell nodded at Lindros who in turn nodded to Griffith, who walked towards the warehouse door. Lindros reached over to close the window blinds, cutting the view of the warehouse off to the office, glaring at Holloway senior as he did so. He didn't like to be watched while he worked and if the boss wasn't going to remain in the office there was no need to leave the blinds open. Lindros and Griffith then left the office and headed off to perform their interrogation.

Jamie slowly limped over to Mitchell's side, drawing a glare from his father, and Mitchell led him from the room.

Soon the office was empty except for Holloway and the just now awaking Hawkins. After a few minutes Holloway sighed loudly and began pacing the room. Hawkins watched quietly, trying his best to ignore him and get some sleep. He opened his eyes when he heard Holloway cease his pacing in front of the couch.

"Do you think Mr Mitchell would…" Holloway began, but stopped short when he saw the gun in Hawkins' hand, pointed at his chest.

"Never talk to me. Ever." The man growled.

Holloway clamped his mouth shut and sat down. This wasn't going as well as he'd hoped.

Both men remained silent from that moment on, Hawkins trying to get some sleep and Holloway fidgeting in his seat. Neither man noticed that the mobile phone sitting on the desk had lit up. The phone belonged to their 'guest', Morrison, and lay on the desk along with the rest of the his effects, including his clothes. The phone hadn't made a sound, hadn't vibrated, but just turned on for no apparent reason.

****

Deblanc lay still, looking straight up at the white ceiling some fifty or so metres above him, a smile on his face.

He had done it. He had regained entry to Sol's Keep.

His split-second decision to leap towards the Portal in Sol's reception chamber had come at a terrible personal cost, but he didn't consider losing his arm to be too great a price compared to what he stood to gain.

The Portal training he'd received before Sol banished him from the Keep had left him with an incredibly fast mind and supremely quick reflexes. The decision to sacrifice his arm was a conscious one, a fair exchange, but he wasn't quite prepared for the level of pain it had caused. The control he now enjoyed over his mind allowed him a limited amount of pain control, the ability to increase the level of adrenaline and endorphins his body produced. But when he'd lost his arm the mental shock had crushed his ability to concentrate, to regulate his physical body.

His broken wrist was less of a problem. The last Portal he'd been through would have detected the damage and realigned his molecules in their correct order, effectively re-setting the break and healing the bruising.

He looked down at the stump below his right elbow. It was a surreal sight, looking at the empty space where his arm used to be. He was convinced he could still feel his hand, but that wasn't possible of course. He looked closely at the stump and saw it was covered by a moulded piece of flesh-coloured plastic.

"Ow!" Deblanc drew his arm close and grabbed at the empty space where his hand should have been. His hand, the one that no longer existed, was a burning ball of pain. As his remaining hand closed around the empty space Deblanc heard a cruel, mocking chuckle coming from somewhere behind him.

He sat bolt upright on the bed and leapt clear, turning as he went… and found himself face to face with Brakus.

Deblanc's eyes narrowed as he glared at the creature and at what it was holding in a selection of its tentacles.

A human forearm.

Or at least the emaciated skeleton of one.

As he watched, Brakus extended one of his slimmer, more dextrous tentacles and bent one of the hand's fingers back against its usual direction. Deblanc let out another yell and his eyes watered as he once again looked down at the empty space where his right hand should be. Brakus made his strange alien laughing sound again and Deblanc glared at him.

"Give me that!" he bellowed as he reached out and snatched the arm from Brakus's grasp, being careful not to touch any of his tentacles. He turned the forearm over in his hand, examining its shape and surface. The bone structure of the arm was all there but the flesh and muscle was underdeveloped, as if it had shrivelled away. At the elbow end of the arm was the another flesh-coloured plastic cap, similar to the one he'd found on his stump. The caps were obviously designed to interconnect with each other. He also knew from previous experience that the plastic caps were also invisibly connected by an intricate network of senders and receivers, sending signals from the arm to his brain and allowing him the illusion of sensation in the limb.

"It isn't quite ready yet," Brakus chuckled as he extended a longer tentacle to retrieve the arm. "But I have got its sensory feedback working at eighty-seven percent."

"I noticed," Deblanc growled. His phantom hand hurt like hell but he couldn't even hold it to comfort himself. "What upgrades are you giving it?"

"Ah," Brakus said slowly as if savouring the moment and dragging his answer out as long as he could. "Well, there aren't actually going to be any enhancements…"

"What? Why not?"

Brakus didn't have time to respond before Deblanc answered his own question.

"Sol," he muttered.

"Indeed. I do not believe you have regained his trust."

Deblanc grunted. How long was he going to be kept out in the cold?

Brakus moved across the room and placed the arm on a workstation.

"Your new arm will be ready in a little under one hour," he rasped as he adjusted an aperture in the wall behind the arm. A pale green light shone from the device, bathing the arm and giving it a ghoulish appearance. Deblanc felt the effect of the beam, a sensation like he'd put his hand into a pool of warm water.

Without moving from his position, Brakus addressed Deblanc in a conversational tone, a tone Deblanc had never heard from the creature before. It made him feel uneasy.

"I wonder how long Sol will be keeping you around, now that Timothy Bruce has entered the Keep," he mused aloud.

Deblanc glared silently, his mounting anger beginning to blot out the pain Brakus had so recently inflicted on him through the replacement arm. The creature began chuckling again and Deblanc started to cross the room. He didn't know what he could possibly do to hurt Brakus, but he felt sure he could come up with something.

He never had the chance to find out.

A portal opened between him and the creature and two men stepped out.

The first man, he didn't know. He was a dark-skinned giant, standing at over seven feet tall, his loose-fitting black clothing doing nothing to hide the man's impressive build. The giant took one look at Deblanc, sneered and then looked around the room, dismissing him with the single glance. He then spotted Brakus and a cruel grin appeared on his face.

"Brakus!" the giant bellowed cheerfully as he set off in the creature's direction. As Deblanc watched, Brakus sped away from the advancing giant and disappeared behind the line of consoles. Deblanc grinned as he watched the Brachyuran flee. This was obviously Kendrick, one of Sol's colleagues from his Rigel War days. Deblanc had yet to meet Kendrick, or the bizarrely named Agent 23 come to that, but he was already thinking he would enjoy working with them. As Kendrick disappeared in Brakus's wake, Deblanc returned his attention to the second man who had come through.

The smile left his face in an instant.

"Hello, Deblanc," said Ted Kane. "Remember me? I'm the guy you punched in the face."

Chapter 15: Lindros Takes His Medicine

Robert 'Bob the Breaker' Mitchell led Jamie Holloway gently by the shoulder. Together, they passed Mitchell's driver, still standing to attention by the Escalade, and emerged from the warehouse's entrance. Keeping close to the building's wall they rounded the corner to find a quiet spot out of the wind and drizzle.

Jamie groaned quietly every time the foot at the end of his plaster covered leg touched the ground.

Mitchell lit one of his fat cigars and offered one to the boy. Jamie shook his head without taking his eyes from the ground. He was wrapped in the same hospital blanket he'd been wearing when his father had signed him out of the hospital and was shivering miserably. Mitchell was still wearing his thick winter coat and it suddenly dawned on him how cold the boy must have been. *Good,* he thought, *that'll make him talk quicker so he can get back into the warm.*

He held his cigar wallet in front of the boy and tried again.

"Want one for later, Jamie?" he asked.

Jamie shook his head as he continued to stare at the ground, but then his head slowly rose to meet Mitchell's eyes.

"There will be a 'later' then?" he asked quietly.

Mitchell was shocked by the question, but reacted quickly and kept his expression neutral.

"Did you have any hand in my son's death?" he asked bluntly.

"No!" the boy gasped.

Mitchell regarded him silently for a moment, staring into his eyes, looking for any hint of a lie, then nodded slowly.

"Then I have no quarrel with you," he said to the boy's obvious relief. "But I do need you to tell me everything you know about the man who did this to me."

Jamie nodded dumbly and looked at the ground once more.

"I will, sir," he said quietly. "He was my best friend."

The comment made Mitchell stop short. He wasn't aware of that. He didn't really know anything about his son's life over the last few years. Perhaps this was a chance to fill in some of the gaps. He motioned to a low wall, running along the side of one of the warehouse's fire exits.

"Sit down, Jamie," he said gently. "Take the weight off your leg." The boy sat down with a groan, his injured leg straight out in front of him. Mitchell sat down beside him. "Ah," he said suddenly, as if he'd just remembered something. He reached inside his coat and produced a packet of Marlboros.

"How about one of these?" he asked. The boy hesitated briefly before nodding. Mitchell took one out and lit it on the end of his cigar before handing it over. He remained silent for a few minutes, letting Jamie enjoy the cigarette while he gathered his own thoughts.

There was so much Mitchell wanted to know. Of course, he wanted to find the man who'd killed Peter and make him suffer, but in that moment, sitting next to this terrified kid, he felt a greater need to learn about his son. Lindros would have started work on his prisoner by now and for the time being Mitchell didn't even care who the prisoner was. He didn't have much faith in Lindros and his cronies but he knew they would be thorough. He'd promised them enough money to ensure that much.

"What was Peter like?" he asked, the question coming from nowhere. The pain and guilt he felt at even having to ask the question threatened to make his voice break, but the anger beneath kept his voice hard and strong. Jamie sat for a moment, staring into the distance as he thought. The teenager looked genuinely sad.

"We were very similar," he began, his voice gradually rising as he spoke, remembering happier times. "We liked the same music and films and everything. But I don't know why we were friends," he said, turning to look at Mitchell. As he did so his voice lost some of its volume. "I was always a bit of a wimp at school, the one getting picked on and bullied. But Peter looked out for me, scared the other bullies away."

Other bullies, Mitchell thought to himself. *So, Peter was considered a bully too*. It didn't surprise him, but he'd never really been sure. Mitchell had had to bail his son out of a few sticky situations in the past and each time he'd tried to beat some sense into him. There hadn't been any trouble for some time and he thought he'd finally learnt to either keep his nose clean or to be better at covering his tracks. It gave Mitchell a small feeling of pride that Peter had at least learned to keep some things secret from him.

"And we were both scared of our fathers," Jamie said quietly, wrenching Mitchell from his reverie. He'd had to be tough on Peter to prepare him for the real world, but did he really want him to be scared of his own father? Mitchell felt suddenly lonely, as if even the memory of who he thought his son was, was drifting further away from him.

Jamie fell silent and Mitchell realised he was worried that he'd said the wrong thing. But he needed to hear it all, to get to know about his son while he still could. He needed Jamie to feel comfortable talking to him.

"You're scared of your father?" he asked quietly, making his voice sound as friendly as he could. But, where Robert 'Bob the Breaker' Mitchell was concerned, there was always a very fine line between 'not angry' and 'scary creepy'. However, this time he seemed to have hit the right side of that line.

"You've seen him," Jamie said, "he doesn't care about me. He never has."

Mitchell nodded silently. He was less than impressed by the way Holloway had treated his son. The man was a parasite, a leach, always looking to latch onto someone for the free ride. Mitchell had met his type many times before and they were always the same - nothing was ever their fault and the world owed them a living. As long as they were happy, everything was right with the world.

"Pity," Mitchell said with a forced grin, "I was going to offer him a job…"

Jamie's head snapped round and he stared at Mitchell in surprise. His eyes widened until he noticed the big man's lip twitching slightly. The next second they were both laughing freely, all the tension between them suddenly gone.

"Did Peter ever talk about me?" Mitchell asked. Jamie stopped laughing and looked suddenly worried, making Mitchell wish he hadn't asked that particular question so soon into their conversation. But to the boy's credit he met his eye as he answered.

"Not really…" he began, "but we didn't talk much about our parents. He *did* tell me his mother moved to Canada..."

"Hmm, yes," Mitchell replied, not wanting to talk about the details of that particular saga. "How about *your* mother?" he asked, deflecting the conversation back at Jamie.

"She died," he answered quietly, a fresh sadness creeping into his voice. "When I was two or three, I think, but dad never told me how. He doesn't like to talk about it."

Mitchell wondered how a man, though he struggled to even *think* of Holloway as a man, could treat his own son so badly. How did this teenager live, not even knowing how his mother had died? In the short time he'd spent in Holloway's company it had become painfully clear how self-centred he was. Other people's opinions and feelings probably never so much as entered his head. Mitchell made a vow to himself to get the information for Jamie before they parted company.

"Sorry to hear that," was all he could think to say. The pair fell silent again and Mitchell found himself fighting to come up with something to say. He didn't know why, but he found himself caring about what happened to this teenager. He wanted to think of something to say to cheer him up, give him some hope for his future.

"Tell me, Jamie," he said, "What do you want to do with your life? Where would you like to be in ten years time?" He'd asked the question because it was the same question he'd asked himself every day when he'd been growing up. He'd taught himself to forget about the immediate future, the things he didn't want to do, and concentrate on where his deeds and actions would one day lead him.

Jamie thought about it for a while but Mitchell recognised his expression to be more one of surprise and confusion than contemplation. Clearly the notion had never occurred to him before. Mitchell remained silent, giving the boy all the time he needed. Finally, Jamie spoke.

"I don't know," he said. "Never really thought about it."

Mitchell waited, but that was all Jamie had to say. He made a mental note to come back to it later. Now was not the time – Lindros would be getting to work on his own questioning and he didn't want to be lagging behind.

"I need to know everything you can tell me about the man who killed my son," he said suddenly. He watched Jamie's expression change from thoughtful to worried to terrified. The boy looked down at the ground and for a split second Mitchell considered putting his hand on Jamie's shoulder to comfort him. He fought back the urge, focusing on the matter at hand.

"We'd just come out of the supermarket on St. Leonard's Road," Jamie began, his eyes tightly closed. "We were trying to buy some beer, but the…"

Mitchell suddenly held his hand out, signalling Jamie to stop talking. "Quiet," he snapped, "Did you hear something?"

Jamie *did* hear something, something he'd heard before. A strange, whispering sound. It was familiar, but where had he heard it before? Realisation appeared on the teen's face and he turned to Mitchell.

"I *did* hear something," he said, "…that night. I heard it that night as well!"

"The night Peter was killed?"

Jamie nodded. "Yeah," he said, "it was just after the guy in green attacked us. I thought I'd dreamt it. It wasn't like anything I'd ever heard before. And it came with a funny smell, like…"

"Like loose electricity… ozone…" Mitchell cut in.

"Yeah, that's it, like what you get with slot-car racing..." he suddenly turned to Mitchell. "How did you know?" he asked.

"Because I can smell it now," was the surprising reply. Jamie hadn't noticed the smell this time, but now he sniffed the air and there it was: Ozone.

"But where's it coming from," Mitchell murmured as he stood and looked around him.

****

Alfred Morrison listened with a sinking heart as the muffled voices from the office increased in volume. They were coming back. Nothing much was said as at least two people left the warehouse and two sets of footsteps headed in his direction.

Lindros and his crony.

"Well, well, well, my friend." It was Lindros. "Sorry we had to duck out for a few minutes, but we're back now and I promise that you have our full attention." There was a cruel and almost excitable tone in his voice. Morrison knew the type, he'd seen them wash out of interrogation training time and time again simply because they enjoyed it too much. They'd lose focus, forgetting it was information they were seeking and not perverse pleasure.

From that moment onwards, Morrison knew his only chance was to remain silent and not give Lindros the satisfaction. Perhaps he'd get bored, though that wouldn't make the day go any easier.

Morrison had made no progress with the plastic bindings. In fact, he'd been trying so hard that he could now feel one of them had worked its way under the skin of his left wrist. It hurt like hell but the pain was getting lost in the overall dull ache that was his entire body. His broken toes were of a far greater concern.

"So," Lindros continued, "who are you working for and what is your interest in the murder of Peter Mitchell."

Finally, some questions.

Morrison remained silent, so Lindros asked the questions again. But this time he punctuated each word with a punch to Morrison's stomach. It was the longest sentence he had ever had to listen to.

Morrison's training took over and a phrase swam to the top of his consciousness.

Name, rank and serial number.

He opened his mouth to give the information, hoping to buy himself some time, time to come up with something. But as he cleared his throat, preparing to speak the words, a ball of material was violently shoved into his mouth. Even before his gag reflex could respond to his tongue being forced backwards, a length of gaffer tape was wrapped around his face, sealing his mouth shut.

Lindros and his friend laughed uncontrollably as Morrison put all his efforts into fighting the urge to throw up.

Bastards. Useless, fucking bastards.

Just for the sake of screwing him around they'd seriously endangered his life. If he puked now he would drown on his own vomit. Dead before he even got the chance to answer any questions.

From now on he wouldn't even give them his name.

From now on he would concentrate solely on what he would do to the bastards if he ever managed to get free.

It was a forlorn hope, he knew, but it was as good a thing as any to keep his mind occupied, to forget about his imminent and painful demise.

Damn it Ted, where the hell are you?

The next thing Morrison heard sounded like a hiccup. From its direction he guessed it was Lindros. But next there was a muffled gurgle, a sound Morrison knew all too well. There was a dull thump, followed by the sound of someone shrieking in pain and surprise before hitting the ground.

The blindfold was pulled from his face and he winced at the sudden brightness of the light assaulting his eyes. Blinking and squinting, he finally began to make out shapes around him and there, inches in front of him was the blurry, grinning face of Ted Kane.

"I leave you alone for five minutes and look at the fucking state of you…" he was saying as he removed the tape gag. Before Morrison could reply, Kane moved behind him and he felt the cable ties being cut free. Kane muttered something about 'fucking amateurs' as he carefully freed Morrison's hands, gently removing the plastic straps from the deep gashes Morrison's struggling had opened up. In places the blood had begun to congeal, effectively gluing them to his flesh.

Morrison groaned as his friend slowly helped him to his feet. His instinct told him they should be running from the scene and laying down suppressive fire, but the calmness in Kane's voice and actions put the notion from his head. His friend was so calm and unhurried that he knew he was safe. He trusted Kane with his life.

Kane wrapped a long coat around his shoulders and he was suddenly reminded of how cold he felt. The pain throughout his body gnawed at him, steadily increasing as the adrenaline left his system. Kane tried to lead him towards the exit but he held up his hand to stop him. He turned around to see what had happened to his tormentors and was surprised to see they were both still alive. Two men stood over Lindros and his henchman.

He'd assumed Kane had arrived with some colleagues from either MI6 or the Regiment, but these two men were strangers to him. One man was pointing a sidearm at Lindros's crony, now slumped against the wall with his eyes closed and his head slumped against is chest. The man with the gun was of average build and held the pistol casually in his left hand. He nodded at Morrison. It was only the slightest movement of his head but it somehow relayed an earnest respect that Morrison found both flattering and confusing. He returned the nod before looking at Kane, his expression a silent question in itself.

"Ah, yes," said Kane, sounding strangely embarrassed. "Alfred Morrison, may I introduce you to our new friend and colleague…Deblanc."

Morrison's eyes widened as his head snapped round to look at the man again. He then looked down at the long coat Kane had wrapped around his shoulders. It was dark green. Deblanc raised his right arm in an attempted a wave but, apparently as much of a surprise to Deblanc as it was to Morrison, the arm ended just below the elbow. Deblanc stared at the stump briefly as though he'd forgotten that fact and lowered it again.

"It's an honour," he said, an embarrassed though honest greeting.

"And this," Kane continued as he gently turned Morrison to face his right, "is Mr Kendrick."

Morrison's eyes widened again as they found the other stranger. He'd briefly glimpsed Kendrick earlier, when his blindfold had been removed, and had just seen the blurred outline of a man. But now that his eyes had fully adjusted, he saw him properly. But the image before him was so surreal that Morrison wondered if he'd been drugged during his interrogation.

Kendrick was standing near the office wall, holding Lindros a full two feet from the ground by the throat. Lindros was desperately clawing at the giant's hand in an attempt to free himself while Kendrick just grinned and winked at Morrison. There wasn't the slightest hint of strain on his face.

"Hello, Alfred Morrison," he said, his voice impossibly deep. "A pleasure to meet you. I trust that you are well?"

"Are you kidding?" Kane burst out. "He looks like a sack of shit!"

"Cheers mate," Morrison muttered.

"Well, you do."

Kendrick laughed a deep, rumbling laugh and Lindros renewed his desperate attempts to free himself. Clearly Kendrick's amusement was making him inadvertently grip his throat all the harder. Lindros launched a desperate kick at Kendrick's stomach.

"I think he's going to be alright," Kendrick said, looking at Morrison and ignoring Lindros completely. He didn't seem to notice Lindros desperately kicking at him.

"I hope he's on our side," Morrison muttered to Kane.

"Well… it's more like *we're* on *his* side actually…" Kane replied.

Morrison chose to ignore his friend's cryptic response. He had quite enough to try to make sense of already. He looked at Deblanc again, trying to imagine what the hell Kane had been up to in the few hours since he'd last seen him.

"How did you find me?" he asked.

"Magic, mate. Magic," Kane grinned. "And you wouldn't want it spoiled by the magician explaining it all, would you…?"

****

"Are you sure?" Robert Mitchell whispered. "Are you *really* sure?"

Jamie Holloway leant against the wall next to Mitchell and grimaced as he stretched up on his plaster-cast leg to see through the small window. The smell of ozone had gone but after quickly looking around the area, Mitchell and Jamie had been drawn to the open window by unidentified voices from within.

"Yeah," Jamie said, with undeniable certainty, "that's the man who attacked us."

"And killed my son…"

"Yeah," he repeated, "the man with the gun and only one arm. But he definitely had two arms when he attacked us… and killed Peter."

Mitchell grunted and slid down the wall to sit on the ground. Jamie followed his lead and slowly lowered himself too. They sat there quietly, Mitchell deep in thought and Jamie in respectful silence. But Jamie had another reason to keep quiet. He was waiting for one of Mitchell's famously violent outbursts of anger.

But Mitchell just sat quietly, his face as grim and frightening as any Jamie had seen.

The man was planning furiously.

****

"There are others in the office," Morrison said.

"Already taken care of," Deblanc announced from across the room. Morrison grunted and looked at Deblanc, trying to decide whether to trust the man who'd been his quarry for so long.

"Two men," Kane said, all business again. "One civilian, currently filling his pants and cuffed to the radiator, and one combatant, injured and sedated. A third man was stationed by the vehicle outside. Also neutralised."

"I don't suppose you found my clothes in there?" Morrison asked, nodding towards the office.

"Yeah," Kane replied, embarrassed that he hadn't thought of it himself. Though he would never admit it, Morrison was pretty much being held up by Kane and Kendrick had his hands, well, *hand*, full with Lindros. So Kane turned to address Deblanc. "Would you mind?" he asked. To both Kane and Morrison's surprise, Deblanc nodded and, after a quick glance at the man unconscious at his feet, trotted towards the office.

"Here," Morrison said as Deblanc passed, "take this." He shrugged off the coat and handed it back. "Thanks," he added tightly. Deblanc nodded as he accepted his coat and continued on to the office.

"What the hell did those bastards do to you?"

Morrison took his eyes from Deblanc and looked at Kane to see what he was talking about. His friend was staring openly at his crotch.

"Oh, yeah," Morrison muttered as he gestured at Lindros, still struggling in Kendrick's grip. The big man didn't appear to be tiring at all. "That wanker bit me…"

Kendrick and Kane both stared at Lindros who had now stopped struggling and whose eyes were darting between the three men surrounding him.

"Charming," Kendrick's deep voice rumbled. "What do you want to do with him?" he asked Morrison.

"Well," he replied, returning his thoughts to matters of procedure. "First, I think we…"

He was cut short as three shots rang out, echoing through the warehouse and making everyone's ears ring. Kane heard someone cry out in pain as he instinctively pushed Morrison to the ground and covered him with his own body. Unfortunately, his quick actions, while shielding his friend from this new and unknown danger, also trapped the P90 between his body and that of his friend, rendering him defenceless. His head snapped up and he looked around, desperately trying to locate where the shots had come from.

Lindros's man, still slumped against the wall where Deblanc had left him was grinning, a smoking pistol in his hand. Before Kane could move, the man fired twice more, sending two more rounds into Kendrick's spine. Kane watched helplessly as the man grinned and pointed the gun at him, so straight that Kane could see straight down the barrel.

"Nighty night," the man said.

Chapter 16: Aftermath

Dead Bang.

That's what they called it when you have a shot lined up that you can't possibly miss. And that was what Ted Kane was looking at right now. The face of his killer was just visible behind the Glock 34 semi-automatic, grinning widely. He'd already shot Kendrick five times in the back, leaving up to twelve rounds in the pistol's 9mm magazine. But he'd only need one.

Kane's mind raced, desperately trying to come up with some plan of attack, some way to survive the next few seconds. He would worry about the seconds after that if he was still alive.

Nothing came to mind. He was prone and in no position to make any sudden moves. He considered rolling to the side, but knew it would take a few seconds to roll clear.

Far more time than it took to squeeze a trigger.

Perhaps he could launch himself at the gunman? He would certainly be killed, but if he was lucky maybe he could gain Morrison a few valuable seconds…

But in the next instant the situation changed radically and so suddenly that Kane couldn't fathom what was happening.

The gunman disappeared in a tangle of arms and legs and practically *flew* to the side. The spectacle reminded Kane of a cartoon, where fighting characters turned into a ball of smoke with limbs sticking out at random intervals. Whatever was happening, it gave Kane a moment of respite that he fully intended to use. Rolling off Morrison's prone form, Kane grabbed at the P90, still attached to the front of his webbing and found its grip. He continued his roll and came up smoothly on one knee, the weapon pointed straight at the bizarre tangle of human forms on the ground in front of him.

He could make out the gunman and one other person in the tangle and his first thought was that Deblanc had returned from the office and jumped the gunman. Kane's finger froze over the trigger as he desperately tried to identify a target in the untidy heap before him.

Less than three seconds had passed since Kane had been lying on top of Morrison and his mind had yet to understand anything that had happened in that time. He was acting purely on instinct.

He took careful aim at the tangle of arms and legs, desperately looking for a part he recognised as belonging to the gunman, but suddenly his aim was lost as a dark shape passed in front of him. A feral roar filled the air and Kane held position, his mind racing.

The shape crossed the floor and lunged at the pile of bodies, lifting one of them clear of the ground and discarding it to one side. It was only when it lunged again, this time lifting the gunman from the ground, that Kane realised it was Kendrick. The giant lifted the gunman by the throat and held his hapless victim close so he could glare into his eyes.

"You *dare* shoot at me?" he bellowed, shaking the gunman vigorously. He slammed his victim into the wall, smashing his skull with a dull thump. He released the corpse and watched it fall to the ground, a trail of crimson gore painting a broad line down the wall.

Kane hadn't moved from his kneeling position, the P90 steady in his grip. He lowered it, suddenly feeling uncomfortable pointing it in the giant's direction. He stared at Kendrick's back and saw no evidence of where he'd seen the bullets definitely strike him. There wasn't so much as a mark on the black material.

Movement to his right suddenly caught his attention. It was Lindros, now sitting on the ground and pushing himself backwards with his feet, desperately trying to escape. A gun was in his hand. Kane brought his weapon around and prepared to take Lindros down, but his aim was blocked once again by Kendrick, now advancing on Lindros.

"Get back…!" Lindros was screaming, raising his weapon in his shaking hands. Kendrick continued to advance and Kane winced as Lindros emptied the entire magazine into Kendrick's chest.

Kendrick ignored the shots and swatted the gun from Lindros's grip before grabbing his throat and wrenching him from the ground. Lindros struggled even more furiously than before and this time aimed his kicks at Kendrick's crotch. He was hysterical, screaming and pleading in equal measures.

Kendrick looked down at where he was being kicked and then into Lindros's eyes. A cruel smile appeared on his face as he reached down with his free hand and grabbed Lindros by the crotch. Lindros screamed louder than Kane had ever heard a man scream before as Kendrick hefted him into a horizontal position, one hand gripping his throat and the other his crotch. Casting his gaze about the warehouse, Kendrick spotted something and his grin turned feral. He walked across the warehouse and hefted Lindros up above his head, preparing to throw him.

"No!" Kane shouted, "We need him to…"

Kendrick grunted as he threw Lindros across the warehouse. Kane's mouth was still open, mid sentence, as he watched Lindros flying through the air.

But he didn't travel far.

After half a dozen metres, Lindros struck a pillar with the middle of his back. He hit it with such force that his ankles struck the back of his head. He was dead before his body hit the ground.

"…answer some questions," Kane finished uselessly as he got back to his feet. He reached down and helped Morrison up. "You okay?" he asked his still-naked friend.

"Yeah," Morrison replied quietly, staring at Kendrick. "I'm *really* glad he's on our side," he muttered.

"Damn!" Kendrick was saying, loudly as usual, as he shook his arms after his brief workout. "I really need to get out more! That was fun!"

Kane and Morrison stared at him, or more accurately, at the front of his shirt. Kendrick followed their gaze.

"Oh, yes," he said, pinching at the material where Lindros had emptied his gun into him. "Inertia fabric. Absorbs most blunt force. No use against energy weapons though…" he added as though embarrassed by the fact. "Bullet's still hurt like hell," he continued as he glanced at Lindros's broken body wrapped backwards around the bottom of the pillar. "Hence my…ah… angry little workout there…"

"Better not let Sol find out..."

Kendrick, Kane and Morrison turned in unison to look at Deblanc, standing in the office doorway. He stepped over to the group and handed Morrison his clothes. "Sol doesn't like what he calls 'excessive violence,'" he explained. "He gets pretty upset about it actually."

"Sol?" Morrison enquired as he accepted the pile of clothes.

"Long story," said Kane. "You'll see." He then turned to Kendrick. "We'd better get back if we're going to make that meeting…"

"Hang on!" Morrison cut him off. "I'm not going anywhere until someone tells me what the hell is going on." He pointed at Deblanc. "Not that very long ago we were hunting this man for a series of brutal murders and now we're best friends?"

"Ah," said Kendrick, looking at Deblanc with a knowing grin on his face, "So *that's* why Sol doesn't trust you. He always did lean a little to the left..."

"Again," Morrison interrupted loudly. "Who's Sol?"

"Well, I *did* think he was in charge of these people," Kane replied, his voice uncertain. "But their chain of command appears to be pretty... well, it's fucked up." He looked at Kendrick, his eyebrows raised. The big man picked up on his silent question.

"I suppose *I'm* in command," he said modestly. "I'm certainly the most qualified. But I've been...away... for a while and Sol's been taking care of things." He looked at Morrison, who by now had almost finished getting dressed, though he was struggling to put his trousers on with his broken foot. Kane gave him a shoulder to lean on. "To be honest," Kendrick continued, "I need to catch up on a few things myself." He cast a significant glance at Deblanc. "I've no idea how many strong our group is now. Sol tends to keep things close to his chest."

Morrison turned to Kane, who gave him a tight nod of acknowledgement. If Kane was okay with this, then Morrison was satisfied. There was still a hell of a lot of things he didn't understand, but hopefully they would become clear soon enough.

"Right," Morrison said, not even attempting to put his shoes or socks on. His mind was made up. "Let's get back to wherever it is you came from so you can explain to me what the hell is going on."

Kendrick, apparently satisfied with the plan, finally started to act like a leader.

"Okay," he said. "Kane and Morrison come with me. Deblanc, you hang back and clear this place of evidence. You should know the drill."

Deblanc stiffened.

"Kane doesn't have a Portal device yet," Kendrick explained, nodding at the new watch on Deblanc's left wrist, "and you have a lot more experience in this... er, country than I do. Plus, I'll need to be there to explain our little side trip to Sol in person. Follow us as soon as you can."

Deblanc nodded, though obviously unhappy with Kendrick's orders. Morrison glared at Kane, who shrugged with embarrassment. For a man supposedly in charge, Kendrick wasn't impressing. And what he did next wasn't a welcome surprise either.

Stepping swiftly up to Morrison, Kendrick spun him around so that his back was pressed up against Kendrick's muscular stomach before Morrison could react. A thick forearm wrapped around his throat and began to tighten. Morrison tried his best to fight his way free, but it was hopeless. Kendrick was incredibly strong.

The last thing Morrison saw before losing consciousness was Kane, standing before him and not lifting a finger to help.

"Was that really necessary?" Kane asked as he stared at his unconscious friend.

"Did you want him entering his first Portal without any training?" Kendrick replied flatly as he manoeuvred Morrison into his arms.

"I was alright..."

Kendrick stood there, his sleeping charge safely gathered in his arms, and regarded Kane with an approving grin.

"Yes, you were," he said, "and it was your idea to activate your friend's communication device to listen in on him." Kendrick looked down at Morrison, reminding Kane of a man gazing at a child sleeping in his arms. God, he was big. "He chooses his friends well."

Kane was taken aback by the big man's compliment. Morrison *was* a good friend, but they'd been thrust together in military service. There had been no question of choice in their friendship.

"We'd better get back before he wakes up," Kane said uncomfortably.

"Yes, and I for one am very much looking forward to hearing Sol's briefing." Kendrick turned to Kane as he fumbled with something in his pocket. "And see how many more strangers he's got hiding about the place ..."

Though Kendrick's tone was emotionless, Kane detected something in the big man's eyes that signalled a new sense of kinship with his fellow soldier. He decided to test their newfound understanding by asking a question he was dying to learn the answer to.

"Why did you name him Sol?" he asked.

Kendrick stared at Kane as though appraising him. He nodded, his mind apparently made up.

"Agent 37, as he was then known, chose this solar system as our new home," he explained. "I named him Sol after your sun and he was suitably flattered." He chuckled to himself. "I told him it was because he was at the 'very centre of our new home' and he accepted the name with his usual humility." Kendrick stopped chuckling and turned to Kane with an expression of mock severity. "And if you tell him I told you this I'll twist your head off… Well, much later he heard me explaining the real reason for the name to 23…" He let his voice trail off, tormenting Kane.

"And…?"

"You know we come from the Rigel system, right?"

"Yes..."

"Well, Rigel is some forty thousand times brighter than Sol. I called him Sol because I didn't think he was very bright. A bit dim to be honest…"

Kendrick roared with laughter as he resumed the fumbling in his pocket. Kane laughed too, though not as raucously, feeling a pang of concern that perhaps Sol wasn't the genius leader he thought he was.

Kendrick hefted Morrison's slumbering form so that he could grasp his hand and offered his other one to Kane. As soon as Kane grasped it, Kendrick announced, "three… two… one…"

A second later, the three men disappeared.

****

Deblanc watched the three men disappear and found himself alone in the warehouse. Well, alone with two dead bodies and three others unconscious.

He didn't like the process of cleaning up after a job but knew it was a necessary evil. At least this one would be quick, contained within a single building as it was. All he had to do was check for surveillance cameras and destroy any hard drives connected to them. It would be a job of minutes.

He stepped into the office and checked that the two men within were still unconscious before turning his attention to the single computer on the desk.

It was as he was removing the back of the computer's base unit that he heard a footstep behind him. He instantly tensed, wondering if Kendrick had returned, but before he even finished the thought something hard struck him across the back of the head and the world went black.

****

Robert Mitchell looked down at the crumpled form at his feet, satisfied with his work. The pistol in his hand, the one he'd retrieved from the ground in the warehouse, had made a satisfying crack as it struck the back of the bastard's head. He dropped it onto a chair and returned to the office doorway.

His head was spinning. Not from the adrenaline produced by striking Deblanc, subduing his son's killer, but from what he had heard. Deblanc and his colleagues were clearly not what they had at first appeared to be. There was something big going on, something he didn't yet understand.

He had told Jamie to stay outside when he'd crept into the warehouse, something the boy was more than happy to do. He wasn't so much concerned for Jamie's safety as unwilling to be hampered by his noisy limping. Now he was glad he had done so. Knowledge was power and he didn't share power with anyone.

"It's alright Jamie," he called out, "you can come in now." He peered into the warehouse to see the boy hobbling in his direction. Satisfied, he returned to the unconscious form of the man who had caused him so much pain.

"Mr Deblanc, I believe," he muttered.

He stood there, staring at Deblanc and trying to feel some measure of victory, some hint of satisfaction at having his enemy lying helplessly at his feet. But he felt nothing. The brief search for his son's killer had taken control of his life and now that it was over he felt strangely deflated, disappointed even.

Before he'd found out about Peter's murder, Robert Mitchell had been feeling the same way about his life in general. He'd accomplished almost everything he'd set out to do and was looking for fresh challenges. Hunting Deblanc had been such a challenge, but now that was completed too.

"Oh boy," he said aloud as he stared down at Deblanc. "Am I going to make you suffer for what you've done to me."

Jamie entered the office.

"Is this him?" Mitchell asked as he turned Deblanc's face upwards with his toe. "Are you sure this is him?"

Jamie hobbled closer and looked at Deblanc's face.

"Yeah," he said. "Definitely."

Mitchell grunted acknowledgement then pointed across the room.

"Want to check on your father?" he asked. Jamie frowned but limped across the room anyway.

Higgins, the man with the injured leg, was still stretched out on the couch. He scared Jamie, though he still found himself glancing at him before his father. He was relieved that his father was unconscious as he approached quietly, fearful of waking him.

"How is he?" Mitchell called from across the room.

"He looks alright," Jamie replied upon seeing his father's chest rising and falling steadily.

"Good."

Mitchell busied himself with binding Deblanc's ankles with a roll of duct tape. "Go to the front of the warehouse and close the shutters. I don't want any interruptions." Jamie nodded and gratefully limped away from his slumbering father.

Satisfied that Deblanc's ankles were secured, Mitchell addressed the problem of securing a man with only one hand. He did this by sitting Deblanc upright and leaning him forward enough to tape his left wrist to his left thigh. Mitchell used plenty of tape, wary of what he'd done to his son and two friends.

By the time he'd finished, Jamie had returned and was standing behind him.

"Take a seat Jamie," he said, a little sharper than he'd meant to. "Take the weight off your leg." Jamie did so without hesitation, making Mitchell feel guilty. The kid had been through a lot. Perhaps he shouldn't be so bossy with him. It was a strange thing for him to think. He'd never felt guilty about the way he'd spoken to Peter, and now it was too late.

Mitchell checked Deblanc's bindings one last time then pulled an office chair over so he could sit facing Jamie. He leant forward, his elbows on his knees, his fingers interlocked loosely.

"Quite a day," he said, his voice light and conversational. Jamie nodded silently. He looked terrified again, as though expecting Mitchell to announce his usefulness had come to an end.

"I want to thank you for your help," he said, to Jamie's obvious surprise. "I couldn't have identified this Deblanc character without you." Mitchell sat up straight and regarded Jamie as if appraising him.

"How would you like to work for me?" he asked, not quite sure what reaction he'd get. Jamie looked shocked.

"What would I have to do?" he asked nervously.

"Nothing you'd need worry about," Mitchell assured him. "I have several legitimate businesses. You could train to run my restaurant or manage the apartments, anything you like. I'd pay you very well and perhaps you could tell me about Peter."

Jamie thought about the offer and during the silence that followed Mitchell was surprised to find himself feeling uncomfortable. His comment about Peter had slipped out unbidden and he needed say something else to break the silence.

"And any job you accepted would come with an apartment," he said, perhaps a little too quickly.

"I'd like that," Jamie said, casting a quick glance at his father. "Very Much."

Mitchell grinned and held out his hand. Jamie reached out to shake it, but as he did so he saw a sudden blur of movement behind Mitchell.

It was Deblanc.

Somehow, despite having his ankles taped together and his one remaining wrist taped to his leg, Deblanc had somehow bounced himself across the floor towards Mitchell. Even as Jamie tried to shout a warning, he watched helplessly as Deblanc leant back and lashed out with his bound feet, catching Mitchell on the back of his head.

Mitchell grunted with surprise, his eyes rolling up inside his head as he fell.

"No!" Jamie cried as he leapt forward, grabbing at Deblanc, momentarily forgetting the pain of his own damaged leg. He landed on Deblanc hard, his hands clawing for his throat. All the fear he had of Deblanc had disappeared. He felt only anger now.

He clawed at Deblanc's face, desperate to hurt him by any means possible. But even bound and missing an arm as he was, Deblanc wasn't about to give up and take a beating. He rolled to the side with such energy that Jamie fell off him and onto the ground. Deblanc continued his roll and came up on top of Jamie where he delivered a quick head-butt before the desperate teenager had time to react. Without pausing, Deblanc rolled onto the ground and sat himself up. A quick glance at Jamie satisfied him that he was no longer a threat. The teen's face was screwed up as he held onto his bleeding nose. Obviously the boy wasn't used to fighting.

Mitchell groaned and started to get up, so Deblanc shuffled forward and kicked out, once again catching him on the back of his head. Satisfied that both of his adversaries were subdued for the time being, Deblanc bent as far forward as he could and used his teeth to attack the tape securing his wrist to his thigh. It was a stretch but he managed to strip enough of the tape away to pull his hand free. After that it was a simple task to free his ankles.

This clean-up job was quickly becoming complicated.

Satisfied that the teenager was no longer a threat, *never was a threat* he corrected himself, Deblanc picked up a chair and placed it over Mitchell's chest. He then toed the prone man's arms out to his sides and, sitting on the chair, placed his feet on Mitchell's wrists, holding him firmly in place.

Mitchell grunted as the weight from the chair's struts pressed onto his chest and stomach, both pinning him to the ground and making breathing difficult. He looked out to his arms and the booted feet holding his wrists in place. He was immobile and helpless as if Deblanc had crucified him on the ground.

A hand lashed out and slapped him, drawing his attention upwards and into the face of the man he hated more than anyone else in the world. Deblanc was leaning on the back of the chair, grinning down at him.

"Well, well, well," he said. "And who might you be?"

Mitchell glared back as he continued to struggle to free himself. How the hell was Deblanc keeping up such pressure on his hands? Deblanc appeared to divine his question.

"There's no use struggling," he said smugly. "I'm on a couple of pressure points here. There's no way you're wriggling free." He leant forward, bringing his face closer to Mitchell's and increasing the pressure of the chair on his chest. "Again," he said, "who are you?"

"I'm the man who's going to kill you," Mitchell grunted through clenched teeth. "Very, very slowly…" He put all the venom he could muster into his voice, trying to make the threat as intimidating as possible. All his years of both subtly and unsubtly intimidating people had led him to this moment. He watched Deblanc for a response, for any sign of fear in his eyes, the slightest twitch. There was nothing, Deblanc just stared back blankly.

"Well," Deblanc said. The bastard was actually grinning. "What nasty piece of shit did I do to piss you off then?" He put more weight on the chair back again, prompting Mitchell for a reply.

"You killed my son!" Mitchell shouted. He could feel his eyes getting hot as he fought back the tears he could now feel pooling in the corners.

Deblanc glanced at Jamie, still lying on the ground, holding his nose and moaning quietly. Deblanc reached over and grabbed the boy's hair, pulling his face round so he could stare at him.

"I *thought* I'd seen you somewhere before," he muttered. He looked down at Jamie's plaster cast and grinned. "Yeah, I remember you and your two friends…" He looked Jamie in the eye a moment longer then slammed his head against the side of a desk and let him fall to the ground, still conscious but stunned.

"So," he said as he returned his attention to Mitchell. "You must be *really* angry with me." His voice was mocking, infuriatingly so, but just to be sure he reached forward and slapped Mitchell across the face. "Yeah… *really* angry."

Mitchell fumed as he desperately fought to free himself. He failed and was rewarded for his efforts by another slap across the face.

"You *do* realise that your son was scum, don't you?" Deblanc asked mockingly and slapped Mitchell again. "You really should be thanking me for putting him out of your misery." Another slap. "And it doesn't say much for you as a parent does it?" Slap. "You look quite well-off..." Slap. "But you can't even raise one boy properly." Slap. "And he *was* a boy." Slap. "Not a man." Slap. "And he cried and snivelled and pleaded for his life." Slap. "And I really enjoyed killing the worthless little shit." Slap. Slap. Slap.

Deblanc leant back and spent a moment watching Mitchell's furious struggling.

"I bet you can't guess what's going to happen next, can you?" he asked as he reached back and picked up the gun Mitchell had discarded earlier. Mitchell glanced at the gun with narrowed eyes as he continued his fruitless struggling. Deblanc slapped him again, much harder this time. All trace of amusement had suddenly disappeared, as though someone had flipped a switch.

"Hey!" he shouted into Mitchell's face. "Pay attention! This concerns you!"

Mitchell stopped struggling and stared at Deblanc, murder in his eyes. He watched as Deblanc removed the magazine from the pistol and threw it across the room. He then slowly slid the top slide back to check there was a bullet in the chamber. This done, he cocked the hammer and held the weapon in front of Mitchell's red face.

"One bullet," he said, his voice lower and sounding all the more sinister for it. "One bullet with which I'm giving you the chance to avenge your scumbag of a son."

Mitchell glared back, stunned and waiting for the cruel twist to come. He had no doubt it was *he* who would be receiving the bullet.

Deblanc leant forward and pressed the gun's muzzle against his own temple.

"Would you like that?" Deblanc mocked him, tapping the gun against the side of his head. "Eh? Mr. Scumbag?"

Deblanc turned the gun on Mitchell, who waited for the world-ending boom he knew would follow.

He didn't have to wait for long.

Boom.

And everything went black.

Chapter 17: Rolling a Hard Six

So that's it then? You're just going to give up and die?

The thought appeared in Mitchell's mind as though spoken by another version of himself. He was held helpless, watching Deblanc killing *him*, just as he had his son. It was a long time since Mitchell had given up on anything and this was the big one, the end of his life.

He heard the gun going off and almost immediately felt a crushing pain in his chest.

That's not right; he shot you in the head didn't he?

The voice was right, but the weight on his chest and sudden darkness couldn't be argued with. He then heard another voice, this time coming from far *outside* his head.

"Fucking die!"

It was Higgins, one of Lindros's men. The one with the leg injury.

The weight on his chest began to lessen and Mitchell considered the possibility that he might not be dead after all.

"He's fucking getting up!"

Higgins again. And he was wrong; Mitchell hadn't so much as moved a muscle. He was waiting for the weight on his chest to lessen enough that he could breath properly. Yes, he was most definitely not dead.

Another shot rang out, and then another. With the third shot in a row the weight on his chest shifted suddenly and somewhere off in the distance he heard a hollow thud followed by someone gasping in pain. Jamie yelled something unintelligible and the weight on his chest disappeared completely.

Another shot rang out. But only one this time, followed closely by a grunt and the sound of breaking bone.

Mitchell took a deep breath. He had no idea what was going on, but at least he was still alive.

The danger hasn't gone, you know… Inertia fabric.

His eyes opened and looked into the face of Deblanc, now standing and glaring down at him. His mocking demeanour had been replaced by one of undisguised fury. But at least the bastard wasn't grinning anymore.

Mitchell glanced over to where Higgins lay, realising that was where the other shots must have come from and hoping that more would follow. But the fruits of Deblanc's last action were clear to see. Slouched against the back of the couch was Higgins, his face a bloody mess. The gun was still in his hand, but was now held loosely in his lap. And there, next to the weapon, was another pistol; the one Deblanc had been holding mere seconds before. It took little more than this quick glance to make it obvious to Mitchell what had happened: For some reason, Deblanc had thrown the weapon at Higgins rather than fire it. But it had obviously struck the gunman with enough force to break Higgins' nose and send the cartilage into his brain.

Mitchell returned his attention to Deblanc, standing silently over him, his face grim. He knew Deblanc was very fast and brutal in his fighting style, while he himself hadn't been in a fight for decades. And it now appeared that he was dangerously creative; why else would he throw a perfectly good gun at someone?

The odds didn't look good, but Mitchell was never one to play the odds. Especially when he was desperate.

"Don't do it Jamie!" he called out suddenly. Deblanc, still slightly stunned by Higgins' shots to his back, snapped his head round and narrowed his eyes at the teenager.

Jamie stared back, wide eyed and confused. Deblanc picked up on Mitchell's trick in a fraction of a second, but by the time he'd turned his head back, his view was filled with the very chair on which he was sitting not ten seconds ago.

The back of the chair struck Deblanc squarely in the face, not hard enough to cause serious harm, but hard enough to throw him off balance. He fell onto his backside, hard, but retaining enough of his senses to turn his momentum into a backwards roll, taking him behind the desk. Mitchell was already moving, reaching for the gun in Higgins's limp hand.

Gun retrieved, Mitchell fired a quick shot in the rough direction of the desk. He wasn't surprised that he'd missed; the shot was purely intended to check the gun was working, was still loaded. All of Mitchell's weapons knowledge came from what he'd seen in movies. They were something he'd deliberately shied away from, distancing himself from the tools of the less savoury side of his life.

He'd never fired a real gun in his life and the buck of the weapon and sheer volume of the shot had surprised him. But now he knew it was working and he set off to outflank the apparently unarmed Deblanc and take a more considered shot.

Inertia fabric.

The words echoed through Mitchell's head as they often did when he was forced to make quick decisions. It was an instinct that had served him well in many business situations over the years. A part of his mind always remained focused on the important issues, whatever the distraction.

He knew from what he'd heard earlier that these people, or some of them at least, were outfitted with bullet-proof clothing. He'd have to aim for Deblanc's head, a much harder shot and his target certainly wasn't going to sit still while he took aim.

The desk suddenly left the floor and flew straight at him. Mitchell dived in the only direction available to him and landed hard on top of Higgins' dead body. Somewhere he heard a cry of fear and pain as Jamie scrambled to get out of the line of fire. He considered telling the boy to get out of there but instead kept his entire attention on Deblanc. Killing him was all that mattered.

Much to his surprise, Mitchell found there was another reason he'd decided not to shout a warning to Jamie. It occurred to him that if he showed any form of concern for the boy, Deblanc might well use him as a hostage or even kill him out of spite. It's what Mitchell would do in his position.

The desk caught Mitchell a glancing blow to the side of his leg, though not enough to bother him, while the computer fell to the ground with a disappointing thump. Deblanc was already on the move and dashing for the office doorway. Mitchell landed hard on his chest but automatically raised the pistol and fired off three shots. The first went wide and the other two even more so as the gun bucked wildly in his hand.

"Shit!"

Mitchell's curse was partly due to his utter lack of marksmanship and partly the realisation that Deblanc was now in the warehouse where he could find any number of discarded weapons among the dead bodies there. He climbed off Higgins and picked up the magazine Deblanc had dropped earlier. The two guns looked about the same and hopefully the magazine would fit the gun he now carried. He didn't dare remove the gun's clip to check in case he did something wrong and it wouldn't fire again. He'd seen people reload guns a thousand times on television and in films – remove the empty mag, put in the new one and pull the top slide back – it looked easy enough but it wasn't worth the risk until he was forced to do so. And he didn't kid himself that the fight would last that long once Deblanc found a gun of his own.

"Keep your head down Jamie," he whispered as he moved towards the door.

Deblanc was nowhere in sight.

The warehouse looked suddenly huge, with thousands of places for someone to hide and the gun felt impossibly heavy in his hand, forcing him to adopt a two-handed grip. But at least it stopped it from shaking quite so much.

Taking a deep breath, Mitchell stepped through the doorway and into the warehouse.

****

Alfred Morrison's eyes snapped open and he was sitting up before he was properly awake. His head was spinning and he had no idea where he was but his mind was screaming a single word at him, denying him the luxury of waking in his own time.

Danger.

Harsh white light assaulted his eyes but he forced them open anyway, blinking away the tears.

"Alright, alright, settle down Al," a familiar voice muttered from somewhere behind him. "You're showing me up."

"What the fuck's going on, Ted?" Morrison was surprised by the bitterness in his own voice, increased by its raspy nature. His throat felt impossibly dry.

Rubbing life into his eyes, Morrison concentrated on the rest of his body, checking for injuries. Everything felt fine with the exception of his sore eyes and throat. He blinked and squinted until he could open his eyes properly.

Strangely, his broken foot felt fine and he was surprised to discover that he could wiggle his toes without feeling any pain whatsoever.

He turned his head in the direction of Kane's voice, his mind racing to put all his questions in order of priority. But as his eyes adjusted all his questions evaporated, leaving his mind a stunned blank. The room he was in was huge and impossibly white. Everything was spotless: the chairs, the strange consoles with their large, floating screens and the bizarrely floating… mechanical things milling about in the air above their heads. The ceiling looked impossibly high.

Kane was there, standing stiffly with his arms folded. At least the bastard had the decency to look embarrassed. But more interesting was the collection of people standing around Kane.

That big bastard Kendrick was there, dominating the space with his sheer size. He stood to Kane's left and slightly behind him, highlighting their newfound allegiance. The giant, there was really no other word for him, also had his arms folded but his expression wasn't one of embarrassment, more like amusement. Morrison glared at Kendrick, but the giant's expression didn't change in the slightest. He obviously wasn't bothered by what Morrison thought of him.

Standing to Kane's right was a woman. Despite being of pretty much normal proportions, though maybe slightly larger than most women, she was no less impressive. She wore an outfit similar to the giant's, though pale grey in colour and of a much sleeker cut. She was obviously in great shape and very athletic. Her shoulders were slightly broader than they could have been, an attribute highlighted by her stiff hands-behind-her-back pose. Her expression was one of polite boredom, making Morrison feel strangely disappointed. He was a happily married man but he still liked it when women showed him some sort of interest.

On the woman's right was an entirely normal, ordinary looking man, probably in his early thirties. He stood slightly behind the woman as though attempting to hide from Morrison's gaze. He seemed terrified and only looked up from the floor for brief moments.

"Welcome to the Keep, Mr Morrison," a voice said from somewhere behind him. He turned to see an elderly man dressed in the same outfit as the woman. A uniform, perhaps. His demeanour was kindly enough but his voice the slightest hint of anger.

"I *was* due to hold a meeting," he said, "explaining our presence here to Mr Kane. But he and Kendrick," he pointed at the giant, "disappeared on a private errand of their own." He looked at Kane and Kendrick as though about to lecture them, his voice carried that sort of tone, but instead sighed in acceptance. Morrison guessed the older man must be the mysterious Sol and in charge of whatever this place was. But the way the other people had arranged themselves suggested they were united in bringing him here even if their boss wasn't.

Kane had mentioned that their chain of command was less than solid and after just a few seconds in their presence, Morrison had to agree. He glanced quickly at Kane as he stood to face the old man. He and Kane would be having words soon enough, but for now he trusted his friend to watch his back.

"And who might you be?" he demanded. He was pretty sure who he was already of course, but took the opportunity to take the initiative, to be the one asking the questions. It was an old tactic, but that didn't mean it wasn't a good one. The old man didn't smile or frown; there was no readable expression on his face at all.

"My name is Sol," he said simply.

"And where am I? What is this place?"

"This is the Keep."

Morrison ignored the answer and held Sol's gaze, waiting for some *useful* information. Sol sighed again and turned to Kane and Kendrick.

"Mr Kane," he said flatly. "Would you be kind enough to bring Mr Morrison up to date? Tell him everything you already know about the Keep and our mission here. I'm going to see what's taking Deblanc so long." And without another word he turned and walked away.

Kane grinned sheepishly as he stepped forward.

"Al," he began, his voice filled with apology. "I know you're probably pretty pissed at me right now…"

He didn't finish the sentence. Morrison turned on him and planted his fist straight into his friend's jaw. Kane fell to the ground with all the dignity of a dropped rubbish sack.

"What the fuck was that for?" Kane shouted as he rubbed his jaw.

"*That* was because I don't want to hit *him*!" Morrison shouted, stabbing a finger in Kendrick's direction. "Now, will someone *please* tell me where the fuck I am and what the fuck is going on?"

****

Mitchell stopped dead in the office doorway.

What the hell was he thinking?

Deblanc could be sitting out there with a gun trained on the opening, just waiting for him to do something this stupid. He returned to the office and switched off the lights. The blinds had already been drawn and he didn't want to present Deblanc with a nice silhouette to shoot at.

His mind raced. He desperately wanted to get a hold of Deblanc and make him pay, but he'd rather not get himself shot in the process. He looked around the office, now in semi darkness, desperately searching for anything that would give him an edge.

"What's happening?" Jamie whispered. "Has he gone?"

"I hope not," Mitchell muttered through clenched teeth. "That bastard's not getting away from me." Mitchell moved over to

Higgins' body and began searching it for any other weapons. "I don't suppose you know anything about guns do you?" he asked.

"A bit," came the teen's surprising reply.

Mitchell's head snapped round and he stared at Jamie. The boy looked uncomfortable, as if about to make a confession. Mitchell stared at him silently. It was the best interrogation technique he knew.

"Peter borrowed a gun once and we went into the countryside to shoot at beer cans."

"Anything like this one?" Mitchell asked, holding out his weapon. Now wasn't the time to worry about his son's secret past. Jamie scrutinised it for a few seconds before replying.

"Almost," he said. "That's a Smith and Wesson 9mm, we were using a Browning. Works the same though."

Mitchell stared at Jamie, shocked and wondering what else he was going to learn about his son. He reached into his pocket and withdrew the extra clip he'd picked up earlier and held it out.

"Will this magazine fit this gun?" he asked. Jamie accepted the clip and examined it briefly.

"No," he said, "This comes from a different gun, but the bullets are the same calibre. I could top up the clip in your gun if you like?"

Mitchell silently handed the firearm to Jamie and watched as the teen ejected the clip and fed it with bullets from the other one. Once done, he slotted it back into the gun, cocked the hammer and handed the weapon back.

"Don't you have to slide the top back?" Mitchell asked quietly. Jamie shook his head.

"No need," he said, "There's already one in the spout. If you slide the top back now you'll just eject it. This way, you get an extra one. There's fifteen in there now."

Mitchell looked from Jamie, to the gun, and then back to Jamie again. He felt suddenly behind the times.

"You any good with a gun?" he asked. Jamie looked terrified all over again. His face drained of all colour and he slowly slid himself backwards on the floor. Mitchell dismissed the idea. This wasn't the kid's problem and he had no right to endanger him. "Don't worry about it," he said as he returned to searching Higgins' body.

But Jamie stood up suddenly and walked to the other end of the couch. He pulled up one of Higgins' trouser legs to reveal an ankle holster containing a backup pistol.

"Just like Miami Vice," he muttered. Mitchell reached past him to take the weapon and compared it to the one he was holding. He slid the top slide back before tucking the weapon in the back of his waistband.

"Just in case," he said quietly as he stood up. He had something else in his hand, something he'd found in one of Higgins' pockets.

"As soon as you hear shooting," he said as he approached the office door, "get the hell out of here." His tone left no room for argument. He noticed Jamie cast a quick glance at his father, still slumped by the radiator. It was a quick glance and the first time the boy had looked at his father for some time. Jamie nodded once.

As he approached the door, Mitchell stowed the object he'd found in his coat pocket. This next step would take an uncharacteristic act of bravery. Sticking the gun into the waistband of his trousers, he stepped out of the office and into the most open area of the warehouse, the large open space where Morrison's interrogation had taken place. He saw no sign of Deblanc.

"Deblanc," he called out, "I need to talk to you." He held his hands out to his sides, palms open and empty. When he heard nothing in response he went to the next part of his desperate plan. "You attacked the wrong person. I came here with a message for you from Sol. I didn't know who you were when I attacked you. I know you killed my son and, yes, I do hate you for that, but you know the stakes are higher than our individual differences." Still no sign of Deblanc. He pressed on. "Sol sent me with news for you, something he wanted only you to know." He heard a footfall from behind and spun around to see Deblanc standing there, barely two metres away and regarding him coolly. He appeared to be unarmed.

"What did he say?" Deblanc said suspiciously.

This was the moment Mitchell had been dreading; part of him was hoping Deblanc had made his escape. Now he stood just two metres from a man who could certainly kill him in the time it took to so much as reach for his gun. He was surprised that Deblanc appeared unarmed, but rejected it as good news because Deblanc was obviously sadistic and preferred the hands-on approach.

Mitchell's mind raced, desperately working to complete the half-plan he'd been forced to instigate. A shootout or physical fight with Deblanc would certainly end in his death; the only difference being the amount of pain he suffered in his last few moments. But he had other weapons at his disposal, things he was much more capable of using.

Knowledge was power and information was weaponry. He'd picked up a few choice pieces when he'd overheard Deblanc's colleagues earlier. Now all he had to do was use that information to gain Deblanc's trust.

He knew several things for certain: Sol was the name of the man in charge. Sol didn't share information easily. And Sol didn't trust Deblanc. He hoped it would be enough for what he had planned.

"Sol sent me to talk with you away from the others," he said, making sure his hands remained in clear view. "I had to follow you and wait until you were alone to deliver his message." He tried to gauge if Deblanc believed his story, but the man remained poker-faced. He pressed on. "My son wasn't involved but you killed him, so maybe you can understand my anger with you. And Sol told me how… aggressive you are in your methods, so I had to make sure you weren't in a position to harm me before I could deliver his message safely. And I'm sorry about that."

He paused, waiting for Deblanc to show some sign of whether he believed him or not. But he wasn't giving anything away.

"Go on…" Deblanc said. Mitchell took a deep breath.

"He said it's time for all his operatives to come in, you included. He wants to put you in charge of an important mission. He didn't tell me what it was though."

Deblanc's face made the slightest of twitches. Most people would have missed it, but Mitchell didn't. Something he'd said had struck a nerve, but whether good or bad, Mitchell didn't know.

"What else?" Deblanc said, a little too conversationally. Yes, his interest was certainly piqued and, hopefully, his trust along with it.

"He said something about you being perfectly placed for the mission, with your combat skills, and that this was your chance to prove yourself once and for all. Whatever that means…" Mitchell let his voice trail off as if he was relaying information he'd pieced together rather than direct quotes from the mysterious Sol. "I don't think he really likes you…" he added, "but he certainly appreciates your skills."

Deblanc snorted and began pacing. His brows furrowed in thought as he moved, his eyes never leaving Mitchell.

"What did he say about my arm?" he asked suddenly.

"Nothing to me..." Mitchell replied. He was grasping at straws; not knowing what Deblanc was talking about, but managed to make it sound like he was searching his memory for details.

"Typical," Deblanc murmured, "you'd think he'd get Brakus onto that as a priority..." He suddenly looked up at Mitchell with slightly narrowed eyes. "Have you seen Brakus recently?" he asked, "Is his hair still green?"

It was obviously a trap, Deblanc's expression said as much. Mitchell's mind raced. He could claim never to have met this Brakus, but that might be an improbability within Sol's organisation; he had no idea what its structure was. There wasn't really any safe answer but he had to say something. His only chance was to guess right and make it sound like he was certain of his answer.

"You know as well as I do that he has no hair," he said, putting a little irritation into his tone. A bluff was worthless unless it was played to the full.

"True," Deblanc answered quietly, "but someone should tell him that beard makes it look like his head's on upside down."

"Yeah, I've often though that..." Mitchell said, adding a little chuckle for good measure. Deblanc chuckled as well and all the tension evaporated. Mitchell had done it; he'd gained Deblanc's confidence.

"Did Sol say anything else?" Deblanc asked, much friendlier this time.

"Not much, he..."

Mitchell was constructing the sentence on the fly, but by the time he'd reached the third word Deblanc had him pinned against a pillar by his throat. Mitchell could feel Deblanc's thumb and index finger pressing into either side of his windpipe, threatening to wrench it from his throat. Deblanc leaned in close, almost nose-to-nose with him.

"Let's start again," Deblanc growled, pinching Mitchell's windpipe for extra emphasis. For a man with one arm he had done an excellent job of rendering Mitchell immovable. He didn't dare move a muscle, but he still had his final card to play. Carefully reaching into his coat pocket, Mitchell wrapped his fingers around the grenade he'd taken from Higgins' jacket pocket. He'd read the words 'High Explosive' on its underside, so he knew it was the exploding type and not a stun grenade. He found the ring-pull and slipped his thumb into it.

Mitchell gurgled a few words at Deblanc. He didn't even try to make them sound like proper words, all he needed was to distract him long enough to pull the grenade pin and blow them both to hell. Deblanc released his grip slightly, though not enough to stop the pain.

"What was that?" Deblanc demanded, his voice dripping sarcasm. "Was that a plea for mercy?"

The pin came free of the grenade, releasing the lever inside Mitchell's pocket.

So that's that, thought Mitchell, *a few seconds to go, but at least I'll take the bastard with me.* He stared into Deblanc's eyes and a smile crept across his face.

He gurgled again and this time Deblanc loosened his grip just enough to allow Mitchell's words to make sense.

"Rot in hell…" he choked.

Chapter 18: Crossroads

Deblanc grinned a feral grin.

"Finally got some..." Deblanc's sentence ended abruptly and his words turned into a scream of pain as his body jerked forward and into Mitchell's. Before Mitchell had time to realise what had happened, Deblanc was moving with impressive speed, pushing himself away and to the ground. As he fell, Mitchell saw the reason for the dramatic turn of events.

Standing in the office doorway was Jamie, his gun still in a two-handed grip, his eyes following Deblanc's rapid movement across the ground.

"Down!" Mitchell yelled as he drew the active grenade from his pocket and tossed it in Deblanc's direction. Even before it left his hand he was moving in the opposite direction, diving for the ground. Just before he hit, the grenade detonated.

If Mitchell thought the gunshots were loud, he certainly wasn't prepared for the grenade's explosion. Red-hot pain tore through the back of his left thigh with enough force to change the trajectory of his dive. He landed with a lung-emptying thump, followed by the jarring impact of his face hitting the concrete. But as much pain as he was in, he still had the wherewithal to push himself onto his side to see what had happened to Deblanc.

Mitchell's ears buzzed and his entire body felt like he'd been dragged through a field of broken glass, but he still forced himself up onto his elbows and then his hands and knees. His legs wobbled and he fell back to the ground, hard, suddenly realising the agony his leg was in. He looked down at his ragged trousers, barely registering the state of his leg within. Blood and pieces of... something plastered his suit and dripped and dribbled onto the ground where he had landed after the blast. He knew enough about injuries to realise the lack of pain wouldn't last for very long. As soon as his body ran out of adrenaline and the shock of the detonation passed, he would most certainly be in agony.

But that was better than the certain death he'd accepted not ten seconds earlier.

Across the floor from him lay the smoking, torn pile that was once Deblanc. Mitchell felt strangely disappointed by his hard-earned victory, exhausted and empty. Pain began to blossom into life all over his body, making him wonder just how badly he'd been hurt by the grenade.

With a groan he eased himself into a sitting position and began checking himself for injuries. His leg was a mess of blood and torn clothing, but on closer inspection didn't look too bad. No major arteries appeared to be cut and most of the blood was coming from shallow cuts left by glancing hits from the grenade's shrapnel. He'd been lucky and, by no design of his own, had placed the pillar between his body and most of the detonation. The rest of his injuries were mere cuts and bruises and a general feeling of being shaken up by the shockwave. Carefully rising to his feet, Mitchell limped across the warehouse to look down at Deblanc.

Deblanc was laying face down on the concrete, where the torn remains of his green coat had become a ragged shroud. He lay several metres from the pillar against which he'd so recently held Mitchell immovable, far too far a distance to have been covered by his desperate dive for cover. The blast must have knocked him flying. There was an unsatisfactory amount of blood around his body, but the wisps of smoke rising from Deblanc's back made Mitchell smile despite himself.

He toed Deblanc over and onto his back so he could look his nemesis in the face once more.

"Is… is he dead?"

Mitchell turned to see Jamie standing in the office doorway, leaning on the doorframe to keep the weight off his plaster cast. His face was whiter than any Mitchell had ever seen and he looked more terrified than ever. The gun was still in his hand, but pointed downwards and away from his body as if he was now scared of it.

"He is," Mitchell replied flatly, his voice devoid of emotion. He felt suddenly tired and wanted nothing more than to go back to the apartment and sleep for days. The day's activities were well outside his usual experience and he wouldn't be looking to repeat them any time soon.

But the day wasn't over yet. They had to clear the warehouse of any signs of what had happened.

"How are you feeling?" he asked as he started towards the office.

"Okay, I guess," came Jamie's uncertain reply as he hopped aside to let Mitchell into the office. Mitchell placed his hand on Jamie's shoulder and felt disappointed and a little hurt to feel the boy flinch under his touch. He removed his hand.

"Don't worry Jamie," he said, "it's almost over." Further discussion was interrupted by exaggerated groaning coming from the far side of the office. Jamie's father was conscious again and determined to draw as much attention to himself as possible. Mitchell sighed as he stared at the pathetic spectacle of a fully-grown man writhing on the ground, groaning in mock pain. Of all the people in the warehouse, he was the one with the fewest injuries.

"You'd better see to your father," Mitchell muttered. "You should find some handcuff keys on Higgins. I'll go and see how my driver is." Jamie nodded and hobbled off across the room. Mitchell stared at Holloway, wondering how someone like him could have raised a kid as brave as Jamie had proved himself to be.

But then his train of thought was disrupted by a sound from the warehouse. He spun around to see Deblanc slowly coming to, groaning as his consciousness slowly returned.

The bastard was still alive.

Forgetting his injured leg, Mitchell moved as quickly as he could over to where he'd dropped his gun earlier. He scooped it up and brought it round to point in Deblanc's direction before pulling the trigger. The gun fired twice, each time missing the prone figure by a clear couple of feet before the third trigger pull was greeted by a low clicking sound. Throwing the gun at Deblanc in disgust, Mitchell was pleased to see the heavy weapon strike his target on the temple before he limped forward as fast as he could to finish the job. Deblanc was briefly stunned by the blow and shook his head to clear his vision just in time to see Mitchell approaching, clawed hands outstretched and grasping for his throat.

Incensed with fury, Mitchell grabbed the still stunned Deblanc and began to throttle him with all his remaining strength. Spittle flew from Mitchell's mouth as he strained his every muscle, focused his every vengeful thought on this one, simple task. Deblanc would die by his hand. Nothing else mattered.

Deblanc, almost all of his remaining strength leeched away by the grenade's concussion, could offer no defence. He grabbed fruitlessly at one of Mitchell's forearms, surprised by how broad and solid it was, but with just one remaining hand he could not deflect it from its grip purpose. His vision began to blacken around the edges as his life began to drain away.

But Deblanc wasn't ready to give up just yet. He always had one more escape plan in reserve, and that was all he needed.

Stretching his arm out straight he raise it from the ground, his movements slow and shaky, and brought the face of his new watch down hard onto the concrete.

Nothing happened and Mitchell continued to choke the life from him.

He raised his arm to try again. His movements were becoming ever slower, his body threatening to ignore his commands.

This would be his last chance.

The watch face struck the ground again, this time with enough force to depress the toughened glass.

Still waiting for his replacement arm, Deblanc had had to have Brakus make a slight alteration to his new Portal summoning device. Obviously, his missing arm made the previous set-up of depressing the three side buttons before activating the switch hidden under the glass face, a useless one. So the new device required the toughened glass to simply be struck with some considerable force, of course, to avoid the device from being activated by accident. The force needed to activate the device had turned out to be a little too high and Deblanc had barely managed it. But manage it he had.

As his vision dimmed to an almost perfect blackness, Deblanc allowed himself a little smile as he felt the welcoming embrace of the Portal as it whisked both him and Mitchell away from the warehouse.

****

Darkness. No light, no sound, nothing.

Not for the first time that day, Mitchell considered the possibility that he was dead. At least he thought it was the same day, it was getting harder and harder to tell how long it had been dark.

The last thing he remembered was grabbing hold of Deblanc's throat.

A word swam into his consciousness, something he'd overheard earlier.

Portal.

Was that where he was now? Was this what it was like inside one of those impossible things he'd heard Deblanc's colleagues talking about?

He tried to think about what he'd heard, about all the weird and impossible things the people who'd trespassed into his warehouse had said. But thinking was hard; his anger was still too powerful. He'd been sure he'd grabbed hold of Deblanc's throat. He was going to tear the bastard to pieces and end this once and for all. But once again, Deblanc appeared to have survived.

Mitchell raged, trapped in the sightless, soundless limbo for what seemed like days. Eventually, his random fury found focus in a series of scenarios in which he killed Deblanc in any number of vicious and bloodthirsty ways. There were no images to the scenarios, just a shapeless cloud of anger that tasted of Deblanc, into which Mitchell poured all his anger and hatred. He could sense the Deblanc cloud writhing in pain under his mental assaults, broken and torn in imagined agony.

With every passing moment his barrage increased in its intensity and with it his ability to focus his imaginary attacks. He received no satisfaction from the process, instead feeling frustrated by the knowledge that he could do better if only he tried harder. It felt like reaching out for some prize only to have it pulled away as his outstretched fingers were about to encompass it.

And as he continued to mentally attack the shapeless, formless thing that represented Deblanc, he became aware that his entire thought process was somehow being changed, improved even, his thoughts becoming sharper and easier to form.

Robert Mitchell had always considered himself one of life's thinkers, a man who planned meticulously, taking every eventuality into account. But he was fast beginning to realise that he'd been deluding himself. He'd been a fuzzy thinker, barely comprehending the true scope of what his mind was capable of. But now, his mind was being laid bare before him, compartmentalised and neatly ordered. He could distinguish between individual areas, different memories. All his plans for the future were laid out before him in various states of completion.

And they all felt ridiculously small and pointless, like he'd been merely playing at life. He felt suddenly embarrassed, as though he was being judged. And he was: by himself, his biggest critic by far. All his accomplishments, his businesses, his fortune, were all suddenly so pointless, no more than childish games.

So what else was there? He'd done his best to kill Deblanc, no one could argue with that. No, that wasn't what was niggling at him. There was something else, a feeling he had always been aware of and accepted as fact but never acted upon.

A sense of potential.

Somehow he'd always known he was capable of so much more, that his intellect was greater than even he gave himself credit for. Yet he'd coasted through life, never bothering to try harder than was absolutely necessary. It was enough that he'd stamped his authority on those around him, that he'd raised huge sums of money and was slowly building an empire.

But why?

What was the point of wealth in itself? What would he do when he had enough money, enough authority over those he chose to surround himself with? It was all so pointless. There had to be something more.

He'd had that thought earlier. Something someone said had made him think along those lines, but the thought had been tenuous and quickly evaporated. It was when he was hiding, listening to the people in his warehouse, just before they'd disappeared into what he now knew to be a Portal. They'd said something about training being needed before using Portals, implying some kind of peril otherwise. But the other man had apparently done so without any ill effects.

Then there was a comment about the giant man having come from the Rigel system. Mitchell hadn't given the words a moments thought at the time, he was far too eager to take his revenge and the revelation that Deblanc alone was staying in the warehouse while the others left had filled his mind completely. But now he thought about the words and what they meant.

These people, or at least some of them, were aliens.

So great had been his desire to make Deblanc pay that Mitchell had completely overlooked the bigger picture. He'd ignored the single most important piece of information he would ever hear.

But now, with his wonderfully clear thought processes, he was able to recall every single fact and inflection of that important conversation. He found that, simply by concentrating on what he'd heard, he could recall every single detail as though watching and hearing it all over again. He could hear the voices, see the people in his mind's eye, even recall the shape and depth of the knot he'd noticed in the wood of the crate he'd been hiding behind.

He felt elated, dizzy with excitement at his newfound abilities and the information he'd been given a second chance to own. Already, a plan was forming in his impressive mind. But it was useless as long as he was trapped inside the endless dark void of the Portal. How was he possibly going to escape it?

But as soon as he thought the question, he became aware of a pale blue light growing around him. It came from everywhere at once, engulfing him. And in the next moment he found himself tumbling into an almost featureless white room.

****

Mitchell let go of whatever it was he was holding onto and straightened up to survey his new surroundings. The room he found himself in was in complete contrast to his warehouse. Everything was a perfect white, making the huge space seem all the bigger. He looked up to the ceiling, wondering where the light was coming from. The ceiling was so high above his head that he felt himself tipping backwards, a momentary attack of vertigo seizing him.

As he lurched forward to regain his balance, Mitchell noticed a strange thing. Or rather, a lack of something. As he looked down he saw that his shoes were missing. Furthermore, an instinctive search of his pockets revealed that everything within was missing. His phone, his wallet, even his cigar pouch and lighter. He looked around, half expecting to see a pickpocket running away from him, but here was nobody there. The second grenade he'd taken from Higgins was still there, he could feel the coolness of the clip touching against his back where he'd hooked it onto the back of his waistband. Also tucked into the waistband was a second pistol he'd collected from the warehouse earlier.

A grin took hold of his face as he surveyed his new surroundings. This was a totally new form of architecture, something he'd never imagined being possible. This new reality was breathtaking, making everything he'd ever strived for in his old life seem petty and pointless. He was going to like it here.

His eye was drawn to movement on the ground before him and his smile evaporated. Crawling away from him was the coughing, weakened form of Deblanc.

The Portal had repaired Deblanc's body of its pre-Portal injuries of course, but he was still suffering from the effects of Mitchell's choking hands upon the pair's arrival in the Keep. Deblanc tried to put as much distance between himself and Mitchell as he could while he recovered from his mauling.

Mitchell watched the pathetic spectacle, savouring Deblanc's painful last few moments of life. It couldn't have worked out better. Stepping forward, Mitchell planted a kick into Deblanc's ribs. Deblanc cringed and his body moved away from the impact, but he didn't make a sound. Frustrated, Mitchell kicked again, harder this time. But still Deblanc made no sound.

"Tough little son of a bitch aren't you?" he muttered as he slowly circled his helpless victim. Mitchell had never felt so satisfied. All his previous injuries appeared to have been miraculously repaired and he wanted to savour the moment. But Deblanc was merely a distraction, something to get out of the way before he could begin his new journey.

Squatting down in front of Deblanc, blocking his path, Mitchell grabbed a handful of hair and wrenched his head back.

"Goodbye, bastard," he muttered, releasing Deblanc's head and standing, preparing to stamp the life out of his nemesis.

But even as his foot rose from the ground, Mitchell's attention was drawn by a familiar sound coming from somewhere behind him. He turned just in time to see a Portal grow into life in the wall and deposit a figure dressed in a pale grey suit. The figure was carrying something, but Mitchell couldn't quite make out what it was.

"Ah," said Mitchell, turning to face the newcomer. "Would you be Sol by any chance?"

The man stared, first at him, and then the prone figure of Deblanc.

"Yes, I am," Sol replied, still staring at Deblanc. "What's going on here?"

Mitchell's mind raced. The trip through the Portal had been a revelation, but now, at the other end, he could feel his newfound clarity of thought slipping away. It felt like a light mist was forming in his mind and clouding his thoughts. But he'd made various plans within the Portal and one such plan was a response to Sol's appearance at this point.

"Your man here went on a rampage," he said, pointing at Deblanc. "He killed several people, including my son." Mitchell waited, watching Sol for a response, all the while staring at the object in Sol's hand, trying to divine its purpose. It didn't appear to be a weapon of any kind, but he kept an eye on it just in case.

Sol said nothing and stepped forward to take a closer look at Deblanc. As he crossed the room, Mitchell got a good look at the object and was stunned to see that it was a human arm. He watched as Sol crouched next to Deblanc and whispered something to him. Mitchell moved in closer, straining to hear Sol's words, but as he neared Sol stood up and turned to face him. His face betrayed no expression as he spoke.

"Where was this?"

"A warehouse in Eastbourne," Mitchell replied, "in Sussex."

Sol grunted to himself and stared at Mitchell.

"That is not possible," he said simply.

"I can assure you it is," Mitchell asserted. "I watched him talking with some other men who then disappeared through some kind of blue light. As soon as they were gone he began killing people." It was quite a statement to be making, but if he was going to capitalise on the few scraps of information he had on Deblanc and Sol, he would have to go for broke. He knew Sol didn't trust Deblanc and that Deblanc had been chastised for excessive violence in the past.

Sol silently considered the words. "And how did you get here?" he finally asked.

"I tried to stop the killings," Mitchell said, adding a note of false confusion to his voice. "I grabbed him and…well, here I am…I don't really understand what happened."

"And why were you in the warehouse?" Sol asked.

"It's *my* warehouse," Mitchell replied angrily. "I *own* it."

Sol regarded him again, his expression becoming suspicious.

"Wait here," he said, "I will take Deblanc for medical attention and converse with my colleagues." Sol looked very dubious now, as if Mitchell had somehow given himself away.

Sol reached down to slowly turn Deblanc over and as he did so Deblanc murmured something Mitchell couldn't make out. He saw Sol stiffen slightly and he knew his story had been debunked.

"Oh, what the hell," Mitchell muttered as he drew the pistol from his waistband and swiftly crossed the room. He strode up to Sol and, without a pause, knocked the older man down with a pistol whip to the back of the head.

"Sorry to be going all 'Plan B' on you," he said cheerfully as he kicked at Sol, now on the ground next to Deblanc, "but you're getting in my way and that is not something I will tolerate ever again."

Sol groaned and tried to defend himself as Mitchell continued his assault, but his hands were batted away as Mitchell leaned forward and continued to lay into him with the pistol butt.

"Sorry to be so… thorough," he said between kicks and pistol whips, "but I need to make this look like friend Deblanc's handywork."

He was just raising his hand again, ready to bring the gun down onto Sol's head for possibly the final time when he heard a familiar clicking sound behind him. He turned and found himself looking down the barrel of another pistol, this time held in the steady two-handed grip of Deblanc. Deblanc was sitting up now and it took Mitchell a moment to realise that Deblanc had fitted the arm Sol had brought him. He had no idea where the pistol had come from, though the warehouse floor seemed as good a guess as any. It must have been hidden in his clothing, but quite why he hadn't drawn it before, Mitchell had no idea.

Mitchell stared at the unwavering pistol and Deblanc's expressionless face behind it. His own gun was still upside down in his hand and there was no way he could turn it around into a firing position in time. He wasn't Josey Wales.

Mitchell was suddenly aware of a gentle groan coming from Sol. He was still alive but neither he nor Deblanc risked so much as a glance in his direction. Both men's eyes were fixed firmly on the others'.

Deblanc continued to hold the gun steadily in his left hand his new right hand slowly reached for the watch on his wrist.

Mitchell followed Deblanc's gaze and saw that Sol was looking straight at Deblanc, a sad expression on his face. He nodded once.

Mitchell looked back at Deblanc, certain that fire would soon be belching from the pistol and ending his life.

Deblanc stared back, motionless except for the single tear that was now rolling down his cheek. Mitchell turned back at Sol, looking for some explanation of what had passed between the two men, but Sol was focused solely on Deblanc, his expression unreadable.

A familiar sound came from Deblanc's direction; a Portal forming. Deblanc glared at Mitchell with undisguised hatred one last time before he disappeared.

Mitchell turned back to Sol, turning the gun in his hand as he did so.

"What the hell just happened?" he demanded as he pointed the weapon at Sol's chest. Sol smiled weakly.

"You have just become trapped here," he said slowly. "There is no way for you to escape and Deblanc will be reporting to the rest of our group within the hour." Sol climbed to his feet and moved over to one of the beds where he sat down carefully. He ignored the gun in Mitchell's hand as though it was no longer a threat and dabbed at the blood spots covering his previously pristine suit.

Something was wrong. Mitchell didn't know what it was yet, but he knew he'd just witnessed something else going on. And he could feel the effects of the Portal drifting away from him, his increased clarity of thought gradually receding. He was becoming ordinary again and he didn't like it.

"You're lying," Mitchell said slowly. "You've sacrificed yourself to let Deblanc escape…"

"Tell me," Sol replied, ignoring Mitchell's comment, "what will your next move be? You're obviously aware of our abilities, the level of technology we employ. What did you ever hope to accomplish by gaining access to my Keep? Even had you gained my trust?"

Mitchell stood in silence. The truth was he'd been so carried away with his improved clarity of thought that he'd not planned this far ahead. He was convinced he could make his plans on the fly, adapting to each situation as it presented itself. But now that he was free of the Portal his thinking had returned to normal and he was trapped.

"There has to be a way out of here," he said, desperately looking around for some kind of doorway or window. "You can't rely solely on Portals."

"Yes, we do actually," Sol replied, his voice infuriatingly calm and level. "And very soon Kendrick will be arriving to…"

"Kendrick?" Mitchell interrupted. "The big guy?"

"Yes," Sol replied, his voice showing no sign of annoyance. "And I'd advise you…"

But he didn't get to finish the sentence. In one smooth movement, Mitchell stepped forward and shot Sol point-blank in the side of the head.

"Thank you," he said as Sol's lifeless body fell sideways and onto the bed. "That's all I needed to know."

He reached down to cover his hands with Sol's blood and wiped a good amount over the front of his shirt. He then sat on the ground next to Sol's bed, gun in hand, and settled down to wait.

Chapter 19: What Has Gone Before

"Let me get this straight," Alfred Morrison said slowly. "You people are aliens and you've come to our planet to hide from a vicious race of floating jellyfish/crab hybrids who get sexual jollies from inflicting pain on others. Am I right so far?"

An embarrassed silence fell upon the construction chamber. Morrison looked to Kane, then Kendrick, then Agent 23 and finally to the young man he now knew as Timothy Bruce. Everyone held his gaze silently with the exception of Timothy who looked to the floor as soon as Morrison turned to him. With nobody answering his question, he continued.

"Look," he said, his voice heavy with exasperation. "I can buy the Portal thing, sort of." He looked across at Kane. "It *does* explain how I got here, though I don't appreciate the check-in procedure," he added, casting a significant glare at Kendrick who at least had the decency to look away. "And this place is, well, impressive to say the least." He looked out across the massive room they were now seated in, the very same room in which Kane had his unfortunate first meeting Agent 23. The drones continued to dart about the space, continuing work on the grey constructions. The sheer size of the chamber couldn't be ignored and the multitude of consoles appeared incredibly advanced, even to someone with Morrison's experience with cutting edge computer systems.

Kane had been the one to explain the story so far, sharing with his friend all the facts he'd been exposed to up to that point. Kendrick had chipped in with occasional corrections and new facts, while Agent 23 remained mostly quiet, appearing almost bored with the whole procedure.

Early on, Kane had suggested introducing Morrison to Brakus but the cranky alien had refused, stating in no uncertain terms that he was far too busy to bother himself with such trivialities. Kendrick threatened to personally escort him to the meeting but Brakus just cut the connection, refusing to talk further.

Timothy Bruce had been asked to sit in on the meeting and listened quietly. He obviously had a serious anxiety disorder and found sitting in the company of even a group this small uncomfortable. Morrison felt sorry for him, but refused to become distracted from the matter at hand.

"What I *don't* understand," he continued, looking over at Timothy, "and please don't be offended by this Tim, is how Mr

Bruce here is the linchpin to some plan to defeat these jellycrab aliens and save our own world from a similar attack." He let the comment hang in the air for a moment and when nobody took the floor, he turned to Kane. "And where, exactly, do *we* fit into all this?" At least this time he got a response.

"Oh, come on," Kane said, a huge grin on his face. "Don't tell me you aren't excited. Intrigued at least?"

But now it was Morrison's turn to remain silent, his usual happy-go-lucky attitude was gone, replaced by a clearer understanding of the gravity of their situation. Oddly, Kane's usual grim demeanour appeared to have been replaced by an almost childlike excitement as if he'd been granted membership to some exclusive club. The two friends stared at each other, each challenging the other to speak. Neither man spoke but Morrison lost the staring game when he threw his arms up in exasperation and began pacing.

"Look," Agent 23 broke the silence that followed, speaking for the first time. "When Sol gets back he can debrief us all and we'll know what's what…"

"Are you telling me that neither of you actually know what Sol's big plan to save the world is?" Morrison addressed Agent 23 directly but also gave Kendrick a significant glare. This time the big man held his gaze, his face grim and his brow indicating a rising anger. "How can that be?" Morrison demanded.

"Look," Agent 23 continued. "You have to understand how we operate and how long we've been on this world. You probably think Sol is much older than either of us." She indicated Kendrick with a nod. "The truth is, Sol is actually several years younger." She let the revelation sink in as she watched an exchange of confused expressions between Kane and Morrison.

Morrison sat down with a heavy sigh.

"Look," he said, "we need to be working together here. I appreciate we're your guests, but *you* have to understand that this is *our* planet." He glanced at Kane as he added under his breath, "and I can't believe I just said that. We need to have an exchange of information: a show of good faith." He turned his full attention to Agent 23, realising she was his best bet. "Please," he said earnestly, "at least give us some background so we're better prepared for Sol's briefing. You owe us that much at least."

Agent 23 looked at Kendrick who nodded once.

"Very well," she said, "I will tell you what we know up to this point." She took a deep breath and looked at Kendrick again before beginning her story.

"After we'd made our escape from the Rigel 4 mission we laid low, hiding our vessel under a rockslide on an uninhabited moon. We all entered a Portal set to reopen after a three week delay, hoping the search for our team would have been called off by then. But we were new to Portal technology and were actually released just under four years later." She watched Kane and Morrison trade raised eyebrows at this statement as she continued. She spoke quickly as if wanting to get through the facts as quickly as possible. "We managed to secure a larger ship and set off in search of our compatriots, but there was nobody left." Her voice was suddenly near to breaking and Kane and Morrison were suddenly aware of the sheer scale of her statement.

"You told me your society was made up of several different worlds…" Kane said quietly.

"It was," said Kendrick, his deep voice also on the verge of breaking. "It took the Brachyurans less than three years to murder or enslave every single being on all twenty three worlds."

"And they're coming here," Timothy muttered, speaking for the first time. It wasn't a question; he was just putting words to the cold feeling in his gut. As soon as the words left his lips he turned pink and stared at the ground again.

"They've been here before."

Kane, Morrison and Timothy all stared at Agent 23, each wide-eyed at her softly spoken revelation. Kane and Morrison exchanged stunned looks before Morrison did the same with Timothy. He was pleased to see the young man hold eye contact with him for a few seconds before looking away. He was glad that Timothy appeared to be gaining some confidence at last, was beginning to join in, but he had to wonder who *wouldn't* be reaching out for support under the weight of such a revelation. He himself could feel the world turning dark and closing in around him.

"You led them here," said Kane, his tone one of realisation rather than accusation. Morrison's head snapped round to look at his friend, then to Kendrick and Agent 23. Both of them looked shamed by the comment.

"When?" asked Morrison. Agent 23 took a deep breath and returned to her narrative.

"After securing our new ship we tried to get in touch with one of our planets. We soon discovered the Brachyurans had quickly gone on the offensive, overtaking our worlds with ruthless efficiency. It seems their original plan to feign friendship and infiltrate our system gradually had been abandoned soon after our failed attack." She looked at Kendrick, who remained grim-faced and silent. "We knew we were taking a huge risk by trying to expose the Brachyuran threat, but we had to do something. As it turned out, all we managed to do was demonstrate the threat our society posed and in response they waged a full-scale war that we had no chance of resisting. Our fleet was scattered and picked off, leaving the planets defenceless outside their atmospheres. They simply stood off and pounded the planets from a high orbit."

Agent 23's chin fell to her chest. Clearly, telling their story was difficult, but Kane's natural impatience would allow her no respite.

"You said they've already visited our world?" he prompted.

This time it was Kendrick who spoke.

"The vessel we stole was one of theirs," he explained. "It was a deep space scouting vessel, the type they sent out on long-haul missions to seek out habitable planets to seize or control. We ran into it by accident and managed to dispose of the crew." He looked at Agent 23, who smiled weakly at the memory. At least something appeared to have gone right during their escape. "We cracked the ship's logs and found reference to a small nine-planet system containing a single life-supporting world. They'd marked the system as unremarkable and the life forms on the third planet as primitive. Your world," he added.

"Charming," muttered Kane. But Morrison didn't feel insulted in the least and a look of realisation appeared on his face.

"So, just how long ago was this?" he asked.

Kendrick smiled and nodded. "I think your friend is starting to get it," he said to Kane before turning back to Morrison. "We set off for what we now know as Earth, knowing it would be safe from the Brachyurans for some considerable time." He paused before continuing. "All of this happened a little over sixteen hundred years ago."

Morrison nodded slowly. He'd guessed it would be something like that. Kane's reaction was much less restrained.

"Bollocks!" he said loudly as he leant back in his chair. "Sixteen centuries?"

"No, think about it," said Morrison. "Using Portals for long periods of hibernation renders time irrelevant. And as they come from a totally different solar system, who's to say their society isn't thousands of years older than ours anyway?" He turned back to Kendrick and Agent 23. "That would have put your arrival at some time during the Dark Ages wouldn't it? And the Brachyuran survey team some time before even that?" He shook his head with a relieved grin. "No wonder they didn't view us as a threat."

Kane grunted. "Didn't they miss their survey vessel?" he asked.

"They're not that caring," Kendrick snorted. "Besides, where would they start looking? It's a pretty big universe."

"Okay," Morrison interrupted, bringing the conversation back on track. "So, you arrived here sixteen hundred years ago. What happened next?"

"We sank our vessel," said Agent 23, "and buried it in the silt at the bottom of the Atlantic Ocean. From there we sent a drilling probe down into the planet's outer core…"

"…which is the liquid layer of iron and nickel found two thousand miles beneath the surface…" Kane said to Morrison, his tone perhaps a little too lecturing. Morrison rolled his eyes in an 'I know' kind of way.

"And," 23 interrupted loudly, "we sent down a Brachyuran chamber crystal to grow the first part of the Keep. Once that chamber was ready we Portalled in supplies and moved into our new home."

"There must have been some kind of plan?" Morrison prompted. "I can't believe you just moved in to hide."

"At that point, no," Kendrick muttered. "What could we possibly have done? Three people and a stolen survey ship against the Brachyuran Empire? I don't mind fighting against the odds every now and then, but there are quicker ways to commit suicide."

"Hang on," said Kane. "Where was Brakus all this time?"

Kendrick and Agent 23 exchanged glances. Kendrick nodded once and Agent 23 picked up the narrative.

"The first time we entered the hibernation Portal, we put Brakus into a separate one. He stayed in there until we could decide what to do with him." She looked at Kendrick again before continuing in a slightly lower voice, as though embarrassed. "Kendrick and I wanted to leave him in there indefinitely. I was angry and blamed Brakus for the destruction of our worlds and Kendrick… well, Kendrick wanted to take more… robust action."

"I wanted to kill him in the most painful manner I could come up with," Kendrick interrupted unapologetically. "You have to remember," he said, "that I was the only one with my pre-mission memories intact. I alone knew how vicious the little bastards were."

"Seems reasonable," muttered Kane, remembering his initial meeting with the alien.

"Obviously you decided against it," Morrison prompted. "What made you decide to keep him around?"

"Sol," came Agent 23's simple answer. When she didn't elaborate, Morrison raised his eyebrows in a silent 'go on' signal.

"The drilling and initial chamber-seeding process took several months to complete," she continued. "During that time Kendrick and I entered hibernation Portals but Sol didn't. He spent the time accessing the Brachyuran vessel's database and learning as much as he could about our enemy, looking for any weaknesses we could exploit.

"And he found something interesting about Brakus." She turned to Kane. "Did you notice the brand on his carapace?"

Kane nodded. "I figured it was some kind of tattoo."

"No," she said, "It was a brand. The Brachyurans are an unforgiving and draconian society. What you saw was a symbol of slavery. Brakus had committed some crime or other and as a result was branded. The mark shows him to be a weakling with no rights within their society. More than that, it actually weakens him physically."

Kendrick chuckled at this point, drawing a disproving scowl from Agent 23. "It means we can hurt him," he said.

"Brachyuran carapaces form an almost unbreakable protective dome," Agent 23 explained, "protecting their internal organs from impact. But in order to brand offenders, an area of the carapace spines are ground away. They never grow back and once gone the dome's integrity is seriously weakened. Whatever Brakus' crime, and he refuses to even acknowledge the subject, he was sentenced to a lifetime of servitude and humiliation. He ceased to be a Brachyuran in their eyes."

"I really have to meet this guy," Morrison muttered. He looked at Timothy and added, "Have you met him yet, Tim?" But Timothy just shook his head, refusing to meet Morrison's eye. It was obvious the very thought of meeting the alien terrified him. Morrison was determined to find a way to ease him into the conversation, but he knew he had to be careful and take his time.

"So," Morrison continued, drawing his attention back to Kendrick and Agent 23. "You released Brakus and convinced him to join you in your crusade…"

"Well, it wasn't quite that straight forward," Agent 23 replied. "But yes, that's pretty much what happened. With Brakus's aid we built a fabrication plant in the first chamber, with which we built the first batch of construction drones." She indicated the drones busying themselves in the air above their heads. "We used raw materials from the planet's outer core to build further chambers in which we set the drones to work, building the equipment you now see around you.

"The process took years, but for the most part it took care of itself. Brakus doesn't require sleep as we know it and being from a race with a life expectancy of hundreds of years, he opted to oversee the procedure with only a few hibernation sessions when fully automated phases of construction could be set up." She looked over to Kendrick who nodded and took up the narrative.

"Sol, on the other hand, became enamoured with your world and took to taking trips to the surface while 23 and I were hibernating. He travelled all over and soon found something of great concern."

Kendrick paused here and looked to Agent 23, possibly for support, but she just lowered her eyes and nodded. But still Kendrick hesitated.

"Go on…" Morrison prompted, a little exasperation creeping into his voice.

"Okay, well, Sol travelled to what you now know as Europe where he discovered an alarmingly well-organised Empire in the process of aggressive expansion."

"The Roman Empire," Kane interrupted a little too quickly and failing to keep a smug note from his voice.

Morrison rolled his eyes. "Yes, Ted," he said patronisingly. "That would be the Roman Empire. Well done."

"Fuck off."

"And," Kendrick interrupted loudly, "they were in danger of creating a single, worldwide society…"

Kane and Morrison exchanged puzzled looks. Obviously this fact was significant to Kendrick and he thought it required no further elaboration. Fortunately, Agent 23 picked up on their confusion.

"There is a common misconception," she said, "that a society advances further in technology and invention during a time of war. This is true, to a point, but imagine for a moment, what a society would be like if it was free from all wars and conflicts." She leant forward slightly as she spoke and a faraway look appeared on her face. "Imagine if a society solved all of its problems of food production, homelessness and religious infighting. How would a society prosper in the absence of all crime and lawlessness? Imagine a society that had nothing to fear from their neighbours and didn't have to waste time and recourses on military matters. Don't you think such society would advance at a faster rate than one jealously watching their neighbours or planning ways to dispose of them in case they one day decided to attack?

"Now, imagine an individual in such a society, free to explore his or her own potential rather than spend a significant portion of their life working to support them self, to simply exist. Think of what they could accomplish. Now imagine the entire world enjoying such freedom. This is what Rome was in danger of becoming and this is why we had to stop them."

Morrison and Kane considered this for a moment with mixed feelings. Morrison thought about his family and how he would feel if they were always safe and comfortable, living to better themselves rather than waste their life away, working some mundane job to keep fed and sheltered.

Kane's first thought was that he'd be out of a job.

"So, what did you do?" Timothy asked quietly, his curiosity piqued. As soon as the words were out of his mouth he looked away, fearful that he'd drawn attention to himself again.

"Well," 23 said to him directly. "Sol drew Kendrick and myself out of our hibernation Portals and explained the problem. It was obvious that, should the Roman Empire advance to its logical conclusion, Earth's technology would advance exponentially and your world would inevitably be viewed as a threat by the returning Brachyurans.

"We had a decision to make. Either let Earth continue to advance, perhaps with our secret help, and hope you became advanced enough to defend yourselves against a Brachyuran attack fleet… or engineer the fall of the Roman Empire."

"You caused the fall of Rome." Timothy murmured.

"We did," said Kendrick proudly. "Sol created the persona of Odoacer and manoeuvred himself into a position of power where he set about undoing all the work of previous rulers. I became Theodoric the Great, his rival and one of my favourite aliases by the way. I even got to strangle Sol to death!" He chuckled at the memory. "In fact, that's why I chose to keep the name. With a slight change in spelling of course."

"Anyway," Agent 23 interrupted, "these and other manipulations on our part brought about the sacking and eventual fall of the Roman Empire and the beginning of what you now know as the Dark Ages."

Kane looked confused again, but this time enlightenment came from an unexpected source.

"Eight hundred years in which no scientific advances were made," said Timothy quietly. He felt on firmer ground now, having spent years of his life reading library books in the safety of his small flat.

"Indeed," said Agent 23 approvingly. "It worked out better than we dared hope. The whole world fell into a dark age of superstition and backwards thinking. Science itself was deemed ungodly and outlawed."

"Which was just as well," Kendrick offered. "Because the Brachyurans came back, looking for their scout ship. Fortunately, we'd long since stripped out a lot of the vessel for components and materials. Everything left had been deactivated and wouldn't show up on their surface scans. Our Keep was far enough within the outer core that it too was safe from detection. They went away, probably satisfied that Earth wouldn't be a problem for several centuries."

"So you reset the clock," Morrison said, "you lost us eight hundred years of invention and advancement. What now? We're not entirely backwards anymore. I'd like to think we could at least give the crabheads a fight if they tried to invade now."

Agent 23 and Kendrick exchanged embarrassed looks.

"Well," said Kendrick, "maybe if…well, you could…" He looked at Agent 23 again and she shook her head firmly. "No, not really, no." Kendrick admitted.

"Great," muttered Kane, "So what have you been up to all this time? What's the plan?"

"That's what we're waiting for Sol for," Agent 23 said angrily. "And before you start assuming we're only here to protect your world, remember that if it wasn't for our intervention you'd all have been tortured slaves or dead long ago."

Kane and Morrison held their tongues.

"Speaking of which," Kendrick said as he rose to leave, "I'm going to see what's keeping him so long." And without another word Kendrick stalked off and disappeared behind a bank of consoles.

"I have a question," Timothy asked quietly once the giant had left.

"Go on, Timothy," Agent 23 said quietly.

"How is it that we can understand what you're saying?" he asked. "Does this place have some kind of translation system or something? I can't believe people from another solar system speak English…"

"Good question, Tim," Morrison said with a friendly grin. "I was wondering that myself." Agent 23 regarded Timothy proudly for a moment, all her previous agitation melting away. If she did hear Morrison's comment she wasn't showing it.

"You're right of course," she said, "that would be too much of a coincidence. Technically, I don't actually speak English and neither do you." She let the statement hang in the air for a moment before continuing. "The language I'm speaking, the language we're *all* speaking, is the universal language of the Rigel system. We introduced it to Europe and finally concentrated it in England during your Dark Ages." She let her attention expand to all three listeners. "Didn't you ever think it odd that, after the huge influence the Roman Empire had in Europe, that you're not all speaking Italian now?"

Chapter 20: Deblanc Must Die!

Kendrick knew something was wrong even before he'd spotted Sol's lifeless body. There was a scent in the air that he knew all too well.

Blood and cordite.

Even before he was completely out of the Portal he was heading towards Sol, his eyes darting about the reception room, picking out details and looking for signs of intruders.

Sol's body was laid backwards across one of the room's many beds in such a way that Kendrick was looking up the length of his body and unable to see the older man's head. As he approached, his hands instinctively rolled into fists. He wished he'd thought to bring a weapon with him but he was no slouch when it came to brawling and he felt especially eager to lay his bare hands on someone right now.

But as fast as he was with his hands and feet, no matter how effective his inertia clothing was, Kendrick knew he couldn't survive a bullet to the head. And that was the lament that entered his mind as he reached the bed and peered over it to see Sol's head, or what was left of it. It looked like a close-range shot, probably point blank.

Behind the bed, hidden from him until he'd come this close, was another man. And in the man's shaking hand was a gun, pointed right at Kendrick's face.

"Don't touch him again, you...!" the man screamed. But his voice trailed off when he saw Kendrick's face. The man was hysterical, the gun shaking and twitching violently in his hand. "Who...who are you?" the man demanded. "Are you with *him*?"

Kendrick raised his hands slowly, his eyes never leaving the end of the gun's barrel. "What happened here?" he said, ignoring the man's questions. It took all of his force of will not to leap across the bed and tear this man to pieces with his bare hands. In the absence of further evidence, it was pretty obvious what had happened.

"Are you with *him*?" the man screamed again, clearly on the verge of a complete breakdown. His eyes were bright red and his nose was streaming. There was blood all down the front of his shirt, suggesting to Kendrick that he'd been cradling Sol's body before his arrival.

"Who?" Kendrick demanded, nodding towards Sol, "Him?"

"Deblanc!" the man screamed, "Did Deblanc send you?"

Kendrick lowered his hands, his face a mask of confusion.

"Don't move!" the man sobbed as the gun wavered dangerously in his hand. "I shot Deblanc and I can shoot you too!"

"You shot Deblanc?" Kendrick murmured. It didn't seem possible someone as panicked as this could get the drop on someone like Deblanc. "Why?"

"He killed Sol!" the man shrieked, and in that moment all his energy seemed to leave his shaking body and the gun lowered. "He killed Sol..." he repeated, this time barely a whisper.

Kendrick was over the bed and had the gun in his hand before the man's final statement was out. The action gave the man a renewed surge of energy however, and he leapt at Kendrick in a feeble attempt at retrieving the gun. Kendrick sidestepped and watched the man fall onto the ground, sobbing helplessly. There was no need for Kendrick to do anything else, the man was no threat, sobbing on the ground as he was.

"Tell me what happened," Kendrick said as he moved over to Sol's side to examine the body. He didn't know what else he could gain from a closer look; it was perfectly obvious he'd been shot in the head from close range.

"Who are you?" the man asked feebly, looking and sounding completely defeated.

"Kendrick."

With the utterance of that single word, the man's whole demeanour changed. He turned around and sat up on the ground, his head in his hands. "If only you'd got here a few minutes earlier..." he whimpered, shaking his head slowly.

"What happened?" Kendrick repeated, his voice surprisingly level and without emotion. He was in a state of shock and struggling to accept what had happened.

"Deblanc," was the stranger's single-word answer, as if that explained everything.

"From the beginning," Kendrick snapped. His temper was suddenly dangerously close to the surface. The man took a deep breath then looked at Kendrick directly for the first time. He looked genuinely relieved.

"You've probably heard of me," he began, "my name is Robert Mitchell..." He paused, looking for some sign of realisation from Kendrick. Of course, it was impossible that Sol had ever said anything about him, but Mitchell threw in the comment as extra detail. He was literally acting for his life.

Kendrick remained silent, giving no indication of whether he believed him or not. Mitchell continued.

"Sol approached me a while ago," he said, throwing in a sad glance at the dead man's body. "He spun me a tall tale and said he wanted me to join him in some bizarre scheme to save the world." He shook his head. "Of course I didn't believe a word of it at first, but he showed me things that couldn't be argued with. Portals, for instance."

Kendrick remained silent, his face unreadable as he watched Mitchell tell his story. Mitchell had no idea if the giant was believing him or not but decided to take his still being alive as a good sign.

"The last time I saw him," Mitchell continued, "some time ago now, he said he'd send someone to come and collect me." He waved his hand at Kendrick. "He told me *you* would be coming to bring me in after he'd put the idea past you for approval.

"But it was Deblanc who came for me."

"When was this?" Kendrick interrupted.

"A little under an hour ago." That put it at about the time Kendrick had Portalled out of the warehouse.

"Go on."

"I knew it wasn't you because Sol had told me a little about you and it was pretty obvious Deblanc was an impostor. I guessed his real identity through things Sol had said about him." He shook his head at the false memory. "Sol didn't seem to like Deblanc and it was pretty obvious the feeling was mutual." Mitchell watched Kendrick as he spoke and was pleased to see the slightest of grim nods when he'd mentioned Sol's opinion of Deblanc. It was a relief because he was fast running out of things he'd overheard in the warehouse. But hopefully the hook was baited enough.

"I had no choice but to come here with Deblanc," he continued, making his voice slightly lower, faking shame. "I knew something was wrong but Sol had told me how effective Deblanc was as an assassin and I feared for my life. I just hoped I could find out what Deblanc was up to. And to be honest," he craned his neck to look up at Kendrick once more, "from what Sol told me about *you*, I hoped you'd be around to deal with Deblanc." He looked the big man up and down, throwing in a little flattery for good measure. "I didn't think you'd have much trouble dealing with him… but you weren't here. There was a fight and Deblanc shot Sol in the head. I hit him a few times but the bullets didn't seem to bother him much and he managed to get away."

And that was about it. Mitchell had given it his best shot. Either Kendrick would believe his story and he'd be in, or he'd be dead within the next few minutes.

Kendrick looked at the gun in his hand, the one he'd taken from Mitchell, looking for a moment like he was going to return it, but then tucked it into his belt instead. *So, he doesn't trust me fully*, Mitchell thought to himself. But he was certainly off to a good start.

"We'd better get back and inform the others," Kendrick said, his voice emotionless once more. His mouth was set firm and Mitchell could see that he was grinding his teeth.

He was in.

He wasn't trusted fully yet, but a quick trip through a Portal would give him time to get his thoughts in order, get his story straight.

Everything was going to plan.

****

Mitchell sat still. Very still.

Surrounding him was probably the most dangerous group of people he'd ever had to deal with, and that said a lot considering the life he'd led.

Kendrick had Portalled him to this huge chamber and told him to sit down in an armchair. Without a word, Kendrick had noisily pulled various other pieces of furniture around to create a semicircle of chairs and couches facing him. At some unseen signal a group of four people had appeared from behind a bank of consoles and headed towards him.

The two men from the warehouse were there with an impressive-looking woman and a younger man who refused to meet his gaze.

"What's going on?" demanded the woman, her voice an emotional mix of anger and concern. "Who's this?" she added, pointing at Mitchell and eying the blood covering the front of his shirt.

"Robert Mitchell?" One of the men from the warehouse muttered, sounding surprised. It was the man Kendrick had choked out in the warehouse, the one Lindros had been interrogating. Mitchell still had no idea who he was and the fact that he seemed to know *him* was worrying. He'd have to adjust his strategy on the fly.

Fortunately, his sense of heightened thought had been increased once more during his second trip though a Portal. And this time he felt even more improved.

"Robert Mitchell is the owner of the warehouse I was held captive in," the man was saying to his colleague. "And the father of the Bexhill murder victim."

The group reached the semicircle of seats and stopped, the woman in the lead. She stared at Mitchell with distain for a brief moment before turning her attention to Kendrick, now looming behind Mitchell, somewhere out of his line of sight.

The armchair Mitchell sat in was both deep and comfortable but those two attributes made him feel suddenly exposed and threatened. It wasn't the sort of chair you could get out of in a hurry.

"Sol is dead," Kendrick stated emotionlessly. Everyone stopped dead and stared at a point several feet above Mitchell's head, an uncomfortable reminder of how big the man was. No one said a word and the room fell silent except for the gentle humming of the robotic devices busying themselves about the huge space. Mitchell had spotted the devices with some interest but couldn't take his eyes from the woman in front of him. And as he stared, he saw her eyes redden as they flashed in his direction. He'd barely even registered her change of focus before she was moving towards him, her hands curled into claws and grasping for his throat.

She was incredibly strong and Mitchell instantly found himself fighting for breath. But even before he could make a vain attempt to free himself, a third, giant hand reached over his shoulder and grabbed both of her wrists, pulling them away from his throat. The woman's murderous glare shifted to Kendrick and for a moment Mitchell thought she was going to attack him next.

"There is a possibility," Kendrick said smoothly, "that Sol arranged for Mr Mitchell to join us on our mission. It also appears that it was Deblanc who killed Sol." The woman's glare returned to Mitchell as she violently shook herself free of Kendrick's grip.

"Who is he?" she snapped as she turned her back on the now gasping Mitchell.

"I'm..." Mitchell began, rubbing at his neck.

"Not you!" she all but screamed over her shoulder as she pointed at the man Lindros had been interrogating. "You, Morrison. Where do you know this man from?"

Morrison stepped forward to have a closer look at Mitchell. "He's a crook," he said. "Deblanc killed his son, for some reason, and he sent his hoodlums out to get him. But they captured me instead and took me to the warehouse." He leaned in closer to Mitchell and looked him up and down. "Your friends didn't treat me very well."

"I can assure you they did so against my orders," Mitchell said indignantly. "It was Deblanc I was after. I have no quarrel with you." He leaned to the side, looking past Morrison to address the woman. "Deblanc didn't like the fact Sol was going to replace him with me and he threatened to 'deal with me' if I didn't turn the offer down." He carefully added a little sadness to his voice and lowered his head slightly. "I called Deblanc's bluff… and he killed my son."

"Why?"

The question came from the woman. Mitchell couldn't read her expression and had no idea whether she was starting to believe his story or not. The secret of a good lie was to sprinkle it with as much truth as possible, but he was fast running out of those truths and entering a cloudy world of lies and manipulation. His next words would have to be good.

"Oh, that's simple," he said bitterly. "I made it perfectly clear that I wouldn't be threatened. Sol wouldn't explain what it was he wanted from me until he knew I was onboard, but I knew it was something important.

"What Mr Morrison said is true. I am a 'crook', but I've never hurt anyone. Sol said he needed someone with my abilities, someone who wouldn't draw as much attention as Deblanc did. I think Deblanc killed my son to get to me, afraid that if he killed me, Sol would cut him off.

"I do know three things for certain," he added, looking at everyone in turn and waiting until he had their attention before continuing. "Sol didn't trust Deblanc. Deblanc killed Sol. And the next time I see him, I will kill Deblanc myself."

He sat back in his chair, waiting for the group's reaction to his bold statement. He'd milked the few scraps of information he'd had for all they were worth and couldn't add anything else until someone spoke and gave him some new piece of information upon which he could build.

But the next comment, coming from the woman, surprised and pleased him in equal measures.

"Do you still want to join us?" she asked. It was all he could do not to grin like a Cheshire cat with a lake full of cream. He stared at her and counted to five in his head before answering, making his voice sound uncertain.

"I don't know…" he murmured. "Maybe after I've dealt with Deblanc for what he did to my son… and Sol."

"If Deblanc can be found," Kendrick's voice boomed from behind Mitchell, making him jump slightly, "*we* will deal with him, not you."

"Then I can't join you," Mitchell replied as he craned his neck to look up at the giant, "and I request that you return me to my home." It was a dangerous bluff, but one he felt he could pull off. It was one thing to be accepted into the group, but another to be begged to stay. He was gambling on their respect for Sol's judgement.

And the gamble paid off beautifully.

"If Sol thought Mr Mitchell would be a worthy addition to our group," the woman said, staring at Mitchell intently, "then that's good enough for me. We will find Deblanc and decide what is to be done with him, together." This last statement was aimed at Kendrick and the giant's silence suggested he had decided to accept her ruling. She looked back to Mitchell. "Will you give us time to explain what we are doing here before deciding whether to stay or not?"

Mitchell pretended to think about it for a few heartbeats before nodding grimly. Her original emotional reaction had been replaced by one of pure logic. She was obviously an intelligent woman and Mitchell was pleased about that. It was always easier to manipulate someone more open to logic than raw emotion.

He was in.

Apparently satisfied with Mitchell's answer, the woman looked around at each member of the assembly. Her voice rose and became filled with emotion. She paced about the room as she spoke, he hands clasped behind her back.

"Today we have suffered a great loss, the loss of someone who can never be replaced. Sol has led us since the beginning, working hard while Kendrick and I remained in Portal hibernation. His tireless…"

"That's all very nice," a bored, raspy voice cut her off, "but there is a matter of far greater concern."

"What is it, Brakus?" The woman snapped, apparently shouting at the ceiling. Mitchell looked around, trying to discover the source of the new voice.

"A Brachyuran vessel has just entered orbit," the voice continued, apparently oblivious to the woman's anger, "and is beginning to scan the planet's surface."

Mitchell's eyes returned to the woman and he watched as her shoulders slumped in defeat rather than anger at the interruption. What she had begun to say was obviously very important to her and Mitchell filed that piece of information away. It would come in handy when he went to work securing her trust and cooperation.

"Have you activated the distress beacon?" Kendrick's voice boomed as he hurried towards one of the room's many consoles.

"Of course," the voice snapped, as if the very question was an insult.

Led by the woman, everyone rushed over to see what Kendrick was doing at the console. Forgotten for the moment, Mitchell allowed his shoulders to slump with relief. This distraction was extremely welcome and any further conversation could only provide him with extra information to use. He eased himself out of the chair and followed the group to the console.

The screen was gibberish, covered in bizarre shapes and moving icons.

"What's going on?" Morrison demanded, staring at the unintelligible mess flashing across the screen.

"Ask 23, I'm busy," snapped Kendrick as he continued to manipulate various switches and sliding controls. His brow was deeply furrowed with concentration and a sheen of sweat had appeared across his forehead. Morrison's attention turned to the woman.

"Well?" he snapped.

Ah, thought Mitchell, *she's called 23. Odd.* The woman turned to Morrison.

"Exactly what we'd feared," she said. "The Brachyuran survey ship we seized appears to have been missed after all..."

"Took them long enough," Morrison muttered. "It's been sixteen hundred years. Why send someone looking for it now, after all that time?"

"Brachyuran survey missions can last anything up to a couple of thousand years," she replied. "Remember the amount of distance they have to cover. It was inevitable that they'd send someone back this way sooner or later." She pointed at the screen. "Unfortunately, they appear to have come here *specifically*. That's not a survey ship. It's a warship."

"What's it doing?" demanded Mitchell. He had no idea what they were talking about, but saw this as a chance to appear to accept the situation as if it wasn't a complete surprise.

Kendrick stared at him for a moment as if appraising him.

"Scanning for their missing vessel and… hmm," he scowled as he activated further controls and stared at the screen, "…technology. That's not good. You humans have advanced a bit further than they tend to tolerate."

"Which means…?" Mitchell prompted.

"Which means," 23 muttered between clenched teeth, "as soon as their scan is complete, this planet will become a valid target for the Brachyuran Empire."

"And…?"

"And, if you're lucky, they will return with a fleet and burn your world to a cinder."

"If we're *lucky*?" Mitchell all but shouted. 23 turned and loomed over him. She was shorter than Kendrick but still an impressive height.

"Believe me," she said slowly, her voice all malice, "that's a lot better than the alternative."

Her statement was left hanging in the air as Kendrick spoke again.

"They're approaching the crash site," he said a little too loudly, betraying the anxiety hiding behind his calm and deliberate movements. "Entering the Mesosphere now…"

"Crash site?" Morrison's friend muttered.

"Where we originally hid the survey vessel," 23 explained. "Though we've salvaged most of the ship and there's pretty much just a distress beacon there now."

"They're passing over the United States!" Kendrick gasped. "Of all the places to do a flyby…"

"Are they still heading for the beacon?" 23 snapped.

"They are."

"Then we don't have much time…"

Chapter 21: First Strike

"Why the hell did you activate a distress beacon?" Kane demanded, fighting to keep the panic from his voice. "Are you inviting them down for fucking coffee?"

"They would have come down anyway," snapped Agent 23 as she glared at the screen in front of them. "This way, they're coming down where we want them to come down…" She spared a quick glance at Kendrick before her eyes returned to the screen and she stared intensely at the unintelligible gibberish there. Kane held his tongue and allowed their alien visitors to work.

"Four minutes," muttered Kendrick, then rose his voice to shout out loud. "Brakus! Is the Net aligned?"

"Obviously," the alien replied from his unseen laboratory. "We should be able to deliver a payload of point eight of maximum."

"Only point eight…?"

"The Brachyurans *did* arrive twenty years ahead of schedule." Brakus droned, more than a little patronisingly.

"Will that be enough?" Kendrick snapped, ignoring the alien's tone.

"I will tell you in four and a half minutes."

"So, we've got four minutes…" Morrison said to Agent 23, breaking the brief silence that followed. "Enough time to explain what the hell is going on here…"

She turned to him, shaking her head. "No," she said flatly, "You don't understand. In four minutes the Brachyuran vessel will be close enough to discover our ruse, at which point she will most likely break for orbit at maximum blast."

"And that's bad?" Kane muttered.

"It is if you don't want them returning with an attack fleet," she snapped. "Now, be quiet and let us work." And with that, the conversation was closed.

"Three minutes, thirty," Kendrick muttered. "How are we doing, Brakus?"

"We?" the raspy voice replied. "I am preparing to fire an unfinished and untested, primitive version of an out of date weapon while you wait and watch. But, I believe I can… Wait. Firing now."

Six pairs of eyes watched the screen intensely as dozens of zigzag lines of white light arced from the edges of the screen and met at a point roughly in the centre.

"Pile it on!" Kendrick yelled and for three full seconds the zigzags continued to touch that unremarkable spot on the screen. One by one they split off from their focus point, gradually winking out until just three remained. One by one these, too, disappeared and the screen returned to its previous state, with more of the alien text scrolling at various points. The room fell silent, totally silent, and only then did Morrison realise that even the robotic drones had ceased their work and disappeared from the chamber.

"Is that it?" he asked, feeling strangely disappointed.

"Ninety-seven-point-eight percent of the enemy vessel has been vaporised." Kendrick announced as he began activating various controls. "The remaining fragments have splashed down in the Atlantic. Sending retrieval drones now." He hit a few more switches then turned to address the group as a whole. "It's over. For now."

"That's it?" Morrison said again. It was what everyone else was thinking. "What the hell happened?"

"The Brachyuran vessel was destroyed." Kendrick announced matter-of-factly. "Well, ninety-seven-point-eight percent of it anyway."

"Just like that?"

"Just like that." But Kendrick's voice was matter-of-fact and held nothing of pride or satisfaction. Kane and Morrison exchanged surprised looks.

"But…?" Kane prompted, ever the pessimist.

"We've burnt out almost half of the atmospheric capacitors," Kendrick announced as he turned away from the console. "We won't be able to reactivate the Net for some time."

"But the emergency is over for today?" Morrison prompted. Kane grinned a tight and bitter grin. How like Morrison to try to focus on the positives.

This time it was the turn of Agent 23 and Kendrick to exchange curious looks.

"For today, yes." 23 murmured.

"So there's no reason not to explain what just happened?" Mitchell asked flatly, sounding impatient to the point of rudeness.

"I suppose not," Kendrick replied as he leant back against the console. He looked at Mitchell briefly, his eyes narrowed, before continuing.

"Do any of you know how many lightening storms your planet experiences every year?" Silence met his question, so he continued. "Anywhere between sixteen and seventeen million. Each producing multiple bolts of lightning. Each bolt carries up to one hundred million volts of electricity, producing in the region of twenty thousand degrees Celsius; roughly three times the surface temperature of your sun." He paused, letting the figures sink in before continuing. "For several decades we've been seeding the atmosphere with orbital capacitors," he made a sweeping gesture, encompassing the huge expanse behind the group. "The grey units you've witnessed being prepared in this chamber."

The group turned as one, each watching the gradual reappearance of the drones returning to work.

"Even now," Kendrick continued, "Brakus is ordering the drones back to work, restocking our supply.

"The blast you've just witnessed has all but depleted the capacitor's load, discharging several decades worth of stored energy. Not all of the planet's lightening of course, people would notice if lightening storms ceased completely, but a significant percentage; mostly collected from the upper atmosphere where they usually go unnoticed."

"Remember we told you how the Brachyuran fleet stood away from our planets to bombard them into submission?" added Agent 23. "How we were defenceless *outside* of our atmospheres? This is why they didn't come any closer. The capacitor network is usually used as a planetary energy supply, but it can be turned into a devastating weapon as well. Unfortunately, electricity dissipates too quickly outside of an atmosphere so it can't be used for planetary defence beyond a certain altitude."

A low whistle from Kane broke the stunned silence that followed Agent 23's statement, but Mitchell read the expression on Kendrick's face and a knot of anxiety formed in his stomach.

"But…?" he prompted. Kendrick met his gaze, but when he didn't respond, Mitchell did so for him. "It's only bought us a little time hasn't it?"

"Yes," Kendrick said. "And a second vessel failing to return from this system will be as good as any signpost to the Brachyurans." He turned to address the entire group. "The twenty years we thought we had before a full Brachyuran investigation in force has just been reduced to months. Possibly even weeks."

"And you've spent the last sixteen hundred years making sure we remained in the Dark Ages!" Kane spat bitterly. "Thanks for your help!"

It was a supremely difficult task for Mitchell not to react to this latest revelation, but somehow he did and even managed to use it to his advantage. His mind was still working at an increased capacity after his second Portal trip and he was calling upon all his guile to make the most of it before his mind returned to its previous state.

"That's not entirely fair," he said, keeping his voice level and filled with calm confidence. "Sol had a plan which he appeared to have confidence in. We may not know its details yet but I'm sure that between us we can work out what it was." He looked about the room, ensuring he had everyone's attention before continuing. "And I think we should get to work sooner rather than later." He addressed Kendrick directly. "I think I should meet with Brakus, see what he knows."

"Are you sure you want to do that?" Kendrick replied, visibly surprised. "Brakus can be something of…"

"It's okay," Mitchell cut the big man off with an outstretched hand and an easy grin, "Sol told me all about our grumpy friend." It was a lie of course, but he desperately wanted an excuse to go through another Portal. He was sure they were having a cumulative effect on his mind and he'd been intrigued by the unseen speaker's apparent authority. Brakus was someone he was very keen to get onside. Any debate on the subject was cut off before it had a chance to begin.

"That would be the most efficient use of our limited time," Brakus's voice rasped throughout the chamber. "I am opening a Portal for him now." And the comm line was cut. Seconds later a Portal opened right in front of Mitchell, cutting his view off to the rest of the group. He leant to one side to peer around it and address them again.

"Right," he said. "I guess I'd better not keep the man waiting." And without any farewells Mitchell stepped into the Portal and disappeared.

"Man?" muttered Agent 23 as she turned to Kendrick. "Just how much do you think Sol told him about Brakus?"

"Might bring him down a peg or two," Kendrick grinned. "I suggest," he continued as he turned to address Kane and Morrison, "that Kane come with me and Morrison and Timothy go along with Agent 23 so we can show you around and fill you in on the relevant details…"

"No," said Morrison, his arms folded stubbornly across his chest.

"What?"

"Not 'relevant details'. Not any more. You owe it to us to show us *everything*. This place that you've built in *our* planet, a planet now in imminent danger of attack from alien creatures we'd never so much as heard of before *you* showed up."

Kendrick was stunned. He looked as if he was about to step towards Morrison, perhaps use his sheer size to intimidate him. But Agent 23 placed a hand on his chest before any such move could be made.

"He's right," she said. "We're all in this together and I for one am very impressed with the native human's ability to Portal without any training or preparation. We may have underestimated them in other areas too..."

****

"Here," Kendrick said as he handed the weapon to Kane, "try this one for size."

Kane accepted the gun, which looked exactly the same as his own P90, still hanging from the front of his combat webbing, and gave it a once over.

"Notice anything different?" Kendrick asked with a proud grin.

Kane completed his brief examination of the weapon then unclipped his own model to compare their weights.

"It's a little lighter than mine," he said as he put his gun down on a nearby table and began field-stripping the new weapon.

The chamber he and Kendrick had Portalled to after the meeting was a new one to him. It was the same shape and colour as all the other chambers, another perfect white cube, but this one was almost empty. With each side measuring about two hundred metres, the only pieces of furniture present were a line of tables and half a dozen chairs. He and Kendrick now stood at the tables, upon which lay half a dozen P90s, the same number of handguns, the same model as Kane's sidearm, and a variety of knives. At Kendrick's end of the table was a small control panel, the nature of which Kane couldn't even guess at.

The main differences, however, were to be found both at the far end of the chamber and high up, near the chamber's two hundred metre high ceiling.

Targets. Hundreds of them. Some were static while others were moving around in a dizzying variety of speeds and formations. Some were cut outs of people, some were simple roundels and others still were cut in a rough approximation of Brakus's silhouette. Kendrick had described the room as his private workshop and playroom and Kane had to admit that he liked it.

Kane continued to strip the P90, with Kendrick silently watching him, until he came upon a hitch.

"This magazine is seized solid," he muttered as he looked down its length. "The bullets are… well, they're… they're not bullets are they?"

"Not the type you're used to, no," Kendrick replied slyly. "Put the gun back together."

Kane did so and as soon as he finished Kendrick took the new weapon off him and placed it on the table. He then handed Kane back his own, original weapon and pointed across the chamber at a series of human-form targets.

"See if you can hit those," he said.

Kane grunted and brought the P90 up to his shoulder. "Easy," he muttered and fired three, three-round bursts. Each burst grouped well, leaving a small triangle of hits on each of his three chosen targets. He grunted again as he strained to see how well he'd done. "Not bad, Ted," he muttered to himself.

"Not bad at all," Kendrick grinned. "Now, be honest, do you usually shoot that well?"

"I'd like to say yes," Kane replied modestly, "but it felt easier than usual."

"Seems to me," Kendrick said, "that someone's been making good use of his Portal time."

Kane grunted again, feeling strangely embarrassed. It was true he'd been spending a lot of his Portal time shooting the leaves off plants in the Kansas cornfields. It had felt strangely wasteful at the time, as if he was playing rather than using the time more productively.

"Whatever you spend your time doing within the Portal remains in your memory. Weapons practice, for example, is never wasted time. As your aim improves within the Portal, your physical memory in the real world is also improved." He pressed a couple of switches on the table's control panel as he continued. "That also goes for strategic thinking and close quarter combat. Something to think about."

That must be why Deblanc is such an impressive and imaginative fighter, Kane thought to himself. Something to work on next time he was in-Portal.

Kendrick hit a further switch and a gentle hum filled the chamber.

"I've turned on the atmospheric conditions simulator," he announced. "Try again with an exaggerated cross-wind."

Kane brought the weapon up again and fired off the same pattern of shots. This time the first burst missed the target completely, the second scored a single, passing glance and the third, two hits.

"Not too bad," Kendrick allowed. "But the first two bursts would have alerted the enemy. You probably wouldn't get the chance to fire a second or third burst." Kane remained silent, glaring down the range and obviously unhappy with his score.

"Try it again with this one." Kendrick handed Kane the new weapon then hit another switch. "And I'll increase the wind speed." Kane brought the new weapon up to the firing position and loosed a three-round burst. All three shots missed the target.

"Try again," said Kendrick. "But this time don't try to compensate for the wind, just aim for the targets as you did the first time."

Kane followed Kendrick's orders and hit the dead centre of the target with all three rounds from his next burst. And the next. And the next. He ceased firing and looked at the weapon in his hands.

"Impressive," he murmured. "Barely any kickback at all. Come on then, you're dying to tell me what you've done to it…"

"The basic weapon is the same," Kendrick explained proudly, "but I've replaced the magazine's innards with a microscopic Portal generator and fabrication matrix." Kendrick paused for a moment, enjoying the confused expression on Kane's face. "The other end of the micro Portal is located on the outside of one of these chambers." He swept his arm to indicate the huge room they stood in, "where it gathers material from the outer core of your planet's interior. An unlimited source of ammunition."

Kane grinned widely.

"So it won't ever run dry…" he muttered, eyeing the weapon with a new sense of appreciation.

"It also has improved optics," Kendrick announced with a grin. "Try the telescopic sight."

Kane did so, peering through the short sight mounted on the top of the weapon. "Seems about the same," he muttered as he moved the gun around, picking out various targets.

"Now try adjusting the focus."

Kane reached up to twist the small dial on the side of the scope. “No need,” he said but tried none-the-less, “it’s set up pretty much…whoa!” Through the sight, the target he’d been looking at disappeared and was replaced by a glaring, plain whiteness. He lowered the weapon with a look of confusion on his face. “What the hell was that?” he demanded.

“Try it again,” Kendrick said patiently, “and this time, turn the dial slowly.” Kane did so and his look of confusion quickly turned to a grin.

“Whoa…” he said again, this time quieter. “That’s pretty impressive.”

As Kane turned the dial, the target he was looking at through the sight was rapidly growing in size. He turned it the other way and it shrank again until the dial hit it’s limit and the view was the same as if there was no sight at all. He looked again and turned the dial all the way in the other direction. Once again the view went white; he was looking at an extreme close up of the featureless back wall.

“That’s very impressive,” he repeated, “but with the focus dial being used for range, what happens if I need to focus in on a target at a certain distance?”

“No need,” Kendrick answered. “The sight measures your eye’s focal point and self-adjusts for each user. It will always be perfectly focussed for any range and the weapon will always hit whatever’s in the crosshairs when you pull the trigger.” Before Kane could respond, he pointed at the fire select switch. “Also, look at the selector. Standard positions; safe, single shot, three-round burst and full auto. I’ve added a fifth option. Try pushing the selector past full auto.” Kane did so and at a nod from Kendrick fired the weapon down-range.

This time the weapon was completely silent.

“Whoa.”

“Effective range is seven kilometres in any mode, in any weather conditions,” Kendrick announced proudly.

Kane looked to the table, at the sidearms sitting there. “And these?” he asked, “Are these updated the same way?”

“They are.”

Kane picked up one of the knives, a medium-length combat model.

“And what does this do?” he asked, trying to keep the excitement from his voice.

"It cuts things," Kendrick replied to Kane's obvious disappointment. "Here, let me show you," he said as he reached out and carefully took the knife from Kane. He then picked up Kane's original P90 and held it away from his body in his other hand. As Kane watched, Kendrick swung the blade in a smooth arc and sliced the P90 clean in half. The front end of the weapon hit the ground with a thump. "Be careful with these," Kendrick warned as he handed the knife back to Kane, "they're sharp."

Kane stared at the blade edge, squinting as he tried to see any sign of damage from Kendrick's demonstration. He saw none.

"The leading edge of the blade is one hundredth of a micron thick," Kendrick explained, "about one ten thousandths the width of a human hair. These blades were created from fragments of surface panels retrieved from our captured Brachyuran vessel. Be careful with them, the metal is a type not found on this planet and as such they're irreplaceable."

"Cool," was all Kane could think to say as he gazed at the knives lined up on the table. "Can I have one?"

****

"This chamber is Brakus's main work area," Agent 23 explained as she led Morrison and Timothy Bruce through the maze of consoles and floating screens. "I don't come here very often myself. To be honest, he still gives me the creeps after all these years."

"I *think* I'm still looking forward to meeting him," Morrison said as his eyes darted about the room, trying to make sense of the alien text drifting up and down and across the screens.

"I'm not," said Timothy, almost too quietly to hear.

"Don't you worry about Brakus," she said, stooping slightly to get down to his eye level, "We have ways of keeping him in line."

"Kane told me about your plastic apron," Morrison said, instantly feeling uncomfortable when he considered the possible connotations of his remark. Fortunately she either didn't realise or chose to spare him further embarrassment.

"The computers in this chamber are each more powerful individually than all the computers on your world combined." She announced with more than a little pride.

"Why are they all covered in that weird alien script if you speak English, or whatever language it is we're all talking now?" asked Timothy.

"Good question," she replied, then paused to gather her thoughts. "The first computer we had was the shipboard one from the captured Brachyuran vessel," she explained. "All Brachyuran vessels above a certain size carry a fabrication matrix, enabling them to make all the spare parts they could conceivably need on deep-space missions. We used the matrix and raw materials from your planet to create enough parts to build several new matrixes, which we used to create more computers and everything you see here in the Keep.

"Because the computers were all copied from the original, they operate in the same manner," she continued. "As to the language itself… well, it's a lot more complex than anything we can speak. Brakus has five mouths and a wider range of frequencies to call upon. Their written language has over six thousand individual characters and their numerics operate in base sixty-four rather than our base ten system."

"So…they're much smarter than us?" Timothy asked.

"Much."

"Great," muttered Morrison. Agent 23 detected the lowering of morale and changed the subject quickly.

"This might interest you," she said as she pointed to one particular console among the many in the chamber. It looked no different from the others.

"What is it?" asked Timothy, suddenly interested.

"It's the Internet."

"Bollocks."

Agent 23 and Timothy both looked at Morrison in surprise.

"Sorry," he said, grinning sheepishly. "You'd think I'd be used to implausible revelations by now."

"We'd had a similar system on our planet for thousands of years," 23 continued, ignoring Morrison's comment. "Quite how yours has managed without it until just twenty-odd years ago, I will never know."

"We *have* had our technology hampered for the last sixteen hundred years..." Morrison muttered under his breath. He walked over to the indicated console and peered at the screen. "So," he said, "what does it do?"

"It's the Internet," she repeated, sounding confused.

"I *know* it's the Internet," Morrison replied, "But what on Earth are *you* doing with it? Online shopping? Gaming?"

"Keeping track of your world," she replied matter-of-factly. "We engineered its creation purely to make our job easier. And," she added, "its very existence makes your planet's security an open book to us."

That caught Morrison's attention.

"Go on…"

23 took a deep breath. "We created the concept of modern banking. We've put forward several security innovations, making pass-codes and documents appear unforgable. Once you can convince someone that both they and their secrets are secure, they cease to be so. There is nothing on this world we can't gain access to."

"Banking…?" muttered Morrison.

"Yes, we have complete control of the world's finances; our computer systems can create phantom money in phantom accounts. We literally have no end of funds, should we ever need it."

"But why would you need money?" Morrison asked, taking in the whole chamber with one expansive hand gesture. "With all of this, why would you ever need anything we have up on the surface?"

"Agents…" said Timothy suddenly.

"Yes, Timothy," said Agent 23. "Agents. It was always part of our plan to create a secret army of agents to prepare for our stand against the Brachyurans. There was no way we could go public with news of their inevitable arrival, the world would descend into chaos overnight. It is a delicate balance," she continued, "but we had to stall your advances in technology in case the Brachyurans arrived unexpectedly, while at the same time worked to prepare you for the battle to come.

"You must have thought it odd," she said, sharing her attention equally between the two men, "that so many of your technological advances have all taken place in the last hundred years or so?" Timothy and Morrison exchanged puzzled looks then turned back to her. Agent 23 sighed as though trying to explain counting to a slow toddler.

"Just over a hundred years ago we completed our deep-space network of listening stations. Little more than cloaked spy cameras really. They were launched to selected points throughout the galaxy where they sit, quietly watching for approaching vessels.

Upon completion of the network we began analysing Brachyuran movements and came up with an estimate of their arrival time." She looked at both men gravely before continuing. "We *had* thought we had twenty years, but, as you can see, they almost caught us out today. Possibly an erroneous course correction or similar led them here, but we'll never know for sure. Fortunately, the capacitor network had also been completed enough for a trial firing, or this day would have ended rather differently..."

"But I still don't understand," Timothy said. "I can see why Mr Morrison and his friend are here, maybe even that Mitchell character, but why am *I* here? What could I possibly have to offer?"

Morrison had been asking himself much the same question.

Agent 23 sighed and placed a friendly hand on Timothy's shoulder. "Only Sol knew why he'd chosen you to be the first full agent. And I for one trusted his judgement completely."

"First agent...?" Timothy muttered.

"That was my understanding, Timothy. Sol saw something special in you. I only hope we can discover what that was ..."

****

Despite his third trip through a Portal, Robert Mitchell was still not mentally prepared for the sight that met him upon his emergence.

"Ah, the mysterious Mr Mitchell," a familiar voice rasped from across the chamber. Mitchell had no idea what to expect from the meeting, had wondered why his meeting with Brakus had concerned the humanoid aliens quite so much. But it wasn't like this in his wildest dreams.

"Uh...yes," he stammered.

The monstrosity that was Brakus drifted across the chamber and came to a stop a couple of feet in front of him. It floated there, apparently observing him, though it was hard to tell with the creature having no eyes as such. Eventually, Brakus tired of the silence and a slim tendril rose from the mess of tentacles beneath his carapace and brushed lightly against the back of Mitchell's hand. The reaction was as instant as it was violent.

Mitchell screamed like he'd never screamed before and lurched away from the creature so violently that his feet became entangled and he fell hard to the ground. He'd never felt agony like it and looked down, half expecting his hand to have been cut off.

But there was only the tiniest of pink marks to show that his hand had even been touched.

"What the fuck was that!" he screamed, cradling his hand to his chest. But the only response was a strange gurgling laughter.

"You humanoids," Brakus rasped, "you're so deliciously fragile."

Mitchell was stunned and had no idea what to say. Why was Brakus attacking him? He didn't have to voice the question though, as the answer came all too quickly.

"Now," said Brakus as he moved closer to loom over Mitchell menacingly, his tendrils dangling over his face. "Why don't you tell me why you killed Sol?"

"What?" Mitchell blurted, instinctively protesting his innocence even before the question had sunk in. "Deblanc killed him, not me!"

"That is not possible," Brakus replied, letting a couple of tendrils dangle dangerously close to Mitchell's face.

"Why don't you think Deblanc did it?" Mitchell pleaded, desperately buying time. Any trace of composure was now completely gone.

"Because," said Brakus, "when Deblanc started to get out of hand, killing for fun as it were, Sol had me make a few…alterations to his brain. He didn't want the others knowing. A few synapses bypassed here, a few removed there… Simply put, when I'd finished with him, Deblanc became incapable of lying. His brain simply won't let him do it. But of more relevance here," the creature continued, "Deblanc was also rendered incapable of killing needlessly. He could defend himself but he couldn't inflict any more injury on someone than they'd already *attempted* to inflict on him. It became impossible for him to use a weapon he'd not retrieved from a person who'd attempted to use it on him first. And," the creature added, moving closer to Mitchell's face to emphasise his point, "it became totally impossible for him to use any type of firearm."

Mitchell's mind raced. He thought of his son Peter, killed with his own knife. About the time Deblanc had him held helpless in the warehouse office, yet giving him the chance to take the gun to free himself and then throwing it at Higgins rather than shooting him. About Deblanc obviously being a cold-blooded killer yet never carrying any weapons of his own. And Deblanc waiting for him in the warehouse, unarmed when there were several guns lying on the ground.

"Why didn't you tell the others about Sol," he finally asked, knowing further denial was pointless.

"Oh, that's simple," the creature replied. "Because they would kill you. And this way, well, you are now working for me, and me alone."

"Why would I do that?" Mitchell asked nervously.

"You have a simple choice. Work for me and enjoy more money and power than your feeble mind could possibly imagine, or die here, now, in an equally unimaginable amount of agony." Brakus moved in even closer. "I assure you, I can make such a death last several days: Several days of unrelenting, unsleeping agony.

"And before you even consider it," the creature added as he moved away slightly, allowing Mitchell the room to sit upright. "The same fate awaits you if I so much as think you're trying to betray me."

Mitchell stared at the creature. This was not going as well as he'd hoped.

Chapter 22: New World Order

Robert Mitchell rubbed angrily at the back of his hand, trying to massage feeling back into it. The tiny pink mark left by the touch of Brakus's tendril had completely disappeared, leaving no evidence that it had ever happened. The creature continued to watch him, continued to make that strange alien version of chuckling. It was a most infuriating turn of events.

"What do you want from me?" Mitchell demanded, not caring what tone his voice carried. His anger was too great.

"I haven't decided yet," came the Brachyuran's offhand reply. "But be assured, I will find some use or other for you." Brakus couldn't have said anything to anger Mitchell more. His glib remark had in one utterance reduced Mitchell from potential ruler of the world to powerless lackey.

"You can't expect me to just sit around doing nothing," Mitchell spat, "while you decide whether you want to get me out of my box or not…" As soon as the words were out of his mouth, Mitchell felt a sharp stab of regret and fear, as a child who'd been too cheeky to an angered parent. The uncharacteristic feeling only made him feel more angry. Brakus froze in the air for a second then turned and drifted towards one of the room's consoles.

"Yes," the creature said, "you're quite right. You've already proved how treacherous you are…" A single tentacle reached up from beneath the creature's carapace and reached towards the console. "But never let it be said that I don't look after my pets…"

At the press of a switch there was the slightest puffing sound of released air and Mitchell's hand flashed to his neck as he grunted in surprise. Had something stung him? For a moment he thought Brakus had brushed one of his tentacles against him again, but he was out of range and the pain of that first touch was still fresh in his mind. This wasn't even remotely comparable.

"What the hell was that?" Mitchell demanded.

"A tracker pellet," Brakus replied matter-of-factly. "From this moment on, my little pet, I will be able to track your movements to the nearest centimetre anywhere on the surface of this wretched little world." The alien returned to Mitchell's side, rising higher from the ground so he could look down on the furious human. "Also," he added, "at your first sign of betrayal or the slightest failure to follow my orders, I will open a Portal beneath your feet and bring you back here. And then," he added as he moved in closer to Mitchell's face, making the man back-peddle, "your slow and agonising death will commence." He made his alien chuckling noise again as he returned to the console. "Which I look forward to greatly," he added, his voice suddenly sounding jovial.

Mitchell glared at the creature, his hands uselessly becoming fists at his sides. He'd never felt so helpless, so enraged.

He'd never felt so afraid.

He considered, for the briefest moment, hurling himself at the creature and causing it as much pain as he could before his inevitable demise. But that wasn't the way he worked, he reminded himself. He was a planner, a schemer and this was just another obstacle to get past, a puzzle of logistics. And now, with his newfound mental capabilities, the potential he now knew to be within himself, it was more important than ever that he *think*. Think like he had never thought before.

All he needed was time and information.

"I won't betray my own kind," he said through clenched teeth. "I won't let you use me to destroy my world." He was pretty sure that wasn't what the Brachyuran was planning. It could have done that long ago without the help of one human being. But with any luck the very idea would be an insult.

It was a dangerous strategy but Mitchell said the words to see if Brakus could be goaded into revealing his plans, to provide some scraps of information. Perhaps he could feign emotional weakness to hide the true nature of his tight and scheming mind. But the creature wasn't going to be so helpful.

"My plans are my plans," Brakus droned, sounding suddenly bored. "And you are nothing but a tool for me to use and discard as I see fit. However," Brakus continued, his voice rising slightly as he returned to the console. "I am true to my word and if you cooperate, you will be rewarded."

The creature activated controls and a panel opened on a different unit, this one next to Mitchell.

"A gift," the creature said as it motioned towards the selection of items now dropping onto the ground beside Mitchell. Mitchell glared at the creature before crouching down to retrieve them. The very act gnawed at his ego, the indignity of collecting the scraps Brakus had deigned to allow him. But as it turned out, they were far from mere scraps.

Mitchell stood up and examined his booty, a selection of bank and credit cards, various other documents and a British passport. Each item carried the name Hugh Mann, though it was his photo in the passport.

"Very funny," he muttered as he realised the name's connotations. "What are these?"

"Your new identity, Hugh," the creature replied as though it was the most obvious of facts. "Robert Mitchell died in an unexplained explosion some twenty minutes ago."

Mitchell/Mann stared at the documents and cards, stunned by the creature's blasé announcement.

"Why?" he muttered.

"A fresh start. Your dealings on Earth, insignificant as they where, have none the less left their mark. Your disappearance was necessary. Forget your life up to this point. It has ended."

"Couldn't you chose a better name than… this?" he asked, not wanting to say it out loud. Brakus ignored him.

"The bank cards will work in any country and use the same PIN numbers as your old ones. They are good for any amount. Congratulations, you are now the richest person on Earth."

That caught Mitchell's attention. He looked at Brakus, wide-eyed and almost scared to believe it was true. But then a thought hit him.

"What about my holdings up to twenty minutes ago?" he demanded, making his voice sound unnecessarily angry, clamping down hard on any excitement he felt about his new-found wealth. The question clearly surprised Brakus: He obviously hadn't given it a moment's thought.

"What does it matter?" the creature replied. "You now have unlimited funds, all the money you could ever…"

"What happened to *my* money?" Mitchell repeated, louder this time. "Where did it go?"

"Nowhere."

"So I can still decide what happens to it?" An idea was forming.

"I suppose…"

"I want everything I owned to be passed on to someone. I want my will changing. Can you do that?"

"Of course," Brakus replied. "But who? Your only heir is dead."

"Jamie Holloway," Mitchell murmured, ignoring the creature's careless reminder of Peter's death. "I want it all to go to Jamie Holloway."

****

Agent 23 emerged from the Portal and stepped smartly to the left. Kendrick appeared next and stepped to the right. The two former Rigellian agents stood silently, flanking the glowing oval. A moment later a third person emerged, though not under his own power. The body of Sol, formerly Agent 37 of the Rigellian Task Force and saviour of the last three members of that doomed mission, entered the chamber, floating on a dais of crisp white material.

The chamber they'd arrived in was the first one created when the trio arrived on planet Earth and it still looked as clean and new as it did on that first day. The remains of the captured Brachyuran survey vessel lay to one side of the small chamber, though there was barely enough material left to fit into Morrison's car and all of it had been used to complete one final construction: a single, multicoloured sarcophagus.

The dais moved over to the sarcophagus where Agent 23 and Kendrick gently lifted their colleague's lifeless form and placed him in his final resting place. Without a word, the two agents stood together at the bottom of the sarcophagus, their hands clasped before them, and looked upon their friend for the final time. Eventually, Kendrick looked at Agent 23 who nodded once. He pressed a hidden switch on the side of the sarcophagus and retuned to his place by Agent 23's side.

Silently and extremely slowly, the sarcophagus lid closed itself as a Portal opened near its head. It then rose several centimetres from the ground and began moving towards the new Portal. Kendrick and Agent 23 watched silently as their friend, colleague and unofficial, though undisputed, leader slowly disappeared into the gently glowing oval, through which he would become one with the molten outer core of the planet Earth; the world he'd pledged his life to save. The Portal winked out of existence, marking the end of the simple ceremony.

The pair stood silently several minutes longer, neither wanting to be the first to move for fear of upsetting the other. Eventually, Agent 23 turned to Kendrick and this time it was he who nodded. They then turned as one and left the chamber.

Sol was gone.

****

Timothy Bruce paced about the reception chamber, wondering what he was going to do next. His life had never exactly been filled with an abundance of choices; he'd just lived each day as it came and concentrated on remaining unnoticed.

One day his life was continuing along its usual, uneventful path and the next… Well, he was still trying to work out exactly what it was that was happening to his life. If these people were to be believed, and he had no reason to doubt them after seeing the things he had seen, then the world was under some kind of threat from alien invaders and he, Timothy Bruce, was somehow pivotal in a plan to save it. He found it almost funny that, once he had actually become important to something, it had been lost with the death of the only man to know all its details.

He had no idea where that left him now, so here he was, aimlessly wandering through the workshop chamber, idly watching the drones going about their work. The MI6 agents had returned to the surface to 'tie up some loose ends', as they put it, and Agent 23 and Kendrick had gone off to perform a funeral ceremony for Sol and hadn't asked him to attend. They also hadn't suggested what he should do with himself. So, after enjoying some snacks he'd found on a half-eaten buffet near the meeting area, he had started to explore.

He felt strangely comfortable in the Keep, probably because he knew there were no other people nearby.

"Timothy?" a voice called to him. It was Agent 23, though the voice seemed to be coming from all directions at once. He looked about, trying to see where she was. "I'm back in the control room," the voice explained. "Kendrick and I would like to have a meeting with you to see if we can work out Sol's plan."

"Okay…" he called back feebly, the familiar sinking feeling returning to his stomach. Agent 23 was okay, she was patient and he felt safe with her, but Kendrick…? The man's size intimidated him a great deal. The two MI6 guys were okay too, especially the one called Morrison. He seemed to make a special effort to be friendly.

But the man called Mitchell? Timothy had a bad feeling about him; he was too pushy and overbearing. Then there was the mysterious Brakus. Nobody had said anything about him, but Timothy could tell from his voice that he was extremely arrogant.

"Would you like to try going through a Portal?" Agent 23's voice continued, shaking him free of his reverie. "Only if you think you're ready of course…"

"Yeah… yeah, okay," he replied, not really understanding what she was talking about but not wanting to appear stupid.

A second later the pale blue disc of a Portal appeared in the air before him.

"Just step into the Portal and we'll see you in a minute," Agent 23's voice explained.

Timothy held his breath and stepped through before allowing himself time to think about what he was doing.

****

"Are you sure that's such a good idea?" Kendrick muttered as agent 23 closed the comm channel. "The kid doesn't really look ready…"

"Sol saw a great deal of potential in him," 23 replied, though not without an edge of concern in her voice. "I'm sure Timothy has hidden depths that we're not yet seeing."

Kendrick grunted his doubts.

"How about the others?" he said. "The soldiers appear capable, especially Kane, but I'm not convinced about Mitchell. The man's a villain. What the hell did Sol think he was doing, bringing him into all of this?"

Agent 23 just shrugged and the question was forgotten as she turned to watch the Portal open across the room from where they stood.

Timothy Bruce stepped out and into the chamber. He glanced around the room once, looking briefly at Kendrick and Agent 23 and then down at his own body. He looked confused. Agent 23 stepped forward, offering him her hand for support.

"Are you alright, Timothy?" she asked. He looked at her hand and then at his own, staring first at one side and then the other. As he did so a grin appeared on his face. It wasn't a pleasant grin. It was almost feral. Agent 23 didn't like the look of it.

"Timothy?" she asked, taking another step forward. "Are you alright?"

His grin widened and his eyes narrowed ever so slightly as he looked up at her.

"Oh yes," he said with more confidence than he had ever felt before, "I'm very well, thank you."

Chapter 23: The Lines Are Drawn

Ted Kane stretched his legs out as far as they would go, which wasn't very far in the passenger seat of Morrison's car. He'd been there for almost three hours, one of those without the heater on for fear of running the battery down. Boredom had driven him to explore every nook and cranny of the vehicle, looking for something, anything, with which to amuse himself.

He'd long since found the carton of cigarettes he'd left beneath his seat. Just a couple of days ago he'd been reliant on the things, had felt anxious if his supply fell below a couple of packets. But since that first Portal experience he'd not given them so much as a passing thought.

Sol had explained the medical advantages of Portal travel, how the device screened your body for abnormalities, removing anything untoward and repairing any damage before depositing you at your destination a mere second later. It was a remarkable thing, a medical panacea and tactical boon rolled into one. He tried to imagine a world where Portal technology was available to everyone, where no corner of the planet was inaccessible and everyone had all the time they could possibly imagine.

That last detail alone was mind-boggling, akin to immortality. And this was the world he now found himself in.

After the Brachyuran warship incident he and Morrison had sought a quiet corner to talk briefly before Kane had gone with Kendrick to talk weapons and Morrison had gone with Timothy Bruce and Agent 23 to talk about the Keep's other resources. As soon as the opportunity presented itself the pair had returned to the surface where they could talk freely and come up with a plan of action. And here he was now, sitting in Morrison's car, parked safely round the corner from Morrison's family home.

Kane felt like he'd just come out of a particularly intense fire-fight. His every nerve was tingling with adrenaline as he tried to come to terms with the events of the last few days. He felt the uncontrollable urge to do *something*, anything rather than sit still. And it was slowly driving him crazy.

Once again he climbed out of the car and paced. Stamping feeling into his feet as the chill wind assaulted his face.

"Damn it Morrison," he muttered, his teeth chattering. "Make it a quickie." He stared through the car window and made a decision. "Fuck it," he muttered as he opened the passenger door and retrieved the cigarette carton.

Seven cigarettes and a lot of coughing later, Alfred Morrison finally emerged from his house and approached the car.

"I see some things haven't changed," Morrison grinned as he nodded at the freshly lit cigarette in Kane's chattering mouth. Kane grunted as he removed the offending item and stared at it.

"Deal's a deal," he said and passed it to his friend. Morrison took it and pushed it between his lips. Two seconds later he was coughing violently and the cigarette was crushed beneath his heel.

"Quitter," Kane muttered as he climbed into the passenger seat. Morrison got behind the wheel and sighed loudly. It was the sort of exaggerated sigh that said he'd just had the best sex in his life. Kane ignored it.

"Well," he said, his voice somewhat disapproving in tone, "now that's over with, shall we decide on a course of action?"

"Oh, come on," Morrison grinned. "We had to celebrate didn't we?"

Kane had to admit that his friend had a good point.

Morrison had told his wife he'd got a plum new job. At least that much was true, but the rest was a fabrication he and Kane had quickly and easily come up with. It was a simple task, imagining the perfect job. Few Special Forces soldiers hadn't fantasised about such things, stuck in a rainy foxhole or marking time on a stakeout.

Morrison had explained to his excited wife that he'd been offered a position training bodyguards for some unnamed sheik in the United Arab Emirates. As well as the six-figure, tax-free annual retainer, he'd said the job also came with countless bonus opportunities. *Big* bonus opportunities. It was the easiest way to explain his absence for long periods of time as well as the sudden and huge wealth his beloved wife and daughter would now be enjoying: all thanks to the Keep's inexhaustible wealth-generating computer systems.

Of course he couldn't talk about the job's particulars to his family: security rendered it a thing of secrets. But by far the best part of it, certainly in his wife's eyes, was the relative lack of danger it presented to Morrison himself. She was now extremely rich and happy that her husband wouldn't be placed in constant danger. It was all her dreams come true and well worth a white lie or two.

"But I *have* been doing a lot of thinking," Morrison announced, much to Kane's surprise. He turned to his friend with a raised eyebrow.

"You were *thinking*… while you were…"

"Yes, thinking… It helps keep the wolf from the door... Don't you think about… mundane things when you're… you know?"

Kane snorted.

"I just want them out the door as fast as," he muttered. "Two condoms and no phone numbers."

Morrison shook his head silently and changed the subject. "Anyway," he continued, "about our new… situation. I think the most important thing we all have to agree on, is to keep all of this new tech under wraps. We can't tell anyone about any of it."

This came as a great surprise to Kane. Of all people, he'd been sure Morrison would want to share the wealth and make the world a better place. In one fell swoop they could revolutionise medical science, end the energy crisis, put an end to war: the possibilities were endless. Kane had drifted into the army because he didn't know what else to do when he'd left school and stayed there for similar reasons, but Morrison had joined because he'd wanted to make a difference, to change the world for the better. Kane was so surprised by his friend's statement that he didn't know what to say and just let him continue.

"It's all very well and nice, freeing everyone up to go anywhere in the world in the blink of an eye, to have all the 'in-Portal' time they could ever dream of, but I've been thinking about Sol's earlier warnings about the dangers of Portal travel. You said he'd told you anyone with an 'unprepared mind', as he put it, would be trapped in a mental limbo and become insane." He turned to face Kane as he continued. "Don't you think it's odd that we've all be fine? You, me, this Mitchell character? And for all we know, Timothy Bruce as well."

"Think a lot when you're on the job, don't you?"

"I think Sol was lying," Morrison continued, ignoring Kane's comment.

But that didn't make sense to Kane, and he said so.

"Think about it," Morrison said, sounding a little too teacher-like for Kane's liking. "If everyone could Portal, could spend as much time as they wanted in an imagined world of their own making, why would they ever want to return to the real world?" But Kane was shaking his head in confusion.

"But that wouldn't matter," he said. "Portal travel takes less than a second in real time. People wouldn't be missed for a second or two."

But Morrison wasn't going to be put off. "Okay," he said. "Look at it this way. Imagine someone, an average Joe in a nine-to-five job at… a power station for example. Do you really think this person could bare to return to work after even a single Portal experience?"

"I suppose not…" Kane admitted, realisation crossing his face.

"How about policemen? Fire-fighters?" Morrison pressed. "Why would anyone do a day of work when they could retreat into a fantasy world of their own imagining? And what about relationships? Who, in the real world, could possibly live up to anyone's fantasy ideal within a Portal?"

"Huh," Kane grunted with a tight grin, "never thought of that…"

"My point being," Morrison raised his voice slightly to break Kane out of whatever sordid little fantasy he was indulging in, "society would collapse and the human race would become extinct in one generation. I think Sol realised that. He *had* been watching and 'guiding' us for several centuries. But, of course," he added, "we might not last even *that* long…"

"Yeah," Kane muttered, all business again. "The small matter of the Brachyurans."

"Right."

The two friends fell silent, thinking their own thoughts and trying to comprehend the sheer size of the problems facing them. Kane was staring off into the distance with unfocused eyes as he broke the short silence.

"And there's another problem," he said quietly. "Closer to home." Morrison turned to face him but didn't speak. Kane continued.

"Sol told me he had some way to keep Brakus in line, something to ensure his loyalty. He didn't get round to telling me what it was of course," he added with a deep sigh, "as usual. But with Sol gone…" He let the words linger, not needing to put voice to his concerns. This time it was Morrison's turn to produce a very Kane-like grunt.

"Hmm," he said grimly. "I did wonder why that… thing… was being so helpful against his own people. He *did* destroy the survey vessel, but I agree he needs watching closely…"

"And we'll have to go comms down on the subject when we're in the Keep. That thing can listen in, and probably see, everything that happens down there from his control room."

"Agreed," Morrison nodded. "We need him more than I'd like to admit but we'd be fools to trust him. And I'm not convinced about Kendrick and 23's commitment. They seem to be treating it all like a game… pissing about with history and the like… Plus," he added, rubbing his chin thoughtfully, "you said Sol had something over Brakus? Did he share this with *them*, or do they think their bullying is keeping him in line?"

Kane grunted agreement. Their Rigellian friends didn't appear to be tactical geniuses. Certainly not compared with Morrison. Kane once joked that his friend was the only person he knew who could follow you into a revolving door and come out first.

Kane nodded towards Morrison's house.

"And did you have enough time to consider the little problem of the Brachyurans?"

"First stage planning," Morrison announced as though reciting a training manual. "Resource evaluation. We go back to the Keep and get Agent 23 and Kendrick… and Brakus… to give us the low-down on all their kit and take it from there."

"Agreed," Kane stated, stiffly staring forward.

"Do you remember when you first joined the SAS?" Morrison asked suddenly. "When you got through Selection and received your posting?"

Kane grunted. "I remember I was glad to see the back of all that parade ground bullshit."

Morrison nodded, but that wasn't what he was thinking about. "No, I mean the freedom the SAS gave you, compared to the regular army? I remember keeping my head down for a while, needing a little time to adjust. I was so used to following orders, or giving orders I knew would be obeyed instantly, that I found it uncomfortable at first. But I came to realise the wisdom in giving highly trained soldiers a lot more latitude, more freedom to plan on the fly." He turned to face Kane as he continued. Something in his voice made Kane concentrate harder on what he was saying. "My point being, that step forward was similar to the one we're facing now. Just like leaving the regular army for the Special Forces, we're being granted a lot more freedom to forge our own path. And just like before, whatever we do, the stakes are going to be raised. But this time we really will be on our own, with no back up."

"No change there, then," Kane muttered. "But speaking of which, what are we going to do about the Keep's… command structure?" This was another matter that had given Morrison cause for concern.

Despite Kendrick's claims to the contrary, Sol had obviously been the Keep's undisputed leader despite appearing to have no leadership qualities. It seemed that every problem that had arisen was responded to in the same way: He'd call a meeting and refuse to discuss the matter until that time. It was as a direct result of this lack of urgency, likely a result of too much Portal usage, and reluctance to delegate responsibilities, that had seen his every plan lost upon his sudden death.

Agent 23 and Kendrick appeared to be lost without their colleague and obsessed with tracking Deblanc down to the detriment of all other matters. Kane and Morrison had already discussed their concerns regarding the pair's allegiance to the world and its threats.

"I *do* have an idea to help refocus them," Morrison said slowly, "to turn their priorities away from Deblanc. Hopefully they'll then be more useful to us."

"Tell me on the way," said Kane as he pointed forwards. "Ready?" He asked.

"Ready," Morrison grinned as he stretched lazily. "If I've still got the energy to drive."

"Fuck off."

****

Robert Mitchell paced about Brakus's control chamber, deep in thought and rubbing furiously at the back of his neck. He was not a happy man, even if he *was* now the richest man in the world.

"I wouldn't rub that too hard if I were you," a cruel voice rasped from across the chamber. "The tracker has a secondary, acid-based explosive function and it's liable to go off if you dislodge it…"

Mitchell's hand flashed away from his neck and a look of panic crossed his face. But this quickly returned to one of anger when the chamber filled with harsh laughter.

"Very funny," Mitchell growled, and when the laughter continued, added, "What do you want from me, Brakus?"

Finally, the laughing ended and Brakus floated into view from deep within his maze of computer consoles and instrument panels. As he drifted closer, Mitchell backed away despite his determination not to show any sign of intimidation. The creature was as grotesque and sinister as he remembered, made all the worse by his unshakable air of superiority.

"Do I need a reason, my pet?" Brakus rasped, his voice gentle and patronising. "If I summon you, you come."

Mitchell held his tongue, fearful the foul creature would brush him with one of its stinging, paralysing tendrils. When he didn't speak, Brakus continued.

"As you know, there is shortly to be a meeting of all Keep members." This was known to Mitchell, so he remained silent. "The meeting is intended to decide upon the next course of action regarding the Brachyuran's expected invasion of Earth." Still nothing new to Mitchell. "However, I predict that this will not be the case." *That* caught Mitchell's attention.

"What do you mean…?" he said. But now it was Brakus's turn to remain silent. It floated in place, apparently regarding Mitchell. Mitchell's mind raced. He had a sudden, unpleasant thought.

"Kendrick and Agent 23 will want to deal with Deblanc first…" he muttered as he began pacing, rubbing his chin in thought.

As terrifying as an invasion by such creatures as the Brachyurans might be, Robert Mitchell couldn't stop thinking about his own, personal danger.

"But… if they *do* find Deblanc…" Mitchell murmured, his brow furrowed in thought. He stopped his pacing and turned to face Brakus. "What if they can make him talk?" he snapped. "He'll tell them *I* killed Sol…"

"They will not find Deblanc," Brakus cut him off.

"How can you be so…?" Mitchell began, but was once again interrupted.

"That is not your concern," Brakus dismissed the question. "However, the rest of the group must be convinced that the search for Deblanc is of secondary importance. This will be your role at the meeting. I don't care how you do it, but you *will* do it."

"But how can…" Mitchell began. He wasn't liking the way his new role within the Keep was turning out. He wasn't used to being the one taking orders.

Before he could even finish his question Brakus moved closer to one of his many consoles and manipulated various controls with one of his more slender tentacles. A Portal burst into life beneath Mitchell's feet and he fell out of the room, his final word ending abruptly as he disappeared.

Brakus allowed himself a brief alien chuckle. It was turning out to be a very good day. He was enjoying his new pet and the death of Sol had changed everything. He would be smiling if his alien body were capable of such a thing.

Yes, Brakus thought to himself, *things are shaping up very nicely.*

The whole balance of power within the Keep had changed. And best of all, the stupid, tentacle-less bipeds didn't even realise it.

Chapter 24: Under New Management

Six people and one alien monstrosity stood, sat or floated in a brooding silence. The chamber chosen for the meeting was the same one Kane had first Portalled to, where drones milled about, constructing the grey devices they now knew to be high-orbit energy collecting satellites. The food tables were still there but hadn't been tidied or restocked, giving the area the feel of a party's aftermath, or more correctly, a funeral wake's sad remains.

Kane and Morrison, the former SAS and later MI6 agents, stood, Kane pacing slowly while Morrison calmly observed those around him. His eyes fell first on Kendrick and Agent 23. The impressively muscled Rigellian warriors appeared subdued after Sol's private funeral service, but he could read in their faces a shared anger and impatience to *do* something. And knowing them, it was something violent to Deblanc when they finally found the fugitive.

Robert Mitchell, the latest arrival to the Keep, sat with a face like thunder. Morrison really had no idea why Sol had brought him in, but the Keep's late principal obviously had his reasons and Morrison felt sure the former criminal would make his usefulness clear in the fullness of time.

But more of a mystery was the presence of Timothy Bruce. Quite what Sol had seen in the shy and unassuming young man, Morrison had no idea. He seemed smart enough, though not overly so, and obviously had problems with anxiety. Having thought that, though, Morrison was now detecting a newfound confidence in the man. As he watched, Timothy Bruce was lounging in his chair and staring at Brakus. It was the first time Timothy had seen the alien creature and far from being scared he appeared fascinated. His very pose, with one arm hanging over the back of the chair, looked so out of character that Morrison wondered if he'd underestimated him. Or perhaps he'd just underestimated the effects Portal travel had on different individuals.

With nobody seeming ready to start the meeting, Morrison cleared his throat to draw everyone's attention.

"First of all," he began, looking across to Agent 23 and Kendrick, "I think I speak for everyone here when I say how saddened I am about what happened to Sol." He allowed his words to hang in the air for a moment as he scanned the faces around him.

But before he could continue with his well-rehearsed speech, Kendrick interrupted.

"Sol's fate is *our* business," the giant warrior rumbled, placing enough emphasis on 'our' to leave everyone in the room in no doubt that this wasn't a subject open for discussion. Morrison saw Agent 23 cringe as Kendrick spoke. Either she was more affected by Sol's death than Kendrick or she didn't completely agree with her colleague's determination to prioritise the hunt for Deblanc. He hoped it was the latter: it would make his next move more likely to succeed.

"I understand that," he spoke levelly to Kendrick, meeting the much taller man's eye. "But we're all here by Sol's design. This is our world," he continued, taking in the human elements of the gathering with a sweep of his arm, "but this is also your home." Here he took the time to make eye contact with both Agent 23 and Kendrick and glanced at the general area of the eyeless Brakus's head. "The truth is, we need each other and we have to address the threat of further Brachyuran visits together or we face certain death." Morrison lowered his voice slightly. "And I think we should put *all* of our efforts into the Brachyuran situation, effective immediately…"

And with those words, the chamber erupted into chaos.

Kendrick strode forward, his outstretched hand curled into a claw and reaching for Morrison's throat. All reason had gone from his face, to be replaced by a fury the likes of which Morrison had never before witnessed. Agent 23 moved slightly faster however, and embraced the giant warrior in a two-armed neck-lock before he could quite cover the distance. Kendrick didn't fall, but the hold Agent 23 had on him certainly appeared to be having some effect. Morrison guessed that such a hold would incapacitate any normal man, but it appeared that even the arteries and windpipe in Kendrick's massive neck were abnormally tough.

Kane wasn't standing still either. By the time Morrison had taken in what was happening between the two Rigellians, Kane had stepped between his partner and the two warriors and had smartly placed the barrel of his P99 sidearm against Kendrick's temple.

"Easy now, big fella," he warned.

As for Timothy Bruce and Robert Mitchell, neither had time enough to do more than widen their eyes: so fast had the situation changed. Brakus simply chuckled his strange, alien chuckle.

But even with Kane's gun pressing to his head and Agent 23 grunting as she hung from his back, both of her feet now clear of the ground, Kendrick continued to slowly move towards Morrison.

"Nothing…" he spat between clenched teeth, "will… stop… me… from… finding… Deblanc… and… making… him… pay… for… what… he… did."

"I understand," Morrison assured him as he slowly back-peddled, his palms out before him. "I really do. But Sol brought us all here for a reason and we owe it to his memory to find out what that was and to act upon it. Besides," he added, "If I'm right, I don't think we have a chance in hell of finding Deblanc on this or any other planet…"

That gave Kendrick reason to pause. He stopped moving and Agent 23 loosened her grip slightly, though her feet didn't return to the ground and Kane's gun didn't waver.

"What do you mean?" Kendrick demanded. Morrison stopped moving backwards and slowly lowered his hands.

"We have to assume that Deblanc is pretty smart…" he began.

"Do we?" Kendrick snorted.

"Why else would Sol have recruited him?" Morrison asked mildly, gently complementing the dead man's memory. The ploy worked and Kendrick relaxed visibly.

"Go on…"

"It stands to reason that anyone competent enough to be recruited by Sol, to carry out the sort of work he was doing, would have to be tactically minded. Agreed?"

"I suppose…"

"So he Portalled out of the chamber when he was backed into a corner…" With this statement, both Morrison and Kendrick turned to look at Robert Mitchell for confirmation. Taken aback by their sudden attention, the man simply nodded his agreement, though Morrison caught the slightest flicker of the man's eyes in the direction of Brakus. *Odd*, he thought, but quickly returned his attention to what he was saying.

"So," he continued, "why haven't we been able to find him? Why hasn't Brakus, with all his wondrous technology not been able to do something so simple?"

This time, Morrison and Kendrick both turned to observe Brakus. The creature stayed dead still and silent, his alien demeanour impossible to read.

"You *have* been looking for Deblanc?" Morrison pressed the creature.

"Of course," came the simple, snapped reply. Kendrick looked back to Morrison, his eyes asking the silent question. *Well*?

"I think Deblanc was smart enough to have a time-delayed Portal set up as an emergency escape route."

Realisation dawned in Kendrick's eyes and his shoulders slumped slightly. Agent 23 slowly released her grip and her feet found the floor once more. Kane slowly removed his gun from Kendrick's temple and took a step back. But didn't holster the gun just yet.

"He's right," said Agent 23 quietly. "Deblanc could reappear at any time, anywhere on the planet." She moved round to stand in front of her friend and put a hand gently on his massive chest. "And when he does," she added, staring up at Kendrick's face, "we *will* find him and bring him to justice…"

And in that moment all the tension left Kendrick's body and his head tilted forward. But whether in defeat or simply to meet the shorter woman's eye, Morrison couldn't tell.

The tension in the entire chamber lifted as well. Kane holstered his weapon as he stepped back to Morrison's side and Timothy Bruce visibly exhaled. Robert Mitchell look very relieved too, and once again Morrison saw the man sneak the quickest of glances at Brakus. But the creature remained as unreadable as ever and Morrison was forced to file it under things to keep an eye on in future.

"So, what do we do next?" Kendrick asked Morrison.

It was only then that Morrison noticed everyone in the chamber was looking at him, with the possible exception of Brakus of course, he couldn't tell. Kane had the slightest of smirks on his face, as if he'd caught his friend with his hand in the cookie jar.

Morrison suddenly realised that they were all looking to him for leadership. He was about to deny that was his intention, to tell Kane to take that smug look off his face, when he realised he didn't know who else in the group could fill the post. What they needed now was a sense of purpose, to get busy and move forward before they fell into disarray. *Further disarray*, he corrected himself.

Mitchell was staring daggers at him for some reason.

Morrison took a deep breath and met everyone's eye in turn before speaking.

"Right," he said, all business. "Kendrick: Take Kane and bring him up to date with your weapons and tactics. And then," he added with the slightest smirk in his friend's direction, "see if you can teach him to fight, get some of that flab off him…" Kendrick grinned an evil grin at Kane.

Before Kane could respond, Morrison had already turned to face Agent 23. "Can you give Timothy, Mr Mitchell and myself a more comprehensive tour of the Keep's systems?"

"Gladly," the agent smiled back. The smile brought a warmth to Morrison's heart, not only because she was such an attractive woman, but because it seemed genuine. It made him feel like they were getting somewhere, already beginning to gel as a group. He looked to Timothy and Mitchell for confirmation and received two nods: one nervous and uncertain, one stiff and curt. But that would have to do for now. At least he'd manoeuvred himself into a position where he could continue his studies of the Keep's systems while at the same time getting to know the two men. With any luck he could discover what qualities Sol had chosen them for.

Finally, he turned to Brakus, still floating silently off to one side. The creature still gave him the creeps.

"Brakus," he said, "can you continue to scan for Brachyuran activity?"

"Obviously," the creature rasped.

"Good. And I'd like you to keep an eye out for Deblanc's return as well. Prioritise this. As soon as you get the slightest sniff of him, of any Portal activity not initiated by any of us, I want to know." He took a moment to throw significant glances at Kendrick and Agent 23. "Deblanc is still a major priority," he said, raising his voice slightly to further press the point home, "and he *will* be dealt with for his actions. But before *anyone* does anything to him," here he looked straight at Kendrick, "I want him fully debriefed. He may have information regarding Sol's plans that we can use.

"Do I make myself clear?" This last comment was directed to the room as a whole. Everyone nodded their agreement.

"Thank you," Morrison said quietly to the group as a whole, though he was pointedly looking at Kendrick as he spoke.

"Right," he said, his voice returning to its previous level. "Let's get to work. We reconvene here in two hours to compare notes. Dismissed."

****

The group slowly dispersed and set about their assigned tasks. Brakus went first, winking out of existence and into a Portal almost before Morrison's final syllable was out of his mouth.

Timothy Bruce allowed himself a secret smile. The creature was in a particularly foul mood; that much was obvious even to him. But what wasn't so obvious, though still detectible if you knew what to look for, was the tension in the crook, Mitchell. Timothy thought about what he'd witnessed while the meeting had been going on: Mitchell's anxiety and furtive glances towards Brakus and the creature's apparent mood. Yes, something was definitely going on between them.

This was an interesting development for Timothy to be keeping his eye on. And that fact alone demonstrated to him what he'd already come to know: His first Portal experience had changed his world beyond all recognition.

He cast his mind back. Was it really only a day ago that Deblanc had first erupted into his quiet and empty life? Events had become more and more surreal after then until, finally, when he thought the Keep couldn't throw anything else at him, he'd entered the Portal.

Upon exiting the device in the control room where Kendrick and Agent 23 were waiting for him, the latter immediately inquired after his health, asking him how he felt. At the time he'd been too stunned to speak and barely listened as she set about explaining how first Portal trips were always hard on the individual and how deeply personal a Portal experience was. She'd explained how he would never be expected to talk about his unless he felt he needed to.

This last comment had been something of a relief. Not because he wanted to talk about his Portal experience, but because he knew he never could. Of course, he had no idea what anyone else experienced, but something told him that his was something unique. But events were moving on and now wasn't the time to think about how he'd got there, but rather what he would do with his new reality.

Mere days ago his only dreams and aspirations had been to get through the current day, to go unnoticed and unmolested by the other inhabitants of Bexhill-on-Sea. The sum total of his ambition, even in his wildest dreams, had been to have friends who he could talk to. Or rather, the ability to actually talk to people. And now, he found himself in a secret underground base scantily inhabited by people who appeared to accept him as one of them. It was the perfect set-up for Timothy and he didn't have to leave it if he didn't want to. The Keep had more than he'd ever need.

He felt happy and for the first time in recent memory began to think about the future beyond today.

He rose from his seat and watched his new friends and, yes, colleagues milling about around him. Kane slapped Morrison on the shoulder, presumably congratulating him on his sudden rise to the top of the Keep's loose command structure. Morrison shrugged him off and appeared to be denying such ambitions but this only seemed to encourage further ribbing from his colleague. As Timothy watched the two men, he wondered what it would be like to have such a friend, someone you could casually insult without the fear of offence, someone you could rely on to be there whatever the situation. And for the first time for as long as he could remember, Timothy realised that he was feeling ambition. He hadn't realised before because the concept had become alien to him. But now he felt a warmth inside when he thought about what he knew himself to be capable of.

"Are you ready, Timothy?" Agent 23 asked quietly, shaking him from his reverie. He was aware of her hand resting on his shoulder as he blinked and looked around, suddenly noticing that the group had split into two huddles: Kane and Kendrick on one side and Agent 23, Morrison and Mitchell on the other. Everyone was looking at him and he felt a little foolish for being caught daydreaming.

"Are you going to be alright taking another Portal trip so soon," Agent 23 continued, her voice filled with concern. He knew she didn't mean to sound patronising, but that was how it felt. For the briefest of moments he felt an uncharacteristic anger welling up inside him and he fought the urge to shrug her hand from his shoulder. He wanted to shout at her, tell her, and everyone else in the chamber, how much he had changed, how confident he felt. He wasn't the same person they thought he was and he wouldn't be putting up with their condescending tones for much longer.

But as quickly as the anger passed through him, it disappeared, to be replaced by a calculating calm. No, it might be better to hide his new outlook on life. It would be better for him if everyone continued to underestimate him until he was ready. But he couldn't resist giving them a little clue.

"Tim," he said in a weak voice, looking to the ground and forcing himself not to grin.

"I'm sorry?" Agent 23 replied.

"Tim," he repeated. "I'd like to be called Tim now. I've always thought Timothy sounded like a child's name but I've always just put up with it." He raised his eyes to meet hers. "But things have changed and I think it's a good time to see the end of the old Timothy Bruce. I'm Tim now."

Agent 23 looked surprised at the comment, which was understandable he supposed. But there was something else behind her eyes, a flash of realisation and possibly… concern? But the moment passed as Morrison spoke up.

"Very well, Tim it is," he said with a friendly smile in his direction. "Shall we get to work?" There were general murmurs of agreement and various individual Portals sprang into life. Kendrick stepped into his without so much as a backwards glance, but Kane paused for long enough to throw Tim an unexpected thumbs-up and a grin before disappearing.

Tim's Portal sprung into life before him and he stepped up to it. He found himself almost buzzing with excitement, as though receiving a low-voltage electric shock. The truth was, he couldn't wait to get back into a Portal. Everything in his life had changed now, and would continue to change for the better. There was nothing at all wrong with his world.

He stepped into the Portal, leaving the outside world behind. Within one second he would step out again in the control room, but not before spending a very, very long time in a world of his own devising.

Tim's Portal was the last but one to disappear from the construction chamber, leaving only Agent 23. All around her, drones continued with their assigned tasks, buzzing around the grey constructions. Their simple, construction-specific programming didn't provide them with facial recognition capabilities, but if they had they alone would have bourn witness to an expression equal parts confusion and concern on the female Rigellian as she stared at the spot where Tim Bruce's Portal had been mere seconds before.

www.ingramcontent.com/pod-product-compliance
Lightning Source LLC
Chambersburg PA
CBHW030403020726
47493CB00003B/921

* 9 7 8 1 8 4 9 9 1 3 4 3 0 *